WILFORD ROKEBY,

CAPTAIN OF THE NIGHT GUARD.

"ONE SHOT FROM THIS," CRIED BUCKINGHAM, "AND THE KING'S GUARD WILL BE UPON YOU."

THE NIGHT GUARD;

OR,

The Secret of the Five Masks.

BEAUTIFULLY * ILLUSTRATED.

COMPLETE.

LONDON:

"BOYS OF ENGLAND" OFFICE,

173, FLEET STREET, E.C.

AND ALL BOOKSELLERS.

The Night Guard;

Or, THE SECRET OF THE FIVE MASKS.

"MURDERED! MURDERED! MY POOR FOSTER-BROTHER!" ROKEBY MURMURED.

CHAPTER I.

A TREACHEROUS ENEMY.

"Who goes there?"

Sharply the words rang out on the clear air of the moonlit, frosty night, as the guard, pacing to and fro opposite the western gate of the palace at Whitehall, challenged what seemed at first a shadow.

The western gate was buried in deep shade, for the moonlight that streamed over the river and the eastern side of the building only served to render more gloomy and chill the portion of it which escaped its radiance.

The guard himself, as he paced to and fro, was one moment thrown out in bold relief by the bright beams and then disappeared for awhile in unutterable gloom. The great city was sleeping; all was very still.

The troopers posted at the different gates almost slept as they walked slowly to and fro, for during some time they had heard nothing but the plash of the river, and the murmur of the guards within, and the waving of the unfrequent trees.

One form only had they seen near the palace, the form of a tall man, habited in a dark cloak, who seemed prowling about without any definite object and who fled or disappeared when challenged.

"Who goes there?" again cried the sentinel, raising his piece slowly, as the dim figure of a man stood half in and half out of the moonlight.

"Is it so dark that you do not recognise Hubert Aveling?" said the newcomer, advancing more into the light.

"I seek Wilford Rokeby. Has he entered the palace to-night?"

"He has not yet returned, Master Aveling," said the guard. "He is on an errand of importance, I believe. He will return by water. Therefore, if you desire to see him, you had best wait upon the stairs yonder."

"I will take your advice, my friend," said Hubert, in a slow, hesitating voice, as if striving to remember something; "but, tell me, did he go alone?"

"He did, Master Hubert, and as he passed the gate he spoke to me. 'Tell Hubert Aveling,' he said, 'if he enters the palace before my return, that I must speak with him this night. If he can meet me without the palace it will be better.' He then quitted me, and passed down towards the river, and since then I have heard no voice save yours. I have seen no one, in fact, but the figure of the tall, cloaked stranger, who, at night times, for weeks past has haunted the precincts of Whitehall."

"Again that form — again that vision!" muttered Hubert, as he turned away. "What can it mean? What terrible peril does this man's appearance foreshadow for me, that I feel this deadly chill at my heart whenever he is seen, even by others?"

Instinctively he felt for the handle of his sword, and then, as if revived by the contact, he walked almost jauntily towards the silent river. But the scene and the atmosphere were not calculated to rouse feelings of mirth or happiness.

The air was, as I have before said,

frosty and chill; the ghostly moonbeams lay upon the still waters, and on the dim country-side across the river, and the few boats moving uneasily under the influence of the ebbing tide, while the tall, dark gables of the palace of James I. frowned dismally over the scene.

"Who goes there?" was the cry which roused him again from his reverie, and turning round sharply, he saw the sentinel with raised musket, and the dark form of the unknown hastening rapidly away.

He was about to follow, but it was of no avail.

Suddenly beneath the shadow of the great building the stranger disappeared, and all was once more still as a city of the dead.

Presently, however, the ring of merry laughter was heard on the river, and then the loudly-chanted refrain of a well-known drinking song.

The sound seemed to rouse Hubert Aveling from his sombre study, and to inspire him with renewed life.

"For a crown that is Wilford Rokeby," said he, and as he spoke, and glanced eagerly along the moonlit waters, a boat came in sight, in which he could see the forms of three men.

They pulled directly towards the stairs, still singing as they came, and in a few moments a young man, dressed in the costume of a lieutenant of the guard, leaped upon the stairs.

"Ha, Hubert!" he cried, "well met! well met! If I had but fallen in your way an hour or two ago we might have glided along the river together. It is a splendid night; the moon has its own way everywhere, and where I have been

I have seen bright eyes and fairy forms enough to keep you dreaming for a week."

Hubert heaved a sigh.

"I wish, indeed, I had been with you," said he. "The hour of waiting I have spent without the palace has brought over my heart all my old forebodings, and the only dream which I have had has been that of the unknown pursuer, who is on my track—for ever!"

"Have you seen him again, then?"

"This night he has been prowling about the palace. His cloaked figure has glided almost unobserved past the sentries, in their semi-sleep; and, still as silence—mysterious as death itself— he vanishes when challenged by the guard. Wilford, I may be mad—and even cowardly, if you *will* have it, but I feel as if this man held my life and death in his hands."

"Not while the sword, which your brave arm has so often wielded, still hangs by your side. But let us dismiss him from our minds for awhile. I have with me an important message for the king; but I have also an important one for you, which I must deliver ere I enter the palace. You can go now," he added to the two boatmen; "to-morrow night, at eleven, I and my friend here will require you."

"To-morrow night!" murmured Hubert.

"Yes, to-morrow night," repeated his friend, as he linked his arm in his, and walked slowly along the river terrace. "At twelve we meet at the Lone House near Linwood. Not one of us must be absent. Buckingham has some new scheme on foot which must be thwarted; and you—whom he favours—must above all be there."

"If I am alive I shall be there to time," said Hubert; "none of you can accuse me of holding back where duty demands my presence, or danger threatens my friends. Tell me the pass-word."

"Simply 'Buckingham.' But of this you will scarcely have need, since I shall be with you. In the meantime I can give you news which will bring joy to your heart, and dissipate your gloom."

"Good news, indeed, then, it must be."

"It is. Lady Laura Clavering is in London, and will be at the palace to-morrow. Ha! even in this ghostly moonlight, I see your face brighten, and your eyes gleam with a pleasanter light. Yes, my brother," added the light-hearted young lieutenant, "yes, Lady Laura will be here in a few hours as one of the new maids of honour, and we shall then see no more of the gloom and despair which seem to have chased away your joyousness for ever. Fare-well, my friend, till to-morrow; I will leave you now, while that smile is on your lip, and I'll warrant when Lady Laura's bright face appears at the western gate to-morrow you will forget all the mystery and horror which appear to be your companions now."

With these words the careless soldier wrung his friend's hand warmly, and making his way towards the palace, disappeared through the western gate.

"So Laura is to return to-morrow," murmured he; and as he thought of the bright eyes, and the glossy hair, and the fairy form of the one he loved, he forgot the strange vision, and the haunting dread, and walked once more towards the river side.

Hubert Aveling, young and full of life and energy, strong in love, hand-some and noble in heart, stood in the moonlight for a few moments by the rippling water, thinking of Laura Clavering, while the cloud, which was to burst over his path and sweep away his mind and being for ever, was gather-ing above his head.

Gone from his thoughts now was the form of the unknown foe, gone from his heart the chill which had before invaded it; and the place of the Figure of Dread was filled by the image of the loved one as he turned towards the palace once more.

Bright and glorious it came before him like the face and form of an angel; then—all was blank!

A dark figure crept out of the shadow of the palace, gliding along stealthily, noiselessly, treacherously; a hand was raised; a gleaming blade de-scended, and with a long shrill cry Hubert Aveling staggered forward.

Only for an instant was conscious-ness left to him—just time enough to draw his sword and face his foe; and then, pierced again in the breast by the knife of his assassin, he fell to the ground—dead.

Shrill and loud went his one despair-ing cry up towards the blue vault of heaven; so shrill and loud that the guards came rushing to the spot before the body of the murdered man had settled itself, as it were, on the pave-ment.

But they were too late to be of service, for the form of Hubert Aveling was alone in its stillness—the assassin had disappeared!

And now, from the guard-room, came rushing excited men with flambeaux, which lit up with a red glow the great square before the palace, and cast an air of picturesque beauty over the scene of horror.

Foremost among them came Wilford Rokeby, his tall figure towering above his men, and his voice, as he called them on, ringing out cheerily on the night air.

His manner was soon changed.

Summoned by a wild, despairing cry, such as was too often heard in the streets of Old London, he had issued from the palace with that careless bravery of heart and recklessness of manner which had ever been the brave fellow's characteristic.

But when the Night Guard gathered round the body, and the red light of the torches fell upon the face of the dead, with its brown curls clustering round his calm, pale features, the heart of Wilford Rokeby swelled with a terrible emotion.

"Murdered! murdered! my poor foster-brother!" he murmured.

Then raising his sword aloft, and gazing up towards heaven, he cried in a loud and ringing voice—

"By the blood of Hubert Aveling, slain in unfair fight, I dedicate this sword to vengeance. As I keep my word, so may Heaven direct my arm! Search round the palace, my men," he added, turning to the Night Guard; "and to the man who finds this traitor, and brings him within reach of my sword, I will give a hundred crowns in gold!"

Eagerly the men spread themselves around the palace, their flaming torches gleaming fantastically as they rushed hither and hither in the moonlight and in the gloom, while Wilford Rokeby and two others raised the body with tender respect, and bore it into the building.

Solemnly, mournfully gazed Wilford at the pale face of his murdered foster-brother, as they laid him upon the table in the guard-room.

They had been children together; they had grown together to manhood; their joy and their sorrow had been shared; and death—the great destroyer of all—was the first to separate their thoughts and beings.

"Oh! Hubert," cried the brave soldier, in a voice tremulous with emotion, as he drew the white cloth over the calm features of the dead, "Oh! Hubert, I have fought for you, and you have fought for me; but never did blows of ours fall so heavily as shall fall my blows upon those who have planned this deed of horror! Heaven will aid me, for my cause is just."

As he was speaking, the Night Guard re-entered.

Their search had been in vain.

Round the palace and down by the river's side they had dispersed themselves, and had sought in every spot where there seemed any chance of discovering the mysterious assassin.

They found him not.

Yet, as if the shield of Satan were spread before him to protect him, the man in the dark cloak had stood beneath the shadow of a closed gateway, hidden away in the black gloom of a heavy buttress, where his form seemed part of the grotesque masonry, and where he could see all without being seen himself.

He had been near enough to see the excited group gathered round the murdered man — near enough to hear Wilford Rokeby's vow of vengeance— near enough to behold the look of savage determination on the face of the young lieutenant.

He waited patiently here in his place of concealment until the Night Guard had passed into the palace, and the heavy western gate had clanged to, and then issuing from the darkness, he stood upon the broad pavement, and whistled long and shrilly.

Standing even thus, boldly and openly in the moonlight, he would have been unrecognisable by any.

His hat was drawn closely down over his brow, his cloak was raised to meet it.

Save two gleaming eyes, which seemed to pierce the darkness, nothing of his face could be seen.

He was a man of mystery, bent seemingly on deeds of desperate evil, and shielded by some evil genius.

As he uttered his shrill warning, he glanced upwards at the wall of the palace.

Evidently he expected—knew, in fact —that his signal would be answered.

He was not deceived.

In a few moments a window was opened, and a white hand and arm was thrust forth.

Then something whizzed through the air, and a packet, small but heavy, fell with a chink upon the stones.

The white hand then waved an adieu, and the casement was closed once more.

The stranger then stooped, picked up the packet, placed it in his bosom, and walked rapidly towards Charing.

CHAPTER II.

THE MAN WITH THE BLOOD-RED HAND.

HUBERT AVELING was dead, and Lady Laura Clavering was weeping in her chamber.

But not for this would a court throw itself into mourning.

A grand ball was to take place at Whitehall on the evening following the murder, and at the appointed hour the carriages of the nobles of England came rolling up to the western gate to discharge the loads of beauty and chivalry which were to grace the gorgeous reception rooms of James the First.

The queen with her ladies already had appeared in the rooms, and been received with those extravagant demonstrations of loyalty which were so characteristic of the times ; but the king was alone in his room, pacing to and fro in evident agitation.

Walking rapidly, with that strange sidling gait which made him always so much an object of remark, the dark-visaged king muttered to himself as he went, stopping now and again to make some vehement gesture, and then hurrying on more rapidly than before.

He had ceased his wandering, and was standing near the large window, when a hand was placed familiarly on his shoulder.

The king started round.

The new comer was the Duke of Buckingham.

"How is this, my lord?" cried James, with a kind of feeble anger, "how have you entered unannounced?"

The favourite smiled.

"Your majesty in general requires no announcement from me," he said, almost sarcastically, and bowing most profoundly ; "however, if your majesty wishes it, I will retire, and send the page in waiting to announce me to your majesty."

"Well, well, Steenie," said the king, relapsing into his usual manner, and calling his favourite by his pet name, "I have no doubt you have grave reasons for desiring to speak to me. Tell me what brings you hither ?"

"In the first place, the queen wishes to see your majesty in the ball-room."

"I will come presently."

"In the second place, Steenie wishes an order from your hand for the arrest of three of your guests."

The king started.

"My guests !" he cried ; "this is most strange and unusual. What will be said of me if I do this ?"

"That you preferred taking precautions to deluging the country in blood, your majesty."

"And who are these guests ?"

"Lord Clarence Tremaine, Lord Claude Mortimer, and the Duke of Rosstrevor."

"Two well-tried English friends, and one of my Scotch adherents," murmured the king. "Are you sure, Steenie, that this is necessary ? Are you sure that I stand in need of this ?"

"Your majesty, I do but advise," said Buckingham, with affected humility ; "but, at the same time, if this is *not* done, I foresee such evils that I, for my own safety, will retire to France. Your majesty's favour is great, but I love my life still better."

The king was much agitated.

The monarch, who wore padding to avoid the blows of assassins, could easily comprehend his favourite's nervousness, but he feared sorely the consequence of these daring arrests.

"And must these gentlemen be arrested to-night ?" he asked. "Cannot this be done without disturbing the harmony of the ball ? Is it absolutely necessary to act thus precipitately ?"

"To-morrow, your majesty, it would be too late, since this very night they meet those who plot against your crown and life. Give me this order, your majesty—believe me, I shall use it well ; or, if you fear to trust me, give me your royal permission to retire from court."

"Steenie, Steenie !" said the king,

sitting down to a table and taking up a pen. "Am I king of England, or are you? Remember," he added, in a tone which for him was unusually stern, "remember, if you assume the crown, you assume also its responsibilities."

The duke smiled.

"I am quite willing, sire," he answered, looking anxiously at the monarch, as he began to trace the words on the paper—

"To the Duke of Buckingham.

"I hereby command you to arrest this night Lord Claude Mortimer, Lord Clarence Tremaine, and the Duke of Rosstrevor, and deliver them into the safe custody of Sir Henry Bolton, Constable of the Tower.

"Witness my hand and seal,
"JAMES R."

"There, Steenie," said the king, with a sigh; "there is the order; but now, ere I deliver it to you, I *must* know the reasons of this haste."

"Those," returned the duke, "I will give your majesty to-morrow, in full; but I have, I can assure your majesty, discovered a terrible plot against your majesty's life, in which those three gentlemen are implicated. I assure you, sire, I would not ask for this order did I not know your person to be in danger. I will ask you one thing, sire, and then, with your permission, I will conduct you to the ball-room. When I entered this room, your majesty was profoundly agitated. Why was this?"

The king placed his hand on the shoulder of his favourite, as he rose and leaned heavily upon him.

"Steenie," he said, in a voice which betrayed much emotion, "Steenie, here is the order. The question you ask I will answer at another time. Kings' heads are none of the quietest; kings' families none of the tenderest; and there may be little sorrows and grievances, and bitternesses which may escape even your notice, and which even the worst of men may take to heart. Let us to the ball-room now."

"Good, sire," said the duke, and, offering his arm to the king, he conducted him from the apartment.

The ball was now at its height.

Fair women and haughty cavaliers filled the spacious rooms; and in one corner was gathered a group which was the observed of all observers.

On a high chair sat Lady Clara Mortimer—the belle of the court—her brown, glossy hair falling in rich curls over her shoulders; her blue, beaming eyes drooping tenderly and gently as it were; her whole manner and presence giving evidence of purity and refinement.

By her side was a young girl some two years younger, whose golden tresses seemed brighter and more golden still as they almost touched the darker tresses of her sister.

Near Clara and Geraldine, the dark and fair beauties, were several brilliantly dressed and handsome cavaliers, whose eyes wandered as if in doubtful admiration from one to the other of the sisters.

One, in particular, seemed to endeavour to monopolise the attentions of Lady Clara.

He was a tall, finely-built young man, of some five-and-twenty years, whose bronzed face and soldier-like bearing seemed to tell that the sword which he wore at his side had seen more than drawing-room service.

He was handsome and noble-looking, but there was a degree of hauteur about him which almost amounted to insufferable pride.

Towards Lady Clara Mortimer his manner was the most gentle and gallant; his proud voice was modulated into the tenderest tones, his attitude was relieved of all its stiffness and self-importance, but ever and anon his eyes flashed and his cheeks flushed as he caught the earnest glance of one who watched him closely —one who had leaned for more than half an hour against a massive pillar, with folded arms and pallid face.

The watcher was Wilford Rokeby, the lieutenant of the Palace Guard.

Presently, as the cavalier was earnestly conversing with the one who seemed to have made so deep an impression upon his heart, a page approached bearing a tiny note.

The page was a youth of some sixteen years, with long fair hair and dark hazel eyes, looking very handsome and noble in his blue velvet doublet and golden embroidery.

Wilford Rokeby, as he saw him, made a movement as if to advance; but, by a glance of significance, and placing a finger on his lip, the boy restrained him.

The Duke of Buckingham's page then approached the young cavalier.

"Sir Huntley Mordaunt," he said, "the Duke of Buckingham sends you this."

Sir Huntley took the note and read it hastily.

Then, crushing it in his hand almost angrily, he thrust it in his bosom.

"Lady Clara," he said, "I must leave you for awhile. The king, you see, has just entered with the Duke of Buckingham, and he has sent for me. For awhile, then, adieu."

He bowed gracefully, and then, with the haughty step which was peculiar to him, he walked away.

Wilford Rokeby, still leaning with folded arms against the pillar, watched him until he disappeared amid the throng.

Then, quitting his post of observation, he approached Lady Clara Mortimer.

"Oh, Lady Clara," he said, in an under tone, "how long is this to last? How long am I to be compelled to see this man—this reprobate—monopolising your attention in my very presence? How long am I to be forced to see him smiling upon you—to see you smiling on him, and foremost in the dance with him—to hear your names coupled as those of betrothed lovers, when your vows have been made to me—when you have given me hope in secret, and so earnestly, so truthfully, as it seemed, promised me that this secrecy and mystery should not last long?"

The young girl's eyes drooped, and her bosom heaved with intense emotion as the young lieutenant spoke, and telltale blushes suffused her pretty cheeks.

"You are too exacting, Wilford," she said; "you forgot our compact. Is it not enough that I love you, that I have promised to be yours, and yours only, and that I ask but patience and constancy? Have I yet given you cause for real jealousy?"

"You have not, indeed."

"Then, why blame me?"

"I hate this Sir Huntley Mordaunt; there is something in his manner and appearance which sends a chill and a dread to my heart. I feel that he is an enemy of ours; I am sure he is meditating evil against you and yours, and I know that he is daily plotting against me."

"You have your own remedy, Wilford," said the young girl, earnestly. "Keep from all conspiracies—from all intrigues which may furnish grounds for attacking you, and then, what can you fear?"

The words of Lady Clara fell heavily on Wilford's heart.

What could *he* answer—he who was so bound up in the deepest and most complicated of plots?

How could *he*, whose liberty hung upon a thread, follow out her instructions?

"I would do anything—promise anything—could I throw off this reserve, and publicly claim my right to be considered your friend—your betrothed husband. But this mystery, which not even you will explain, weighs heavily and painfully on my heart."

At this moment a youth, habited also in the costume of a guard, approached with a careless air, and, after bowing with graceful nonchalance to the ladies, clapped Wilford on the shoulder.

"Where is your gaiety—where is your joyousness, friend Rokeby?" cried he. "This is no place for sorrow. If it is Hubert Aveling's death that preys upon your mind, be at rest, when you remember that there are brave hearts and bright swords to avenge it!"

"Oh, it is very well to give advice, Launcelot Courtenay," returned Wilford Rokeby, "but not so easy to take it. I cannot drive from my mind the remembrance of the pale, still face of my friend upturned towards the sky. And this Sir Huntley Mordaunt; he, too, is another source of anxiety to me. Besides other reasons which I have for disquietude in regard to him, I feel an instinctive belief that he is connected in some way with Hubert Aveling's death. Ah! Great Heaven! See—as he approaches now from the further end of the room and removes his glove—see how the blood lies thick upon his hand! Just God! do my eyes deceive me, or is this man walking red-handed among us, unnoticed and unchallenged? It is *no* delusion—no delusion! See, Launcelot, see! I am not deceived."

Launcelot gazed earnestly in the direction indicated by his friend.

"I see nothing," he said; "calm yourself; be advised by me. Men have been committed to the Tower for a less offence than a quarrel in the king's palace."

Wilford took no heed of his companion's words or the frightened looks which Lady Clara Mortimer cast upon him.

His eyes were riveted upon the advancing cavalier.

Rightly or wrongly, the hand of Sir Huntley Mordaunt appeared to him dyed in blood, which seemed, as he approached nearer and nearer, to lessen in colour until, as he stood close to Wilford Rokeby beneath the bright lamp, there was but a bright red spot upon it!

This spot, however, was enough for Wilford.

He forgot where he was.

The presence of the king, the queen,

and their courtiers, the thronging pleasure seekers, the fact of his being in the palace, the danger which attended a rupture with a royal favourite, such as Sir Huntley Mordaunt undoubtedly was—all—all was swallowed up in one wild, frantic thought, and, rushing forward, he seized Sir Huntley by the wrist.

"What means this insult? Why do you seize my hand?" cried Mordaunt, in terrible anger.

"For the blood that is upon it!" exclaimed Wilford, wildly, as he pointed to the spot where he had seen the stain.

It had vanished!

"Merciful powers! it has gone," he said. "But Heaven has warned me, and I will follow out its commands."

"You are mad!" whispered Launcelot Courtenay. "Pay no heed to him, Sir Huntley; the death of his friend last night has well-nigh turned his brain."

Sir Huntley frowned fiercely.

"Your friend," he said, "must pay for his madness. At midnight, Lieutenant Rokeby, I will meet you beneath the Tower wall."

"I will be there," cried Wilford Rokeby; "and may Heaven, which has heard my vow of vengeance, guide my arm aright."

At this moment the page of the Duke of Buckingham approached, while at the further end of the chamber a singular commotion took place, and the mailed forms and gleaming guns of troopers mingled with the gay throng.

"Lieutenant Rokeby, the king has need of you," said the page.

"At twelve o'clock I will be at the Tower, Sir Huntley," repeated Wilford, as he walked away, fearing to look at the pale face and drooping form of his mistress.

With the king his business was brief.

The order was given to him to convey Lord Claude Mortimer, Lord Clarence Tremaine, and the Duke of Rosstrevor to the Tower, and, before he had recovered from his surprise and grief at being compelled, among others, to lead Lady Clara's brother into captivity in the gloomy fortress, he found himself at the head of his men, and already on the road.

The Duke of Buckingham watched him as he departed. Then he called his page.

"Wilford Rokeby and his friends," he said, "meet this night at twelve. Follow him, and tell the Governor of the Tower to see that this madcap lieutenant does not leave the place till morning. Tell him that the king's life depends upon his prompt obedience, and *I* will guarantee that he loses no favour with King James."

The boy bowed and quitted the room; and, in a few moments, a light skiff was bearing him towards the Tower over the waters of the silent Thames.

Unseen by him, a boat, containing several armed men, pushed off at the same moment, and followed eagerly in his wake.

THEN CLASH WENT THE SWORDS TOGETHER.

CHAPTER III.

THE FAIR UNKNOWN!

THE young page sped onwards rapidly from the Palace of Whitehall, never dreaming of those who followed him so eagerly and determinedly.

Under the guidance of the Duke of Buckingham he had been led into many and strange adventures; but on this occasion there seemed no real cause for pursuit, and he never once looked out for enemies.

As he neared Old London Bridge, however, he became conscious that he was followed.

The boat containing the armed men had rapidly gained upon him, and as soon as it had shot through the dreary arches, and passed into the dark waters of the pool, they drew up close, and challenged him.

"Young sir, a word with you," said one of them, standing up in the boat as it jarred against the light skiff; "whither are you bound?"

"My business is that of my master," returned the page, boldly. "I tell it to no one."

"Well answered," replied the other, "but somewhat indiscreetly, since we are here in numbers sufficient to compel you to do our bidding. Tell us at once," he added in a sterner and more commanding voice, "tell us at once whither you are bound, from whom you come, and what message you bear, or I shall seize your papers, and maybe plunge you head foremost into the water."

The page drew back as far as he could in safety, and unsheathed his light sword.

"Back!" he said, "I take no man's commands but my master's. Back, or I will show you that I can fight as well as keep a secret. The lamb, you know, can sometimes defeat the wolf."

"You refuse, then, to do my bidding?" said the other, savagely.

"I do."

"Then your foolhardiness is your own enemy," exclaimed the man, and with these words he sprang into the boat so violently and recklessly that it rolled agitatedly to and fro.

But the page was not thus to be taken at a disadvantage.

His light sword parried skilfully the fierce thrusts of his opponent, and it was not long before the cavalier found that his adversary was one with whom it would be folly to trifle.

"My friends," he cried, "this young whelp fights like a madman. Come, one of you, and drag him down into the boat. I would not harm him, but in a few moments we shall have our enemies upon us."

In an instant the boat rolled again under the weight of two of the other men, who sprang into it simultaneously.

"We'll soon pull him down, the young

imp!" cried one of them, running nimbly along the edge of the skiff, while the other balanced it.

The page saw his danger.

Resistance was vain.

One wild glance he cast round him—one glance, as if to discover if any possible help was near, and then he sheathed his sword.

His enemies lowered their weapons.

Naturally they imagined that he was about to deliver up the papers of which they were in search, and experienced in their hearts a secret satisfaction at being enabled to obtain them without further harm to the brave page.

They were deceived.

Passing rapidly to the extreme end of the boat, he stood for an instant facing them.

"You think," he cried, "that you have conquered me. You are wrong. What I have entrusted to me I never part with, except with life. See, then, how I achieve my end, or devote my existence to these dark and rushing waters."

With these words he sprang from the skiff, and plunged into the deep river.

His pursuers stood for a moment in utter bewilderment, as his light form disappeared in the black eddies.

But they soon recovered their self-possession.

"That is always the way with you, Giles Lambert," cried one of the men. "You are too squeamish in these affairs. One shot would have settled it all."

"You are a murderer in your very heart, Job Mulford," returned the other. "I will *not*—as you know well—resort to such means, if others have a chance of success. Let us follow this madcap. We must overtake him ere he reaches the shore, or, at any rate, before he can climb up yon rough and slippery bank."

With these words, he sprang back into the large boat, and they once more began to pull rapidly in the direction of the river's edge.

The page, meanwhile, when he leaped into the dark stream, struck out lustily for the shore.

He was a good swimmer, and had no fear of not being able to achieve his purpose; but the remembrance of the enemies who were near to him, and who were pursuing him for a purpose, which was to him an enigma, caused him to swerve every now and then from his course.

Presently, as he heard the voices of his pursuers nearer, and knew that they were gaining ground, he imprudently deviated from the direction he had taken, and began to float with the tide.

In doing this, his head struck against a floating log, and he became insensible.

What time elapsed between the time when he sank senseless down—down into the depths of the river—and the moment when he awoke, he was unable to say.

Certain it was, however, that when he recovered his consciousness, he was in a well-furnished and well-lighted room, and the voices of two persons in earnest conversation fell upon his ears.

Awaking thus suddenly from a stupor, deep and heavy as death, it would not have been surprising if our young friend had sprung wildly to his feet, and sought an explanation of his position.

But he did not do so.

Prudence came rapidly to his aid, and

HUBERT AVELING,

THE VICTIM OF SIR HUNTLEY MORDAUNT.

checking the exclamation which rose to his lips, he lay still and listened.

One glance only he took at the speakers.

This glance showed him that one of them was the man who had been addressed as Giles Lambert, and the other a lady, half masked.

Lambert was young; but the age of the lady was undistinguishable.

Her hair was dark—at least, the little which could be seen beneath her hat seemed dark—her figure was slender, and her voice was soft and pleasant.

More he could not tell.

"Giles," said the lady, "you have done well. I could not have wished this young life to have been shed in my service. He is a brave young lad, and was, after all, but doing his master's bidding. However, he is safe, and we need say no more of that. The duel will now take place, and may Heaven defend the right!"

Giles Lambert smiled.

"You seem confident in the issue of this combat," he said.

"I am."

"And yet should you be wrong—should Sir Huntley Mordaunt prove more than a match for your brave champion—what then?"

"Then," cried the lady, pressing her hand over her bosom, and glancing upwards towards Heaven, "then I must ask Providence to save his soul and to seek me another as brave as Wilford Rokeby. Oh! Giles Lambert, you little know me, if you think that I can forgive this man. Shall I, who loved Hubert Aveling so well, permit this assassin to walk red-handed among us—to lisp

sweet nothings in women's ears, and receive honours and rewards at the hands of the king? No, no, Lambert; were I an assassin as he is, I would soon rid the court of his hated presence; but as it is, I will leave it to those who can honour a woman's love, and pity her sorrow and her despair."

"And yet," said Giles Lambert, "yet you have no proof of his guilt."

"Proof!" cried the masked lady, still pressing her hand over her breast, "proof! What need have I of proof, when my heart here tells me what it does? Oh! I need no more evidence, Giles Lambert. There is something within my bosom which tells me that Sir Huntley Mordaunt is the assassin, and nothing, till the day of doom, would make me alter my belief. No, no; he must die. The young blood he has shed—the bright heart he has stilled—the loved voice he has hushed for ever, call to me to avenge him, and, by the great God—who rules us all— I swear to answer to this cry! If Wilford Rokeby dies, and I can find no other champion, then I myself will destroy him!"

Giles Lambert thought a moment, and then answered her in a voice which had in it a strange intonation of bitterness—

"Some long time since I came to London, a poor adventurer and without friends, and won my way to a position in the king's army. I was then foolish enough to cast my eyes upon a lady far above me. She rebuked me then, and declared she would never forgive me. I will earn her forgiveness now. If Wilford Rokeby dies this night in your cause, I myself will take up the gage of vengeance, and dedicate my life to Sir Huntley Mordaunt's destruction. Fear not, lady—I shall say no more. The very thought that I am fighting for one who possessed your whole heart would make love in me impossible.''

The masked lady extended her hand.

The page observed it.

It was very small and very white, and had upon it an emerald and ruby ring—a peculiar ring, with the head of a snake glittering treacherously over the pretty finger.

"You have long since merited my forgiveness," she said, "else I would not this evening have invited your assistance. But—if you act as you now promise me—you will entitle yourself to my life-long thanks.''

"One favour you can grant me now," said Lambert.''

"Name it, and if I can grant it, you may rest assured I will.''

"I wish for a password by which, at any time, I can gain admission to your presence.''

The lady smiled.

"A strange request, truly," she said; "yet it is one I can scarcely refuse. I will give you, then, the same password which admits Buckingham always to the presence of the king.''

"And what is that?''

" 'The king and the favourite !' ''

"A thousand thanks," said Lambert, raising to his lips the white hand he had till this moment retained; "and, depend upon it, these words will never be used except for your benefit. I will now hurry down to the Tower, and see that Wilford Rokeby has fair play in this duel. Although I do not suspect Sir Huntley of this murder, I fear me he would not be particular as to his method of ridding himself of an adversary who proved troublesome. Adieu, my lady—or, shall I lead you to your coach ?''

"I will go at once to my coach," returned the unknown; "but this page —what is to be done with him? Is he safe here ?''

"Yes; as soon as we are gone, Gertrude Laverne will awaken him. The narcotic I gave him will scarcely cease its working until this deadly scene is over. Now, my lady, I will lead you to your coach and then——''

"Silence !" she interrupted, placing her finger to her lips.

"Yes; my word on that," he said. "I will never reveal to any one this meeting. Nor will I return to the palace until I can bring news of the result of this duel.''

They then quitted the room together.

The page waited until they had passed away ere he moved from his recumbent position.

Then springing to his feet, he searched in the bosom of his doublet to see if the letter from Buckingham was still there.

It was gone !

"Ah !" he cried, "I see the plot now; but never mind. I have the watchword — the same she said that opens the king's door to Buckingham. This may prove to me far more useful than she would imagine; and now, since they are gone, I will follow in their wake, and see from afar this duel which I cannot prevent.''

So saying, he arose, and as noiselessly as he could, made his way across the room towards the staircase which the companions had descended.

He was not challenged, and in a few moments he found himself once more in the cool night air.

"The narcotic acts but weakly," murmured he, as he hurried towards the Tower. "I shall yet be able to witness this fight. Ah! for the many slights you have put upon me, Sir Huntley Mordaunt, you may be paid this night."

The words had scarcely left his lips, when the light of torches fell upon the bosom of the dark river, and the clash of arms was heard.

"They are at it already," exclaimed the page, as his pace increased to a run; "I must be quick, or I shall lose the best of it."

CHAPTER IV.

A DUEL TO THE DEATH.

On leaving the Palace of Whitehall, Wilford Rokeby and his men, escorting the prisoners to their dark and gloomy homes in the Tower, entered a large boat and made all speed towards London Bridge.

Wilford, brave, stalwart soldier as he was, could not repress a sigh as he passed down the uneven stairs, and saw the water plashing up at his feet.

It was here that on the night before he had met his friend, Hubert Aveling; it was here he had bidden the watermen meet them to take them together to the Lone House at Linwood; and now he was passing down to the water's edge, alone as it were, the escort of prisoners and the Avenger of the Early Dead!

As he sat himself down in the boat by the side of Launcelot Courtenay, who insisted upon accompanying him, he cast one long, lingering, tender glance at the windows of the palace.

He was going upon a dangerous mission.

The man upon whose hand he had seen, cr fancied he had seen, the stains of blood, he had defied to mortal combat, and in less than an hour he was to meet him beneath the battlements of the Tower.

It was no common duel they were to engage in, no ordinary exchange of cuts and thrusts in which a flesh wound would be enough to satisfy honour.

This was a battle to the death, in which the utter annihilation of the one would alone wash out the terrible hate of the other.

"You are serious, Wilford," cried Launcelot, turning to his friend as gaily as if nothing was about to happen.

"I have reasons, have I not?"

"I do not see them."

"You are vastly unobservant, then, my dear Lance," said Wilford. "In the first place, my foster-brother, my dear brother, Hubert Aveling, is dead; he who has fought side by side with me; who has before now saved my life and my honour. Is that no reason?"

"Yes," cried Lance, with much emotion, "yes, it *is*. But you shall *not* want for a friend to aid you, or an arm to assert your honour while Launcelot Courtenay lives !"

"I know it, Lance. But then I have other reasons. You are aware how deeply I love Clara Mortimer ?"

"I am; and you will win her."

"I am conducting her brother to the Tower."

"He must be saved."

"By whom ?"

"By you."

"By me, who within an hour may be lying stark and stiff by the river's side, slain by Sir Huntley Mordaunt's sword."

"Why, Wilford," exclaimed Lance, "this humour ill befits *you*; you who are so brave and dauntless, ever the foremost in the fight, the most reckless adventurer, the most daring soldier. You will *not* die; you will not—*shall* not fail! Think of this villain; think of poor Lady Laura's stricken heart, of Hubert Aveling's pale face, and then tell me, *will* you fail ?"

Wilford Rokeby laughed bitterly.

"Oh! you mistake me," he said. "You mistake me altogether, Lance. I feel no tremor of the heart, no wavering of the arm. When I think of this man who has the blood of my friend upon his hand, I feel the strength of a giant, the heart of an immortal being! I speak only of death, because — if Heaven will but permit it to be so— nothing but death shall part us. One or the other of us shall this night measure his length upon the banks of this dark river, and there breathe out his last plea for Heaven's mercy, or his last appeal to a friend to take up the gauntlet of revenge."

"Ah! there speaks my brave friend !"

cried the light-hearted Launcelot. "I hope that nothing will be suffered to interfere with this meeting. I for one would not be absent from it for the world, for if *you* love Clara Mortimer, *I* also love Geraldine. But hush! Let us say no more. Lord Mortimer is observing us."

Wilford Rokeby readily acquiesced in this, for he had no desire to talk.

His mind was occupied with but *one* thought—his eyes had but one sight before them, and when at length the boat stopped, and grated against the stairs at Traitor's Gate, he sprang up like one in a dream.

He was the first to alight and knock at the dark, iron-bound doorway.

Then he turned to help the prisoners out of the boat.

"Lord Mortimer," he said, as he pressed the hand of Clara's brother, "this is my *duty*."

"For which," returned the young noble, haughtily withdrawing his hand, "you need make *no* apology."

Before any further explanation could be given, the black portal was swung open, and three armed men appeared.

"What want you ?" asked one.

"I am Wilford Rokeby, Lieutenant of the Guard at Whitehall. I bring three prisoners to the Governor of the Tower. Admit them."

The three prisoners walked haughtily into the stone passage, which clanged dismally under their measured footsteps.

Then the Night Guard entered behind them, and the heavy door was swung back into its place once more.

The further preliminaries were soon arranged.

The warrant for the detention of the three prisoners was read to the governor of the Tower; they were then given into the charge of warders and placed in separate cells, and the Night Guard proceeded to take its departure.

The sentinel began to lead the way towards the Traitors' Gate.

"Stay !" cried Wilford, "I have business elsewhere. Let us depart by the gate which admits us to Tower Hill."

On reaching the outside of the dreary prison—the Bastille of Old London—the young lieutenant ordered his men to halt and form.

"My men," he said, "in all emergencies I have found you ready at the word of command. We have yet more business to perform ere we return to the Palace of Whitehall. Last night, as you know, your other lieutenant, Hubert Aveling, was foully murdered. I have discovered his murderer. I cannot bring him to justice, but this night —in a few moments—when the clock yonder in the turret strikes the hour of midnight, I meet him beneath the Tower wall. I have my second here— no doubt Sir Huntley will bring his friends. To you I leave it that we are not interrupted."

A loud murmur of approbation at once showed to him which way their sympathies led them.

He was a favourite with his men, and he had expected nothing else.

"Have you your torches with you ?" he asked.

For answer, the men drew from their belts the long twisted rope-ends, which the Night Guard always carried.

"Shall we light them ?" asked one of them.

"Yes, light them and follow me," said Wilford. "Hark !—there is the first stroke of twelve. We shall be too late."

It was scarcely a minute, however, before the flambeaux were blazing merrily, and the party hurried down to the water's edge at a point where the outlying battlements of the Tower afforded a place of temporary concealment.

It was a dark, romantic spot—just such as men in such a humour would have chosen—a spot where the water threw a heavy shadow over the bank, and almost mingled it with the water.

Sir Huntley Mordaunt was punctual to his time.

Just as the Night Guard reached the appointed place, a boat neared the shore, and several cavaliers sprang out, foremost among them being Sir Huntley himself.

He halted a moment, as if in surprise, as he saw the assembled men ; but, as if not caring to exhibit any emotion which might be construed into fear, he quickly recovered himself, and advanced.

"We are both punctual, Lieutenant Rokeby," he said ; "we had better lose no time in commencing."

"Certainly not," exclaimed Rokeby, who had already drawn his sword ; "I am prepared. You see I have torches here, which will give us both fair play."

"An excellent plan," said Sir Huntley, drily.

Then, casting their plumed hats to their attendants, they both advanced fiercely.

It was a scene of thrilling and romantic interest—the grouped cavaliers; the steel-clad soldiers; the rugged battlements; the rushing river; the two eager combatants; all illumined grandly by the red glow of the torches; while, up above, the deep blue sky and the twinkling stars looked down in silent watchfulness upon man's fierce conflict with man!

As I have said before, this was no ordinary duel—it was a combat to the death!

The two men advanced savagely—impetuously.

Their gleaming eyes, their pale faces, their white lips, their very attitudes told that they meant no surrender—no mercy!

The spectators held their breath for a moment in eager expectation.

Then clash went the swords together — clash — clash — clash; thrust for thrust, parry for parry.

The merry jingle of the steel was a mockery, as it were; every plunge was meant as a death-blow—every parry was but the breathing point before a desperate lunge for life!

Clash—clash—clash!

Quicker and quicker still were the sounds that went echoing over the silent river!

Hotter and hotter grew the strife; more stern the features of the foes; more set their lips; more ghastly their pallor!

"For love and revenge," thought Wilford Rokeby, from the first.

"For dear life's sake," was soon the thought of Sir Huntley, as his dauntless foe pressed upon him.

The cavaliers on the one side, and the Night Guard on the other, looked on eagerly.

Sir Huntley Mordaunt now began visibly to give way, and as each step of vantage ground was gained, the eagerness of Wilford Rokeby appeared to increase.

Wounded slightly, and seeing the jaws of death opening, as it were, to receive him, Sir Huntley was rapidly pressing in among his own friends, losing his self command, parrying his foe's thrusts weakly, and making desperate but ill-judged lunges.

This was the time.

Raising his sword aloft—gleaming now in the light of the torches—Wilford Rokeby prepared to give the final stroke of vengeance, while the spectators on either side, panting, and breathless with eagerness, watched the actions of their respective friends.

The cavaliers would willingly have interfered to save their friend, although, as it was "a duel to the death," they had no right to do so.

But they dared not.

The Night Guard, mail-clad and armed with long stout swords, were on the other side to see justice done, and the slightest interference on the part of Sir Huntley's men would have been the signal for a fierce onset.

So, gladly as they would have shielded him or hurried him off to the boat, or in some way or other obtained him breathing time, they were compelled to remain inactive.

They were soon relieved from their anxiety and alarm, however.

Scarcely had Wilford Rokeby raised

his gleaming sword, when there was a sudden rush of feet, and several men flung themselves down from the battlements, while others hurried up, and pressed their way into the very midst of the scene of combat.

At their head was the Governor of the Tower.

"How, now, gentlemen!" he said. "What's this? Do you not know it to be high treason to fight here upon the king's ground?"

Wilford bowed.

"Justice can *never* be treason, sir," he said.

"Ah! it is you who fight—you, a lieutenant of the Guard, who should know better. Who is your opponent?"

He glanced round, but could distinguish no form in particular as that of Rokeby's adversary, for the cavaliers had now gathered round their friend, and were hurrying into the boat.

Wilford Rokeby, whose sword was still unsheathed, was maddened by the sight, and advanced eagerly towards the retreating throng.

But the Governor of the Tower stepped before him.

"Back!" cried he. "Back, Lieutenant Rokeby, or I shall take on myself to arrest you. At another time, and in some other place, you may renew your duel, but not beneath this Tower, where I hold jurisdiction on behalf of His Most Sacred Majesty. See, your opponent is gone. It is too late; therefore, take my advice, and, for this night, desist from your enterprise. Remember, too, what an example you are giving to your men."

Scarcely a word of this long-winded and pompous speech was heard by Wilford Rokeby.

His eyes were wandering over the silent water, striving to pierce the dark shadows, among which the boat of Sir Mordaunt and his friends was fast disappearing.

His mind was wondering how soon another chance of fight would present itself, and bitterly cursing the interference which robbed him of his prey.

"Well, well," he said, as he again sheathed his sword, "I must defer this meeting since you have so inopportunely stepped in to prevent it."

Then he passed rapidly up the incline, and, without paying any further heed to the Constable of the Tower, addressed himself to Roderick Brandon, the sergeant of the Night Guard.

"Roderick," he said, "I have most important business to transact this night—business which prevents my returning to the palace for some hours. I am even now behind my time, and I wish you, therefore, to take the men home without me."

"Good, sir; and if the king sends for you——"

"Say that the three prisoners are safely lodged in the Tower. Of this duel, however, not a word."

"Fear not, sir," returned Roderick Brandon. "We never speak of night adventures to any. In these stupid times a little change is pleasant enough; and if it were not for such scenes, why, our life would be as monotonous as that of a monk. Does Mr. Lance Courtenay go with us?"

"No, no. I go elsewhere," returned Lance.

"Good-night, then," continued Wilford, "and remember, above all things, as you value my friendship, silence!"

The men now at once took their places in the boat, and the two friends, having seen them disappear on the dark stream, parted with mutual good wishes, and started in opposite directions.

Wilford then made his way to a hostelry, near the sombre state prison, which frowned over the rushing water.

Here he knocked up the grumbling host, and obtained a horse, a sorry-looking nag, but good enough for the occasion.

He then drew around him his long cloak, so as completely to conceal his dress, and as soon as he had quitted the inn, and reached a somewhat secluded spot, he placed upon his face a mask, which nearly covered his features.

This mask was of a green colour, and when seen in the light gave to the wearer a most peculiar and even unpleasant appearance.

Taking his way towards old London Bridge, then a dense mass of quaintly-shaped houses, he proceeded at a rapid rate along its rough roadway, paying no heed to the muttered curses of the disturbed gate-keeper, and on reaching the Surrey side of the river, he dashed away as quickly as the strength and willingness of his steed would allow, along the dark and lonely road.

Soon after this, the growling bridge-keeper had to leave his comfortable room to allow the passage of a second traveller, who was also masked, with a *brown* mask, and who seemed in as great a hurry as the first.

Again a third came—this one in a *black* mask—a tall, broadly-built man, whose beard hung long below the domino.

This was the last; and the three men, having taken the same road, all was still.

The Lone House at Linwood, which was the point to which Wilford Rokeby was pressing, was situated some six miles south of the Thames, and stood by itself in the midst of a mass of densely-foliaged trees.

Its builder seemed rather to have sought a shelter than a healthy home, for its foundations were sunken in a damp and greeny hollow, which before had been a pond, where toads and frogs and efts had disported, and which now in the rainy season was little better than a bog.

Upon the earth, which on all sides was much higher than the place where the foundations were sunk, grew tall, and densely-growing trees, around whose massive trunks coiled parasitical plants, and among which were thick masses of tangled undergrowth.

It was to this strange abode that Wilford Rokeby was now hurrying, and it was not very long, even on such a sorry nag, ere he reached the almost impenetrable barrier which surrounded it.

He knew it well, and, therefore, after glancing quickly around to see that no one was watching him, he suddenly dismounted, passed between two trees, and dragged his unwilling steed after him.

Then, having fastened his horse to a tree, he broke through the tangled underwood, and approached the dark-looking house where, for months past, the Five Masks had held their strange and mysterious meetings.

"IN THE KING'S NAME, ARREST THAT MAN!" CRIED SIR HUNTLEY.

CHAPTER V.

THE FIVE MASKS.

AFTER one more glance back to see if any one was following, Wilford Rokeby proceeded on until he reached the door of the house, where he knocked three times with a peculiar intonation.

In a moment the door opened, and a man in the costume of a trooper appeared on the threshold.

"The password?" he said.

"Buckingham," returned Wilford Rokeby.

"Good," cried the Guard, "you are the first."

"They are late, then."

"They are. Something, perhaps, may have detained them—some duel or some arrest."

"True, true," said Wilford, as he passed on down a broad but gloomy passage.

Instinctively the thought occurred—could these fellow conspirators of his have been among the friends and enemies who had clustered beneath the Tower wall but a short time before?

In the old house they saw not each other's faces—knew not each other's names. They acted silently—secretly.

Betrayal was almost impossible, unless one betrayed all; no special or personal enmity had any room here for its malevolent action.

As he thought thus, the trooper ushered him into the room where the Five Masks held their meetings.

It was a large, darkly-panelled chamber.

The ceiling, as well as the walls, was of a dull brown, and the windows were all built up, so as to exclude—with the light of day—the prying eyes of enemies.

At one end was a round table, where the conspirators sat without any distinction.

The rest of the hall was left—for a reason which will be explained hereafter—entirely blank.

A few minutes only elapsed before another arrival came—a man dressed in every way like Wilford Rokeby, with the exception that his mask was brown.

He merely bowed to the first comer, and took his seat.

Then another, and another, and another, and the door closed.

These last three had black, yellow, and red masks.

Silently they took their seats at the table, and, after a few moments, one of their number rose.

"Unknown friends," he said, "the WHITE MASK is absent. He will no longer take his place among us. He is dead!"

"How know you that?" asked the Man in the Brown Mask. "We give no names, and when we die out from the Society we pass, and make no sign."

"The WHITE MASK must have either

betrayed us, or have known of his approaching death. He sent word *himself* of his death. His name was Hubert Aveling."

As these words were pronounced, the door was blown open by a fierce gust of wind; a chill air invaded the apartment, and, as Wilford Rokeby started up and glanced towards the portal, a tall figure glided noiselessly over the threshold.

"Dead or alive I will be with you," Hubert Aveling had said. And he advanced now towards the table to keep his plighted word.

He wore a mask, truly, upon his pale and haggard face, but it was the White and terrible Mask of Death!

The four masked men who surrounded Wilford Rokeby gazed at him in undisguised wonder.

To their eyes there was no apparition. All they felt was the cold, chill wind which had swept in so fiercely; all they saw was the swinging open of the great door, and the undisguised emotion of the young Lieutenant of the Guard.

"What ails our Brother of the Green Mask?" asked the Red Mask. "Without there! has any stranger been admitted?"

At the voice of him who seemed to take the position of chief, the trooper who had charge of the outer gate ran in in alarm.

By this time, however, Wilford Rokeby's excitement had, in a great degree, subsided.

The figure of his friend, who had advanced so warningly, so noiselessly, so pale and ghastly towards him, had now vanished, and Wilford sank down into his chair, as exhausted by that momentary excitement as if he had passed through the fiery and glowing ordeal of a second duel for life.

"Did I hear your voice, sir?" asked the soldier, as he entered the chamber, and approached that portion of the table where the Red Mask sat.

"Yes; I wish to know whether any one has been suffered to enter our place of meeting unsummoned, and without giving the watchword?"

"No, sir. Since the Four have entered, all has been still as death, except when a sudden wind burst into the corridor, and swept open the door."

"'Tis very strange," muttered the Red Mask; "nevertheless, we cannot waste time now in fathoming the mystery. Retire, and see that you keep good watch."

The man having retired, and the door having been once more closed, the Red Mask addressed himself to Wilford Rokeby.

"Brother of the Green Mask," he said, "may I ask the cause of your emotion? It is due to the Society that you disclose it."

"I will," returned Wilford, boldly. "You were speaking of Hubert Aveling; you mentioned him as being either a coward or a traitor. He is neither."

"You know him?"

"I do. He was my best and dearest friend. Of that, however, I will say no more. Suffice it, that as you spoke of him, the door swung open under the influence of a mighty wind, and I saw him enter, his features disguised by the White Mask of Death! He came in noiselessly, gliding towards me, and, at the sound of your voice, vanished. That is my explanation. By the very rules of our band I am excused from saying more."

The masked brethren bowed in acquiescence.

"And now," continued Wilford, "as one of our number is gone—as one brave heart has suffered—let us be careful how we increase our number. For the present let us remain as we are. Let us not run the risk of admitting traitors."

To this proposition the band willingly agreed; and, after awhile, they proceeded to the business of the evening.

This business it is not my purpose to explain here.

It was most secret—most important—most mysterious.

Great names were freely used; the inmost recesses of great hearts were searched; lords and ladies who were at that moment of the still night sleeping the sleep of innocence or sin, were spoken of as if those who sat masked and mysterious around the table in that dark and gloomy house were their bosom friends, and could see into their very heart of hearts!

Just before the dawn broke over the country, the four separated.

Wilford Rokeby was the last but one to quit the place.

The miserable horse which he had borrowed at the old inn near the Tower was quietly awaiting him, nodding asleep among the long grass, and half hidden by the tangled brushwood; and it was not long before our hero was riding as fast as his steed would carry him along the road to London.

At Bartley Cross he halted to partake of some refreshment.

There were two reasons for this.

In the first place, he felt faint and weary from the excessive excitement and labour he had undergone; and, in the second place, he fancied that, during his ride, the figure of some unknown foe had hovered near him.

The voice of his murdered friend seemed to whisper to him of evil threatening him; and then again behind him came the clattering of horses' hoofs and the dull echo of the footsteps far away.

As he drew up at the inn door, he took a glance around him.

The spot was a dreary one.

The inn itself was one of those old places which are seldom, if ever, seen at the present day; built of blackened timber, with quaint little diamond-paned windows, and a sign which swung gloomily and drearily to and fro in the wind as if it was watching its own reflection in the waters of the black pond below.

Opposite it was a high wooden fence enclosing the further end of the ground of Bartley Manor—a massive gabled building, now tenantless—so that the view even from the top windows was obstructed by a dull prospect of nothingness!

The sounds of horses' feet had now ceased; so, having removed the green mask from his face, and cast his long cloak over his shoulders, Wilford Rokeby dismounted from his steed, and then knocked at the door of the inn.

After some grumbling, one of the upper windows was thrown open, and a head was protruded.

"Who's there?" growled the voice of

some one who had evidently been disturbed in the middle of a heavy sleep. "Who's there ?"

" A traveller in need of refreshment," replied Wilford.

" Well, well," said the landlord, " I can't see in this light what you are like, but I suppose you are what you say. We have guns and dogs here remember, if you seek to do us evil."

" Fear not," said Rokeby ; " I seek but a moment's refreshment, and shall then continue my journey, and leave you in peace.   Quick, my friend, unloose the door, for I am cold and thirsty."

In a very few moments the door was opened and Wilford had entered.

As he did so, a second horseman came up with such a rush, that the feet of his steed, as he spurred it on and then suddenly stopped, splashed up the water of the still dark pool.

He, too, alighted, and, fastening the bridle of his horse to a hook near the post of the door, entered, and called for refreshment.

On seeing Wilford, he turned his back towards him, and persistingly kept his face averted, so that our hero could see nothing of his features.

There was something in his manner, however, which roused Wilford's suspicions ; and, excited as he was by recent events, he was not inclined to allow the slightest circumstance to escape his attention when once it had been attracted.

Clouded as his life promised to be, he was resolved to endeavour to fathom, as far as possible, the reasons for this darkness.

Moving,   therefore,   towards   the

stranger, he tried, by an easy manœuvre, to catch a glimpse of his face.

The effort was vain.

As he neared the stranger, so the latter moved away, and, having drank up hastily the strong ale he had ordered, he made once more in the direction of his horse.

Now was the time.

Without waiting for any change for the piece of money he flung down, Rokeby sprang after the stranger, and confronted him just as he leaped into the saddle.

" Ha !" he cried ; " it is as I suspected.   Sir Huntley Mordaunt, defend yourself !"

As he spoke, he drew his sword and stood prepared, as if expecting his enemy to dismount and confront him.

The face of Sir Huntley was greatly agitated.

" This is no time for quarrels," he said. " I will not, and cannot remain !"

Wilford seized the bridle of his horse.

" You must, and shall remain," he cried. " We were interrupted before, we shall not be so interrupted again. We are alone now, man to man ; let us end this feud once and for ever."

Whether Sir Huntley Mordaunt had some special reason for avoiding him, or whether he remembered unpleasantly the deadly thrusts of Wilford's sword beneath the battlements of the Tower, it would be difficult to say ; at any rate he seemed resolved on *this* occasion not to hazard an encounter with his enemy.

Accordingly he gave a sudden wrench to the bridle, and, in an instant, the spirited horse he rode reared upon his hind legs, and Wilford Rokeby **was** flung violently backward.

Sir Mordaunt then put spurs **to his** horse, and rode desperately **away.**

Pursuit was useless.

The horse which Wilford Rokeby rode was, I have said, a sorry jade, which he had borrowed at an inn, and he, therefore, made no attempt to follow his enemy.

With feelings of anger and despair, he saw him passing away in the distance, and disappearing amid the misty atmosphere which the warm sun of morning was. calling up from the earth.

"You have escaped me twice," he cried, bitterly; "you shall not escape me always. My vow is registered before Heaven, and, in spite of the love whose loss I risk, in spite of the *world* I will avenge my friend."

How in that moment, as he cantered slowly in the wake of his deadly foe, he regretted that he was not seated upon the back of his own brave mare, Black Meg, which had carried him to **victory** on many a desperate field !

CHAPTER VI.

THE MYSTERY OF THE COAT OF MAIL.

LEADING from one of the state rooms at Whitehall to the chamber where, upon the night of the ball, the Duke of Buckingham had held his conference with King James, was a long corridor, in the very centre of which was a large bow window overlooking the river terrace, and forming a deep **and dark** recess.

Along the walls of this dimly-lighted corridor were hung strange old pictures, some representing the voluptuous beauties of the Court, others the grim, stern warriors who had won their title by their swords, or effeminate favourites who had crawled gently up the high hill of fortune.

You could scarcely distinguish their features in the misty light, and they seemed, therefore, at first sight, to be ghostly beings peering out from the heavy shadows.

What added more to the weird-like appearance of the place were the rows of coats of mail standing bolt upright against the walls, to keep watch over the pictured chivalry and beauty above them—bright, glittering armour, be it said, but here and there exhibiting dents and fractures which told that they had been used in no child's play.

Gazing at them, you could have almost seen the faces which once filled their now empty casques, and the strong hands which once grasped the heavy lances which now lay listlessly against the shoulder-pieces.

It was about ten o'clock at night **on** the second evening after the ball **and** the duel beneath the wall of the **Tower.**

The Palace was comparatively quiet.

The queen was in her own room listening to the pleasant chattering of her maids of honour.

The king and Buckingham were closeted together, speaking of the arrests which had already caused considerable excitement within and without the Palace.

Nearly all in the great building were engaged in some business which kept them to their own rooms.

At the hour of ten, however, just as the last reverberations of the clock rolled over the silent river, the door at one end of the long corridor opened, and a lady entered.

It was Clara Mortimer.

Cautiously she closed the door behind her, and glanced up the long, dimly-lighted passage to see if any one was there before her.

All was quiet.

She and the grim old pictures and the relics of the dead knights were there alone together.

Having satisfied herself of this, she made her way to the point where, as I have said, a deep recess was formed by the large bow window.

Here she ensconced herself as if for concealment, and looked out upon the dark scene which lay, as it were, at her feet.

She could see little distinctly.

The rolling river and its bank beyond, and the terrace, and the far-off houses, were all blended in an almost undistinguishable mass; but of sounds there was now and then an abundance.

The roll of wheels; the tramp of the Night Guard; the jingle of weapons; the exchange of passwords, and now and then a burst of laughter from some gay rollickers without, smote upon her ear as she listened.

Presently there was a sound nearer at hand.

It was in the corridor, and seemed like the heavy breathing of some concealed person.

She clasped her hands to her bosom in fear, and glanced quickly round.

No one was near her.

Heavy curtains fell over the windows, truly, but there was no room for anyone to hide himself behind th..m.

Whence, then, came the sound?

She had heard it certainly; and yet, throughout the length and breadth of the corridor there was no living being but herself.

With a shudder, she murmured,

" Oh ! how I wish he would come. What can detain him ?"

Then, as she prepared to return to her place at the window, she started with affright once more.

One of the coats of mail seemed to have shifted its position, and to be closer to her than it had been when she first entered.

With her heart leaping tumultuously in her breast, she returned to the casement and watched ; but, whether it had moved or not before, it now remained as still as death.

" It must be fancy, " thought she, " and yet I feel terribly uneasy."

She was soon, however, relieved from her position of alarm and loneliness.

Just as—to her wildly gleaming eyes—the atmosphere of the old corridor became darker, and the scene without

The Night Guard;

Or, THE SECRET OF THE FIVE MASKS.

"HE IS WALKING TO HIS DEATH," MUTTERED THE GAOLER.

more dismal and fantastic and the eyes of the old portraits more life-like, the door at the further end of the passage once more opened, and a man entered almost noiselessly.

It was Wilford Rokeby.

"Ah! Clara," he cried, rapturously, as he advanced to meet her, and drew her to his breast; "you have not then deceived me. Oh! what an age it seems since I have met you and embraced thus before."

The fair girl was fluttering and trembling like a frightened bird in his arms.

"And even now," she said, "I know not if I am doing rightly. It must be but a brief meeting. Sir Huntley Mordaunt is more watchful over me than ever; and I fear, too, his growing favour with the king bodes you no ultimate good."

"I have thought so myself," returned Wilford; "but tell me, dearest, why this sudden alarm? You are trembling and panting as if some unexpected terror had overwhelmed you. What is it?"

Clara smiled up into his face.

"You will think me foolish no doubt, Wilford," she said; "but, since I have been in this corridor, I have experienced a feeling of overwhelming dread, and just now I heard a sound as of the heavy breathing of some man concealed here."

"A man concealed here!"

"So at least it sounded," continued Clara; "and then, when I examined the place to endeavour to ascertain where the sound proceeded, I fancied that the coat of mail which had stood

some four yards from me had advanced from among the others, and approached me. At any rate it was out of the line."

"Which was it?" asked Rokeby, eagerly.

"The one which is now just behind you."

Wilford turned hastily, and glanced at it; while the young girl, as her eyes fell upon it, uttered a cry of fear, and started back.

"The coat of mail stands in a line with the rest," exclaimed Wilford Rokeby.

"Yes, yes!" cried Clara Mortimer, "it has moved again. There is some fearful mystery here!"

Without another word, the Lieutenant of the Night Guard began an examination of the suspicious figure.

But he could discover nothing.

All seemed fixed and solid.

"This is a strange mystery, indeed," he said, turning to Clara, who, with eager eyes, was watching his movements. "*I* cannot fathom it. Are you certain that it has moved?"

"I could swear it."

"Strange, indeed!" murmured Rokeby. "Can there be spies upon my track? Can those who have sworn to be my friends have betrayed me?"

Clara placed one hand on each of his shoulders, and looked up into his face.

"Betrayed you, Wilford!" she said. "What have they to betray? Have you neglected my advice, and embroiled yourself in the unhappy intrigues of the day?"

"Clara," he said, "you pain me when you ask these questions, because

I cannot answer them. I am a true friend to my country; whatever intrigues I may join in are *in* the interest of England, not against it. More than this I cannot say."

"Then if you are England's true friend, you can be no friend of Buckingham's," said Clara.

Wilford smiled.

" *You*, then, have discovered that the favourite is his own friend and the friend of no one else, " said Rokeby. " Well, well, it matters little to me whether Buckingham or Huntley Mordaunt are favourites if I only view it in a political light. But the vows of the heart are different; they *must* be fulfilled, and there is one of these men who must fall."

As he spoke thus, and Clara was looking up into his face, admiring his noble features as they glowed with excitement, there was again the sound which had so startled Clara Mortimer before.

A low, suppressed sigh.

"By Heaven! I heard it then, " exclaimed Rokeby. "I must investigate this matter. We must have no secret passages for spies in Whitehall. The king shall know of this."

Approaching the mailed figure once more, he endeavoured to shake it upon its pedestal.

It was immoveable.

"The sound must come from another spot," said he, in a whisper to Clara. "The wall is thin in some part. It has been built so, or altered so purposely, to enable spies to overhear what is said in this corridor. But no matter, I have uttered no treason. My right hand is ever at the service of my country, and, while I can say this with an honest heart, I surely can have nothing to fear from the shafts of intriguing enemies. Oh! Clara, how glad I shall be when you can throw off the mask of coldness you wear—when you will no longer deem it necessary to deny the love I really believe you have for me."

"Would that it were so; would that I could cast off this reserve," she answered, gazing tenderly at him. "I feel as if, at this moment, some great danger was threatening you, and though my protection would avail little against any enemy, it would be some satisfaction to share the peril with you."

Scarcely had the words left her lips, when there was a sudden commotion outside the door at the end of the corridor, and ere they could utter a word of surprise, Sir Huntley Mordaunt entered, followed by six of the Night Guard, under the command of Launcelot Courtenay.

Sir Huntley Mordaunt advanced towards them with a swaggering and insolent gait, such as would be no part of a gentleman's manners in these days, but in those times was not considered unbecoming.

"I regret," he said, "I regret exceedingly, Lieutenant Rokeby, to have to interrupt your interview with this lady, but my duty to my king compels me. Lady Clara Mortimer, allow me to lead you hence."

Lady Clara made no movement except to cling more closely to her lover.

He was in danger now, and she cared not who knew of her love.

The old feeling of shame and reserve was all gone from her now, overwhelmed in the one idea that he was about to suffer unjustly, and that she was powerless to protect him—powerless to comfort him, except by the confession of her love.

Wilford Rokeby's hand moved at once towards his sword.

"This lady will remain where she is," he cried. "Tell me at once what you desire of me?"

Sir Huntley Mordaunt bowed ironically.

"I desire to spare this lady's feelings," he said. "I again ask will Lady Clara Mortimer allow me to lead her away?"

She made no answer.

She could only cling nearer to her lover.

"Lady Clara desires to remain, Sir Huntley," replied Wilford Rokeby. "Speak on, therefore, and quickly, too, as I desire—in such a presence as yours —to have as short an interview with you as possible."

As he uttered these words, he drew his sword, as if to enforce the truth of his words, forgetting, in the heat of his passion, that he was in the king's Palace; forgetting that it was high treason to draw his weapon in such precincts; forgetting how he was compromising both himself and Lady Clara Mortimer, by yielding to his feelings.

"Very well, Master Rokeby," said Mordaunt; "since you insist upon this lady being a witness of these proceedings, let it be so. Launcelot Courtenay, that person is charged with high treason.

In the king's name I command you to arrest him."

Lance advanced a few steps, while Clara clung more closely to her lover, with the energy of despair.

"Have you the warrant, Sir Huntley?" he asked.

"I have," replied Sir Huntley, raising his finger, and pointing towards Wilford, though he avoided his gaze, as if he feared to meet the fiery glance of his eye. "Here it is. See, now he has his sword in his hand. That is high treason in itself. Your orders are to take him hence and lodge him in the Tower. See that it is done at once."

Lance, whose face had turned deadly pale, as Sir Huntley Mordaunt spoke, advanced now sorrowfully towards his friend.

"Wilford," he said, "I must do my duty. I must ask you for your sword."

Gently Rokeby disengaged himself from the tender embrace of his beautiful mistress.

"Clara," he whispered, "be of good cheer. Heaven will watch over me, and punish the guilty."

She pressed his hand eagerly—lovingly—bravely.

"And I, Wilford, will save you if all others desert you!" she murmured. "Keep up your brave heart. Fear nothing from this man. I can do much —much more than you think—and if I cannot, I know those who will aid me."

"Laura Clavering for one!" said a voice, deep, solemn, and earnest, ringing with a weird-like sound through the old corridor, and coming none knew whence.

All started, and glanced around them.

No one but the prisoner and his mistress, Sir Huntley, and the Night Guard was there.

"Who spoke?" asked Sir Huntley Mordaunt, sternly.

Lance Courtenay looked at him with a glance which plainly told his feelings.

"*You* can answer that question better than any, Sir Huntley," he answered. "No one of my men spoke. It is a warning voice, may be, from another world, which you may have more reason to dread than any here. Wilford, let us go. The atmosphere of this place suits me not."

Sir Huntley eyed him fiercely.

"Remember," he cried, "that your head itself would be forfeited were you to permit his escape. See that he is lodged safely in the Tower, and that on his road thither he holds no communication with any one; otherwise, the king's displeasure will fall upon you."

"I shall comply with the warrant," returned Launcelot Courtenay; "but further I shall do nothing. I shall place my friend in the safe custody of the Constable of the Tower; but as for

communications on the road, I know nothing of them, and can take no cognizance of your words. Come, Wilford, let us be going."

Clara Mortimer still clung to him.

With the other hand she made an imploring gesture to Sir Huntley.

"Oh! Sir Huntley; spare him this —spare him this shame, and me this misery. You know he is innocent; for my sake plead with the king that this most unjust arrest shall not take place."

Sir Huntley avoided her gaze.

"With you," he said, "I will speak another time. As to the justice of the arrest, it is not for me to judge. Launcelot Courtenay, do your duty, and when you come back from the Tower, see that I know of your return."

He folded his arms with a smile, and watched the Night Guard as they closed round their prisoner and led him away.

Then, as the door clanged to dismally behind them, and he saw the tearful eyes of Clara Mortimer and her clasped hands, he said, in a tone of savage triumph—

"Clara Mortimer, through *you* Wilford Rokeby is consigned to the Tower — through *you* his doom is sealed. Nothing now can save him."

CHAPTER VII.

THE LEAGUE OF TRAITORS.

THE night following the arrest of Wilford Rokeby a man might have been seen walking hurriedly up and down the open space before the palace.

The sentinels who were keeping watch eyed him suspiciously.

Although he did not attempt any disguise, they one and all had the same thought—that he was the mysterious assassin who had destroyed the life of Wilford Rokeby's foster brother—Hubert Aveling.

They had no means of challenging him, however.

Whenever he saw that he was observed, he moved away and did not come again until they had almost ceased to look for him.

Presently he was joined by a second figure, and then the two walked away in the direction of the river terrace.

Here their forms were lost in the darkness, and the men, tired with watching, sought for them no more.

The two figures were those of Sir Huntley Mordaunt and Leonard Fairfax, second constable of the Tower.

"Well," said Fairfax, as soon as they had reached a spot where they were beyond the reach of prying eyes, "I have placed the prisoner in safe custody, as you wished me; but I cannot understand what good you have done by it."

"Good! Is he not my deadly enemy?" cried Sir Huntley.

"Yes; but he is the enemy of Buckingham also. For my part, Sir Huntley, I fancy that you have made a false move."

"Explain yourself," said Mordaunt, "for I confess I am at a loss to understand you."

"I can, easily; this Wilford Rokeby is no friend of Buckingham's, as I have said. He favours the king and quietly and secretly defeats Buckingham's plans. The duke would gladly see the abdication of James and the accession of Charles. Rokeby keeps the king informed of the interviews between Buckingham and Charles; and should Buckingham fall from favour, Rokeby is the one who will have the most aided in his defeat. Why, then, do *you*, who are so interested in the fall of the favourite, and who so eagerly desire to take his place—why do *you* seek to remove from Buckingham's path his greatest stumbling block?"

Sir Huntley was much moved, though he endeavoured to conceal his feelings.

"I have my reasons," he said, "reasons which I cannot now explain. This Rokeby is my most dangerous and deadly foe, and if the king's justice will not overtake him, I *must* rid myself of him. By fair means or foul he must be destroyed."

For a few moments the two men remained silent.

There was between them an instinctive feeling that something terrible was meditated; and yet neither cared to be the one to explain it to the other.

At length Leonard Fairfax spoke.

"Sir Huntley," he said, "you speak in riddles. You say that by fair means or foul this Wilford Rokeby must be destroyed. Do you wish to assign this task to me?"

"Listen, and I will tell you. You remember well, no doubt, that on one occasion you showed me over the Tower, and explained to me its hidden secrets."

"I remember the occasion well," replied Leonard Fairfax.

"No doubt, since it was on that day that you sacrificed one of your best friends to serve your own interest."

"Let that pass; proceed," said Leonard Fairfax, sternly.

Sir Huntley smiled.

"Well, you showed me dungeons where the light of day had never penetrated, where cold and damp crippled the prisoner's limbs, as the exclusion of light and the silence crippled his brain; strange staircases leading to mysterious subterranean chambers, unknown to any save those highest in authority; cells where men might have shrieked in very madness, and been unheard even by their keepers. And then you showed me another place—a long, dark, dismal passage, leading—nowhere! Do you remember that also, my friend?"

"I do," said Leonard Fairfax, with a shudder; "at the end of the passage is a deep well, and those who fall into its dark and mysterious depths can never extricate themselves. But why speak of this?"

"Because this is my plan. Let Wilford Rokeby imagine that you desire to aid his escape—let him pass along this passage—let him fall—let him remain there, and then—you know the rest—oblivion for ever!"

"It is a horrid piece of treachery," said Leonard Fairfax, with another shudder; "if *I* were his enemy, I would sooner meet him fairly face to face than resort to such means as those you name. However, I will not presume to teach you. You know your own scheme best."

"It is too late to teach me. When I am resolved upon a certain course, it would take more than your words to change me."

"Then he is to die?"

"If the king does not order his death, he must not leave the Tower alive!"

Fairfax bowed.

"It shall *be* so," he said, "providing ——"

"What?" asked Mordaunt, sternly.

"That you keep your word with me. When *you* are in the place of Buckingham, I want a high post in the palace, and the hand of Geraldine."

"Both shall be yours," returned Sir Huntley. "Fear not. Such friends as *you* are not easily forgotten."

"And are readily put out of the way," thought Fairfax.

He said aloud, however—

"Good-night, then, Sir Huntley. Within a week this enemy of yours shall be no more."

Sir Huntley nodded, and turned away.

His mind was racked by strange and conflicting emotions.

"Oh !" he murmured, as he walked rapidly along the margin of the river; "oh ! how I wish that my path was rid of this man. The very thought of him curdles my blood. Ever and anon, when I am alone, the stain of blood which he sees upon my hand appears also to my eyes. Can it be that Heaven has thus marked me out for destruction, by placing upon me this stain of crime, or can it be my wandering fancy leads me into this cruel error ?"

Thinking thus, he walked on until he arrived at the palace, and reached the point where Hubert Aveling had met his violent death; and where also, it will be remembered, the packet had been thrown from the window by the white hand of some unknown one within the dark old building.

Here he halted, and, having glanced furtively round him, whistled loudly.

After a moment the white hand was again protruded, and a packet came with a whirring noise downwards till it chinked upon the pavement as before.

Sir Huntley watched the hand as it waved three times ; then, picking up the packet, he took from it a key, which he placed in his pocket.

After this, he raised his hat so as to disclose more fully his handsome though sinister features, threw his cloak carelessly over one shoulder, and walked boldly into the palace.

The Night Guard in the entrance hall presented arms as he passed.

Hating him in their hearts, they yet were compelled to do him honour, as the expected successor of Buckingham.

Taking their signs of respect with insolent assumption, he passed onwards,

and, ascending the broad staircase, made his way towards the corridor where the arrest of Wilford Rokeby had taken place.

Rapidly proceeding along this, he reached the door at the other end, and entered a small chamber, which was now tenantless.

Here he paused and listened.

Then after a moment, he drew forth the key from his pocket, and, approaching a door at the other side of the room, opened it and entered a small antechamber.

It was a small dark place, which seemed placed where it was merely to make up a certain corner of the building, or as a means of acting the spy upon persons conversing in the three chambers adjoining.

It had a little, strangely-shaped window overlooking the river, and in one corner was a high cross of dark wood, carved fantastically, and bending down protectively over the brightly-polished floor.

He had scarcely entered, when the door on the opposite side opened, and a lady appeared.

She closed the portal cautiously and noiselessly behind her.

The new comer was young, very young.

Scarcely more than eighteen summers had passed over her head, but her form was moulded in a rich and voluptuous mould, and might have passed as that of a far older woman.

The jewelled hand which had twice flung from the palace window the key of the little chamber, swelled up into an exquisitely-formed arm, which again merged into a lovely bust, surmounted by a head of classic shape and a face of perfect symmetry.

Blue eyes, golden curls, sunny features; such as might have belonged to an angel !

And yet, within that fair bosom beat a heart bold in its determination—resolute in its hate—cruel in its revenge !

Sir Huntley advanced towards her with a smile, and taking her hand, raised it to his lips.

"Genevieve," he said, "it is a pleasure indeed to see your face again."

"Oh! what a courtier! what a flatterer you are !" she answered, "and how false are all your words."

Sir Huntley looked at her with a glance of surprise.

"False, Genevieve! Nay, say not so. If such were really your belief, you would not meet me here."

"Nay, then you are wrong," replied Genevieve St. Clare, relapsing into sternness. "It is for this purpose I came. Listen to me, Sir Huntley, and do not interrupt me. I am one of the queen's maids of honour, truly, and beyond her majesty I have no one to protect me. My friends being dead or banished, I have been left alone in the world; but this very loneliness makes me brave and resolute. I will *not* be deceived. I will not be duped. I will not bring you tidings which enable you to mount the golden ladder of success, while you are openly—before my very eyes—paying your court to Lady Clara Mortimer, and cruelly deceiving *me*."

Sir Huntley still held her hands, and gazed deprecatingly at her, as she stood before him with flashing eyes and heaving bosom.

"Genevieve," he said, "you are mad. You know it is for policy alone that I pretend this love for Lady Clara Mortimer. You, and you only, possess my heart; for you I am seeking honour, distinction, power——"

"Is it for me," interrupted Genevieve, "that you clear from your path Wilford Rokeby, Clara Mortimer's lover, in order that the field may be open to yourself? Oh, Huntley, if I did but dream that you were playing me false, I would bring down upon your head such a tempest—such a whirlwind, that you would gladly fly to the uttermost part of the world to escape from it."

"Calm yourself, Viva," said Sir Huntley, soothingly. "Calm yourself, you have nothing to fear. Wilford Rokeby seeks my life; it is for that reason I desire his absence from court, and for none other I can swear."

Genevieve eyed him with a look of doubt and contempt.

"I feel sadly inclined to doubt you," she said; "and, if I *did*, I should despise and hate you. Through *me*, through the tidings I have brought you, you have attained to your present position; and, mark me, Huntley, if you deceive me, through *me* you shall fall. There is *one* thing you must do at once to appease me—to prove your truth—and, if you do not fulfil that, our paths can separate for ever."

"Dearest Viva," murmured Sir Huntley, who was greatly moved by her words, though he did not wish her to perceive it, "you know that anything in reason I will do for you. Tell me what this is you demand."

" The immediate release of Wilford Rokeby from the Tower of London !" said Genevieve St. Clare, boldly.

Sir Huntley dropped her hand, and started back in unfeigned astonishment.

" You are jesting, surely, Viva !" he said, earnestly.

" Not jesting, Huntley, I can swear it. Grant this, or we meet no more as friends !"

" Listen, Viva," he said. " Lord Claude Mortimer, Lord Clarence Tremaine, and the Earl of Rosstrevor have been discovered in a plot to destroy the king's life, and my Lord of Buckingham has obtained their arrest. Wilford Rokeby, as you know, is an enemy to Buckingham and a friend to King James. Now see how matters work. Buckingham arrests three powerful nobles; they are innocent; their release and pardon will hasten his downfall, while I add to my favour in the king's eyes by punishing the enemy of my rival; and by doing so, moreover, I work myself into the good opinion of Buckingham. Wilford Rokeby seeks my life; he brands me openly as a murderer; he insults me in the royal presence. While matters are thus; while my very existence is only safe by his absence, and so much good also will accrue to me through it, I cannot grant this. I cannot even dream of granting it. Do you not see the truth of my words ?"

" I do not," said Genevieve, firmly; " and I still keep to my resolution. The release of Wilford Rokeby must be granted, or an eternal separation must take place between us."

Sir Huntley was greatly moved.

" You do not see," he answered," how hard are the terms which you impose upon *me*."

" They are easy terms enough."

" Not so, indeed, Viva," cried Sir Huntley; " I may do all I can—I may do all I *can* with the king, and yet may not obtain the prisoner's release."

" I do not look at it in the same light as you do, Huntley," persisted Genevieve St. Clare. " *You* obtained his arrest, and you can obtain his release. I will not, therefore, change my mind; the order, then, or an eternal separation between us."

" If I get this order, then, you will forgive me ?" asked Mordaunt.

" I will."

" Then, in that case, Viva, it shall be done. I will at once proceed to the king's chamber and make such a representation to him as will secure Wilford Rokeby's release before the week has passed."

" You promise this ?"

" Upon my honour—upon my love. And now, what news have you for me ?"

" Scarce any. Buckingham and the French envoy have had words, and the king is alarmed and displeased. The Prince of Wales, too, passed him coldly to-night on the grand staircase, and it is the talk of the whole court. The queen is much disturbed, and the king has for some hours been in earnest conference with Lord Henry De Lancy."

" Good," said Sir Huntley; " my plot works well. And now, sweet Viva, adieu. Here is the key. In two nights I shall require it again. At the hour of nine I shall be below as before. Adieu !"

He passed his arm round her waist, and their lips met in an ardent kiss.

Then the young girl passed through the door, and left Sir Huntley alone.

"So, so," he murmured, as he walked towards the window and looked out; "so, so, my plot works, and Buckingham will fall. And this girl here—this Genevieve St. Clare ! What a weak, silly fool she must deem me to yield so quickly—to consent to the release of Wilford Rokeby, when it cost me so much anxiety and even peril to obtain his arrest ! She little dreams that by her own pertinacity she has hastened his destruction. The king shall order his release truly ; but that being done, my friend, Leonard Fairfax, will see that he leaves not the Tower alive. And then he being dead, then, Clara Mortimer, you are mine—mine for ever !"

CHAPTER VIII.

THE SECRETS OF THE TOWER.

WHEN Wilford Rokeby arrived at the Tower of London, he entered by the same gate through which Lord Claude Mortimer, Lord Clarence Tremaine, and the Earl of Rosstrevor had been ushered by the Night Guard to their gloomy cells some nights before.

After an affectionate parting between him and Lance Courtenay, he was led by his gaoler into a room—if such it could be called—which was scarcely ten feet square, and so low pitched, that he could touch the ceiling with his fingers.

The damp of years and years gone by had eaten into the stone in different places, and left holes through which rats could steal and fight for the few crumbs which fell from the prisoner's scantily supplied table ; while altogether there was a slimy atmosphere—a chilly air, like that of a vault—which would have been far from being agreeable even in a habitation which was not a compulsory one.

A little lamp was allowed him while he partook of his meals.

During all the rest of the time he was left in total darkness.

People read of the Bastille, and tremble at the stories of horror and misery connected with it.

They hear of men thrust into the cells of that hideous prison at an early age, and there remaining until their eyes have grown dim, and their hair has grown grey, and their brains have been clouded, and their poor hearts chilled.

And then, congratulating themselves, they say—

" Thank Heaven, such things never happen in free England."

They are wrong.

Within the precincts of the gloomy Tower as many hideous crimes lie hidden as ever disgraced the worst periods of French history.

The gaoler who presided over this portion of the building was a fit representative of the sins which might have been perpetrated within its gloomy precincts.

The dark passages; the lightless dungeons; the torture chambers, represented scenes of horror; old men cut down on the brink of the grave; young, brave hearts stilled while yet they beat the strongest; homes desolated; sweet bosoms chilled for ever; hope—love—glory rendered a mere vision and a dream.

The gaoler was such a one as might have figured chief in all such scenes.

His frame was broadly built, with shoulders square, heavy and massive; long, muscular arms and legs, like those of a gladiator, with immense calves and protuberant joints.

His head was set upon his trunk like that of a bull, with a thick, short neck; while his hair, red and stubbly, added to the intensely disagreeable nature of his appearance.

His nose was thick and round, while his low forehead and his ugly mouth were concealed, the one by the elf locks, and the other by the heavy moustache which fell over them.

The only small features were the eyes, which were round and reddish in colour, like those of a ferret.

His voice—gruff and harsh—dissonant as a cracked bell, rang out gloomily and drearily, and echoed along the subterranean passages of the Tower, where never a sound of the life without greeted the ears of the wretched prisoners.

With this man Wilford soon found it impossible to converse.

He pretended utter ignorance of all that was transpiring, both within and without the Tower, and answered (when he condescended to answer at all) in monosyllables only.

It was on the fourth night after his imprisonment, that a lady, wearing a mask, and a veil also, which half enshrouded her figure, approached the western gate of the old fortress, and walked boldly up to the gate.

" What want you, my damsel ?" said the keeper of the door, with insolent familiarity.

" Civility first, admittance second," returned the lady, haughtily. " See! here is the king's order."

The man glanced at it.

Then he bowed lowly.

" I beg pardon, my lady," he said, " pass on. Travick, what ho there ! Travick !" he added, shouting to the warder at the inner gate, " admit this lady; she bears an order from the king."

" An order to see a prisoner named Wilford Rokeby," said the second warder, reading. " Here, Lockster," he continued, turning to the gaoler, who, among them, generally went by the name of Red Ben, " this lady is to see the new prisoner."

The man rose with the surly growl which was as characteristic of his nature as his ugliness.

" I wish people 'ud come to see my birds a little earlier," grumbled he, as he led the way along the dark passage, where the sound of their footsteps echoed dismally, and sent a chill to the heart of the lady as she advanced. "Here, this way, my lady; down these steps. What's there to be frightened of? Come on, it's darker than this presently."

As he spoke, he lighted a small flambeau, and, proceeding down several steps, led the way along a dismal corridor beneath the earth, whose atmosphere was like that of a charnel house.

"This is the place," he said, as he opened with his jingling keys the iron door of Wilford's cell. "Here, you within there! Here is a lady to see you. Be quick there; ten minutes is all the time allowed."

"What, all in darkness!" murmured the lady, with a shudder.

"Aye, aye; we don't give our birds too much light. It hurts their eyes. Here, prisoner, you can keep this torch while the visitor is here. Stick it against yonder pillar. There's no fear of its burning the ceiling. The flame is like yourself—not very likely to make its way through the stone."

Then, with a loud laugh at his own coarse joke, he clanged to the heavy door, and was gone.

The lady now threw aside her mask and revealed the features of Lady Clara Mortimer.

"Oh, Clara! dearest Clara!" exclaimed Wilford, as he embraced her. "This is indeed kind. I was thinking of you, and wondering if I should ever again behold in the light of day that face I love so well. I have been here but a short time, but it seems to me an age. It is so cold, so dark, so hopeless."

"It *is* cold and dark, dear Wilford," said Clara, "but not hopeless. I bring you hope."

"Alas! I fear you err, Clara," responded Wilford. "Hope cannot dwell here. It is left without. It has never yet crossed the threshold. While I breathe the air of this place, I can believe nothing but that death is in store for me."

"Then you need no longer give way to such gloomy thoughts. The king will pardon you. I know it. To-morrow—perhaps this very night—you may be free."

"And if you are wrong?"

"There are those within these very walls who will aid your escape."

Wilford's eyes brightened.

"I would rather escape in that manner than trust to any pardon obtained through Buckingham or Sir Huntley Mordaunt. But, tell me, who is my friend here?"

Lady Clara leaned towards him, and whispered eagerly the name of Leonard Fairfax.

Oh! how bitterly would she have called down curses upon her own tongue had she known to what a traitor she was committing him!

"You mean the deputy-constable of the Tower?" said Wilford.

"I do. He has already received orders from one whom he will obey; therefore, fear nothing," said Clara, smiling up at him.

Wilford pressed her little hand, and looked smilingly into her bright eyes.

"Hope has forced its way in at last," he said; "from your bright presence it could scarcely be absent."

As he spoke the heavy step of the ruffian gaoler was heard advancing slowly up the passage.

It sounded like a death knell!

In a moment the air seemed more chill—the cell darker—the hope of escape more distant, and instinctively Lady Clara clung more closely to her lover.

"I feel now as if some evil would separate us after all," she murmured. "This dark and gloomy cell banishes my hope as it banished yours. That villanous gaoler, too, is in himself enough to inspire dread and horror."

"He can inspire no horror in me," said Wilford, "while *you* are with me; and, with the hope at my heart of being able soon to quit this gloomy dungeon, and be once more in your presence, I shall be able to fancy myself once more breathing the sweet air of freedom."

At this moment the jingle of keys was heard, the door was once more swung open, and the gaoler appeared.

He looked with a look of intense hatred at Wilford Rokeby's fine features and noble form as he stood erect, with Clara, now re-masked, clinging to his arm.

He hated handsome men.

Knowing well his own hideousness, feeling that his heavy and distorted features were the reflex of his hideous and distorted mind, he hated to see upon the faces of others that openness and nobility of feature which spoke of a heart within throbbing with generous emotions.

"Now," he said, in a surly tone, "the time is up. My lady, I must trouble you to come."

Clara made no reply, but, with a hard pressure of Wilford's hand, turned to go.

The gaoler strode in and seized the torch.

"Cannot you leave the light?" asked Wilford.

"You know I can't; it's against the rules," answered the gaoler, and closed the door rudely.

Once more everything was buried in darkness; and he was left alone with his thoughts.

Three more days passed.

Three days of silence, gloom, and wretchedness.

On the evening of the third day, about an hour after Red Ben had brought his last meal, the heavy footstep of the gaoler was heard again.

Wilford listened anxiously; for after his supper all was, in general, quiet for the night.

"It must be some new prisoner," thought he; "or, maybe, it is a summons to the torture chamber."

He rose to his feet from the pallet bed upon which he had been lying, and stood staring at the door through the darkness.

In a few moments it was opened, and the gaoler entered, closing the portal behind him.

There was a leer upon his features, and a manner about him altogether that made Wilford feel uncomfortable; a dread, indeed, invaded his heart, and he asked, as he moved away—

"What want you?"

The gaoler burst out into a loud laugh. "Ha! ha!" he cried, "you fear me? But you are wrong. I come to give you liberty."

"Jest not," said Wilford, "with a man who is at your mercy."

The gaoler sat down on the bench at the bottom of the pillar.

"I am not jesting," he said; "I come here to aid you in escaping. I have the authority of Mr. Leonard Fairfax; but I must make one little bargain with you."

"If you want money, you can have it," said Wilford; "I will see that you are well rewarded."

"No, no," said Red Ben, with a peculiar smile, "no, no, I don't want money. I only want you to promise that, whatever happen, you will never reveal to a living soul who let you escape. Still, if you do get off all right, a few golden pieces would not be unacceptable."

Wilford placed a purse in his hand.

"There is gold," he said, "and with it you have my promise."

"Very well," said the man, placing the treasure in his pocket, "very well. Follow me, and remember, silence! One word might betray all. I will conduct you to the end of a passage leading to the river. At the end are six steps, and at the bottom of these steps a boat is waiting for you. Come."

He opened the door, and closing it behind him, led the way along the echoing passage.

At the end of about forty yards they descended about six feet more, and entered a corridor which was narrower and damper still.

At the extremity of this was a third corridor, dark and still as the grave, save with the echoes of the plashing river, while far away a faint glimmering light could be distinguished.

"We are arrived," said the gaoler. "Proceed quickly. I will watch here to see that no one follows."

Wilford waited for no more.

Naturally he suspected nothing, and, without a word, he plunged into the darkness.

"He is walking to his death," muttered the gaoler, as he held his torch aloft and listened with a leering smile upon his lips.

For some moments nothing could be heard but the echoes of the fugitive's footsteps.

Then there was a loud cry—a splash of some heavy body falling into water, and all was still again as a grave.

"'Tis all over with him," muttered Ben Lockster, with a smile, as he prepared to quit the corridor. "There's no fear now, for dead men tell no tales."

The Night Guard;

Or, THE SECRET OF THE FIVE MASKS.

WILFORD ROKEBY, SWORD IN HAND, RUSHED INTO THE BALL-ROOM.

CHAPTER IX.

THE SECRET LETTER

WHITEHALL was once more brilliant with lights.

Youth and beauty had again gathered in the large and splendid saloons to do homage to royalty, and at the same time to enjoy itself thoroughly.

Regardless of the prisoners who languished in the Tower, the palace was illuminated for a ball as on that dark and gloomy evening when Hubert Aveling had met his death near the western gate.

The queen, pale and ill, even then sickening with the premonitory symptoms of her premature death, was in the ball-room, as were the king, Buckingham, and Prince Charles, who, by the death of his brother Henry, was heir-apparent to the throne, and, as the Spaniards declared, far more king than his father.

The king was leaning on the back of his queen's chair when Buckingham and the prince approached.

Both seemed excited, and the former held in his hand an open letter.

"Sire," said the duke, "I have here a letter from Lord Hammond."

The king started and seemed annoyed, but he quickly recovered his equanimity.

"Ah! Steenie," he said, "is all well?"

"Excellently well, your majesty," said the duke. "The Commons will grant the money required for the war with Spain, and we shall be able at last to teach these Spanish ambassadors what the power of England is."

"That is good," said James, nervously, evidently not speaking from his heart. "You manage the Commons well, Buckingham. I will consult with you again to-morrow.

"I doubt, my lord," said the queen, "whether the king is prudent in listening to such counsels."

The duke bowed.

"Your majesty, perhaps, is imprudent in trying to thwart them," he said, meaningly.

James did not hear this remark.

His eyes were wandering restlessly towards the door, as if expecting the arrival of some one of importance.

The queen's eyes, however, flashed fire.

"My lord," she said, "you must remember that the greatest favourites have been committed to the Tower for insolence."

Again the Duke of Buckingham bowed sarcastically.

"And your majesty," he said, "should also remember *that queens have been beheaded in England.*" *

With this daring speech, Buckingham turned away, and, overcome by the pleasure inspired by his own boldness, took Prince Charles's arm, without even saluting the king.

---

* This is an historical fact.

King James observed now the queen's agitation, and asked its reason.

In a few words she explained it.

The king's face flushed deeply.

"This is in our very palace!" said he, in a low tone of anger. "I have suffered this long enough. I shall listen to more sage advice. To-morrow morning Buckingham shall see that I am King of England still."

At this moment, Genevieve St. Clare entered the ball-room with Sir Huntley Mordaunt.

Sir Huntley bowed deeply before the king, and Genevieve walked up to the queen's chair.

The king seemed now more agitated than ever, and kept his eyes fixed anxiously upon Mordaunt, as he disappeared among the throng.

Then he beckoned Genevieve to his side.

"Well, my fair conspirator," he said, "have you the letter?"

"I have, sire."

"Quick; give it to me then," cried the king, impatiently. "I am all eagerness to read it."

Genevieve St. Clare looked anxiously round.

"Your majesty," she said, "I must be careful. One knows not in this palace what prying eyes are upon you."

"True, true," replied the king. "Come nearer. See! they are about to dance; now give it to me."

She slid it quickly into his hand, and the king placed it in his pocket.

Great king! that feared in his own palace to receive a letter unknown to his favourite!

Then, as the music swelled forth, and the dancers moved through the spacious saloon, he quitted the scene, and made for his own chamber.

There he opened the letter — the famous letter of Ynoiosa, the Spanish ambassador.

The letter told James how Buckingham was plotting against him; how England was governed by three powers — Buckingham, Prince Charles, and himself—himself being last and least; how, to secure the affection of his people, he must dismiss this duke, who openly boasted of his power, and assumed to himself more power and authority.

Within this letter was a second.

It ran thus :—

"A longer and more particular relation of the doings of Buckingham, and a detailed account of his conspiracy against your majesty, and also the doings of *another arch traitor*, was delivered into the hands of Wilford Rokeby that night he was arrested and conveyed to the Tower. If *he* dies, mark well that it is the work of this traitor."

"Arch traitor!" he murmured. "Whom does this mean? But it matters not. Wilford Rokeby has my pardon, and will be here this night. From him I shall learn all."

He read the letter again, and then held it to the flame of the lamp.

Watching the letter until it was consumed, he muttered, in impotent wrath—

"Would that my enemies could burn also like that."

After a few moments he recovered his composure, and returned to the ball-room.

No one had noticed his absence, and

he accordingly took his seat as before by the side of the queen.

It was a strange collection in that room.

In one corner were the king, the queen, and Genevieve St. Clare, plotting against Buckingham.

In another, Sir Huntley Mordaunt plotting against Buckingham.

In a third corner, Buckingham plotting against all ; while Clara Mortimer and Laura Clavering were watching and waiting for the end.

"Clara," said Laura, "this place sickens me — chills me to the very heart."

"And why ?"

"It reminds me of that other night, which followed the murder of my beloved. Oh ! how it embitters my heart—how it makes me tremble with hate—when I see yonder, smiling at the ladies, and talking familiarly with all, the man whom *I* feel to be the murderer of my Hubert."

"Ah ! I fear not," said Lady Clara. "Wilford will avenge him."

"Wilford Rokeby ! he is in prison."

"He is not. By this time the king's pardon has reached him, and he is free. I know it."

Unknown to them, unseen by any, Sir Huntley Mordaunt had crept near.

Behind a broad pillar he concealed himself, and eagerly drank in the words of the two beauties, the one of whom he loved so dearly, and upon the other of whom he had cast a shadow for ever.

Hurriedly he walked away, as he heard Clara's words, to a part of the room where Leonard Fairfax, deputy-constable of the Tower, was standing talking to some gentlemen.

"Fairfax, a word with you," he said, hurriedly.

Fairfax smiled as he walked away with him.

"You seem troubled, " he said. "What is it ?"

"I hear that Wilford Rokeby has escaped."

"Escaped, has he ?" returned Leonard, sneeringly. "Who told you that ?"

"I have just heard it."

"From whom ?"

"From Lady Clara Mortimer."

"Then Lady Clara Mortimer has told you false. Wilford Rokeby never knew of the king's pardon ; but was allowed to escape by me. He passed down the dark passage this very night, and fell down—down into that place of which you so forcibly reminded me ; but, hark ! what is that ?"

As he spoke, there was a loud outcry without the ball-room ; the clash of swords, and the sound of many voices.

After this there was a rush of feet, and a man, sword in hand, rushed into the ball-room.

His hair was dishevelled, his face pale, his eyes wild and bloodshot.

Muddy water dropped from his ragged clothes, and his hands, torn and bleeding, showed how fierce had been his struggle for life.

He glared round at all, and when he spoke, his voice was harsh and thick.

But all knew the face, and all knew the voice.

It was the face and the voice of Wilford Rokeby.

King James and his courtiers gazed in wonder at the strange apparition breaking thus suddenly, sword in hand, into the midst of a royal assembly.

All expected a scene.

But they were disappointed.

The letter of the Spanish ambassador, Ynoiosa, had paved the way for Wilford's forgiveness, even if he had outraged royal etiquette more than he had done.

"What means this, Lieutenant Rokeby?" said the king, rising from his seat. "Can you, Lieutenant of my Night Guard as you are, pretend not to know that this is no proper manner of presenting yourself before the king?"

"Your majesty, my appearance and my drawn sword mean no insult to you," said Wilford Rokeby, passionately. "They mean that you and I also have been betrayed; they mean that when I had received your pardon, I was lured into a trap. I was induced to hazard an escape from the Tower, and was thrust into a living tomb. That tomb, I fear me, can tell more tales of massacre than your majesty knows of. At any rate, it was too full for their purpose to succeed, and I clambered out, fought my way against two armed sentinels at the Tower stairs, and here I am. I have fought my way into the palace, too, for the guard was changed below, and knew me not."

The king glanced in amazement at the bold young captain as he spoke.

"With half his spirit," he thought, with an inward sigh, "I could conquer the world."

Inwardly his heart was beating with eagerness to speak in private to this bold and daring officer, and to receive from his hands the letter which contained so much news of interest to him.

At the same time an inward voice told him that he was bound to resent, or, at any rate, pretend to resent, the manner in which Wilford Rokeby had entered his presence.

"Under other circumstances, Wilford Rokeby," he said, "your manner of entering my palace would amount to high treason. But on this occasion we have little difficulty in forgiving you. My seal and signature having been attached to your pardon, my royal word is passed, and no one had a right to prevent your entrance into the palace. To-morrow evening I will speak to you on important business. At eight present yourself to me, and you shall be admitted. And now, pray see to your attire and join our revels, that all may see how freely and truly you are forgiven."

While Wilford Rokeby, having bowed to the king, departed to rearrange his dress, satisfied by a peculiar sign which James had made to him that it was imprudent to say more at that moment, Sir Huntley Mordaunt drew Leoeard Fairfax aside.

"You have deceived me," he said.

"Indeed no. I swear it."

"Then how comes this braggart here?"

"Heaven only knows, except it be that he bears a charmed life, and Providence is preserving him until he slays you. I gave full and particular instructions to Ben Lockster, and if he has not fulfilled them, I cannot be blamed. I know that he led him to the verge of the passage and bade him advance, for I watched the whole scene myself, and I could have sworn that I heard a loud and piercing shriek as from one in mortal agony. Who knows, Sir Huntley, how chance may yet throw him in your way? Be not too hasty."

"I am not too hasty," returned Mordaunt, in a tone of voice which clearly showed his anger and malignity. "No, no; I act upon a plan. I only fail when I trust to others. However, I shall know better, let us hope, next time."

So saying, he moved away, and proceeded towards that part of the room where he saw Genevieve St. Clare in close conversation with Lady Laura Clavering.

Wilford, meanwhile, had passed towards his own chamber, anxious, as may be imagined, to return into the royal assembly—to see Clara—to move once more among free people—to enjoy, in fact, the fulness of his triumph over his enemies.

The young page, who, it will be remembered, had carried the letter to the governor of the Tower on the night of the duel, now followed noiselessly in his footsteps.

Wilford was so busy with his thoughts, and his own heavy boots made such a clanging noise along the passages of the palace, that he could not detect the slight sound made by the page's feet.

Walter Hastings—for such was the name of Buckingham's young favourite—was enabled, therefore, to advance to the door of Wilford's chamber without being perceived.

Concealing himself in the window, he watched the young captain of the guard as he entered; and then approaching the door, he began slowly to unfasten it.

He knew well what danger there was in acting the spy upon Wilford Rokeby; but, nevertheless, he did not hesitate.

Cautiously opening the door, he peered in.

By the light of a dull lamp, he saw Wilford Rokeby attiring himself for the ball, and casting aside the torn dress in which he had first made his appearance before the king.

Now, then, was the time.

He had been commissioned by the Duke of Buckingham to extract from Rokeby's pocket the much-dreaded letter from Ynoiosa, and well knowing the importance which his master attached to its possession, he resolved to take it at all hazards.

So he stealthily approached the chair where Rokeby had placed his clothes.

He forgot one thing, however.

Wilford Rokeby, standing before the mirror, could see all that passed.

Yet, though he did see all, he took no notice until Walter Hastings had searched vainly in every part of the clothes.

Then he turned, and, moving hastily to the door, prevented the page's exit.

"Young Hastings," he cried, as the youth stood before him with pale face, and the conscious look of one discovered in a mean action, "tell your master that when *I* take charge of papers of importance, I do not carry them loose within my pocket. Moreover, if necessary, I destroy them sooner than they shall fall into the hands of my enemies. Whether I have done so or not on this occasion I do not say; in fact, I would not gratify him by telling; but let him know that I discovered you, and shall know how to guard against such treachery for the future."

He then opened wide the door, and, without another word, the boy passed out.

"So, so," said Wilford, smiling to himself, as he completed his dressing for the ball. "So, so. My lord duke fears this letter. The king, maybe, will have more reason than he imagines to thank me for my loyalty."

With a true smile of happiness, Clara Mortimer greeted her lover as he once more entered the royal ball-room.

On this occasion she cast aside all restraint, and, taking no notice whatever of the fierce looks of Sir Huntley Mordaunt, welcomed Wilford as one rescued from the jaws of death.

"Oh, how happy it makes me to see you once more free and in favour," she said

"*My* greatest happiness is being free and with *you*," returned Wilford.

Clara smiled.

"You flatterer," she said. "But truly, Wilford, if you love me, as you say, you will take this misfortune that has overtaken you, and from which you have so miraculously escaped, as a warning for the future."

"A warning of what?"

"Not to meddle needlessly in intrigues. Let Buckingham and his enemies fight out their quarrels between them. Neither the one nor the other are worthy of your risking your precious life."

Wilford bent over her.

"To-morrow," he said, "Buckingham will fall."

She smiled incredulously.

"Nay, then," said Rokeby, "it is true."

"How know you it?"

"Because I carry in my pocket the document which will prove his ruin."

"Be it so then," returned Lady Clara Mortimer; "grant that you are right. Who will take his place?"

"Sir Huntley Mordaunt."

"Your greatest foe—an assassin—a traitor!" exclaimed the young girl, passionately. "Are you mad, that you talk of aiding him to rise?"

It was Wilford's turn to smile now.

"He will fall as quickly as he rises," he answered. "Come," he added, as he passed his arm round her waist, "come, let us join the dancers, and leave politics until to-morrow."

"YOUR DISGUISE IS USELESS; I KNOW YOU WELL!" CRIED WILFORD.

CHAPTER X.

TRACKED BY TRAITORS.

THE next morning rose brightly and sunnily over Old London.

Few among the head intriguers in the Palace of Whitehall had slept during the night which preceded that dawning.

The Duke of Buckingham, on his part, had already noticed the growing coldness of the king, and visions of downfall and public disgrace were already floating before his eyes.

Sir Huntley Mordaunt, on the other hand, had observed this also, and was already, in his mind's eye, scanning the glory which attended the post of first favourite.

The partizans of both were eagerly waiting till morn, while Prince Charles and the king, his father, dreamed of the Spanish ships, and the Spanish legions, which were to be arrayed against the hosts of Great Britain at the mere word of a court favourite.

Passing down the corridor at the hour of eleven, Buckingham paused for a moment at an open window, to gaze out upon the square in front of the palace where he beheld the king's carriage standing opposite the grand entrance.

A dark frown overclouded his brow.

"The king going out, and without me!" he muttered; "it must surely be a mistake. Yet, no; there is Prince Charles. I must see to this."

Hastily descending the stairs, Buckingham reached the vestibule just as the king made his appearance.

"Is your majesty about to leave London?" he asked, bowing respectfully.

"Yes, my lord; I am going to Windsor," replied the king, endeavouring to be haughty.

"And may I not be permitted to accompany your majesty?" asked he.

"I desire you, my lord," said James, "to remain here at Whitehall. I go with Prince Charles."

Buckingham's heart beat wildly at these words.

He knew well that the king's object was to separate him, at any rate for a time, from the prince, and he resolved, even if he descended to humility, to endeavour to prevent this separation.

The king, meanwhile, turned his back ostentatiously upon his favourite, and, taking the arm of Prince Charles, walked towards the carriage, while Buckingham remained upon the steps.

For an instant the duke was stunned.

He knew not what course to pursue.

In a few moments more, however, he summoned to his aid that humility—those tears which had often done him such good service; and, hurrying towards the carriage, he affected to weep.

"Your majesty," he cried, "let me entreat you to tell me why I am thus cast from favour. Let me know my error, and, if I have really been guilty of wrong, I will confess it."

The king averted his head.

"I desire you to remain in London," he said.

Then Prince Charles gave the duke a look full of significance, and the coach drove off.

For a few moments the duke, in a state of confusion and distraction, gazed after the carriage in which the king had already begun to weep.

Then, rushing hastily into the palace, he summoned his page, and, without further word to any, rode off to Wallingford House.

Sir Huntley Mordaunt had seen all this.

His black heart was already brimful of triumph and hope.

In his fancy he already saw himself prime minister, wielding, in fact, more than sovereign power, dictating not only to the king, but also to the governments of foreign states.

To his mind also came the dream which of all others was the most pleasant to his mind.

He should now be able to crush Wilford Rokeby, and marry Lady Clara Mortimer.

As for Genevieve St. Clare, her occupation would be gone when once he became court favourite, and he therefore feared neither her resentment nor her vengeance.

He had scarcely reached his private chamber after the public disgrace of Buckingham, when two notes were placed in his hand.

The one was from Genevieve.

The other was from King James.

The latter he opened eagerly, and with trembling hands.

It was very brief; but it contained a world of news for him.

"The king desires the presence of Sir Huntley Mordaunt at Windsor to-morrow."

"Windsor!" he exclaimed, pressing his hand to his brow, as if a sudden thought had occurred to him. "Windsor! I must start to-night. What a strange fatality is this! The one who, first of any, stood in the way of my accession to the splendid property I so much covet is already swept from my path. The second is thus thrown, as it were, into my grasp. This night the deed must be done; then, with honour and riches, the favourite of the king, and the possessor of the fine revenues of Farnley Manor, I shall be able to hold my own against all the petty intriguers of this court. And now, sweet Genevieve, what say you?"

Her note was also very brief:—

"At six this evening, I will give you the key through the window in the usual manner. I *must* see you on a matter of vital importance."

"So, so! a king first, and a fair lady afterwards," said Sir Huntley. "She brings me court news, no doubt. What care I now? The news I wait to hear will be the pleasantest, and, indeed, the only news I care to listen to—Buckingham's dismissal, and my entrance to his place. However, Genevieve *must* be humoured awhile, or she might be dangerous."

The day soon wore away, and at length evening came, and after passing through the guards, who saluted him as one in whom they recognised the future favourite of the king, he walked out upon the river terrace.

The Night Guard watched him jealously as he walked by them.

They felt, as it were, the chill of murder in the air as he passed.

Scarcely one of them was there who did not feel an instinctive desire to rush upon him and strike him to the earth, for scarcely one of them doubted the fact that he was the assassin of their friend, Hubert Aveling.

For some few minutes Sir Huntley paced to and fro upon the terrace.

Then, as the clock chimed solemnly forth, he returned towards the palace wall, and stood upon the pavement just beneath the window from which Genevieve St. Clare had so often flung the key of the private chamber.

Hardly had the last echo of the clock died away when the white hand was thrust through the opening, and the packet fell as usual with a ring upon the ground.

Sir Huntley glanced round quickly, picked it up, and, re-entering the palace, was soon once more in the little room with Genevieve St. Clare.

He approached her smilingly, and, taking her hand, raised it to his lips.

"You are deceiving me," cried the young girl, snatching her hand away.

"I am not. I swear it."

"Nay, swear not. You are deceiving me, and you know it. I have heard—no matter from whom—your plot with Leonard Fairfax to rid yourself of Wilford Rokeby. I know who was your base instrument, and I know,

too, how absurdly and deservedly your infamous plan failed. You have broken faith with me in this—you may break it with me in other things."

"You have been made the victim of a plot yourself," replied Sir Huntley. "I have nothing whatever to do with any scheme to destroy Wilford Rokeby, in whose fate you seem to take so great an interest. But tell me, why did you ask me to meet you here to-night?"

"I am in no humour for jesting, Sir Huntley," cried Genevieve St. Clare, while a bitter and a cruel smile played over her beautiful features; "I come to offer you conditions of peace."

"Of peace!"

"Aye, of peace. You will either consent to do what I say or I shall disclose to the king the whole of your plots against him. Do I not know that your only desire is to crush Buckingham? Do I not see that when Buckingham is crushed, you will worm yourself into the favour of Charles; that then you will destroy the king, and with the weak prince as monarch of England, Sir Huntley Mordaunt will be paramount?"

"You are mad, Viva!" cried Sir Huntley, in alarm, "to speak thus loudly of such treason in the king's palace. For Heaven's sake lower your voice."

The young girl's eyes were flashing, her lips white, her bosom beating with emotion.

"You do well to stop me," she cried; "you do well; for you know that if found here your head would be forfeited. But you shall listen to me, or I will give the alarm and we will suffer together."

"Speak on, Viva, but in a lower voice," said Mordaunt, suppressing his anger.

"Be it so, then. My conditions are these : either Wilford Rokeby shall be free to marry Lady Clara Mortimer, or *Lady Clara dies !*"

Sir Huntley started in astonishment.

"What mean you ?" he cried. "Would you assassinate her yourself, or would you place her murder in my hands ?"

"It would not come amiss to you," she answered ; "it would not be the first innocent blood that has been shed by you or through you. Therefore, to me it is useless and absurd to express such horror. Besides, the other alternative has no horror in it."

Sir Huntley Mordaunt with difficulty suppressed his emotion.

"Why," he asked, "are you so anxious for this marriage ?"

"You know," she answered. "Think you, sir, I am so blind a fool as not to know that you love this Clara Mortimer while you are pretending to love me ? I am not one with whom you can trifle, and you shall know it. Make me this promise, then, or to-morrow the king shall know all."

Stifling the anger in his breast, Sir Huntley bent over her and kissed her.

"I promise," he said, "this marriage shall take place. I shall send Wilford Rokeby away from court, and so I shall not be in constant fear of his jealousy and anger. And now, as I have promised this, will you forgive me ?"

"I will," returned the young girl, "I will ; but, before a month is over Lady Clara's head, you must permit this union to be consummated."

"I promise this," said Sir Huntley. "And now, I must say adieu ; I have this very night to proceed to Windsor. One kiss, and we must part."

He embraced her, whispered a few false words of love, and she passed into the inner room.

"Foolish girl," he muttered. "Madly as she threatens, she knows not half my power, or she would cower before me. It is not Lady Clara Mortimer who will die, but Wilford Rokeby and Lady Genevieve St. Clare—one of them, perhaps, this very night."

So saying, he passed away **into the** corridor without.

As he did so a figure slowly moved from behind the curtains, and followed in the wake of Genevieve St. Clare.

This stealthy watcher was Lady Laura Clavering.

CHAPTER XI.

A WILD RIDE FOR FORTUNE.

QUITE unconscious of the fact that his plans had been overheard, and full of his own hideous schemes of murder and treachery, Sir Huntley Mordaunt passed away from the room where he had been closeted with Genevieve St. Clare, and descended to the guard-room.

Here he glanced round at all the men, who saluted him respectfully, until his eye rested upon one who sat by the fire — a tall, raw-boned, red-haired fellow, with a scowling, unpleasant face.

"Here, Andrew Foster," said Sir Huntley, "I want you. The king has sent for me to Windsor, and you must accompany me."

The man rose at once.

A peculiar sign from Sir Huntley showed him that he desired speech with him.

The would-be favourite passed towards his private chamber, and the trooper followed him.

"Andrew Foster," said Sir Huntley, when they were alone, "I am going to Windsor. Do you remember who lives upon that road?"

"I do not," replied the man; "though I shall soon remember if you but refresh my memory a little."

"I will," said Mordaunt, dropping his voice somewhat. "Hubert Aveling having been disposed of, the only one who stands between me and the for-tune I so greatly covet is Sir Edgar Farnley."

"Ah! yes; I remember well now," cried the man; "the old man, your uncle, who lives at Farnley Manor."

"The same," replied Sir Huntley. "Well, as I have said, the king this night desires my presence at Windsor, for my Lord of Buckingham has sorely fallen, as you know, from favour, and has retired to Wallingford House. If you choose to earn money as you have earned it before, I can find you a job."

"I see; you will visit the old Manor House?" said the trooper.

"Yes; we will rest there on our way to Windsor Castle."

"And in the morning the old man will be dead," returned Andrew Foster, with the coolness of an old hand.

"Precisely; but do not talk so loudly. In this nest of intriguers one can never be safe from listeners. Get ready our horses at once; bring them round to the western gate, and we will start directly. But stay; you yourself must undertake this matter."

The man laughed.

"I see," he said, "you do not wish to deepen the stain upon your hands?"

Sir Huntley frowned.

"Just so," he exclaimed. "I say again, if you undertake this matter, you must do it yourself; I cannot interfere in it. I can protect *you* if you are discovered, but you could do nothing to save me if *I* were suspected."

"All right, Sir Huntley," said the man; "I will do all you wish. On the road you must explain the details of your plan."

"I will do so. And now proceed at once to the stable, and select two of the finest horses. Get me, if possible, Black Meg."

"Do you mean Lieutenant Rokeby's favourite horse?" asked the trooper.

"Yes, his charger."

"It is not in the stable, Sir Huntley; I believe Mr. Rokeby is out with it."

"Never mind; any other will do. And mind, if you see Rokeby enter while you are getting ready the horses, do not satisfy him as to the road we shall take. I have no desire to meet with him to-night."

"Shall I inform you when the horses are ready, Sir Huntley?"

"No; I will descend to the door and wait your coming."

After seeing that his pistols were ready for use, Sir Huntley Mordaunt descended to the western gate, where he awaited impatiently the arrival of his horses.

It was not long before Andrew Foster brought them up.

They were tall, finely-made animals, and seemed fresh, and prepared for any amount of work.

"Now then, Andrew," said Mordaunt, as he sprang into the saddle, "now for a fortune for me, and for you also, if you do your duty."

"Fear not," replied the hired assassin. "My method of earning a livelihood is a sure and safe one. Let us proceed swiftly, for fear that we might be followed."

They saw no one as they passed away from the palace, truly.

But, nevertheless, they were followed, and that quickly.

Hardly had the sounds of their horses' feet died away, before two mounted cavaliers quitted Whitehall, and rode off rapidly after them.

These were Lance Courtenay and Wilford Rokeby.

Little dreaming that they were followed thus by those whom of all others they dreaded, Sir Huntley Mordaunt and the trooper proceeded rapidly on their way.

Their horses were fresh and strong, and they got over the ground easily.

The last glimpses of London, therefore, soon faded away, and gave place to green fields and rolling hill-lands, which, even in the darkness of the night, could be distinguished from the dull level just around London.

On arriving quite in the open country, where there was no fear of being seen, they stopped their horses, and each unrolling a bundle which had lain upon his horse's crupper, placed around him a large horseman's cloak, and donned a black mask.

"Thus attired, there is no fear of discovery," said Sir Huntley. "Have courage, Foster, and ere morning dawns, *you* will have gained what to you is a fortune, and I shall have cleared from my path every impediment which exists to my attaining to Farnley Manor and its riches."

The trooper laughed coarsely.

"Fear not, Sir Huntley," said he.

THE NIGHT GUARD;

Or, THE SECRET OF THE FIVE MASKS.

"TWO HORSEMEN ARE COMING IN HOT HASTE," CRIED THE GIRL.

" You've given a job in my hands to do, and I shall do it—never doubt it."

" Do you see yonder lights ?" asked Mordaunt.

" I do, Sir Huntley."

" Those are the lights of Farnley. We have not far to go. They will now be in their first sleep, and we shall stand every chance of being able to enter unperceived. Let us hasten."

They pressed forward accordingly, and it was not long before they reached the high thick hedge which skirted Farnley grounds.

Here they dismounted from their horses, and fastened them securely beneath the shadow of some tall and thickly-foliaged trees.

" They will be safer here than if we took them to the door of the house and left them," said Sir Huntley. " Something sinister may occur, and in that case, it will be better to run across the grounds on foot where we cannot be seen."

" True," said the trooper. " True, Sir Huntley; you are a good schemer. I am ready."

Then the two men, unequal truly in rank, but equal in sin, moved forward through the night-shrouded grounds on their errand of crime.

CHAPTER XII.

PASSING AWAY.

Sir Edgar Farnley, the obstacle which Sir Huntley Mordaunt spoke of as standing between him and fortune, was some sixty years of age.

He had served his country in many ways.

Abroad he had been a diplomatist and a soldier too.

At home he had meddled in politics until he had sickened of them, and disgusted with Buckingham, and those around the king generally, he retired to his old house at Farnley to spend the rest of his life in peace.

He had been a hale and hearty man all his time until lately, when some inward complaint had taken from him his strength and his spirits too, and rendered him nervous, irritable, and hypochondriacal.

On the night when Sir Huntley and his hired bravo were gliding stealthily, as it were, towards him, like venomous serpents, he had been seized with a sudden and painful attack, from which the doctor scarcely gave him any hope of recovering; and he had seized the little time left to him on earth to make a will disposing of all his wealth.

Still and white lay the old man on his dying bed.

Everything around him was of the most luxurious kind; of spotless white and of polished oak; of bright gold and of dark pictured panels—were the objects upon which the cold moonlight gleamed through the diamond-paned windows.

The best of wines; the best of food; the kindest attention, all were his.

But of what avail were they now?

The poor heart would soon be still; the poor eyes would soon be closed; the voice which had thundered forth its orders on the battle field would soon be silent—for ever!

And on the brink of this Eternal River, which he was so soon to cross, there was no gentle hand of love to sustain his weakness; the mother's hand—*that* had long since vanished; the wife's hand—*that* had never existed!

Only a memory there was of a lovely face—and a lovely form—bright eyes—bright golden curls—bright smiles, and tender tones—the memory of a delicious hope which had never become reality!

> "Oh! for the touch of a vanished hand,
> And the sound of a voice that is still!

He had, as I have said, attentions from those around him; but to *his* mind the only touch he longed for was the touch of that Vanished Hand, and the voice he longed to hear, was the voice that had been stilled long—long ago!

The will was made now, and only the doctor remained in the room.

The old man upon his bed of death was so still, that the physician walked towards his bedside, and leaned over him.

"Are you sleeping, Sir Edgar?" he said, in a low voice.

Sir Edgar opened his eyes.

"Yes, I was nearly so, good Master Levison," he said; "leave me to myself now, for I would fain sleep. I may in this slumber pass from the mortal world into that other bright region, where those I loved are waiting and watching for me. Take my hand, therefore, Levison, and press it. You have been a friend to me, and Death levels all distinctions."

The doctor took the hand of the dying man and pressed it.

"Good sir, you may, and I think will, live till morning," he said.

"'Tis well. I may yet see, then, the red sun breaking over yonder hills. Well, well, doctor, if it be not so, I am content."

"You are happy in your mind?"

"Yes, yes; quite happy."

"You are satisfied with your will?"

"Yes; it is an act of justice."

"Adieu, then, for the present," said Doctor Levison; "I will retire, as you wish it. In three hours I will enter again."

"Do so; but do not disturb me," returned Sir Edgar, in a faint voice.

"I will not," said the doctor, as he turned down the lamp.

Then, as he passed away and closed the door behind him, he murmured—

"He who would disturb you, old man, must come soon, or you will be disturbed no more in this world."

Meanwhile, Sir Huntley Mordaunt and Andrew Foster, the trooper, came gliding gently across the grounds until they reached the main entrance.

This was about an hour after Doctor Levison had quitted the chamber of his patient.

They knocked gently at the door, and a serving-man made his appearance.

The old domestic gazed in surprise and in alarm, moreover, at the two strange cloaked men who thus presented themselves at such an unseemly hour at the door of Farnley House.

"What seek you, gentlemen?" he said, somewhat timidly.

"An interview with Sir Edgar Farnley," returned Sir Huntley.

The servant raised his hands.

"It is impossible, sir," he cried. "He is on the point of death; he must not be disturbed, and——"

"Peace!" cried Mordaunt, sternly, as he drew forth a paper with the royal seal. "See, here is the king's order. If well enough, I can take him hence. Show me the way to his room, and—stay, I know it myself. Go, enter that chamber, and remain there. Stir not, on your peril."

The old domestic hesitated, and glanced nervously at an inner door.

Behind the door were several serving-men, with whose assistance he could easily drive the intruders forth into the night.

But he was left no chance.

The trooper drew from his belt a pistol, and held it to the old man's head.

"Bind him," he said to Sir Huntley, "while I prevent him from making any outcry."

Tearing a piece of the servant's doublet, he tied it over his mouth, and then drove him into the inner room.

Here the heavy curtains afforded strips to fasten his hands and feet, and he was left bound and helpless on the floor.

Sir Huntley now led the way up the stairs.

He knew well which turning to take, and they had soon noiselessly ascended, passed along a dark corridor, and, having laid aside their cloaks, stood at the door of the chamber where the dying man lay in his last mortal sleep.

Sir Huntley opened the door.

All within was very still and very dark, for the lamp shed but a feeble light over the large bedchamber, and all objects were but indistinctly visible.

"Enter," he said to Foster, "enter, and complete the work."

He stood holding the door with one hand, while with the other he pointed towards the room.

The assassin drew his sword, and, after a moment of hesitation, walked boldly into the chamber.

Sir Huntley then quickly closed the door on him and walked away towards a part of the dark corridor where the moonbeams struggled in through a narrow window upon the floor.

Here he leaned and gazed out at the night.

All was very still without; save the rustling of the trees and the sighing of the wind, nothing was to be heard.

All was still, too, within the house for some time, until Sir Huntley became impatient and looked ever and anon at the door of the bedchamber, as if fearful that his emissary's heart had failed him.

Presently, however, a sharp, shrill cry rang out upon the night, and Sir Huntley started and gazed eagerly down the passage.

Suddenly the door was flung violently open, and Foster appeared.

His looks were disordered, his mask was gone, and he rushed forward as if he had entirely forgotten that he was on a secret expedition in which noise-lessness was one of the chief necessities.

Sir Huntley seized his arm as he ran towards him.

"Hold, madman!" he cried, in a thick, hoarse whisper; "do you not remember that discovery now would be destruction to us both? Tell me quickly what is the matter?"

"When I entered the room first," said the man, still keeping his eyes upon the half open door, "all was still. The chamber was almost in complete darkness, and the lamp on the table was so shaded, that its rays took scarcely any effect.

"Presently I heard a sound.

"It was the old man speaking, murmuring faintly the name of 'Laura' in his sleep.

"I approached! I raised the knife! I struck!"

"And he is dead?" said Sir Huntley, eagerly.

"Stay; listen. Something must have unnerved my arm, for when I struck, I missed his heart. He looked at me, and said in a low voice—

"'Man, thy cruelty was unnecessary.

Death had his hands already on my heart.'

"And then—oh, 'twas horrible!—he fell back dead! and as he died, and the moonlight played upon his features, he seemed so like my own father that I cried out and fled.

"And as I fled, a voice, coming whence I know not, exclaimed—

"'This deed shall be remembered against you!'"

"Fool! how you tremble!" exclaimed Sir Huntley. "Follow me quickly, or we shall be discovered and ruined."

The man laughed coarsely and insolently.

"It is easy for those to play the braggart who have hired others to spill blood, and have seen not the face of the dead. But lead on; I follow."

Sir Huntley bit his lip.

But he made no reply.

He knew well that this was no time or place to resent an insult.

Turning quickly, therefore, and drawing his sword, he descended the stairs, and led the way once more into the dismal grounds.

It was very dark out there, and Foster, upon whose nerves the face of the dead old man had had a most terrible effect, trembled as the leafy boughs whispered to him, and the twigs touched him, and the moon wavered the shadows on the broad path; but Sir Huntley, who had more nerve and strength of mind than the bravo, strode sturdily along towards the high gate of the country-house, near which they had left their horses.

As they passed out into the high

road, there was a rush of feet, and two figures sprang forward, sword in hand.

The new comers were Lance Courtenay and Wilford Rokeby.

"We are just in time," said Wilford.

"You may find that you are just too late," returned Sir Huntley, with savage irony. "Stand aside, and let us pass. We know you not."

"Think not to disguise yourself," said Wilford. "Your cloak and mask are not sufficient to deceive us. We both know you well, Sir Huntley Mordaunt, and that cowardly assassin who is with you—Andrew Foster. This time you shall not escape with life."

CHAPTER XIII.

THE BATTLE ON THE DARK ROAD.

As Wilford Rokeby uttered his fierce threat, Sir Huntley glanced hurriedly up the road in the direction of the horses.

His first thought was flight.

He was no coward, to be afraid of a man's sword; but, in spite of this, he was far from desiring a second combat with Wilford Rokeby.

The stain upon his hand he had now almost persuaded himself he could see at times; and there was within his heart a superstitious feeling, which made him loth to engage in any conflict with the sworn avenger of Hubert Aveling.

But escape, at any rate at present, was out of the question; and he therefore was compelled to stand his chance.

Turning his back towards the horses, so that he might yield ground towards them, he withstood the fierce onslaught of Wilford Rokeby, while Lance Courtenay, with equal fury, attacked the trooper, Andrew Foster.

The sound of strife rang out clearly on the night air, and, in a very few moments, lights were seen moving about in the old house.

Still they fought on fiercely, Sir Huntley and his man backing, as he had before determined, in the direction of the spot where they had left their horses.

In the darkness there was a great difficulty in parrying the blows, and, more than once, all four of the combatants received wounds, which, though slight, were sufficient to draw blood, and inflict damage upon their clothes.

At length, having contrived to arrive at the spot where their steeds were fastened to the trees, Sir Huntley and his man made a bold stand.

Now came the heat of the fight.

Sword to sword! Clash, clash, clash! —eyes fiercely gleaming—hearts wildly beating—blood coursing like wildfire through their veins!

Suddenly Sir Huntley stopped.

This was the opportunity.

"At length I have you!" cried Wilford Rokeby, fiercely.

Then dashing forward, he struck up the sword of his adversary, and, seizing him by the throat, prepared to thrust his weapon through his heart.

But it was not yet to be.

The evil genius which seemed to protect Sir Huntley once more was there to befriend him.

Just at the moment when the gleaming blade would have stilled the voice of Hubert Aveling's murderer for ever, two dark figures sprang over the hedge, and Wilford Rokeby was thrust violently back.

"What is this? what is this, gentlemen?" cried one of the new comers; "murder, eh—murder?"

The speaker was a stout, elderly man, evidently a gamekeeper or ranger by his dress, and was, in fact, no other than the head ranger at Farnley Manor.

"Stand aside, fool!" exclaimed Wilford, angrily; "the man I was about to kill is an assassin; he deserved his death, and see now he is escaping."

Sir Huntley had sprung from the ground in an instant, and in another few moments he and the trooper were in the saddle.

"Take my advice," cried the former, to those who had interrupted the fight; "seize those men, secure them. Sir Edgar Farnley has been murdered, and they are his murderers. I heard them debating of it but now."

So saying, he put spurs to his horse, and dashed away with Andrew Foster on the road to the "Ferry House."

"Curse your folly for interfering," said Wilford, as he pushed aside the man who had spoken to him; "you know not what mischief you have done. These are two assassins—two murderers—and I was but about to avenge a friend's death by thrusting my sword through his craven heart. But he shall not escape me. Lance, let us return for our horses, and follow them."

They turned rapidly, and walked down the road in the direction of the old house.

Near this their horses were fastened to a tree.

"Now, then, Black Meg," cried Wilford, to his mare, who whinnied joyfully at his return, "now, then, my beauty, you must show them what you can do when you are put to it. Come, Lance, we will catch these villains ere they are able to reach Windsor."

As he spoke these words a throng of armed servants pressed out into the high road.

"We shall have trouble here, Lance," said Wilford; "keep your pistols in readiness. See, these meddling fools are whispering with them, and pointing to us."

"We had best charge into their midst," said Lance Courtenay; "our steeds will easily carry us through yon crowd of hirelings."

"We will try," said Wilford; "let us charge now."

Settling themselves in their saddles, they put spurs to their horses, and dashed forward.

They had drawn their pistols to fire

in case they were molested, but they were not required.

On seeing the two friends come dashing towards them, the crowd of servants opened, and allowed them to pass on along the dark highway in pursuit of their cowardly foes.

More than one shot whistled past their ears as they proceeded, but none took any effect.

Away they went at a tremendous speed.

Their horses were fresh after their rest, and they needed very little incitement to make them fly over the hard, clear road.

The point to which Sir Huntley and the trooper were making was a ferry-house, kept by an old man, his son, and daughter, who worked a boat large enough to take men and horses also over the Thames, which, near Windsor, was very narrow.

Upon any urgent occasion, and in the day time especially, it was very easy to swim a horse across, but there was no means of fording, as the water was extremely deep.

In the night-time, however, the river was very dangerous, in consequence of the reeds and rushes that grew in clumps among its rushing waters.

Sir Huntley and the trooper found everything in complete darkness when they reached the spot.

Not a single light appeared in the windows of the ferry-house.

However, the fugitives—for such, indeed, they were—stopped not to think long, but knocked loudly and peremptorily at the door.

Old Jonas Thatcher was a curious fellow, and generally slept in his clothes, and, as the saying is, "with one eye open," and it was but a minute before he popped his grey head out of the window, and demanded—

"Who's there, at this ungodly hour?"

"One who must see the king to-night, and has the king's orders with him. Quick, let us have the boat out."

"Patience, patience, good sir," cried the man; "I must rouse my son and my daughter. But fear not, I will be with you in a few moments."

To those who wait time passes on leaden wings.

It seemed an age to Sir Huntley Mordaunt, but it was in reality but a few minutes before old Jonas Thatcher with his son, Benjamin, and his daughter, descended to the boat-house.

The young girl, a pretty maiden of some seventeen years, but now looking very dazed and pale through being awakened out of her sleep and suddenly brought out into the open air, had a torch in her hand which she held aloft to enable her father and brother to find the oars and boat-hook.

The scene was a very picturesque one.

The ruddy glow of the torches falling upon the figures of the two horsemen and the boatmen, cast their shadows, quivering and dancing, on the ground, while the rippling river, the nodding, rustling reeds, and the strangely-built old house and the trees overhanging it, were all illumed by the flickering flame.

It was not long before the unwilling horses were dragged on board the boat.

The wherry being laden heavily, however, it was a matter of great effort to start, and, for some time, it would not move, although Sir Huntley and the trooper also added their strength to that of the boatmen.

"Curse these delays," cried he, savagely. "Why are not more men kept to assist in this ferry? Why are people's lives and fortunes to be left at the mercy of a boy and an old dotard?"

Jonas Thatcher looked at him angrily, and put down his oar.

There was anything but the look of a dotard about him as he did so.

"If you are dissatisfied, there's the bridge at Datchet, miles on, if you wish it," he said, coolly.

"No, no; there's no time now, we must push off. That girl, there; cannot she help?"

The old man shook his head.

"You would not allow one of your children or your sister, brought up daintily at court, to risk her life on a dark river at night, neither will I venture the life of my child upon its dreary bosom—my child, who is the image of one I love, even better than I love her. No, no; king's messenger or not, you don't find Jonas Thatcher doing that. Now, then, Benjamin, work with a will. There we have it; push again; that's it. She's clear, and across we shall go right merrily."

The heavy boat glided away now from the bank, and, carried forward by its own impetus, it was soon passing rapidly away.

The young girl still stood on the bank with her torch raised aloft.

She was very fond of her old father, and scarcely liked the idea of trusting him with such ill-looking men as Andrew Foster and his masked companion; and it was with feelings of the utmost uneasiness that she watched the boat as it faded away in the darkness.

As she stood there with the torch shedding its light over her pretty little form, and the picturesque landscape round her, there was the sound of horses' feet along the hard highway, and in a few moments two horsemen dashed up.

These were Lance Courtenay and Wilford Rokeby.

"Have you seen two men—one masked, and the other dressed as a trooper—pass this way, my fair damsel?" asked Wilford of the frightened girl.

"Yes, sir," answered the maiden, timidly; "there they go—in father's boat."

"Is that your only boat?"

"Yes, sir."

"Follow me, then, Lance," cried Wilford, and, without an instant's thought, he leaped his horse into the dark and rushing river.

CHAPTER XIV.

THE SHOT IN THE DARK.

IF the loud splash into the waters of the Thames had not told Sir Huntley Mordaunt and Andrew Foster that they were followed, they would have known it from the shrill and piercing shriek which rose from the lips of the ferryman's daughter.

She could see from the excited faces, and the excited manner of both Wilford Rokeby and Lance Courtenay, that they wished no good to those whom they were following, and she at once thought of the danger which her father and her brother would run out upon the dark river.

Sir Huntley heard her cry, and turned at once.

"Ha!" he cried, "we are pursued. Andrew, can you see them?"

The trooper glanced anxiously in the direction of the bank, and soon descried the figures of the two friends, as their horses struggled on after the boat.

"They can't overtake us on the water," said Foster.

"No," said the old ferryman; "but, when we get to shore, there'll be a delay for some time to get the horses to land, and then they may overtake us."

"True," cried Sir Huntley; "true. Andrew, you are a good shot, and can you see them sufficiently plainly to pick one of them off?"

"I don't believe I can."

"Give me your gun, then," said his master; "I will try *my* hand at it. If my aim is but as correct as my hate is, it will go hard with one of them."

He seized the short gun from the hands of the trooper, and took steady aim.

All his hate, all the deadly passions of his mind, were concentrated in that aim.

A delight crept over his heart.

A warm glow of anticipated pleasure pervaded his frame.

Then he fired!

The flash lit up the river, and, amid the echoing report, there mingled a wild, shrill cry.

"Just Heaven! you have shot my child!" cried the old man, springing up.

"Madman; keep to your oars," cried Sir Huntley, pressing him down savagely. "See you not yonder body struggling in the river? It is not your daughter, it is my foe. Your child must have cried out in alarm."

His words were true.

The shot which he had fired, though it had missed the rider, owing to a lurch in the boat, had struck the horse and pierced its brain, and as the fugitives watched their pursuers, they could see Wilford struggling in the eddying river.

"We are saved, now," cried Sir Huntley; "his friend will remain to aid him."

It was not long before they reached the opposite shore and landed.

There was no sign of pursuit.

Lance Courtenay, in fact, had too much to do to rescue his friend to think of his enemies, and as they dashed along the road to Windsor once more, not the faintest sound of horses' feet could they hear.

"Rokeby is foiled again, Foster," said Sir Huntley, as the great outer gate of the royal castle clanged to after them, "and dead for all we know."

"If he is not now, he shall be by sundown to-morrow," returned the trooper; "I'll answer for that, if I'm a living man."

"If you act up to your vow, you shall receive a fortune for your reward, Andrew," said Mordaunt, earnestly.

"Good," said Foster; "I'll watch for him, and somehow or another I'll warrant me that I catch him in such a manner that he shall not escape me."

They had now reached the inner gate.

The sentinel in charge looked earnestly and fixedly at them.

"What want you?" he asked.

"The king," replied Sir Huntley.

"The king!" repeated the man, in astonishment.

His surprise was not at all to be wondered at, for, mud-covered, disordered, ragged, and bloodstained, the two companions in crime looked most unlikely persons to be admitted to the king's presence.

"Yes, my friend," said Sir Huntley; "yes, we desire to see the king, although we are in this sorry plight. We have been set upon by ruffians on the road,

or we should never present ourselves at the castle in this guise. See, here is my order; therefore let me pass, and let word be sent to his majesty that I am here."

The man glanced at the order, and having satisfied himself that it was signed by the king, he called another man, with whom he conferred for a moment in an undertone.

The latter then turned to Sir Huntley.

"Will you walk this way, sir?" he said. "*You* can remain here in the guard-room," he added, as Andrew Foster was about to follow.

He conducted Mordaunt along a passage to a small chamber.

"Enter here, sir, and wait a few moments, and I will bring you the king's answer," said the man, civilly. "What name am I to give him; and what message?"

"Say that Sir Huntley Mordaunt has arrived from London on important business, and that he desires an audience, if his majesty will graciously accord him one. You can say that I have been waylaid and maltreated on the road, and am in a very strange condition; but I beg his majesty to see me."

The man bowed and retired.

Sir Huntley paced quickly to and fro on the polished floor of the small oak-panelled chamber.

The messenger was gone but a few moments, but those few moments seemed to his eager mind an age.

Presently the man's footsteps came echoing along the stone pavement of the passage; and Sir Huntley's impatience became then so great, that he rushed to the door and opened it, before the man had time to enter.

"Well," he said, "well, what says the king?"

"His majesty sends his best love to Sir Huntley Mordaunt, and desires him to follow me."

The man bowed again, and, turning, led the way along the corridor through which he had just come, and then up a narrow winding stone staircase into a room fitted as a bedchamber.

Sir Huntley gazed round him in astonishment upon being ushered into this small, low-roofed, quaintly-appointed room.

"Surely," he said, "the king will not meet me here?"

The man bowed again with provoking politeness.

"The king, Sir Huntley, desired me to lead you hither, and to bring you other clothes. He also says that at this unreasonable hour he cannot see you. In the morning his majesty will be most pleased to grant you an audience."

"His majesty will not see me!" exclaimed Mordaunt, in complete surprise.

"Such are his majesty's words; not until the morning," replied the man.

"May I send another message, then?" cried Sir Huntley.

"The king said that he was not to be disturbed this night," said the other.

Sir Huntley muttered something which sounded very much like a curse.

"Send me up my man in a few minutes," said he, "and bring me, in the meanwhile, those clothes. I shall not attempt to rest or sleep this night."

The man bowed silently and quitted the room.

In a few minutes the man returned, bringing with him some clothes for Sir Huntley's use.

He placed them on a chair, and then said, with another grave bow—

"How soon would you wish to see your attendant, sir?"

"In about another quarter of an hour," replied Sir Huntley.

"Very good, sir; he shall attend you," said the servant; and then, bowing again, he quitted the room.

"Confound that fellow and his bows," cried Mordaunt, as he hastily donned his clothes; "there is a spice of sarcasm in his manner that I like not. I hope I am not deceived. And yet," he continued, "yet this refusal of the king to see me seems to bode me no good. I should have imagined that immediately after Buckingham's disgrace he would have been glad, nay, eager, to learn the news. Never mind; I must have patience. I know the king far too well to hurry him."

As he spoke, there was a loud knocking without, and the clanging of a bell.

Sir Huntley rushed to the window, and gazed out upon the night.

All was very dark.

The courtyard below was quite still, and, even if it had not been, he would have been unable to perceive what was going on in its gloomy depths.

He heard presently, however, the clatter of horses' feet upon the hard pavement of a yard at the side of the other one, and then loud voices at the door, after which all was once more quiet.

In a few minutes Andrew Foster entered the apartment.

His clothes had a somewhat better appearance than when he had entered the palace; but his appearance was still that of a man labouring under severe excitement.

"What ails you?" cried Sir Huntley.

"Why, the Evil One himself must preside over the life of Wilford Rokeby. He is here."

"Wilford Rokeby here!"

"Yes, sir, he is. I saw him enter a moment ago. And, what is more, he asked to see the king, and was at once admitted to his presence."

"And I have been refused!" exclaimed Sir Huntley, passionately, as he paced to and fro in his little chamber. "What means this? Am I to be made another victim of this king's caprice?"

"It seems as though Wilford Rokeby, and not you, will be the king's next favourite," said Andrew Foster.

"Do you know in what chamber the conference is held?"

"Yes; in the yellow chamber, at the end of this very corridor."

"Have you courage enough to proceed thither and listen at the door?"

"I have."

"And if you are discovered, what then? What excuse will you make?"

"I will say that I have lost my way. I will go at once."

The assassin then passed out of the door, and, with his usual stealthy movements, glided away towards the king's chamber.

CHAPTER XV.

THE CONFERENCE.

WHEN Sir Huntley Mordaunt fired the shot across the river, the horse on which Wilford Rokeby rode—his favourite mare, Black Meg—uttered one cry, and rolled over into the water.

It was a position of great danger.

The horse, truly, did not struggle, for its death had been instantaneous; but our hero's legs were entangled in the stirrups, and the young Lieutenant of the Night Guard was plunged head foremost in the rushing stream.

But Wilford was not one to lose his presence of mind.

Dragging himself by a violent effort towards the body of the dead animal, he tore the stirrups away from his feet, and had just succeeded in freeing himself entirely, when Lance Courtenay seized his arm.

In another moment he was drawn up upon his friend's horse, and they were making, in all haste, towards the shore.

They were now but a short distance from Windsor Castle, but, in spite of this fact, the jaded horse could not proceed at any great speed beneath the weight of its double burden, and it was, therefore, some time (as has been shown) after the arrival of Sir Huntley at the king's castle, before our hero and his friend reached the ancient palace.

"There seem to be robbers upon the road to Windsor to-night," muttered the guard, as Rokeby and Lance Courtenay passed in wounded and ragged.

"It strikes me forcibly that those gentlemen have fallen out among themselves," said another; "these are queer times in every way. Perhaps that mysterious murderer who they say haunts the precincts of Whitehall, has come to pay the king a visit at Windsor."

Meanwhile, Rokeby, having left his friend Lance in a waiting-room—the same in which Sir Huntley Mordaunt had been placed—was conducted straight to the Yellow Chamber, and in a few moments was joined by the king.

"You will excuse my attire, your majesty, I am sure," said Wilford Rokeby, bowing. "I have been attacked and nearly murdered on the road."

The king smiled.

"You came to me in some such guise before," he said, "at my palace at Whitehall."

"Yes, your majesty," replied Rokeby, "and through the same cause. Sir Huntley Mordaunt was the one who bribed the deputy-constable of the Tower to inveigle me into a pretended escape, and I fell down into a hideous, yawning pit, full of all manner of abominations. It was so choked, however, by the relics of former crimes, that I contrived to clamber up the reeking sides of this pesthole, and reach the top of the stairs leading from the Traitors' Gate to the river. Here I found two sentinels standing still and silent like statues, as if they were expecting some one. I endeavoured to glide past them, but it was in vain; they heard my step, and attacked me. I had no weapon, but I flung myself with despairing energy against one of them, and succeeded in seizing from his grasp the sword with which he had threatened me. With this, I fought my way against the other soldier, and, finding a boat at the bottom of the stairs, I leaped into it, and rowed off."

"And did they not pursue you?" asked the king, who was deeply interested in his recital.

"They had no chance. I was too quick for them, and I arrived, therefore, at your palace unmolested. At the gate, however, I was again attacked. By the orders of Sir Huntley Mordaunt the guard at the door was changed, and I was refused admittance. It was then I took the liberty of drawing my sword, and forcing my way to your presence."

"A liberty I have long since forgiven," said the king.

Rokeby bowed low.

"And you have been again attacked by Sir Huntley?" added James.

Quickly and briefly Rokeby detailed the history of the wild ride from London; while, as he spoke, a stealthy step approached, and a head made its appearance at the partly open door.

The king frowned darkly as he listened, but he made no comment when Rokeby finished his narrative, only saying—

"And now, Rokeby, for the letter of which you spoke."

Wilford handed it to the king, who read it eagerly.

"This confirms what you have said to me. This Huntley Mordaunt is a traitor; he is in secret conspiracies against me. He has accepted heavy bribes to place dishonest men in high offices, and now he seeks the position from which I have ejected Buckingham. This shall not be; I will refuse him an audience. It would be worse for me at my age to cast myself into this man's hands than to submit to the dictation of Buckingham and my own son. I will restore Buckingham to favour, and do all I can to persuade him to calm the overheated blood of our Spanish friends."

"As you please, your majesty," said Rokeby, "as you please. Will you then return to London?"

"No, no. I will see Buckingham here; I must obtain an interview with him before any further is said by him to the Spanish ambassador. I would not willingly allow this country to drift into a war with Spain; but, on the other hand, I do not wish it to drift into revolution."

"Revolution! What means your majesty?" said Wilford, in surprise.

The king lowered his voice.

"I mean," he said, "exactly what I say. Sir Huntley Mordaunt is engaged in two conspiracies. The first is to destroy Buckingham—you are aware of the existence of that one; the second is a more desperate and more villanous one than this. It is a plot to destroy *my* life, to place my son Charles in my place, and ultimately to destroy him also, and substitute a government, over which Sir Huntley would be chief ruler. We must thwart his plans at once."

"You utterly surprise me, your majesty," said Rokeby. "But tell me at once how I can serve you."

"I will. You must return to London at daybreak. I will send word to this traitor that he must leave this palace. He will gladly do so to save his own neck. I will give you a letter to the Constable of the Tower, ordering the release of the Earl of Rostrevor, Sir Clarence Tremaine, and Lord Claude Mortimer; secondly, a letter to the Duke of Buckingham, asking his attendance at the Castle, here, with all possible speed. You must depart privately, and see that you are not followed."

"You may depend on me, sire," said Wilford Rokeby, bowing lowly.

"I know it," said King James, "and you shall see that I can reward you. Though old and much perplexed with the intrigues of my most ungodly court, I can observe how matters stand. You love Lady Clara Mortimer, the ward of Sir Huntley Mordaunt? You shall have her."

Wilford's eyes glistened.

"Sire," he said, "that is all the reward I ask."

"Then that reward you shall have. Some mystery at present overshadows her young life, and prevents her acting as boldly as she would wish; but this

THE NIGHT GUARD;

Or, THE SECRET OF THE FIVE MASKS.

SIR HUNTLEY GLIDED GENTLY BEHIND THE TAPESTRY.

mystery will soon be cleared away, and Lady Clara Mortimer shall be yours. And now retire to your room, and take your rest, that you may be well and ready in the morning to perform my service. They may call me old and feeble, as they do in the letter which you brought me, but the traitors shall see that I am King of England yet!"

"You have the traitor here; why not arrest him at once?" said Wilford.

The king smiled.

"I have my reasons," he said, "which some day you will know. Retire now, as I wish, and at dawn I shall expect you."

The head of the listener at the door now disappeared, and Wilford Rokeby, after bowing to the king, quitted the chamber.

Andrew Foster, meanwhile, glided away unperceived along the corridor, and re-entered his master's room.

Sir Huntley Mordaunt was, as may be imagined, all impatience.

"Well," he cried, "what news do you bring me? Good news, let me hope."

"Bad, very bad. I have overheard all. The king has found out that you are betraying him; he will refuse to see you, and in the morning he will send you word that he desires you to retire to London and await his return."

"Madman! you have been dreaming," cried Sir Huntley Mordaunt, savagely.

"I have not; I give you only the simple truth as I heard it. If you will but give me time, I will repeat all that passed."

"Speak on, then," said Sir Huntley Mordaunt, impatiently.

The man told his story.

"Good," said Sir Huntley, when he had finished his information, "good. We must, at the hazard of our lives, put a stop to this adventure. There is some traitor in the camp, and this traitor I suspect to be Wilford Rokeby himself. I will send to the king early in the morning—see that I wake in time to do so—and we will, on receipt of his majesty's answer, proceed at once in pursuit of these traitors."

The next morning at length dawned over Windsor, gilding its grey old turrets, its stately gardens, and broad terraces, the silver river and green woods, but not awakening Wilford Rokeby.

He needed no wakening.

That had been for him a strangely sleepless night.

The words of the king in reference to Clara Mortimer had roused in his mind a feeling which was not easily to be subdued; and even when he did succeed in catching fitful slumber, his mind was incessantly filled with visions of the face and form he so much loved.

He had scarcely roused himself, when a man entered his room.

"Here is a letter from his majesty," he said. "You and your friend will follow me to a place where you can obtain refreshment, after which his majesty wishes you to go on straight to London. Here are the letters which you have to take with you."

He gave into Wilford Rokeby's hands a large packet, which our hero placed in his breast, after which he descended with his guide to the chamber where breakfast was prepared.

There was on the exterior of the packet a letter addressed to himself, which at the breakfast table he read.

It ran thus :—

"I suspect that you are watched. When you leave the palace, therefore do not take the London road, but proceed as if you were making in the opposite direction. Defend these letters with your life, seek no quarrel, and depend upon the gratitude of

"JAMES R."

After partaking of a hearty meal, Wilford Rokeby and Lance Courtenay mounted the fresh steeds which were provided for them, and quitting the castle, cantered away in a direction opposite that towards London.

The morning was a magnificent one.

The air was clear and balmy, and over the wide country, and the grey towers, the nodding woods, and the gently winding river, the warm sun of morning shed its golden and beneficent light.

Away our heroes cantered until, arriving at a cross road which was of a soft and clayey soil, Wilford suddenly drew rein.

"I have an idea," he said; "see yonder hut, Lance ?"

"Yes."

"That is a smithy. We will hasten thither and have our horses *shod, with the shoes placed backwards.* In this manner we shall put our enemies completely off the scent. We must seek no quarrel now, as we are on the king's business and must depend for the time more upon our stratagem than upon our swords. Come, let us hasten. See how our horses' footmarks show upon this heavy soil.

The ruse will, I am sure, succeed admirably."

"It is a good notion, indeed," said Lance Courtenay; "it must be put in practice at once."

In a few moments they reached the old smithy, a quaint old structure which formed, as it were, the commencement of a village.

In answer to their summons an old man appeared at the door.

He readily comprehended their meaning, and, being told that he would be paid well, he quickly set to work, at the same time calling from the inner recesses of his small tenement a fine-looking girl, who glanced in some surprise and alarm at the travellers.

"Keep a good look-out towards Windsor, Catherine," said he; "these gentlemen have no wish to be seen. They are on the king's business, and expect to be followed by ruffians who will attempt to rob them."

Reassured by the smiles of the handsome strangers, she ascended a small hillock by the side of the road, while Lance and Wilford seated themselves upon a bank.

"This is a strange business, Wilford," said Lance; "we are becoming king's messengers, instead of lieutenants of the guard."

"True, true, it would seem so," returned Rokeby; "but never despair. The road leads to Clara and Geraldine, and happiness for both."

The change of shoes was soon effected, and the old man was just putting the finishing touch to the last hoof, when the girl cried out, at the same time pointing down the road—

"Yonder, from Windsor, come two horsemen, in hot haste. See."

"Let them come," said Lance, not moving from his seat.

Wilford, more excitable than his companion, sprang up at once, and clapped his hand to his sword.

"Oh, it's all right, master," cried the old smith; "presently the high hill yonder will hide you from them, and then you must start. They'll never think of following you. These shoes'll put 'em off the scent, never fear."

Mounting their steeds, therefore, the young men paid the old smith his reward, and having waited until their pursuers dipped into the hollow beneath the hill, darted away at full speed.

They had not quitted the spot more than a quarter of an hour before Sir Huntley Mordaunt and Andrew Foster rode up upon their panting steeds to the door of the smithy.

"Old man," cried Sir Huntley Mordaunt, "I am in search of two traitors, one of whom has made an attempt upon the king's life. Have you seen two horsemen pass this way?"

For a moment the old blacksmith hesitated.

Was he mistaken?

Had he been taken advantage of by two enemies of King James?

But one glance at the hang-dog, ruffianly face of Andrew Foster decided him.

"I have seen no such persons," he said; "if you choose to look, you can see for yourself. The soil of the road will tell its own tale. No travellers can have passed this way."

Sir Huntley cast his eyes upon the ground.

From the direction of the castle horses certainly had come, but none seemed to have departed.

The tracks of Lance and Wilford's horses—*shod backwards*—appeared also to lead from London.

Sir Huntley and his villanous companion were for the moment taken aback.

"You keep horses here, then?" he asked.

"Yes; go in and see, if you disbelieve me," said the old man. "There's my mare and neighbour Larkin's horse in yonder stable. The one came from Windsor this morning, and the other from Langton yonder. But I can't stop talking here all day. Is there anything I can do for you, gentlemen?"

"No, not now," said Sir Huntley.

And making a sign to Andrew Foster, he turned his horse's head, and proceeded back by the way he had come, which was the nearest way to London.

On arriving in London, he proceeded at once to the palace; but here all was quiet.

No one had heard or seen anything of Lance Courtenay or Wilford Rokeby.

They, in fact, had come to town by the longest route, and Sir Huntley and his villanous associate were far in advance of them.

Evening at length once more closed over the palace, and, after searching in every spot where he imagined it possible he could discover Wilford Rokeby, Sir

Huntley Mordaunt retired in exasperation to his room.

"He has escaped me—he has foiled me again!" he muttered, as he flung himself into a chair by the open window; "but to-morrow night there is another meeting of the Five Masks. It is high time that another should be added to the number. I propose Andrew Foster as the fifth, in the place of Hubert Aveling; and, with the opportunities which will then be given him, I do not doubt that he will soon be enabled to dispose of this last enemy of mine."

As he spoke, there was a knocking at the door of his room.

"Come in," he said, and Andrew Foster, the trooper, entered.

"They have arrived," he said; "both Lance Courtenay and Lieutenant Wilford Rokeby are in their rooms. The palace is quiet. I can easily pass into their chambers and dispatch them."

"No, no; not in the king's palace. To-morrow night Rokeby goes upon a long and solitary journey. That will be the time when we can watch and attack him. He *must* be dispatched; but not here. It is far too perilous an undertaking. Leave me now; at six to-morrow evening I will see you again."

The man bowed, and withdrew from the chamber, and in a few moments Sir Huntley Mordaunt followed, and proceeded in the direction of the little chamber where he had so often met Genevieve St. Clare.

He had no sooner placed his hand upon the latch than a tall female figure confronted him.

This was Lady Laura Clavering.

"Stay!" she cried, as she stood before him with pale face and angry gleaming eyes, "*I* have a word to say to you. Wilford Rokeby is *not* your last enemy; you have also to dispose of *me*."

CHAPTER XVI.

LADY CLARA'S SECRET.

SIR HUNTLEY MORDAUNT drew back with a look of surprise as Lady Laura Clavering confronted him.

"What want you with me?" he cried. "I have an appointment; an important one it is, moreover, with another person."

Lady Laura smiled.

"That appointment will not be kept," she said; "Genevieve St. Clare will not see you."

"And, pray, madam, how know you this?"

"Because she directed me to meet you, and tell you this," returned Lady Laura. "In the brief time which your journey to Windsor has occupied, she has discovered your treachery; and she has resolved no longer to imperil her reputation and her life by these secret meetings."

Sir Huntley Mordaunt bowed sarcastically.

"And pray, madam, why has she selected *you* to give me this message?" he asked.

"Because, sir," she said, while her eyes flashed fiercely upon him, "because she knows well that Lady Laura Clavering has sworn to avenge the death—the murder—of the one she loved; and because, therefore, I am always ready to thwart and baffle you. Oh! Sir Huntley Mordaunt, oh! were I a man, the sun should never rise again until I had sheathed the sword of vengeance in your craven heart. My blood courses hotly through my veins when I look upon you; my brain reels; my fingers long to clutch some deadly weapon. I must leave you, for when I am in your presence I see the features of my murdered lover—the dark pavement where his still form lay amid the red stream which has stained your hand in this world and your soul for ever."

Sir Huntley started and looked in nervous dismay at his hand; but ere he could reply, Lady Laura had hurried away, and walked with a quick though a majestic step down the corridor.

He now once more placed his hand upon the latch of the door, but it was fastened firmly from within, and resisted all his efforts.

"She has told me nothing but the truth," muttered he, as he walked away in the same direction as that which had been taken by Lady Laura Clavering.

On passing the chamber which she had entered he heard earnest voices within, and saw, too, that the door was placed so ajar that he could creep behind the heavy tapestry without being seen.

"I may discover something here," he said; "I will enter and listen."

Gliding, therefore, into the room, he pushed the door to after him, and crept behind the tapestry.

No one observed him.

The three persons who were within the chamber were far too much employed to observe anything.

Sitting on a high chair was Lady Laura Clavering, while at her side, seated on a low stool, and leaning on her friend's knee, was Lady Clara Mortimer.

Standing up, with one hand upon a little fancy table, was Genevieve St. Clare.

It was a picture of great beauty—the picture of three lovely girls, dressed in the fashionable costume of the day, with low-necked dresses, displaying their pretty shoulders, sweetly-toned necklaces glittering on their swan-like throats, and costly bracelets circling their rounded arms.

With their faultless forms—their bright features—their earnest expressions—they formed, indeed, a tableau, upon which even the villanous heart of Sir Huntley Mordaunt might have dwelt with pleasure.

But there was no pleasure mingled with his emotions.

Hatred for two; a baffled passion for one; such constituted the feelings of his heart as he gazed upon them.

"Clara," said Lady Laura Clavering, as if continuing a conversation, "it is but just that you should tell us this secret which you have so jealously kept.

Genevieve has unburdened herself of all she knew—she has entered the list of Sir Huntley's enemies—I, as you know, am a declared foe of that treacherous assassin, and therefore it is but just that you should confide to us the reason of this man's power over you."

Sir Huntley smiled triumphantly behind the tapestry.

"She dare not tell," he murmured to himself.

He was wrong.

"Well," said Clara, "to you as friends—as friends who have aided me, and who still are willing to aid me—I may safely and justly confide my secret. Close yonder door, Genevieve, for listeners abound in this palace."

Sir Huntley's heart beat wildly as the young girl turned and approached the door.

Discovery would not only take from him the chance of learning secrets which would doubtless be of advantage to him, but it would hasten his downfall and his dismissal from the palace.

Neither of the three girls, however, suspected the presence of a traitor, and having looked out into the corridor and then closed the door, Genevieve St. Clare returned and sat down on a low stool near her friends.

"Now, be quick, Clara," she said, "for the queen may summon us."

"I must begin from the beginning," commenced Clara. "My father, Lord Ernest Mortimer, was about forty years of age when he first became acquainted with Sir Huntley Mordaunt, and for a time they were fast friends. Different as they were in temperaments, they, for some reason or another, were always together, and at length the terrible fruits of their intimacy became apparent.

"My father was an ardent admirer of free institutions, and, wrongly enough, he imagined that the time had come for abolishing monarchy in England.

"In spite, therefore, of the earnest solicitations of my brother Claude, he engaged in a conspiracy, which Sir Huntley affected to join and aid by all his influence. He did the reverse. He was simply leading him deeper and deeper into the pitfall.

"My father at last so involved himself, that there only remained two courses—to make the attempt at once or to fly. He was suspected; spies watched him everywhere, and he resolved to hazard a rising with the few bold spirits who had gathered round him, and trust to the feelings of the people to join him.

"Sir Huntley selected this moment for his first essay.

"He had repeatedly expressed to my father and to me his unbounded admiration for me; but he had not as yet stated his wish that I should be anything more to him than a friend.

"My father was quite taken by surprise when Sir Huntley spoke of me as his wife, but said he would consult me. You may guess my answer. I was not sixteen, and he was twenty years older. I indignantly rejected the idea, and told my father that I would rather die than marry a man who was leading him into trouble, and who, moreover, possessed a character which I could never respect.

"My father, who loved me dearly, at

once informed Sir Huntley Mordaunt of my decision.

"Sir Huntley was very indignant, and even threatening, but neither his anger nor his threats availed with Lord Mortimer.

"He remained firm, and for the time the subject dropped.

"A few weeks after this the unfortunate rising took place.

"With about six hundred followers Lord Mortimer marched at daybreak against the town of Danesborough, took it, and raised the flag of freedom upon its walls.

"But of what avail was this?

"The people were not ripe for rebellion; King James was not sufficiently unpopular, and, before evening, a strong body of troops, aided by the citizens, drove my father and his friends from the place he had seized.

"In front of the town walls the rebels made a final stand, but in vain.

"They were, ere nightfall, driven from before Danesborough in disastrous rout, and each man had to save himself as best he could.

"My father, one of the last to quit the field, made all haste to his own home.

"He had not arrived more than two hours, when a loud knocking was heard at the door, and, looking out of the window of the room where we were talking earnestly about the chances of escape, we saw that the house was surrounded by troopers.

"In a few moments more there was the clattering of heavy boots in the passage below, and Sir Huntley Mordaunt entered our room.

"He was alone, but the triumph which glittered in his eyes showed to us that he was in command of the troops without.

"'Lord Mortimer,' he said, without casting even one look at me, 'I arrest you in the king's name!'

"'You!' cried my father, 'you who have professed to be my friend.'

"'Yes, I,' returned Sir Huntley. 'Prepare to follow me at once. I have an order, signed by the king, to seize you wherever you may be found, and to execute upon your person, without further trial, the judgment due to traitors.'

"I rushed forward.

"'Oh! have mercy, Sir Huntley,' I cried, 'have mercy. For the sake of your old friendship, permit my father to escape!'

"'There is one condition, and one only, on which I will consent to aid your father in escaping.'

"'Name it, then,' I said, although I almost feared from his look and his manner what it would be.

"'Your hand.'

"'My hand!' I cried, shrinking back.

"'Yes,' he said, 'your hand. Give me that, and I will enable your father to escape, and find for him a refuge also.'

"My father glanced at me for a moment, hesitatingly; but only for a moment.

"Then, turning proudly to Sir Huntley, he said—

"'No; I will not purchase my freedom by sacrificing my daughter's happiness. No; let your men come and lead me away. The child whom I love shall never live to curse the father's folly and cowardice.'

"His words decided me how to act, and, running across the room, I flung my arms round his neck.

"I will consent, dear father,' I whispered. 'I will crave a long delay, and, during *that* delay, who knows what may occur to release us from the power of this man?'

"Then, before my father could reply, I advanced towards Sir Huntley.

"'Is there no time left us for thought upon this matter?' I asked.

"'None,' he answered, sternly; 'there are others who will betray me if I granted any delay. Answer at once, or it will be too late.'

"'Well, then, Sir Huntley,' I said, 'to save my father's life, which is dearer to me than my own, I will consent; but, even to this consent, there must be *one* condition. I am now sixteen; I will *not* marry you until my nineteenth birthday.'

"'I agree,' said Sir Huntley, 'also on condition that your father makes a will, appointing me as your guardian. He must then be supposed to die and quit the world for ever as Lord Mortimer. He must reside, however, in England, lest, when he escapes to a foreign country, you should forget your word to me. Agree to this, Lord Mortimer, and you are safe.'

"'Yes, yes,' I cried, as a loud clamour was heard below, 'I do agree—we both agree. Be quick, and save my father.'

"As I spoke there was a rush of feet up the stairs.

"Sir Huntley himself was perplexed.

"'Have you no secret closet where you could hide awhile? Think quickly.'

"'There is none such here,' I said, in an agony of fear.

"'My lieutenant knows you not,' cried Sir Huntley, suddenly; 'I shall name you to him as Lord Henry—your brother.'

"With this he went to the door, opened it, and admitted his lieutenant.

"Jasper,' said he, 'this is Lord Henry Mortimer, the brother of the rebel. I can extract from him nothing but that Lord Ernest has fled. I suspect, however, that he is somewhere concealed in this house. Send our men away to scour the country. Do *you* guard the front gate, and *I* will see that this gentleman and lady do not stir hence.'

"The lieutenant bowed and withdrew.

"'That man suspects something,' said Sir Huntley; 'he came up the stairs blusteringly, and he has quitted us quietly. Now be quick, Lord Mortimer; make out the paper I require; and do *you*, Lady Clara, while this is being done, don a suit of your brother's clothes.'

"I hastened to obey his bidding, and by the time they had made out and signed the papers, I was ready.

"My signature, also, was appended to the document, and then Sir Huntley opened the door, and led the way down the stairs.

"On nearing the front door, he saw that egress was impossible, and we escaped by a back way, and made towards Sir Huntley's own mansion at Claverstone. I will weary you no longer with details. Suffice it to say that my father has remained at Claverstone Abbey ever since, in the disguise my of a steward, while I have been at Court. When I declare my dislike to him (and he cannot fail oftentimes to see unmitigated abhorrence of him) he threatens to deliver my father up to justice. The king is inveterate against him; his pardon cannot be hoped for, and my nineteenth birthday will arrive in three months. Oh, this horrid— this odious marriage! You know— you know well how I love Wilford Rokeby, and how he loves me. It will break his heart and mine."

And, as the poor girl uttered these words, she burst into a flood of tears, and bent her weary head upon her friend's lap.

"Poor Clara!" murmured Laura, joining in her tears. "And yet pity is not for you as it is for me. While there is life, there is hope. Your Wilford lives, while my Hubert is dead, lost, lost to me for ever. But think you this marriage *must* take place?"

"It must, it must. I love Wilford dearly; but my father—I cannot, will not sacrifice him. How could *I* live on in happiness with a vision haunting me day by day—a vision of his poor grey head upon the scaffold-block? Oh, no, Laura, there is no hope for me."

There was silence for a few moments. Then Genevieve St. Clare exclaimed with sudden eagerness—

"There *is* hope, Clara; there *is* hope. If your father went abroad, this marriage need not be consummated."

"True, true!"

"Then we must send him from England. Why should he be immured in Claverstone Abbey, when we have brave hearts who can rescue him? Sir Huntley is in London. Wilford Rokeby, Lance Courtenay, and Giles Lambert must rescue him, take him from the Abbey, and aid him in escaping to France. We will act promptly and secretly, and our plot will not fail."

Little did she imagine that behind the tapestry was listening one from whom, of all others, she would have kept her plans secret, who would be enabled thus to baffle their scheme, and who, even now, was triumphing in his discovery of their secrets.

Little did she think how his evil eyes glistened, and his evil heart beat, as he heard the words which fell from her cherry lips.

"Your plan is a good one," said Lady Laura. "I can answer for Giles Lambert, and Laura can, I know, answer for Wilford Rokeby, and his friend, Lance Courtenay. We will leave it to you, Clara, to speak to Wilford, and settle the plan of action, and the time for its execution."

"I shall see Wilford, I hope, to-night," said Clara, "and I will tell him your plan. I think it a good one, and I thank you for it, dear Genevieve; but I have a strange presentiment that this hateful marriage will yet be consummated."

"Your presentiment shall prove a true one," thought Sir Huntley, as he listened. "This very night I will remind you of the approach of this dreaded birthday. And yet will I allow this plan to be placed in train. A better chance of destroying Wilford Rokeby could not present itself than will be given me on this journey to the dark and dismal Abbey of Claverstone. Good, Lady Clara. You yourself shall deliver your lover into my hands, and then, when we are married, either I will make you love me, or I will break your proud spirit for ever."

In a few moments after this the women's conference broke up, and Sir Huntley Mordaunt was left in the room alone.

He soon made his way out unperceived and hastily proceeded in search of Andrew Foster.

CHAPTER XVII.

ON THE TRACK.

ANDREW FOSTER was sitting by the guard-room fire, scowling darkly at the men who had been his comrades, but who now were only compelled by Sir Huntley's influence, to receive among them one who was a known enemy to Wilford Rokeby.

Sir Huntley interrupted him in his reverie.

"Andrew," he said, "I want you."

The man rose rather sullenly as he spoke.

He did not care to be disturbed, but Sir Huntley Mordaunt was not a master to whom he could deny any attention.

"What want you to-night, sir?" he said. "Any new journey to undertake?"

"You have hit upon it rightly. Follow me, and I will explain everything."

The man, who saw in his master's words the prospect of further emolument, relaxed the frown which had settled on his face, and followed Sir Huntley out into the night.

Passing down upon the river terrace just where he had walked upon the evening when Hubert Aveling was murdered, he took a rapid survey of the palace, and then stopped.

"Andrew," he said, "are you quite sober and steady?"

"Yes, Sir Huntley."

"Then, to-night you have a wild and a dark ride to take for me far away towards the North of England."

"Then, how about to-morrow evening?"

"That is all altered. Listen now, and do not interrupt me. Circumstances have happened this night which have changed all my plans. There is a plot afloat to destroy my fortune and my life—a plot to take from me all my hopes in this world—to wrest from me the only woman I ever loved, and I must act decisively, and this very night, or I shall be outwitted. You know Claverstone Abbey?"

"Yes; your own house."

"The same. That is where I desire you to go. I wish you to go there without the knowledge of anyone. You must pretend to retire to rest, and then slip round to the stables, and get out a strong and swift horse. I will, meanwhile, prepare a letter for my steward —the old German, Hans Leffler—and he will put the place in a state of defence."

"Is it likely, then, to be attacked?"

"It is. Wilford Rokeby and his friends purpose attacking it ere long; but I will be there to confront them when they do arrive. Be ready in two hours, when they change guard, and I will meet you here. Go now, and I will follow you presently."

As he spoke his eyes caught sight of a light dancing on the waters of the river.

It was only a faint speck, but he could tell that it came from the palace.

Glancing back suddenly, he saw a lamp being taken away from one of the windows of the palace, and then a dark form sprang from the terrace upon which they had been standing.

"As I live, that is Wilford Rokeby!" said Sir Huntley; "if we had but known it, we might have put a stop to their scheme at once. But regrets are useless. Meet me here in two hours well armed, and I will give you a letter."

At the time appointed, Andrew Foster, mounted upon a strong and tall black steed, started from Whitehall, and sped away in all haste towards the north.

Meanwhile we must return to Lady Clara Mortimer.

After the women's conference had broken up, she proceeded to her own room and wrote a short note to Wilford, bidding him watch upon the river terrace until she showed a light, when she would meet him in the corridor, where, upon a former occasion, he had been arrested.

He lost no time when he saw the light glistening on the wavelets of the rushing river, but, hurrying into the palace, ascended eagerly to the place of meeting.

At any time he would have greeted with eagerness a summons from one he loved so well, but he could tell, from the tone of her letter, that she desired to speak to him of some important news, and he was, therefore, more anxious than ever to meet his betrothed.

Clara did not lose much time in her explanation of the scheme which had been suggested by Genevieve St. Clare, and it may be imagined that Wilford eagerly acceded to it.

"I blame you, Clara dearest," he said, "for not telling me of this before. Had I known the possibility of saving your father, I would have attempted it long since."

"And when will you go, Wilford?"

"In three days. I cannot to-night, because the king is not in London; to-morrow night I am engaged upon business which I dare not neglect; but on the day after to-morrow, King James returns to London, and I will ask him for leave of absence."

" And you can answer for Lance Courtenay's help ?"

" Aye, and that of Giles Lambert as well."

" And you will promise to take care of yourself?" she whispered.

" For your sake, and for the sake of the happiness I hope for," he said.

It was during the fond embrace which followed that a hasty step was heard approaching.

"That is Sir Huntley's step," said Clara; " quick, fly—yet no. Hide in yonder recess—here by this statue—and hear what he says."

As she spoke, she led him towards the high mailed figure, which, upon the former occasion, she had fancied she had seen move.

Scarcely had they neared it when it turned suddenly round, and a soft hand seized that of Wilford Rokeby.

" Quick! this way," said the voice of Laura Clavering; " we can hear all here."

And he had hardly realised to himself the strange phenomenon, when he found himself descending two or three steps, and then closed in by a wall of iron.

There was only just enough room for himself and Lady Laura to stand upright, but they could both hear by applying their ears to a kind of grating in the square pedestal of the statue.

" I have in this place heard all the intrigues of the court," said Lady Laura, "and I came here to-night to see how far you adhered to your old friendship for Hubert. You are a good and true friend, Wilford Rokeby, and

you will be rewarded for it. But hush, here he comes !"

Sir Huntley, on entering the corridor, advanced with a cynical smile towards Lady Clara.

" Ha !" he said; " I am afraid that I have disturbed you in a pleasant tête-a-tête. I have, however, something most important to speak to you about. Do you remember what time is approaching ?"

" I do, alas !" said Lady Clara, gazing down upon the ground, while her hands clenched together, and her bosom rose and fell with the intensity of her emotion.

" You will be nineteen in three months. On that birthday you are bound to be my wife, and I do not intend to give you even twenty-four hours' grace. On that day you will become my wife. Do you remember this ?"

" I do," said Clara; "but why tell me of it now—why remind me of it, when you know that it sends a thrill of horror through my heart ?"

" I will tell you. The king has been informed by some enemy of mine, that I am engaged in plots against his life; and, just as I fancied myself rising to the summit of prosperity, I have fallen into disfavour. When the king returns to London, I fear me I shall be dismissed for a time from court. In that case I shall retire to my house at Claverstone, and shall leave you at court. By the time that nineteenth birthday of yours arrives, I shall have made every preparation for receiving you at Claverstone as its mistress, and I shall expect you to arrive there on that morning. Now do you comprehend me?"

"I do, sir."

"And mark me," he added, sternly. "Mark me, if I find that you are deceiving me, your father's life shall pay the forfeit. Marry me now in love, if you will, and I will obtain his freedom and his pardon; but, if you hate me, it shall make no difference. I will be your husband, if life is spared to me to be so. Remember, moreover, that there is no chance of escape. Whatever you may say—whatever you may plead, I have the king's written order—*his order for your father's death.*"

Clara trembled at the angry passion so evident in his eyes as he uttered these words.

"You have my promise," she said, "and I am in your power. I will do as you wish; and now permit me to retire."

He seized her hand, and raised it eagerly to his lips.

Bad man, assassin, and traitor as he was, he really loved her.

"Oh, Clara, Clara!" he cried, passionately, "if you knew how much I loved you, you would never hate me as you do. Bad as you may think me, badly as my actions may speak for me, I am your slave, your humble slave in heart. In your presence alone I feel weakness; you alone would inspire me to live a nobler and a better life."

Clara turned from him in contempt.

"The past," she said, "can never be wiped out. May I retire?"

"Yes," he said, dropping her hand, and arousing himself, as it were, into his former sternness, "yes, you may retire; but remember the nineteenth birthday."

With a shudder of evident fear and disgust, Lady Clara turned and quitted the corridor, while Sir Huntley, with a look and walk which plainly denoted how greatly his black heart was triumphing, passed slowly away in the direction he had come.

"Oh! Lady Laura," cried Wilford, "how my heart longed for a chance of crushing him. My good sword seemed to tremble in its scabbard as he spoke. But that I should have betrayed you, I would have sprung from my hiding-place and confronted him here in the king's palace."

"It is better to leave matters as they are," said Lady Laura. "I have a few words to say to you; but come, let us leave this hiding-place, it is none of the pleasantest."

Touching a spring by her side, she caused the pedestal of the mailed figure to revolve out of its place, and, ascending one or two steps, they once more entered the corridor.

"Now," said Lady Laura, "what I have to say to you is very brief, but it is important. I have discovered that Sir Huntley Mordaunt is about to despatch Andrew Foster to Claverstone Abbey. He evidently, therefore, suspects some plot against him. This Foster, as you know, is attached especially to Sir Huntley; although he has endeavoured, since his expulsion from the corps (which took place, as you know, some time since) to claim fellowship with his former comrades. He is an atrocious villain, and I should not wonder at any crime which he committed. You must, if you wish to succeed in your plans, start for the Abbey to-morrow night, before any great preparations can be made for your reception."

"To-morrow night," said Wilford, "is a most untoward one to choose. I have an urgent and special call elsewhere."

"It must be cast aside, then, for this enterprise," returned Laura, vehemently; "remember in whose cause you fight—think that delay is dangerous."

"True, true," said Wilford; "I must endeavour to go to-morrow, and so I will instruct my companions. If the king returns to London to-morrow morning, I will at once ask for leave of absence."

Wilford Rokeby's thoughts when he parted with his fair companion were most distracting.

Never since the establishment of the society of the Five Masks (whose secret we have yet to reveal) had he been absent from a meeting, and, suspecting what he did as regarded one of its members, he was now more anxious than ever to attend regularly at their mysterious gatherings.

But, on the other hand, all his hopes in life were centred in the enterprise which was now placed in his charge.

To save Clara's father from the position in which he was now placed at Claverstone Abbey, was not only to foil one of Sir Huntley's favourite schemes of villany, but was also to give to him as wife the one he dearly loved, and to crown, in fact, his earthly happiness for ever.

He was saved, however, from any long discussion with himself on the subject, for, on that night, a messenger, *whom none saw and whose footsteps none heard*, placed upon his table a small note, in which the meeting of the Five Masks was postponed for two weeks.

Free thus to act, Wilford Rokeby waited impatiently for the arrival of the king, who, as he had anticipated, came to the palace the next day.

To one who had performed such services as Wilford Rokeby, permission was readily granted; and, on a dark and somewhat stormy night, the little band of adventurers, consisting of Wilford Rokeby, Lance Courtenay, and Giles Lambert, set off towards Claverstone.

CHAPTER XVIII.

THE ADVANCE ON CLAVERSTONE.

THE high-mettled chargers on which Wilford Rokeby, Lance Courtenay, and Giles Lambert quitted London for Claverstone Abbey, carried them swiftly and steadily over the hard road, and it was not long before they left the towers and quaintly-built houses of the metropolis behind them, and emerged into the open country.

The moon was now spreading its

THE ✶ NIGHT ✶ GUARD;

Or, THE SECRET OF THE FIVE MASKS.

"I AM SHOT!" CRIED LANCE COURTENAY, FALLING BACK.

silver sheen over hill, and meadow, and stream, and their way, therefore, was easy before them.

Their hearts beat high with hope.

Wilford Rokeby himself saw in the success of their adventure the utter defeat of Sir Huntley Mordaunt; the triumph of himself and Lady Clara; the union of their hearts for ever, and the destruction of him whom he regarded as the assassin of his poor friend, Hubert Aveling, whose pale, cold face, upturned towards Heaven in the sleep that knows no wakening, was ever before his mind.

It seems outrageous that a man, known by so many to be a villain, should have been permitted thus to go at large—unchallenged and unpunished.

But he had unfortunately, at this moment, a power over them which they could not resist.

They might, truly, have disclosed publicly the facts they knew; they might have branded him before the Court as a murderer, and adduced proofs which to many minds would have been convincing.

But what then?

Sir Huntley might be crushed, and yet in his very downfall have the triumph of destroying Clara's father, against whom the king was inveterate.

At present, therefore, although convinced in their own minds that he was a guilty man—a perjurer—an assassin, they were compelled to depend upon their own exertions, rather than any public exposure at Court.

Wilford, therefore, seeing in the release of Clara's father such golden promises for the future, was, as may be

imagined, most intensely eager to see the towers of Claverstone Abbey before him.

Lance, on the other hand, the lover of Geraldine Mortimer, Clara's younger sister, who was absent from home at the time that the great cloud fell upon her father's house, was equally anxious to press forward; while Giles Lambert, who loved Laura, the betrothed of the slain Hubert Aveling, had an interest in victory which he regarded as even greater than theirs.

As the gentle dawn, therefore, descended over the smiling country, the adventurers, with mutual accord, strained their eyes towards that portion of the horizon where they expected to see the grey towers of Claverstone rising up clearly against the sky.

Their suspense at length became so great that, believing that they must have missed their way, they paused at a little inn, and, calling out the landlord, asked in what direction they might expect to arrive with greatest speed at the Abbey.

The man glanced in some surprise and distrust at them; for, although Sir Huntley Mordaunt was known to have been in high favour at Court, his retainers did not bear the best of names on the country-side, and, in fact, many tales of reckless plunder and outrage were whispered of freely in the neighbourhood.

However, he growled out a direction, and it was not long before, with feelings of mutual joy, they saw the towers of the castellated mansion rising up out of the grey dawn of the morning.

"We have arrived at last," cried

Wilford Rokeby, as he pointed towards the high gate on the other side of the drawbridge. "Unless Sir Huntley, by some strange perverseness of fortune, has been able to steal a march upon us, we shall be able to enter here without hindrance."

The place was indeed a picturesque one.

The house was built upon the summit of a wide-spreading hill, which on one side went gently down to the edge of a stream, and on the other inclined to a great wood.

On one side the tops of the trees nodded gently in the glowing light of morning, while on the other the fine old turrets of the mansion were bathed in rosy splendour—rising like a fairy tower above a still and peaceful lake.

The whole appearance of the mansion was that of an old castle which had stood the storms of time, and the assaults of armed hosts ; a place which had its wealth of traditionary glory, and could show a bold front to the foe in this its old age as it had done in its youth.

It was a picture of fine, grand beauty, and it would at any other time have impressed them with serious thoughts; but now they were only dreaming of the strange secrets which were hidden within its precincts, and the results which would accrue to them when these secrets were discovered and made patent to the world.

The three friends rode slowly up the incline, and approached the Abbey without seeing a living soul either on the ramparts or at the windows or gate.

This quietude, however, did not last long.

They had scarcely time to remark to each other upon the extreme silence of the place, when the portal was swung open, and two armed troopers appeared.

The three friends halted, and were about to speak, when a third form made its appearance at a window above the gateway—a mysterious form with a mask over its face.

It waited for no speech, and gave no challenge, but, raising its arms swiftly, fired at the friends.

"I am shot," cried Lance Courtenay, falling back upon his horse.

"Cowardly villain !" murmured Wilford, as he turned to aid his friend, who, pale and disordered with pain, had fallen into the arms of Giles Lambert.

Then, leaping from his horse, he hurried to a stream which bubbled along over bright pebbles at the foot of the incline, and brought some water for the fainting man, whose arm hanging listlessly, helplessly by his side, proclaimed itself to be broken.

Leaving him there under Giles Lambert's care, he advanced on foot towards the mansion, leading his horse by the bridle.

The troopers still stood at the door.

" What means this cowardly reception ?" he cried. " Is it your habit to murder your visitors without asking questions ?"

" What want you here ?" asked one of the armed domestics.

" To speak to the steward."

" Then you can't speak to him," returned the man, coarsely. " Our master is not here, and, during his absence, we open the door to no one whom we know not."

" Very good. We will return again,"
said Wilford. " When does your
master arrive?"

" We do not know; we, in fact, do
not expect him."

" Expect me, then," returned our
hero.

And leaping on his horse, he turned
its head towards the country once
more.

As he galloped off three shots
whistled after him; but, as if bearing a
charmed life, he pursued his way un-
harmed, and soon reached the side of
Giles Lambert, who was proceeding
slowly away with his wounded friend.

Not far from the mansion was an inn
situated on the edge of the wood, and
here they at once entered.

In a wild and sparsely-inhabited
neighbourhood, such as this was, it was
a matter of difficulty to find a doctor;
but at last a leech was found, and in a
very short time the broken arm was
set.

Lance smiled as he looked upon the
useless member.

" Thank Heaven!" he cried; "this
is but the left arm. I have still the
sword-arm free."

" You shall not be permitted to use
it," said Wilford Rokeby.

" Indeed, then, I shall," replied
Lance. " Wherever *you* go *I* go. My
one arm is quite enough to vanquish a
cowardly assassin."

As soon as the night fell, the three
friends, who had partaken of some
hours' rest, issued from the old inn, and
proceeded on foot towards the Abbey.

Walking over a stubbly and tangled
heath, they found progression extremely
difficult, and it was some time before
they arrived beneath the walls of Claverstone.

Everything was very still, and the
bright moon falling upon the tree-tops,
and the towers of the Abbey, and the
purling streams, and the dewy hill-tops,
formed a picture of exquisite beauty.

But our adventurers took no heed
whatever of this.

Their eyes were wandering eagerly
over the walls, to see the best means of
ingress, and presently, with an exclamation of joy, Wilford Rokeby beckoned
them to follow him.

Stopping at a point where the moonlight, falling on the moat, showed it to
be spanned by a fallen tree, he pointed
to the wall.

It was covered to its summit with
thick and strong ivy.

" There," said Wilford Rokeby, "there
is a method of entrance. Providence
has placed in our hands an easy mode
of access. Let us advance at once."

All three advanced towards the fallen
tree, which bridged the stream.

" Stop, Lance," cried Wilford, placing
his hand kindly on his friend's shoulder,
" you must not attempt this escalade.
Your arm is far too painful to render it
safe for you to try. I and Giles Lambert will climb up and admit you by the
postern gate."

" I can climb easily enough by one
hand," said Lance. " I cannot bear to
think of remaining here, inactive, while
you, my friends, are in danger."

" Think, Lance, that such an attempt
on your part would only cripple our
exertions, and I am sure you will consent to wait," said Wilford. " See

yonder gate. We will climb over, draw the bolts, and admit you at once."

"Very well," said Lance, "very well; but do not leave me waiting here long."

"No, no. Fear not. We will be as quick as circumstances will allow. Now, Giles, come with me, and when the sentinel yonder has passed to the end of the battlements, we will climb up."

The two friends now advanced quickly forward, and hurrying over the frail bridge, they reached a portion of the wall where the ivy grew the thickest.

Here they halted, and taking a strong hold of the creeping plant, began to ascend.

Slow and noiseless was their ascent, and dangerous, too, for every now and then some part of the ivy became detached from the mortar, and swung them backwards, till they hung dangling over the yawning depth beneath them.

But the parasite had in general taken a pretty firm hold of the old building, and, after a long and tedious ascent, they at length reached the summit of the wall.

The heavy tread of the drowsy sentinel pacing slowly along the rough stone pavement could now plainly be heard.

He was close to them.

This was a moment of terrible anxiety.

The ivy which had borne their more rapid ascent might not endure a constant strain.

Yet, what could they do?

To advance now would be to court discovery, for, long ere they could silence the guard, the whole Abbey might be aroused.

They had not long to wait.

The slow and measured steps at length faded away in the distance, and they raised themselves eagerly above the parapet.

No one was near, and in another moment they were upon the battlemented terrace, hurrying towards the steps which led to the postern.

They had reached the steps, and were descending, when the tramp of a second sentinel was heard.

"Lie down," said Wilford, "and let him pass."

They quickly stooped and laid themselves down beneath the dark shadow of the wall.

The man, however, passed on unsuspectingly.

He had no suspicion—in fact, he could have no suspicion that enemies were so near.

The road being now free to them, the two friends hurried down the steps, and unfastened quickly the bolts of the postern.

Lance Courtenay, who was eagerly waiting outside, was soon admitted, and the gate was closed.

The bolts, however, were not again shot.

"We will leave this open," said Wilford, with a smile; "we may find it useful."

Advancing now along the courtyard, they reached the second terrace, and climbing up the stone steps, carefully approached one of the windows.

The window, an old and rickety affair, was not properly closed, and our adventurers found no difficulty in forcing their way in.

On entering, they found themselves in a dark and gloomy corridor, the end of which they could not see, for not a single ray of light broke in upon the gloom.

"Now," whispered Lance, "how do you mean to proceed? If this house is teeming with armed retainers, it would seem that we are throwing ourselves into the trap deliberately."

"Fear not," said Wilford; "I have provided against that. But, come, let us advance. The first man we meet we must seize, and, on pain of instant death, force him to lead us to the steward, Lord Ernest Mortimer."

So saying, he led the way towards the end of the passage.

He had no sooner reached it, however, than the door was flung open, and three armed men appeared.

One of these was Andrew Foster!

CHAPTER XIX.

THE FIGHT IN THE DARK.

THE three friends drew their swords, and stood ready for action.

"What want you here?" cried Foster. "Are you come for plunder?"

"We are not. We wish to see the steward," replied Wilford.

"You should come by the front gate, then, like honest men," returned the trooper. "I see nothing but plunder and villany in this entrance by a back gate. Retire, or our swords shall drink your life-blood."

Wilford's answer was a scornful laugh.

"On, my friends," he said, "on, before these chattering fools awaken the whole house."

There was no further delay.

Advancing quickly, the three friends rushed upon their foes, and drove them back towards a part of the corridor where there was abundant room for the play of their weapons.

Here began a deadly and determined fight.

Our rash friends heeded not the noise which the clash of the weapons sent echoing away along the passage; they were engaged in a deadly battle, and their only object now was victory.

Not a word was spoken.

It was a battle to the death.

Lance, in spite of his wounded and useless arm, singled out Andrew Foster, and, remembering the unsuccessful combat he had had with him upon the dark high road, he was resolved to recover his laurels, which the folly of the keepers of Farnley had lost to him.

But they were not long left thus— three to three.

Suddenly, in the heat of the battle, there was heard the rush of feet, and presently the doors were thrown open and six armed men dashed into the open space.

One of them was masked.

It was he who had fired at the window upon Lance Courtenay.

The three friends saw at once that the odds were fearfully against them, and both Lance and Giles glanced in wonder at Wilford Rokeby, who, with a mocking laugh, retreated towards the window.

Throwing this open suddenly, he raised a small horn, which he had suspended at his belt, and blew a long, shrill note.

Then he returned to the combat.

The fight was, of course, a most unequal one—nine to three.

But, on the other hand, those who had so suddenly appeared were mostly common troopers and domestics, armed on the moment, and they could not, therefore, pretend to compete with skilled and brilliant swordsmen like Lance, Wilford, and Giles.

The three friends, therefore, in spite of numbers, were able to hold their own until suddenly, before any of their enemies expected it, a shout was heard without the casement, then a rush of feet once more, and, with cries of " To the rescue ! To our captain's rescue !" four of the Night Guard burst into the passage.

"Now," cried Wilford, " we are on equal terms, and Heaven defend the right !"

There were only still seven to nine, but Wilford Rokeby thought not of this.

With fiery ardour, the three adventurers and their reinforcement attacked the defenders of the Abbey, Wilford, as if by instinct, singling out the masked man, and Lance singling out Andrew Foster.

In Wilford's mind there was a strange thought.

The masked man was dressed as an ordinary military retainer, and assumed no authority over those about him, yet, in Rokeby's heart, there had arisen a conviction that he was none other than Sir Huntley Mordaunt.

Whether this suspicion was correct or not, the masked man had to stand his chance as such, for Wilford attacked him with most fierce and uncompromising ardour, so much so that he was compelled to give ground at almost every exchange of thrusts.

Gradually yielding ground, the mysterious trooper had retreated towards the further end of the passage, when a cry arose from his friends, and glancing hurriedly towards the others, he saw Andrew Foster transfixed by Lance Courtenay's weapon and fall backwards upon the ground dead.

The one-armed swordsman had at length proved too much for the former trooper.

The death of him who seemed throughout to be a kind of leader among the other men, created some amount of confusion, and as, with a groan and a fearful distortion of his features, he breathed out his last breath in a terrible curse, friends and foes paused to observe him.

This moment was at once taken advantage of by the masked trooper.

Leaving the spot where he had placed his back against the wall to receive the fierce onslaught of Wilford Rokeby, he fled down the passage.

EAGERLY LANCE REMOVED THE MASK.

Wilford was after him in a moment, sword in hand.   But it was too late!

Before he could see even where he had gone, the wall appeared to open and shut, and he disappeared.

In vain he searched everywhere around him.

The wall appeared perfectly solid, and, except a wild, mocking laugh, which seemed to wring dully through the masonry, all signs of his enemy were gone.

"We must settle these other fellows, and proceed to search this house," thought he, as he returned into the thickest of the fight.

The noise of battle was now so great, that it was quite evident that all the retainers of Claverstone Abbey were assembled together, for, had they not been so, the din would certainly have gathered all of them to the scene of conflict.

"Now, my friends," cried Wilford, "we must make an end of these fellows."

The battle after this did not last long.

The domestics, alarmed at the flight of the masked man, and awed by the terrible death of their comrade, fought but wildly, and at last, when one of their best men fell beneath the sword of Giles Lambert, they drew back and surrendered.

Quickly disarming the men, they thrust them into an adjoining chamber, and locked the door.

"Now," said Wilford, "the place is ours; the next thing to be done is to search it.   Follow me."

They proceeded at once along the dark passage, where, with little more than the moonlight, they had fought the battle, until they reached the basement of the building.

Here they began their examination.

They were met during their survey by several female domestics; but it was evident, as regarded the male servants, that they had already disposed of all of them.

Having fastened the women in another room, and having, therefore, the whole place in their power, they quickly passed from one chamber to another, seeking in every chamber, but finding nothing.

Neither the men nor the women would say one word as to the whereabouts of the steward, and they were left, therefore, to their own resources.

They wandered to and fro in the house without discovering anything.

At length, however, just as they were almost in despair of finding anything, a long, shrill wail broke out upon the night air—a wailing cry so terrible, so fearful in its intensity, that one and all halted to listen.

"What can that be?" cried Lance Courtenay, starting back.

"I know not," said Wilford Rokeby; "but, to me, it sounds like the cry of some creature in mortal agony.   Hush! let us listen again."

The men all became silent.

In those days of dark superstition they were not so ready as now to find easy explanations of things, and rather sought for them in all that was mysterious, wild and wonderful.

"It is the cry of a spirit—of some poor soul, perhaps, who has been murdered in this place."

Such, among the troopers, was the general opinion, and even the three friends themselves waited in awe-struck expectancy.

It came soon again, shrill, piercing, heart-breaking as before.

"It is a woman's voice," said Wilford, "and one in captivity, it seems to me; but, where she is, is a mystery I cannot fathom."

He passed around the walls, and tried them everywhere, and at length in one spot he fancied that it sounded hollow.

"I think we have it now," he said; "we must force our way through here. If we do not succeed in discovering the steward, who knows what else we may discover?"

The men wanted no further reminding.

With their swords and knives they commenced an onslaught upon the wall, and it was not very long before they had made sufficient impression to enable them to take out brick by brick.

When they once began this they found no difficulty in making their way into an inner passage, or ante-chamber, which was wrapped in the most complete darkness.

They had no sooner entered here than the noise, which had once more ceased, recommenced again; and then, instead of a shrill cry, it merged into a wild and plaintive song.

"Some poor creature is immured here, no doubt," said Wilford Rokeby; "perhaps from her we shall be able to learn more than from all the rest. Come, friends, let us work with a will. Who knows how soon the masked man who has escaped may bring a host of enemies against us?"

The partition between them and the concealed female was now but a frail one of wood, and by the united efforts of the friends and their followers, it was soon broken through.

As they succeeded in entering the chamber, a sight met their eyes which caused them to pause in astonishment.

Standing in the centre of a well-furnished room was a woman, still young, dressed in the fashion of some years past, her beauty faded out of her eyes and her face and her form as the gloss had faded from off her dress, looking for all the world like a thing of the past, which had survived its time, and was forcing itself unpleasantly, undesiredly, into the present.

There was a peculiarity about her dress which told how long ago the robes around that fair but faded form had been made.

It was a dress which told a story.

There was a history in the faded tinsel on her sleeves; in the faded, broken wreath, which mockingly was twisted still among her tangled hair; in the roses which nestled among the torn and ragged lace about her bosom.

There was a story of love and hate, and deep emotions; of strange, wild feelings struggling for the mastery; of hopes crushed out in their very blossoming; of a heart that had been lightsome and joyous, until a cloud had overshadowed it and blotted out the glow of young, eager life for ever.

It was a sight which would have saddened any one to see, and which, taken with the death of Hubert Aveling, in the pride and the bloom of youth, overcame its beholders with a sickening emotion of hate and contempt for Sir Huntley.

For what could this poor creature, in the hey-day of youth and beauty, have done towards this remorseless villain that she should be thrust away in the very hour of joyousness, in the very dress which spoke of her pleasure, and left to moulder away amid the darkness of those subterranean vaults?

She did not seem at all alarmed at the aspect of the armed men, but looked with a quiet, curious, smiling look upon them.

Wilford approached her respectfully.

"Madam," he said, "are you a prisoner?"

She laughed a low, guttural laugh, and shook her head.

But she made no reply.

"Will you come with us?" he added, in a kind tone.

She at once held out her hand, and, poor mad, distraught creature that she was, tripped forward as if she was taking the first steps in a dance.

As she passed on into the dark passage, she turned and glanced back, as if she had forgotten something, and then, pressing her hand to her brow, while a flood of tears burst from her eyes, she advanced with them.

To Wilford's mind the discovery of this person could be looked upon as proving nothing.

But there was evidently a mystery, and with the prize—a prisoner whom Sir Huntley evidently desired to conceal —their journey was certainly not a fruitless one.

Having now searched in every chamber in the house, they resolved to take their departure.

Without releasing any, therefore, except the female domestics, they hurried out by the front door, and with their strange prize made their way across the country towards the inn where they had left their horses.

Their fair companion, although so distraught in mind, gave them no trouble.

She advanced willingly, and never spoke a single word until they neared the hostelry.

Then, tearing her hand from Wilford Rokeby, who had been leading her, she exclaimed, as she pressed her palms wildly over her brow—

"The seventh stone—the seventh stone! Oh, Heaven! I have forgotten it!"

The three friends started, and glanced at one another in wonder.

"The seventh stone!" exclaimed Wilford. "What can she mean? What do you wish, madam? What is the seventh stone?"

But the idea was gone.

The faint glimmer of intellect had departed once more from her; and passing her arm through his, she smiled vacantly and proceeded on.

"Lance," said Wilford Rokeby, as they advanced again towards the inn, "something tells me that our journey is not in vain."

"Have you fallen in love with your beautiful companion?"

"A truce to joking," cried Wilford. "We have failed to find the steward, but we have succeeded in discovering this lady, who has evidently been hidden away for years in that secret cell. If Heaven but grants her reason once more, we may discover secrets which will bring Sir Huntley Mordaunt to the scaffold."

On reaching the inn they found the landlord in a state of great agitation and alarm.

News of the deadly conflict at Claverstone Abbey had been brought to him by a man who was in the habit of selling things to the servants, and to him numbers of the attacking party had been magnified into a hundred, and their characters given as plunderers and marauders.

"Have you been attacked, gentlemen?" he asked, as they entered.

"In very truth, we have," said Wilford; "but why ask you that question?"

"Because news has come to me that the whole vicinity is crowded with desperate marauders, who have broken into Claverstone Abbey, murdered some of the servants, and caused the master to fly for his life."

"The master!" said Wilford Rokeby. "He has not been there."

"His ghost has, then, sir," replied mine host.

"His ghost! What mean you?"

"That his ghost or himself rode by this door not two hours ago with his steward."

"By Heaven, we are foiled!" said Wilford, fiercely. "Tell me, which way did he go?"

"He went towards the north," returned the landlord. "But it's of no use to follow, for, about two miles hence, there is a cross road, and there can be no knowing which of the four turnings he will follow."

A hasty consultation took place now among the three friends, and it was resolved to return to London with their companion, and place her in some spot where she would be well cared for, and remain, moreover, in strict seclusion.

After partaking of some refreshment, therefore, the friends and their followers started, Wilford Rokeby taking before him on his horse the lovely woman whom they had saved.

For some time their way lay over a level, easy road, and they saw no one, either friend and foe.

On nearing London, however, a dark line was seen to extend completely across the highway, and on nearing it they saw that it consisted of mounted men.

"Stand to your arms, comrades!" cried Wilford Rokeby; "we have fallen upon an ambuscade."

CHAPTER XX.

BEN LOCKSTER ON THE WATCH.

THE Night Guard were not slow, as may be imagined, in obeying the orders of their lieutenant, and, in an instant, their short guns were in readiness for action.

The line of men who had spread themselves across the road to oppose them were many in number, but they were foes which these brave fellows had learned to deride.

By some manœuvre, Sir Huntley had succeeded in carrying away Lord Ernest Mortimer, and he had also obtained the services of above ten men, who, armed with muskets, and swords and pikes, were placed on the silent highway to dispute the passage to London.

"Wilford," cried Lance Courtenay, as he advanced to the front of the battle, "Wilford, *you* must not engage in this conflict. You have the charge of that fair lady, and, with that precious burden, it is quite impossible for you to fight. We must dash forward, break their line, and you must fly off to London with the lady."

"It goes sorely against me to give those caitiffs the pleasure of seeing my back," cried the young lieutenant.

"True; it may do so," said Lance, "but remember that these cowards would be certain to attack you first of all, and, in the mêlée, your fair companion might be wounded, and, perhaps, killed. No, no, Wilford, in this case

you must yield the command to me. Your great enemy is not here, and you have, therefore, no excuse for risking this lady's life."

"Be it so, then," returned Wilford; "let us charge at once."

Drawing themselves into a compact body, they dashed forward at a swift pace upon the men who had formed now closely across the road, with their pikes extended to receive cavalry.

But the ten men resisted bravely.

Little as Lance Courtenay thought of them in his reckless, impetuous mind, they were of stouter mettle than those who had defended the abbey against them, and, finding that their horses only inconvenienced them, Lance ordered his men to dismount.

They might, of course, have sprung through the hedge, and thus endeavoured to make good an escape; but the idea of flight was one which they could never dream of entertaining.

In addition to the brave spirit which always animated them, Lance saw among them the masked trooper who had so mysteriously disappeared in the dark corridor at Claverstone.

"Now," thought he, "now I shall be able to solve the secret—whether this masked fellow is Sir Huntley Mordaunt, or some one who for the time has assumed his name for the purpose of turning us off the scent."

As soon as the two friends and their men had descended from their horses, the battle began with great fury, and in a very short space of time a sufficient break had been made in the ranks of the enemy to allow Wilford Rokeby to pass through, and gallop away along the winding road.

As he passed away in safety, in spite of the bullets which were discharged after him, he took his plumed hat from his head, and waved it aloft in triumph.

A loud cheer from the Night Guard answered this demonstration of success; and the combat was renewed with redoubled fury.

While the others entered generally into the combat, Lance Courtenay attacked the man in the mask, whom he already regarded as his special enemy.

The disguised trooper fought well.

He was evidently an adept in sword practice, and Lance soon found he was no mean adversary.

The passes of both combatants were brilliant and quick, and loudly resounded the echoes of their clashing swords over the neighbouring meadows.

At length Lance began to have the advantage.

His youth gave him activity, and his eyes, too, were keen as those of a hawk.

He kept his glance fixed on his foe, and, at length, succeeding in taking advantage of him in an unguarded moment, he wounded him slightly in the arm.

The pain, and the sight of his own blood flowing, exasperated the disguised trooper so greatly that he became rash, and began to make wild and fierce thrusts.

Now was Lance's time.

"Now," thought he, "I will secure to myself the honour of avenging the death of Hubert Aveling."

A few more parries—a few more echoes from the clashing swords—a gleam of bright steel, and the sharp weapon was run up to the hilt in the body of Lance's foe.

Uttering a cry of terrible agony, the man fell back, as Lance withdrew his weapon, and, with a groan, expired.

Eagerly Lance leaned over him, and removed the mask.

As he did so, he uttered a cry of anger and disappointment.

Sir Huntley Mordaunt had outwitted them after all.

The features of the slain man were those of a stranger.

"Foiled—foiled once more!" cried he, as he dropped the mask again, and turned to aid his men.

There was no time, in fact, to indulge in much thought.

The men who had formed the ambuscade were, as I have said, men of good mettle, and fought stoutly and well.

For a long time the combat seemed very doubtful; but, at length, the superior discipline of the Guard prevailed, and their enemies were gradually driven back.

Back—back slowly towards the hedge they retreated, and, at last, when three of their number had fallen victims, they yielded up their arms.

"No mercy to any," cried Lance Courtenay, "unless we are informed

THE * NIGHT * GUARD;

Or, THE SECRET OF THE FIVE MASKS.

," RESISTANCE IS USELESS," SAID THE SERGEANT OF THE KING'S GUARD.

whither Sir Huntley Mordaunt has fled."

"We know it not," said one of the men, "unless, indeed, he has returned to Claverstone Abbey."

"Fool! do you think I shall believe such silly maunderings as these? Tell me at once, or death shall be the portion of all."

As he spoke, he seized the fellow by the throat, and shortened his sword so as to drive it at a moment's notice through his body.

"Mercy!" said the man, "Mercy! Sir Huntley has returned to London."

"You know this?"

"I know it by hearing him tell my master so!"

"And who went with him on his journey?"

"Only one old man—his steward, I believe."

"And do you know to what part of London he was bound?"

"I swear I do not."

"Then you may go; though Heaven only knows whether I have not been tricked by a knave. If it is so, it will be well for you to avoid my presence should there be any chance of our meeting."

"No, master, you will find that what I have told you is correct. He has returned to the king's palace, but whether he will take with him the old man, I cannot, of course, tell you."

"To horse, my men," cried Lance, "let us lose no time. No doubt Lieutenant Rokeby is awaiting us not far off."

Without a moment's delay, the troopers, who, with the exception of one man, had escaped almost without a scratch, were once more in the saddle, and galloping away along the high road, over which the bright morning sun was now casting its golden beams.

The friends were some hours before they saw anything of Wilford Rokeby; but, at length, on approaching an inn in what is now the populous district of Islington, they beheld him seated outside upon a bench, scanning the high road with eager eyes.

He started up joyously as he saw them approaching, and waved his hat above his head as a loud cheer rang out from the lips of his companions.

In a few minutes Lance Courtenay was beside his friend.

"Where is the lady?" he cried.

"She is within, resting," said Wilford; "we can now start. Have you seen anything of Sir Huntley Mordaunt?"

"I have not," returned Lance; "the masked man whom we imagined to be Sir Huntley was a stranger after all. He was one of those who formed the ambuscade, and I attacked him fiercely. It was only when he was dying, and I tore his mask from his face, that I found that I had been duped."

"Nevertheless, Sir Huntley Mordaunt *was* at Claverstone," cried Wilford Rokeby. "He must have changed his disguise, so as to throw you off the scent. But come, since he has thus foiled us, we must press on towards London, and place this lady in safety. I shall not feel at rest in my mind until I know her to be far beyond their reach."

With these words, he entered the inn,

and in a few moments returned with the mad lady, who gazed around in wonder, though not fear, at the assembled Guard.

"We had better get her another steed," said Wilford. "It will seem so strange to enter London with a lady before one on a horse. Landlord, can I have a horse?"

"Yes, sir. We have a fine one in the stable. John, get thee out Brown Bess, quickly."

It was not long before the animal was brought out with a lady's saddle upon it, and Wilford Rokeby led his strange companion up to it.

But here was another mystery.

No sooner had her eyes caught sight of the animal with its lady's saddle, than a deadly pallor overspread her cheeks, her eyes glared wildly, and she flung her arms around Wilford's neck.

"Oh! no, no!" she cried. "No, no! Not that! Not that!"

No persuasion could induce her to mount; and, after a short delay, Wilford Rokeby was compelled once more to take her before him on his horse and gallop away towards London, as before.

It was night-time before they reached that portion of the town where their fair companion was to be left, and they were, therefore, able to approach the house they desired to reach without attracting any special attention.

While riding along in the open day they had been subjected to many stares, and many remarks, moreover; but now, shrouded by the deep darkness, they made their way towards the house unobserved.

The place where Wilford Rokeby intended to convey the one whom they had so mysteriously discovered in the vaults of Claverstone Abbey was a house near the Tower, which was kept by an old man and his wife, whom he knew to be trustworthy.

Mr. and Mrs. Markham, in fact, had been domestics in his father's house, and had on many occasions done him a service, while he, on the other hand, had supplied them with money at times when they had been in poverty.

At the house of these worthy people, therefore, they pulled up, and having lifted the lady off her horse, Wilford Rokeby led her towards the door, and knocked loudly.

The door was opened by an old man, with long white hair, who stared in some surprise at the lady.

"Ah, Mr. Rokeby," he cried, "I am glad, glad indeed to see you, though you come with such a host at your back as would lead one to suppose that you were in peril."

"We have been, good Markham, but not now, although this lady is in peril each moment she remains in the street. I wish to leave her in your special charge, and, depend upon it, you shall be well paid."

The old man bowed, and opened the door wide to admit them.

"Remain without, Lance," cried Wilford, "and watch for our foes. We know not whether they will not spring upon us at any moment."

"True," said Lance, "true; I will remain here, although at present all seems clear, and not a soul in sight."

He was right in this respect.

No one was in *sight*.

Yet, nevertheless, solemn and still as seemed the place, they *were* watched, for behind a stone projection at the corner of the house, a man was crouching, so near that he could not only see their movements, but hear the words they used.

He heard Wilford Rokeby's words, and saw the lady descend from the horse, and yet, though the soldiers tramped to and fro, so near him, they could see nothing of him.

He was evidently watching there for some one, and as evidently resolving to keep in utter concealment.

Meanwhile, Wilford Rokeby entered the house, and, ascending a dark and rickety staircase, was ushered into a room, which, though poorly furnished, was not destitute of comfort.

Here an old woman was crouching over a fire, looking very venerable with her white hair falling around her faded features.

She glanced up with a smile of greeting as she saw Wilford Rokeby—a smile which speedily changed to a glance of surprise as her eyes fell upon the face of the lady, whose wild eyes and vacant features proclaimed the absence of that mind which alone vivifies and gives soul to our mortal framework.

"Ah! Mr. Rokeby, how gladly I greet you," said the old woman, rising, and curtseying low; "and this lady—this is not the Lady Mortimer?"

"She is not, good Mistress Markham," he said, "she is not; it is one who has been sorely wounded in heart and body—the victim of cruel injustice,

I believe—the victim of that one whom above all others I hate, and upon whose body my sword, under good Providence, is bound to wreak a proper and a deadly vengeance. She is one, Mistress Markham, whom I will deliver into your care, and I will pay you well, handsomely, for your care of her. But there is one stipulation."

"And what is that, Mr. Rokeby?" asked old Markham.

"That no one, not even your nearest and dearest friend, must know of her presence in this house. No matter what you are told, and what bribes you may be offered, you must allow no one to know of her residence with you. If ever she again falls into the hands of her enemies, I am sure that her life would not be safe."

"You may depend upon our secrecy and discretion," said old Markham. "We have a chamber where the poor lady can remain in perfect security. She has been used to be confined in vaults, and will think the room in which I will place her a palace. Mrs. Markham, will you take this lady with you to the upper room?"

As the old woman took the lady's hand to lead her away, the latter cast at Wilford Rokeby an anxious and wistful look—a painful glance, which seemed that of one who was parting with a dear and valued friend.

A tear dropped from her eye as she passed out; but, as if before this she had been subject to the dominion of some woman whom she feared, she went away without a word.

Wilford Rokeby then, having arranged some further details with old

Markham, quitted the house, and, joining Lance Courtenay, rode off towards Whitehall.

As soon as the Night Guard had passed away from the dismal vicinity of the old man's house, the figure which had been crouched up in the recess rolled out from the darkness, and rising up under the light of the lamp, revealed the features of Ben Lockster, the gaoler, who had watched over Wilford Rokeby in the Tower.

Any one who had seen his face would have observed upon his features a smile of demoniacal meaning, as, rubbing his hands, and muttering some words to himself, he advanced towards the door of Markham's house.

Here he looked around him, and having ascertained that no one was near, knocked at the door.

Markham himself opened it.

"Ah! Lockster," he said, with a voice full of nervousness, "what brings you here? How do you contrive to be absent from the Tower at this hour?"

"I am not at the Tower now, except in the day-time, since the escape of Wilford Rokeby from his dungeon," said Ben. "Leonard Fairfax, I suppose, will not trust me. However, if you have a minute to spare, I have something to tell you—a secret of great importance."

The old man did not, in spite of this, open the door any wider.

He was evidently loth to allow his visitor to enter, because, knowing his character, he was aware that he would never quit the house if he knew that there was a secret concealed within it.

"What does it relate to?" said Markham.

"To the lady who has just been brought into your house by Wilford Rokeby," returned Ben Lockster. "If you want destruction and disaster to fall upon your head in your old age, you will keep her with you."

And, with these words, the sturdy gaoler pushed his way in, and closed the door behind him with a menacing and determined look upon his swarthy and hideous features.

CHAPTER XXI.

THE SECRET OF THE FIVE MASKS.

On the second night after the return of Wilford Rokeby from Claverstone Abbey, he received a summons to attend a meeting of the Five Masks at the old house on the Dover Road, and he at once proceeded upon his journey.

There was in his mind a firm conviction that some crisis in the affairs of the Secret Society was approaching, and he resolved upon this occasion to discover, if possible, the truth whether or not Sir Huntley Mordaunt was one of their number.

Much as he disliked and contemned Buckingham, he preferred even him to Sir Huntley.

Buckingham, by his reckless administration, was plunging the country into foreign and domestic difficulties; he had created ill-feeling in Spain, and discontent in the minds of the English people; but there was no knowing into what a position the affairs of England would be thrown, were such a man as Mordaunt permitted to assume the reins of government.

There seemed, truly, for the moment, no fear of such a catastrophe; but the king was so fickle, the tide of events was so swift, that a change might be made in the administration of affairs almost in a few hours.

The purpose of the Five Masks being, by constant meetings and mutual revelations, to counteract the influence of Buckingham, it seemed truly a disastrous affair if Sir Huntley should be discovered to be one of their number.

Yet how could he be driven from among their number?

How could he be expelled without breaking through the first principle of the society, which was that no member of it should unmask?

All these thoughts flitted through his brain as he rode swiftly along the Dover Road and made all haste towards the old house where the Five Masks invariably held their meetings.

The night was a very dark one, but he could tell from the extreme silence that he was not followed; and he therefore advanced boldly towards the hedge, pressed his way through, as he had done before, and knocked at the door.

The same sentinel as on the former occasion answered his summons.

" What is the password?" he asked.

" The third night!"

" Good! Enter."

Wilford Rokeby then at once entered the dark and echoing corridor and passed into the large chamber, where he found that, as upon the last journey he made thither, he was the first who had arrived.

He was not long, however, without a companion.

The great gate without swung open once more; the loud voice of the sentinel challenging a new comer was heard, and the tramp—tramp—tramp of heavy boots was heard along the corridor.

Twice this was repeated, and then the three who had arrived sat down at the table, where they at once commenced business.

" The time has arrived for business, and the Red Mask has not made his appearance," said the Green Mask, rising; " perhaps he may have heard from some one that he is intended to be the subject of this night's conversation."

" Let us give him another half hour," replied the Blue Mask; " in a man's absence it is scarcely fair to try him."

" That is true," said the Brown Mask; " let us wait."

The time soon elapsed.

Yet no one appeared.

Then the Green Mask rose again.

" Brethren," he said, " there is reason to believe that the Red Mask is betraying us, or at any rate, is using our power for his own aggrandisement.

Now, this cannot be suffered. Our purpose in thus secretly meeting, is to save the country from the complications in which the machinations of Buckingham would cast it. We have all a suspicion who the Red Mask is, and we have seen how knowledge has been used which could only have emanated from us. If the Red Mask is he whom we suspect him to be, he is not a fit and proper person to remain in our society. I vote, therefore, that he be expelled from this society, unless, by unmasking, he proves that he is not the person whom we suspect him to me."

"But, if he is that person, and we expel him from our society, we shall be at once betrayed," said the Brown Mask.

"You forget," said the Green Mask, "what expulsion signifies. Before quitting this house in safety he will have to fight singly with us all. It is only over our bodies that he can escape. You remember the terrible oath we all took, that if ever one of our members was found to be betraying us, he would have to pass through this ordeal, and either he or we should die?"

"We remember," said the Brown and the Blue Masks.

"And do you vote for his expulsion?"

"We do; but we had been better pleased if he had presented himself, and undertaken his own defence."

"He is here," cried a loud voice.

Then the door was flung open, and the Red Mask stalked into the room.

Advancing to the table, he said—

"I have heard your last words. Tell me what is my crime."

"You are suspected of having be-trayed the society, and of being Sir Huntley Mordaunt—a man who, by our rules, is one of the proscribed, whose ruin we are bound to compass. You know the oath which you took when we first met you in this house, and you are now required to fulfil its provisions. You must prove that you have not betrayed us in the first place ——"

"That will take time," replied the Red Mask.

"True; but the second provision can be complied with now."

"What is that?"

"That you unmask at once, and prove to us that you are not Sir Huntley Mordaunt, or be expelled the society; the latter of which means, as you know, that you will have to fight us singly before you can make your escape."

The Red Mask drew back, as if fearful that one of his fellow conspirators might snatch his mask from his face.

"Which do you choose?" asked the Green Mask, sternly.

"This new ordeal of battle you have created," said the Red Mask; "or, if ye are not all cowards, a respite until I can bring forward my proofs of innocence."

"In order that you may have time to betray us to the king? No; unless by unmasking you can prove that you are not the one we suspect, we shall insist upon this ordeal at once."

"Be it so, then," said the Red Mask; "be it so."

And, as he spoke, he retreated, and drew his sword from its scabbard.

The Green Mask advanced to the door and called aloud to the trooper, whose echoing footsteps were soon heard approaching along the corridor.

"Friend," said the mask, "there will be fighting and clashing of swords here, and perhaps the groans of dying men. See that no one interrupts us. As for yourself, no matter what happens, come not hither. Be yours the task to watch the door, and see that no strangers, attracted by any sounds, enter to disturb us."

The man bowed. He evidently understood the matter well.

"It shall be as you say," said he; "no one shall enter."

Then the door was closed, and the three conspirators returned to the table.

"We must draw lots," said the Green Mask, "who is first to do battle with this man."

He took three pieces of paper, and wrote the numbers 1, 2, 3, on them.

Then he flung them into a hat, and they drew out the lots eagerly; none more eagerly, be it said, than Wilford Rokeby, who earnestly hoped that he would be enabled at last to meet his inveterate foe face to face in a position where he could not escape his vengeance.

But it was not to be, at any rate at present.

"I have drawn Number 1," said the Green Mask. "Friends, stand aside, and let me try my best to do battle in the cause of justice."

Wilford and the Blue Mask accordingly seated themselves at the table, and the Green Mask, advancing boldly towards his foe, crossed swords with the Red Mask.

Both seemed animated with the same ardent feelings, and, without a moment's delay, the combat commenced with fierce and vengeful fury; with such fury, indeed, that the clashing of the swords resounded loudly through the old house, and rang out upon the night air.

There was little fear of interruption, however.

The road without was lonely, and, in fact, was little frequented, except by the mail coaches and the prowlers who followed them for the sake of plunder.

The room within was occupied by those who were burning with impatience for their turn.

With eager eyes and bated breath they watched the fight.

It was conducted with great ardour on both sides.

The Red Mask, who saw before him a resolute and brave adversary, was urged to the exhibition of his best and most brilliant strokes; and his swordsmanship was admirably correct.

The Green Mask soon saw that he had before him an adversary of no mean importance, and he fought warily and carefully, though to an unpractised eye there would have seemed to have been no time left between the thrusts and parries for any judgment or consideration.

It was difficult to say which was the better swordsman.

Their weapons glanced rapidly, flashing about like sparks of fire, and one adversary retreated as the other advanced so quickly, that it would have been quite impossible to say which was gaining the advantage.

Above the clashing of the bright swords could be heard the heavy breathing of the antagonists, whose every sense and muscle seemed to be exerted in the desperate conflict.

Presently a difference began to be perceptible.

The Green Mask began gradually to give ground, and, as may be imagined, the Red Mask was not slow to take advantage of ths fact.

He began to press his adversary more closely.

Step by step the Green Mask yielded, until at length his back was to the wall.

His strength had now almost entirely gone, and the Red Mask found him an easy prey.

Raising his gleaming blade suddenly aloft, he struck down the sword of his foe, and rapidly thrust it through his shoulder.

The Green Mask fell, but the Red Mask had no time to dispatch him.

" Hold !" cried the Brown and the Blue Masks. " That's enough !"

Then, rushing forward, they lifted their wounded friend, and carried him towards the table.

" You can rest," said the Brown Mask to the victor; " you can rest while we attend to our friend. I am your next foe."

It was an hour before the Green Mask was enabled to speak, even though they tended him with the greatest kindness.

During that time the Red Mask sat moodily apart.

At the expiration of an hour, however, Wilford Rokeby—the Brown Mask —approached him.

" Now, Sir Huntley," he said—" for I feel that you are he—it is my turn. My heart yearns for vengeance. My sword leaps in its scabbard with joy, at the prospect of drinking your life-blood. Come !"

Their swords were crossed instantly, but, ere one thrust was given, the door was flung violently open, and the masked sentinel rushed in.

" Hold, gentlemen, hold !" he cried. " You are betrayed !"

CHAPTER XXII.

THE WHITE MASK.

" Hold, gentlemen, hold !" he cried. " You are betrayed !"

These words, uttered in a voice of evident alarm by the sentinel, caused the combatants at once to desist from their conflict.

There was no time now for settling mutual quarrels—each and all were compelled to look to the common good and defend a common cause.

Retreating, with their swords drawn, as the sentinel closed the door and pressed against it, they prepared for some deadly encounter with unknown foes.

" Who comes ? What mean you by betrayal ?" cried Wilford Rokeby.

"I mean this," said the man, who was panting, as if after some violent struggle; "I mean that the house is invested by the king's soldiers—that in another moment they will be in this room! Fly, gentlemen, while there is yet time."

"Fly—we cannot! There is no means of outlet save through that door," said the Red Mask. "Hark; they come. We must defend ourselves, gentlemen; death is preferable to discovery. Let us stand back here against the wall."

The words had scarcely left his lips when there was a loud knocking at door.

"Open, in the king's name!" cried an imperious voice without.

Then, before they had time to comply with the demand, the door yielded to a strong pressure, and a number of soldiers entered.

The first who came in belonged to the Night Guard of Whitehall—Wilford Rokeby's own men.

Their leader, Wilford's inferior officer, advanced towards the centre of the room.

"Gentlemen," he said, "I demand your swords."

"For what reason?" demanded the Red Mask.

"It has come to the knowledge of the king that a treasonable conspiracy has for a long time been in the course of development in this place, and this night he has received positive information that a meeting would be held here. If this conspiracy does not exist, you will, of course, consent to accompany us without resistance."

"Sir," cried Wilford Rokeby, "you are labouring under an error. The king also, has been misinformed; we have no treasonable designs against the king; we are rather friends than enemies of his majesty; but we cannot consent to accompany you. Masked to each other, we must remain masked to the world; and if you insist upon endeavouring to force us to accompany you, we will fight to the death rather than consent."

"You are mad, sir," exclaimed the leader of the King's Guard, "you are quite mad. We are here in numbers, and all resistance is useless. You cannot even hope for victory."

"We can die," said Wilford Rokeby, placing himself in position.

"And is this the decision of all?" asked the officer, with some emotion.

"It is."

"Then your blood be on your own heads," he answered. "Soldiers, seize those men."

The men at once advanced with their swords drawn.

It seemed a hopeless combat.

Far away down the passage gleamed the sharp points of pikes, and the glittering blades of swords, and the polished steel of helmets.

Yet the four masked confederates thought not of surrender.

Their weapons were raised; the conflict was just about to commence, when there was a strange clicking sound in the wall behind them; the tapestry was flung aside, and a tall, commanding figure entered, wearing a white mask.

Both the conspirators and the soldiers

drew back aghast as the strange form stalked into the midst of them.

"What means this?" he asked, in a loud and solemn voice.

"Who are you?" demanded the leader of the King's Guard, falling back in awe.

"I am the White Mask—the Fifth Mask," said the new-comer. "I come to save my friends. Follow me quickly," he added, turning to the Four Masks. "Fear nothing, for I will save you."

As he spoke, he moved towards the spot where he had appeared first.

The Masks turned to follow him, and they had nearly reached the wall before the king's men had recovered from their stupefaction.

Then, however, they threw off their lethargy and advanced.

"On, my men," cried the leader; "let us not be deceived by a mockery such as this. Follow me!"

A solemn, chilling dread had fallen on their hearts as the strange apparition made its appearance.

There was something so noiseless in its coming, something so solemn in its voice, something so strange and supernatural in its appearance altogether that, in those days of superstition, they may be forgiven for feeling an unpleasant dread of coming in contact with it.

At the voice of their leader, however, they recovered their courage, and rushed forward once more to the attack.

They were again foiled.

The mysterious being was more than their match after all.

Hardly had they made one step forward when a sudden darkness overspread everything.

The lights in the room and in the passage went out, and everything was in complete and utter gloom.

"Follow me," cried the White Mask to his friends.

Then, taking Wilford Rokeby by the hand, he drew him through the tapestry through an opening in the wall, and down a staircase, which, from its dank and unwholesome smell, seemed truly to be the entrance of a charnel house.

After descending some ten or a dozen steps, they found themselves in a long corridor, which, at first composed of stone, gradually merged into softer and more yielding substance, and became ultimately a tunnel, bored through the damp earth itself.

The Masks had no time to ask any questions.

Heedless of all, save the necessity of eluding those who would capture them and bear them in humiliation to the palace, they pressed on, led by the voice of their strange conductor, whose presence had cast an awe and a chill upon their hearts, as well as upon the hearts of the King's Guards.

Who could it be?

Was the spirit of Hubert Aveling revisiting earth to save them?

No matter.

He was evidently a friend, and, although it seemed strange indeed that he should be possessed of their secrets sufficiently to don the White Mask, and enter so strangely their place of meeting, he nevertheless was saving their lives, and the present was no time to question him.

At length, after plodding through a heavy, clayey soil, and stumbling over numberless obstructions, they came to what seemed an impassable barrier.

The White Mask, however, seemed perfectly acquainted with all the ins and outs of the place, and, advancing to what seemed a part of the wall, he pushed it, and a door opened, admitting a strong gust of the keen night air.

"Go now," he said, "you are free. Remain for no excuse, but make straight for London."

"And who are you?" asked the Red Mask. "Will you not tell us the name of our preserver?"

The White Mask shook his head.

"No," he said; "ask no questions, but fly while you have time. You know that your enemies surround you, and that you have no time for parley. Another time, and I will tell you all."

Three of the Masks waited no further words, but waving their hands in token of adieu, they rushed away across the dark moorland, towards the spot where they had concealed their horses.

Wilford Rokeby lingered still.

There was a strange yearning in his heart towards the being at his side, who stood now tall, still, unearthly in the misty moonlight.

"Stranger," he said, "will you not tell me who and what you are? I would willingly brave danger to listen to your tale."

"No, Wilford Rokeby."

"Ha! you know my name!" exclaimed the lieutenant of the Night Guard, in astonishment.

"I do. But, as I have said, I cannot and will not disclose to you my name. I am one, as you may believe, who watches over your interests—one who has grievous reasons to know the villanies of Sir Huntley Mordaunt—one who will save you again, but whose heart, chilled by sorrow, desires no communication with the world."

"Sorrow has not chilled your better feelings," said Wilford.

"Not to you, perhaps; but enough of this," said the White Mask. "You must away; and my time is also precious. See there, among the mist which rises over yonder road, dark forms are gathering. Those are your enemies. Go, now, and be as discreet as you are brave."

He turned from his companion to look in the direction which he pointed out to him, and saw distinctly the forms of men gathering together.

But when he glanced back, the White Mask was gone.

He had heard nothing, and seen no movement, and, with a strange feeling in his breast, he moved away, and hurried across the dusky heath, with his sword still grasped tightly in his hand.

CHAPTER XXIII.

THE MYSTERIOUS LADY.

My readers will remember that Ben Lockster, the gaoler of the Tower—or Red Ben, as he was familiarly termed, in consequence of his red shock head of hair—made his appearance suddenly at the house of old Mr. Markham, on the night of the return of Wilford Rokeby from Claverstone, and forced his way into the passage.

Mr. Markham gazed at him in evident alarm.

"It waxes late, Ben," he said, "and to-morrow I can speak to you better."

Red Ben laughed.

"No, no!" he said. "I never put off until to-morrow what can be done to-day. Besides, you know well that I cannot quit the Tower, except at night. During the day I am engaged every moment, and, therefore, I must speak to you at once."

"But I do not see," began old Markham, nervously, "I do not see that you have anything of importance to say."

The gaoler's brow contracted with a fierce frown.

"Old man," said he, "you ignore my words. I told you that you are even now engaging yourself in an enterprise which may cost you your head, and if I can save you from it I will, especially as you are without reason, and without benefit to yourself, injuring a friend of mine. We will enter here and talk."

With these words the brutal gaoler, who had led Wilford towards the pitfall in the Tower, stalked boldly into the adjoining room.

"Now," said Markham, following him, with an angry look upon his face, "be quick and tell me your business, for I am sick and weary."

The gaoler, whose face—red and bloated—showed that he had been drinking, sat down by the fire.

"In the first place," he said, "you have a lady in this house."

"My wife."

Red Ben laughed.

"Well, well," he said, "we don't deny that. Mrs. Markham is a lady in her way; but I allude to another, a young and beautiful woman."

"I know of none."

"You lie, Markham, you lie!" said Red Ben. "But to proceed. I will tell the story. You can spare yourself the trouble of answering, which will save you also the trouble of telling falsehoods.

"I say again," he pursued, "that you have in this house a young and beautiful lady. She is mad—so at least you think—but she is not. She only assumes madness. She is an enemy of the king. She is, in fact, none other than Lady Flora Harcourt, the wife of Lord Harcourt, who was executed not long since for attempting to poison the king's ministers at a banquet. Surely you remember the fact?"

"I do."

"You remember also, I have no doubt, that Lady Flora was suspected of being the chief mover in the terrible transaction, and she escaped the house just after the plot had been discovered.

"Till this day she has never been found, until now she has suddenly turned up as the friend of Wilford Rokeby, who brings her to your house for safety. Do you know what the king has promised to all who harbour her?"

"I know not."

"Death, on Tower Hill!"

The gaoler paused to watch the effect which his plausible story took upon his listener.

Old Markham's face turned very pale, and his eyes glared wildly for a moment.

But he soon shook off his alarm.

"Ben Lockster," he said, "I do not give credence to your tale."

"And why not?"

"Because I am certain that Wilford Rokeby would not place me in such danger."

The gaoler laughed coarsely.

"Ha, ha!" he cried; "you have more faith in your friend than I have. I would not trust him with the safety of a dog which I prized. But please yourself. You tacitly admit that you have a lady here, and as a large reward is offered for her apprehension, I shall inform the king where she is to be found."

If old Markham had not confessed anything before, his manner now would have betrayed him.

He turned very pale, and his hands trembled as he pointed to the upper part of the house.

"Do you wish to ruin a woman—an old woman on the brink of the grave, who never harmed you?"

Ben laughed.

"Oh, as for that, I'm not particular," he said; "but I can tell you one way in which you can save yourself from all fear of harm."

"What is that?"

"Divide the spoil."

"I do not understand you."

"Give her up to justice."

The old man raised his hands upwards.

"And betray Wilford Rokeby?" he cried. "Never! never!"

"What is Rokeby to you?"

"What is he to me? I will tell you," cried old Markham, "I will tell you what he is to me. He has been a good master, a friend, and a saviour. He is the son of one whom I respected; who was a kind father, a good husband, a good master; and, when he died, young Master Wilford did all he could to make me happy in old age. He saved the life of my only child once at the risk of his own, and shall I betray him now? No; let them kill me; let them stain the axe of justice with an old man's innocent blood, if they will; but I will not have it on my conscience when I die that I have betrayed and ruined my best and only friend."

"Very well," returned the gaoler, who, in his coarse and villanous mind, was already concocting a new plan of treachery, "very well; as you refuse, well and good. If you are determined to cast yourself headlong into the gulf, why, of course, I won't try any longer to save you. I have told you that you have in your house a proscribed murderess—the wife of an executed felon—and I have told you how to save your neck. If you refuse to take advantage of my warning, be it so. I will say no more. Good night!"

He rose to go, with a lowering, leering look upon his face.

Old Markham stood leaning on the back of his chair, gazing at the flickering fire.

"You are resolved, then?" repeated Ben Lockster, halting at the door.

"I am. Go."

"Then, depend upon it, it will not be long ere you receive a visit from the king's guards."

"Let them come," said the old man, resolutely. "They will find no Lady Flora Harcourt here."

Ben Lockster said no more.

He saw that Markham had made up his mind to preserve his secret, and, with a sullen and savage heart, he quitted the place and made towards the Palace of Whitehall.

"I will see that Sir Huntley knows this," he said; "and I will propose to him a scheme by which he can recover possession of this lady without compromising himself. I must work myself into the good graces of Sir Huntley Mordaunt; and this, I am assured, is the way to do it. Curse that Markham! I thought the bait I had cast out would have taken him; but it did not. There is more craft in the old

fellow than I ever gave him credit for."

His journey to Whitehall, however, was fruitless, and he was compelled to return unsatisfied to the Tower, for Sir Huntley was either not within the Palace, or he had business which he cared not to leave, even at the instance of one of his hired bravoes.

On the evening after the strange and unaccountable appearance of the White Mask at the old house on the Dover Road, Wilford Rokeby came face to face with Sir Huntley Mordaunt in one of the corridors of the palace.

Wilford had just quitted Clara.

She had wept to him in very despair.

The period of her marriage with Sir Huntley Mordaunt was rapidly approaching; as the dreaded time came nearer, and her father remained still in danger, she saw before her nothing but the certainty of the fulfilment of the fearful sacrifice.

The anger caused by the sight of her sorrow doubled, when he saw the face of the traitor who had returned to the palace to intercede in person with the king, and beheld the right hand, which seemed to his eyes blood-red against the delicate white lace which encircled it.

"Ill met, Sir Huntley," he cried, "ill met. We should meet out upon the ramparts yonder, or in the street, where my sword might pay the deadly debt I owe you."

Sir Huntley smiled.

"We are well met, Lieutenant Rokeby," he said, "excellently well met. I have to tell you that your newly-born

THE NIGHT GUARD;

Or, THE SECRET OF THE FIVE MASKS.

GENTLY THE MEN RAISED THE BODY OF WILFORD ON THEIR MUSKETS.

No. 9.

favour with the king will be but short-lived."

"How know *you* that? You, at least, have no power to destroy it," returned Wilford, in contemptuous accents.

"I fancy you are wrong in that," said Sir Huntley, with a sneer. "I have the power to destroy it. I shall lay before the king the fact that you have broken forcibly into my house, slain my servants, and I shall demand redress."

"And I, on my part, shall declare that, in doing so, I discovered in your house a lady who is now mad through your ill-usage; but whom, I believe, to be a person you have little desire to meet."

Sir Huntley turned deadly pale.

Up to this moment he had been entirely ignorant of the fact that the mad lady had disappeared from her dismal prison.

He had, as will be remembered, fled away with Lord Ernest Mortimer long before Wilford Rokeby had emerged from the Abbey of Claverstone, and from that moment he had received no tidings from home.

"Ha!" continued Wilford, with a smile of triumph, "I have succeeded at length then in proving to you that my power is equal to yours. Accuse me to the king, and I will bring forward the lady who will for ever crush your hopes in regard to Lady Clara Mortimer. She will have no difficulty in proving her identity."

"Curses be upon you!" cried Sir Huntley, savagely. "You are ever stepping in to foil me, but I will yet

prove to you that I am master over you in this palace. I know secrets which the king will pay for by restoring me to favour; and the first step I shall take to assure myself happiness and power will be to order your head to the block. Ha! Who comes here?"

The door at the further end of the corridor opened at this moment, and one of the Night Guard entered.

In his hand was a note.

"A letter for Sir Huntley Mordaunt," he said, bowing.

Sir Huntley took it eagerly, and, opening it, read it through.

"Ha, ha!" he exclaimed, as he scanned it again; "this is excellent—most excellent!"

It was from Red Ben, the gaoler, and in it he disclosed to Sir Huntley the important discovery he had made at the house of old Markham.

Sir Huntley was so delighted at the discovery that he thus made, that he was about to express his triumph to Wilford, but he prudently checked himself.

"Tell the bearer of this," he said, "that I thank him much, and I will see him in the morning."

The trooper bowed and withdrew, and Sir Huntley prepared to follow him.

Wilford stepped in his way.

"Stay, Sir Huntley!" he cried. "If you are a man, do not quit the place like this. Give me the satisfaction I ask for. Come with me now—both of us alone—and without aid or countenance of friends, and fight me this duel to the death, which both of us desire."

Sir Huntley smiled.

"Young man," he said, "your blood is overheated, and you seem to dream and talk of nothing but fierce and desperate conflicts. I refuse, as I have refused before, to pit my valuable life against that of a beardless boy."

"Then, thus," cried Wilford, fiercely, "thus I charge you with base treachery and cowardice! If nothing else will force you to the combat, then this insult shall!"

And, as he spoke, he flung his glove violently into the face of his enemy.

The hot blood mounted to the cheek of Sir Huntley, as the glove fell to the ground, and his sword leaped like lightning from the scabbard.

"By Heaven!" he cried. "Though it is in the king's palace, I must and will avenge this outrage!"

With a smile of joy, Wilford drew, and approached him.

But they had no time to cross their weapons.

Again fate interposed between them in the shape of Lance Courtenay and four of the Night Guard changing duty.

"For the love of Heaven, gentlemen," he cried, rushing in between them, "put up your swords! The king comes this way."

CHAPTER XXIV.

THE MYSTERY OF THE SEVENTH STONE.

On the following evening, about nine o'clock, when Wilford Rokeby was relieved by the second officer, Lance Courtenay, he made his way in all haste towards the house of old Markham.

He had noted well the triumph which had illumined Sir Huntley's face when he received the note from the hands of the trooper, and he felt assured that something evil was foreboded by that glance of delight.

The nineteenth birthday of Lady Clara Mortimer was fast approaching, and it was evident that something must be done before then to prevent the hateful consummation which Sir Huntley Mordaunt so much wished.

Although he knew nothing of the antecedents or the identity of the strange lady whom he had rescued, he felt certain that in the discovery of *her* secret lay the secret of power over Sir Huntley.

On arriving at the door of old Markham's house he knocked eagerly.

The old man himself opened it to him.

"Ah! Master Wilford," he cried, "I am glad, so glad you have come. Suspicious characters have been loitering about here this night, and I fear very much that some evil is intended. Enter here, and I will tell you all."

Entering the room into which Red Ben had upon a former occasion forced himself, Wilford Rokeby sat down by the fire, while the old man narrated to him the incidents of that evening.

Wilford listened with much concern.

"This is bad," he said, "very bad; but, nevertheless, we must defeat him. Keep a good look-out, and I will proceed upstairs and see the lady. Is Mrs. Markham there with her?"

"She is, Master Rokeby. You know your way up?"

Wilfred smiled assent, and ascended the stairs quickly.

Admitted to the room, he paused for a moment in admiration and surprise.

The few hours of repose—the change of air—the alteration from the dark vault to a comfortable lodging, had already wrought their effect upon the mysterious lady, and now, with her rosy cheeks, and her bright eyes, and her coral lips, and her splendid form, she was an object of beauty and attraction such as is not often beheld.

She sprang up as Wilford entered, and shaking her long, wild, glossy hair over her lovely shoulders, approached him, and threw her arms around his neck.

"My brother!" she murmured, looking up confidingly in his face.

"Are you happy?" he asked.

She shook her head, pointed with a vacant look around her, and then suddenly bursting into tears, withdrew her arms, and returned to her seat.

"Poor soul! she is always thus," said Mrs. Markham, "always thus except when her mind is running upon this seventh stone—this strange mystery, which seems to be her life's torture."

At the mention of the word she sprang up again.

"The seventh stone," she cried, painfully; "oh! the seventh stone!"

Then she walked rapidly to the wall, and then paced slowly back, and pointed to the ground.

"You understand, my brother," she said "the seventh stone—papers—happiness—peace—peace to my weary, weary heart."

Then she clasped her hand to her brow, and wept again, swaying herself to and fro, in an agony of sorrow.

"I begin," said Wilford Rokeby, "to see the dawning of a great light upon my mind. She speaks of papers. They must be at Claverstone Abbey, and to Claverstone I will go once more. My only fear is that she will not be safe here when I am away."

"I dread that Ben Lockster, greatly," said Mrs. Markham. "He is a villain and a traitor."

"I know it," said Wilford Rokeby, as he paced to and fro, excitedly; "yet what is to be done? I know no one else whom I could trust, and in whose house she would be safe and respected."

"Stay," cried Mrs. Markham, approaching the window, and throwing it open. "See yonder light?"

"I do."

"That is the house of one Ellen Fortescue, a friend, a true and honest friend of mine."

"Has she children?"

"She has."

"And is she poor?"

"She is; and she would be faithful as the sun. I will speak to my husband of this, for it is in my mind that she would be better able to save this lady from intrusion than we."

"It is a good thought," said Wilford Rokeby, "and if there were a back way to this house, I might visit her without suspicion."

"There is a back way," answered Mrs. Markham, smiling; "but, see, it lies along yonder parapet which crosses you dizzy height, where a false step would dash you forty feet down upon the hard and flagged stones. Along that parapet you could reach Mrs. Fortescue's house, and enter by a back window; but it would be a sadly perilous path if pursued."

"I have passed through greater perils than that when in pursuit of others," said Wilford. "But, hark! What is that?"

Mrs. Markham turned pale, and, hurrying to the door, passed out upon the landing, where a window overlooked the sill in front of the house.

Immediately that she opened the door loud cries were heard below.

"Open in the king's name!"

Three times the summons was re-peated loudly and imperiously. There was no further delay.

Fast and furious fell the blows upon the old door, and Wilford Rokeby rushed to the window and looked out.

One glance sufficed to show him the peril of the situation, and he withdrew his head.

Below, in the dark street, which was here illuminated by a lamp, was Sir Huntley Mordaunt, with a body of men dressed as troopers.

"By Heaven, we are trapped!" said Mrs. Markham. "Oh! Mr. Rokeby, my poor—poor husband! He will be ruined! He will be executed! Oh! what shall we do?—what can we do?"

Wilford Rokeby thought a moment.

As he did so, the loud blows of the men without resounded on the door.

"In a few moments," he said, as he strode back into the room, "in a few moments the door will give way, and the house will be crowded with soldiers. Follow me. I will save her, if I die in the attempt!"

CHAPTER XXV.

THE MYSTERY UNRAVELLED.

"WHITHER are you going?" demanded Mistress Markham, in eager accents, as Wilford Rokeby rushed to the other window.

"You say that yonder light burns in your friend Mistress Fortescue's house?"

"I do; there, yonder, where the lamp burns, you will find her," replied the old servant.

"Good. I am going there."

"Along the parapet?"

"Aye, along the parapet. My head is sure, and my step is sure also. As soon as we have quitted this room, close the window and draw the blinds, and I will save this lady, and you and your husband. Fear not, I will go safely."

He quickly approached the lady.

"Come with me," he said.

She obeyed him like a child.

Leading her by the hand to the window, he leaped out, and helped her out after him.

Then taking her in his arms, he passed away along the narrow path, with fifty feet of black darkness yawning on one side, and on the other a plain wall, which offered no means of support for the whole distance.

He had not been a moment too soon, for hardly had he started—hardly had Mistress Markham closed the window—when the door below was burst open with a crash, and Sir Huntley Mordaunt rushed into the house.

At his back were a number of men, disguised in the costume of the king's guard.

"Sir," cried Sir Huntley, sternly, "you have outraged the dignity of the king; you have refused to open when entrance was demanded in the king's name; you have risked your liberty and your life!"

"Heaven save his majesty, say I," returned Markham; "I would do nothing to cast an insult upon him; but I did not hear you. What seek you, gentlemen?"

"We are going to search the house," replied Sir Huntley. "Now, my men, follow me, and lose no time."

The old man raised his hands, as if in utter amazement.

"Search my house!" he cried; "and, pray what for? What crime have I been guilty of that I should be subjected to a search in the middle of the night?"

"You are accused, and strongly suspected of harbouring a traitress and a prisoner, by name Lady Flora Harcourt," replied Sir Huntley Mordaunt. "If you are innocent, we shall be most happy to apologise for our intrusion. If you are guilty—if we find her here—we shall convey you with her to the Tower."

Sir Huntley then turned to his men, who at once began spreading themselves over the house, quite regardless of the earnest protestations of innocence which the old man kept uttering as he stood in the custody of one of the morose-looking troopers.

Eagerly Sir Huntley proceeded from room to room, but found nothing.

At length, on reaching the top chamber, they discovered Mistress Markham sitting quietly by the fire.

The window was closed; the curtains were drawn; and there was not the slightest evidence to show that there had been a sudden and desperate flight.

"Mistress Markham," cried Sir Huntley, sternly, "where is the lady whom you have concealed here? Quick! and direct me to the chamber where you have placed her, or the king's vengeance will fall upon you."

"I do not understand you, sir," said the old lady, with assumed innocence. "I know of no lady, save one who came the other night and went away the next morning. She was a beautiful creature, God bless her; but she wasn't right in her mind."

Sir Huntley looked fixedly, searchingly, into the face of the old woman as she spoke, but he could detect nothing. Mistress Markham was a far better actor than her husband, and had far more control over her feelings.

"You swear that you have no one concealed here?" he said.

"I swear, by all my hopes of Heaven!" returned Mistress Markham, solemnly.

"I fear our errand is in vain, Lockster," said Mordaunt, turning to Red Ben, who stood by his side; "you must have been misinformed."

"I was informed by no one," said Ben sullenly, "I saw her with my own eyes."

"Yes; it seems you saw her, and forgot to watch the house. She has since then escaped. Curses on my folly for not thinking that this fatal error might happen! But never mind—the proofs are wanting. I can defy him still. Come, Lockster, let us be going; to remain here longer is but to cast suspicion upon us; and for many reasons, as you know, it will be well for us not to be found here."

Any further search would have been simply useless.

They had sought in every chamber; had examined every nook and corner; had tried the walls; but all to no purpose.

It never occurred to them to open the window and to look out along the dizzy parapet, else, just as they entered the room, they might have seen the casement in the house opposite opened to admit two forms; then closed, and the light extinguished.

Wilford Rokeby had foiled his foe again, and in great discomfiture Sir Huntley and his men retired.

The mad lady seemed to take everything that Wilford did as a matter of course.

She had recognised her danger, and clung very close to him as he carried her along the narrow parapet, above the black, yawning gulf; but on reaching the house, and being placed in another chamber, she at once settled down to her position as before.

It may be imagined that the sudden entrance of a cavalier and a lady, through a window, created some consternation in the minds of the occupants of the chamber—a young lady and her mother, who were just about to retire to rest.

Rapidly, and briefly as he could, Wilford explained the situation, and bade the lady appeal to Mistress Markham on the morrow, if she had any doubts as to the truth of his word.

"I do not doubt you," said Mistress Fortescue; "but I fear I am but a poor protector for this lady. I am a widow, and, with the exception of some young apprentices, I have no one to protect the house. However, they will never suspect me, and I shall keep my own counsel. When shall I see you again?"

"In two days. Meanwhile, here is some gold—let her not want for anything," said Wilford Rokeby. "Be assured you are doing a good action; let that strengthen you to do all you can for her."

"Be assured I will," returned Mistress Fortescue; "both I and my daughter here will tend her as if she were one of our own flesh and blood."

After waiting awhile to give Sir Huntley's men an opportunity of completing their search and going away, Wilford Rokeby quitted the house, and made his way towards the palace.

The mad girl had put her arms

around his neck, and wept, and kissed him at parting, and called him brother, as she had done before, when he had first quitted her.

"I am certain," he said, to himself, "I am certain that this young girl is Sir Huntley's wife; that she has been subjected to some terrible outrage, which has deprived her of reason; and that she has lost by a violent death some one she dearly loves—either a lover or a brother. Not another night shall pass without my proceeding to Claverstone, and discovering what this mystery of the seventh stone means. Delay now would give time to foil me, and still further imperil Clara's position."

Lance was just changing guard when he reached the palace, and he at once confided to him his proposition.

Lance Courtenay eagerly caught at the idea of his friend.

"There is one difficulty, however," he said, "and that is, that the king may object to our both being absent at one time."

"Captain Malcolm will set this part of the matter right," said Wilford; "at any rate, prepare yourself to go; for I have sworn to seek out this mystery, and seek it out I will, if I lose my life in the attempt."

Lance Courtenay grasped his friend firmly by the hand.

"My dear Wilford," he said, "you know that I shall not disappoint you. I will accompany you, even if by so doing I offend the king."

The leave was granted more easily than they imagined.

Giles Lambert was left in command of the troop, the captain, Malcolm, being ill; and after darkness had begun to shadow the earth, the two friends started upon the road, which they knew well, towards Claverstone.

On this occasion they were not observed, and consequently not followed; and, therefore, though abundant difficulties stared them in the face, they had at least the satisfaction of knowing that any delays on the road to the Abbey would be avoided.

The night was very dark, and there was no need of any disguises.

Along the shadowed roads they scarcely met a soul.

Honest people, in very truth, had retired to rest, and those whose business it was to prey upon their fellows kept back in their lurking-places, content rather to lose their chance of spoil than run the risk of an encounter with two such fine-built, well-armed young fellows as our friends Wilford Rokeby and Lance Courtenay.

Arriving in the grey of the morning near Claverstone, they resolved to give no chance to their enemies of discovering the fact of their presence in the neighbourhood; and spurring their horses, therefore, into the dense wood which skirted the Abbey, they tethered them, procured them some grass and water, and lay down to snatch a few hours' sleep.

The warmth of the midday sun awoke them from their slumber amid the green leaves, and, refreshed by their rest, they partook of the provisions they had brought with them, and waited patiently for night.

At length it came—a dark and gloomy one, like its predecessor—and having placed their horses at a point where they knew they could find them, they proceeded cautiously towards Claverstone Abbey.

All was solemn, black, and still, as on the occasion of their former visit.

"How do you intend to enter?" asked Lance Courtenay.

"By the ivy, as we did before," replied Wilford; "but we must, this time, be more discreet, else we stand a great chance of being trapped. We have no assistance to depend upon from without on this occasion."

"True; but along those dark and gloomy corridors there is every chance of concealing ourselves, even if any of the retainers pass that way. I remember well the tall, dark statues which I mistook for men in ambush."

Approaching the Abbey, they crossed the moat by means of the fallen tree, and began ascending the ivy as they had done before.

The sentinel was pacing to and fro, slowly and solemnly as before, but by the shadows of other figures, not far distant, our adventurers could see that the guard on the outer walls had been trebled since the date of their gallant adventure.

They knew their way now, however, and it was not long before they had crept along the battlements under the shadow of the wall, and reached the steps leading to the postern.

Here they were compelled to lie down while the sentinel passed.

Then, when his solemn footsteps had died away, they sprang up, and made rapidly for the window, which on the former occasion they had found to be so easily opened.

A light was shining within.

"We are outwitted, I fear," said Lance.

"Not so," whispered Wilford; "we must not suffer ourselves to think of failure. Let us approach and look in."

Cautiously making their way to the casement, they peered in.

Seated near the blazing fire was an armed retainer, fast asleep.

The lock of the window had not been renovated, but a guard had been placed within instead.

"He sleeps," said Wilford. "We must enter gently, and surprise him."

He pushed the glass slightly, and the casement yielded.

The man started in his sleep, but did not awake.

"He sleeps soundly," said Wilford Rokeby. "There is nothing to fear. Let us enter."

Pushing gently against the casement, they succeeded easily in opening it, and having passed into the room, they closed the window after them, and cautiously approached the man from behind.

Suddenly seizing him, Wilford Rokeby held him, while Lance Courtenay presented a pistol to his head.

"Silence, on your life," said Lance.

"What want you?" asked the man, in a subdued voice.

"It matters not," answered Wilford; "but you may know this much, we do not come for plunder. We are here for no evil purpose, and shall harm no one if we are not molested. Quick, Lance, bind and gag him, and let us proceed on our errand. Presently the guard will be changed, and may pass through this way and discover our presence."

Lance Courtenay at once produced a large silk kerchief, which he bound tightly round the man's mouth.

Then he secured his hands and feet.

"And now," he said, "we must conceal him somewhere. Should he be found thus gagged and bound, we should be at once discovered."

A deep, dark recess in the room presented to them an easy mode of concealment; and in a few moments they were proceeding along the corridor, in the direction of the vault where they had found the mysterious lady.

No one opposed them.

The house was buried in supreme silence.

The inmates, in fact, save the watchers and the sentinels, had retired to rest, and they had the place entirely to themselves.

The spot was soon reached.

Scarcely any alteration had been made, except that some of the rubbish had been cleared away; and the vault was, therefore, far more easy of entrance.

"We are in luck," said Wilford Rokeby, as he drew from his pocket a dark lantern; "but we must be as quick as possible, else we may be found and trapped in this subterranean tomb, from which, it strikes me, we should find it difficult to make our way out."

The light of the lantern illumined a dark, dismal vault, reeking now with damp through the absence of all fire, where the stones were placed irregularly and in broken lines, and where certainly the search for any special one promised to be no easy task.

While Lance stood watching at the door, Wilford Rokeby commenced his search.

He began counting from the door.

Then, with the aid of a small crowbar, he raised the seventh stone.

It revealed nothing.

Again he counted from one of the pillars, and then from the other.

But he found nothing.

"We have come upon a fool's errand," he said, as he desisted from his efforts. "This seventh stone may be found in some far different place to this. It may be in her own home, or some churchyard, or anywhere but here."

"Stay!" said Lance; "I fancy that I have discovered something. See, there are thirteen stones, counting diagonally, from corner to corner; the centre stone is therefore the seventh stone from any point. Strike it with your crowbar, and see if it sounds hollow."

Wilford Rokeby eagerly approached the spot, and struck the centre stone with the heavy iron.

It gave forth a hollow sound.

"By Heaven! it is true," he said, "this place is hollow. We have discovered what we seek. See," he added, joyfully; "see—see this casket! it is open, and here are papers. Quick, Lance, let us examine them. Even in this position of danger, I cannot depart without ascertaining whether they contain the documents we so desire to find."

Lance left his post of observation, and, approaching his friend, held the lantern, while Wilford opened the casket and unfolded the papers.

"By Heaven !" cried Rokeby, with a smile of joy, "this is a marriage certificate, dated two years back, *the certificate of a marriage between Sir Huntley Mordaunt and Lady Esther Malcolm.* Malcolm is the name of the captain of the Night Guard. By St. George, this mystery is thickening rapidly. What if we discover her to be some relation of that hot-headed Scotchman ? It will go ill with Sir Huntley, methinks, if it be so."

"We can easily ascertain that," said Lance ; "but let us depart now. We have discovered enough to save Lady Clara Mortimer from the hands of her bitterest foe. Let not our success be marred by unnecessarily exposing ourselves to danger."

"True. You counsel rightly," said Wilford, "though I, in the exultation of the moment, feel as if I could, single-handed, meet a host of enemies. We will away now, and defend our newly-found treasure with our lives."

Extinguishing the lantern, they proceeded cautiously back towards the chamber where they had left the man gagged and bound.

Leaving him where he was, they eagerly leaped out of window, and hurried away in the direction of the open country, scarcely as cautiously as before.

In a few minutes more, with hearts bounding with the thoughts of the success they had achieved so easily, they were galloping away towards London, to bear the glad tidings to Lady Clara Mortimer.

Little did either of those brave hearts imagine what a cloud of dark and terrible sorrow would fall upon them ere two suns had dawned !

CHAPTER XXVI.

THE COIL OF THE SNAKE.

EVEN now a public *exposé* of Sir Huntley Mordaunt was an impossibility.

Though such an exposure might effectually have prevented, or, at any rate, postponed indefinitely, the marriage of Lady Clara Mortimer with Sir Huntley, it would at the same time have been difficult to prove the identity of the mad lady with Lady Esther Malcolm, and it would of course have precipitated the doom of Lord Ernest Mortimer.

Until, therefore, he was enabled to see Captain Howard Malcolm, the commander of the Night Guard, who was now in the north of England, Wilford Rokeby resolved to keep his secret from all but the band of friends who were as anxious as he for Sir Huntley's destruction and his success.

On the evening after his return to the palace, he made his way to Lady Clara's room, and was at once admitted.

"Clara," he said, "I bring you good tidings. Your marriage with Sir Huntley Mordaunt is impossible."

Lady Clara's face brightened up at once as she threw her arms around her lover's neck, and looked up tenderly in his face.

"Ah, Wilford," she cried, "this is, indeed, glad news you bring me! But are you sure—are you certain that you are right?"

"See," said Wilford Rokeby, showing her the paper; "here is the certificate of the marriage of Sir Huntley Mordaunt with Lady Esther Malcolm, the lady whom I saved from Claverstone Abbey."

The bright smile deepened into a look of radiant delight, but faded away after a moment.

"I fear, Wilford," she said, "that we are no further advanced than we were before."

"Why so?" said Wilford.

"Because, although this precious marriage of Sir Huntley's would, of course prevent my marriage with him, if we could make it public, we dare not publish it, because of my father's terrible danger. There would be no compromise then, and nothing would prevent his bringing my father to the scaffold."

"In my great joy I had forgotten this," said Wilford, mournfully.

"Be not desponding," said Clara; "we are on the road to success. What we have now to do is to discover the place of my father's concealment—and then we can bid defiance to Sir Huntley and all our enemies. You have done much for me, Wilford, but I trust in your energy and courage to accomplish this also."

"The time is very short," said Rokeby, gloomily; "but I will not be daunted by circumstances. Yet, surely, if the marriage day arrives before we can succeed, you will not become the bride of a man who has already another wife?"

"Heaven only knows what I shall or can do," said Lady Clara; "but hark! some one is coming; we must part. Be discreet and brave, as you always are, and I shall fear nothing."

They snatched a brief but fervent embrace, and Wilford Rokeby quitted the room.

Gloomily, and with a depression of feelings, for which he could scarcely account to himself, he quitted the palace, and walked out upon the terrace, on which the shadow of the dark night fell heavily.

It was a specially still and lacklustre night, for never a star was visible, and never a ray of moonlight fell upon the pavement or the palace that towered above, or the rushing river which flowed gushingly away towards the sea.

All was still—solemn, chilling, in its silence—and little calculated to raise the spirits, and involuntarily the thoughts of Wilford Rokeby flew back to the time when, near that very spot, his dearest friend, Hubert Aveling, had met his death at the hands of the man of whom his thoughts were ever busy now.

He could see the scene once more— the dark and rugged pavement; the pale face; the still form; the hurrying Night Guard casting the glow of their torches upon the figure and the features of the early dead ; he could hear the tramp of the troopers, and their exclamations of astonishment and sorrow as they carried Hubert Aveling gently to the guard-house within the palace of Whitehall.

He was just standing, gazing at the river, when he was startled by a slight noise, and turning quickly, he beheld a tall cloaked man standing by his side.

One glance at his face sufficed to show him who it was.

It was Sir Huntley Mordaunt.

"Well met, Sir Huntley!" he cried, drawing his sword; "now, at least, there is a chance of our paying this mutual debt."

Sir Huntley drew back.

"I come to speak to you," he said, "of matters of grave importance. Let your hot temper subside for once, and let us talk reason."

As if to enable Wilford Rokeby to see his enemy more distinctly, the moon broke from behind a heavy bank of clouds, and shone full upon the spot where they stood.

Sir Huntley could see how stern and pale his antagonist was.

"Sir Huntley," cried Wilford Rokeby, "I have sought and longed for this opportunity, and now I have obtained it, I will not allow it to escape me. You can have no information to give me that I should care to hear. All your words and actions are knavery and deceit. Your whole life is a lie; and unless Heaven is against me, and fate interposes to stay my arm, this very night shall see the end of our feud. Upon this very spot I will fight you to

the death. Draw, if you do not wish me to drive my sword unresisted through your craven heart!"

Sir Huntley was compelled to do as he was bidden.

To escape was impossible, and drawing his sword, therefore, with a loud and desperate oath, he prepared to ward off the furious attacks of his foe.

In an instant the flashing steel was crossed, and despite the fact that at any moment the Night Guard might be upon them, the two men fought like madmen, their hearts beating wildly, their eyes gleaming savagely, the blood pulsing like wild-fire through their veins.

The moon now remained bright and beautiful in the fast clearing heavens, and the two combatants could, therefore, see how to parry and thrust as well as they could have done in the day time.

Both fought with desperation, and stoutly and courageously, but it was not long before Wilford Rokeby began visibly to gain the advantage; and Sir Huntley was compelled to retreat along the terrace, in the direction of Whitehall Palace.

Eagerly Wilford Rokeby pressed upon him, and more eager too and desperate became his strokes, until at length, suddenly, by a swift and brilliant stroke, he wrenched his enemy's sword from his hand, and sent it whizzing through the air.

For one brief instant there was a deadly pause.

Sir Huntley was completely at the mercy of his declared foe.

Then Wilford's voice went thrillingly through the night air.

"Now, ere I pass my steel through your dastard heart," he cried, "I will assure myself that I am not deceived. Here on this spot, where my poor friend was murdered, I will assure myself that I am acting with justice."

So saying, he made a spring forward, and after a brief but violent struggle, tore the glove from the right hand of his adversary.

A bright stream of blood flowed from it and fell upon the ground.

"Heaven directs me!" cried Wilford Rokeby. "The blood is still upon your hand. Die, cowardly assassin! Die the death you merit!"

The bright steel was raised, the death-blow was descending, when there was a report—a flash—and Wilford Rokeby fell back upon the ground, flinging his hands above his head, and uttering a piercing cry of agony.

At the same moment, Red Ben, the gaoler of the Tower, rushed forward, and seized Sir Huntley by the arm.

"Come quickly," he said, "the Night Guard are upon us!"

"Give me your knife, and let me finish the work," cried Sir Huntley Mordaunt, in a voice of eager hate.

"No, no! Fear not. He is dead!" returned Red Ben. "I have paid him now for the trick he served me at the Tower. Come, if you are not mad! See, there is the first of the guard with a torch in his hand. Come."

Dragging the reluctant nobleman from the spot, Ben forced him away just as Lance Courtenay and the Night Guard, attracted by the pistol-shot, rushed out.

It was the old scene again.

There upon the ground, with his face upturned to the sky, pale and blood-stained, like that of Hubert Aveling, lay Wilford Rokeby, senseless and cold, lying upon the very spot where his friend had lain before him.

"Great Heaven, what have we here?" cried Lance Courtenay, as he rushed forward. "What, Wilford Rokeby! Oh! just God, can this be true?"

He threw himself on his knees by the side of his senseless friend, and, as he gently raised his head, his cheek paled, and a tear stole into his eye.

"Poor Wilford," he murmured. "Poor friend! What awful fate is here! What fearful doom is hanging over all I love and value in this world! Oh, cursed fate, that you should die and I not be here to save you or revenge your death!

"He is dead," he added, as he rose again, speaking in choking and hoarse accents; "he is dead, my men. Raise him tenderly, and bear him away upon your muskets. I will return at once when I have relieved the guard."

The men obeyed in solemn silence, raising the body of their leader as gently as they would have raised that of a child; while Lance Courtenay stood gazing upon them and him with an expression of bitter sorrow and agony upon his face.

"Oh, Wilford!" he murmured, as his eyes fell upon the features of his friend, pale, and convulsed with terrible pain, "you have left behind you one who will avenge you, even if he has to kill your cowardly assassin in the presence of King James himself."

Compelled, by his duty, to leave for a time the scene which was so memorable of disaster and death, Lance Courtenay moved gloomily away along the dark pavement which skirted the palace.

The men who were with him shared strongly in his bitter feelings, and marched slowly and silently along.

More bitter, however, were the feelings of those to whom the pale and convulsed face of their leader, as they bore him along upon their muskets, brought home the desperate deed of villany which had deprived them of him.

Slowly they bore him to the palace, into the guard-house, among the wondering soldiers, and laid him on the same table that had, months before, borne the body of the murdered Hubert, and where, with the torches falling upon his friend's pale face, Wilford Rokeby had sworn his oath of terrible vengeance.

They had scarcely done so, when a slow step advanced along the passage, and Lance Courtenay entered, and walked slowly and solemnly up to the body of his old friend and comrade.

CHAPTER XXVII.

THE TEMPTER.

For some time Lance Courtenay gazed in bitter sorrow on the face of his friend; but presently, with an eager start, he sprang forward towards the table where Wilford Rokeby had been laid by the troopers.

"He is not dead!" he cried. "By Heaven, he is not dead! See, his chest heaves! His eyes open! Archer and Elliot, fly quickly for the leech. God be praised! my friend will yet be saved!"

He bent tenderly over his friend as he spoke—tenderly and gently as he would have bent over a dying sister, and watched eagerly for the opening of the eyes, which seemed to him now the best beloved in life.

Presently, the large, handsome eyes of Wilford Rokeby opened painfully, and gazed slowly round.

"Where am I?" he asked, as his gaze rested on his friend.

"In the palace, with friends," said Lance. "Fear nothing; the assassin who attacked you——"

"Is he taken?" asked Wilford Rokeby, in eager accents.

"No; but I will give an account of him ere long. I saw him not, but, nevertheless, I can well guess who it was who attacked you."

"It was Sir Huntley Mordaunt," answered Wilford, faintly. "But, since Heaven has granted me my life, let me entreat of you not to attempt anything against that man—at least, for the present."

THE ✦ NIGHT ✦ GUARD;

Or, THE SECRET OF THE FIVE MASKS.

"YOUR MAJESTY," CRIED WILFORD, "I ACCUSE THIS MAN OF MURDER."

No. 10.

"I would kill him, even in King James's presence!" exclaimed Lance Courtenay, vehemently, "I have sworn it."

"That," said Rokeby, smiling, "was no doubt when you believed me dead. You see my life is spared. Let me, therefore, preserve also my peace of mind. This man's doom must come from my hand and no other."

At this moment, the man of medicine entered the guard-room—a bent, white-haired, quaintly-dressed man, who would have certainly been taken rather for an astrologer than a doctor in later days.

A brief examination sufficed to show that Wilford Rokeby had received a most desperate wound in the shoulder, which bade fair to keep him to his bed for some time.

From the guard-room he was taken carefully and tenderly into his chamber in the palace, where he was visited by King James himself, and where he was left under the special care of Laura Clavering, Genevieve St. Clare, and Clara Mortimer.

To the king he declared himself unwilling, for the present, to give the name of the one whom he suspected to be his assailant.

"Let me but recover my strength," he said, "and I will at once disclose his name to you, and ask of your majesty permission to fight him to the death."

Carefully did Laura and Genevieve nurse the wounded man; Clara herself visiting him often, even when it was not her turn for watching.

Under such tender treatment, and with the attention of the most skilful surgeon of the period, it may be imagined that Wilford Rokeby soon began to progress favourably towards recovery, and, with a bitter feeling of anger and disappointment, Sir Huntley Mordaunt saw his last attempt at assassination foiled, as all the others had been.

In this emergency—knowing well what a terrible secret Wilford held in his possession—he came to a desperate resolve, and determined at once to make a bold stroke, which, without involving himself, would destroy his enemy for ever.

To this end, he looked around him for some one who would aid him in his evil scheme, and none presented itself more fixedly to his mind than Genevieve St. Clare, the one whom he had so often and so bitterly deceived.

True to his evil mind, true to his utter misconception of the purity of woman's nature, he imagined himself able, by his treacherous promises, to wean this young girl's heart from its right path and make her the willing victim of his criminal purposes.

One evening, just as Genevieve St. Clare had assumed her position by the side of Wilford Rokeby's bed, a light knock was heard at the door, and a royal page entered, bringing her a letter.

Wilford Rokeby was fast asleep, and the lamp was turned low, and it was necessary to rise and approach the table where it stood in order to peruse it properly.

Slowly and noiselessly she walked across the carpeted floor until she reached the table, turning ever and anon to see whether the rustle of her dress disturbed the patient.

Her noiselessness lasted not for long, however.

She had no sooner indeed cast her eyes upon the letter, than a cry escaped her lips and she sprang back.

The letter was from Sir Huntley Mordaunt, and it ran thus—

"MY DEAREST GENEVIEVE,—Since I deceived you, I have known not a moment's happiness, and nothing, moreover, has appeared to thrive with me. I wish to meet with you this evening, that I may tell you all I feel in regard to you, and how much I repent the past. You only shall possess my heart, dearest Genevieve, in future; you only shall be my wife. Clara Mortimer shall be nothing to me henceforth, and in all my future good fortune, *you* shall be the only sharer. All I ask of you is the accomplishment of what I spoke to you long since, the destruction of Wilford Rokeby. He lies in bed wounded and helpless. You are his nurse; it can easily and readily be done. I shall be in the Black Corridor at ten this night. Meet me there.

"HUNTLEY MORDAUNT."

"Villain! Double-dyed villain!" murmured Genevieve.

Then she turned to the page.

"Tell Sir Huntley that I will be there and will do his bidding. Oh! coward assassin!" she added, as the page withdrew, "has it come to this, then, that you try to trade upon my weak heart to compass the destruction of Wilford?"

She pressed her hand over her heart as she passed to the bedside once more and sat down.

"Oh! how could my heart have been so false, so utterly false to itself, as to have ever loved this man? No matter, I will deceive him; I will pretend to fall in with his views, and thus I will compass, not Rokeby's ruin, but his. Be still, my heart, we have brave work to do this night."

Eagerly she waited the arrival of Lady Laura Clavering, to whom she disclosed the scheme which Sir Huntley had proposed to her.

"And are you going to pretend to fall into this plan?" asked Laura.

"I am, in order to defeat it. If I refuse, he might find agents more treacherous and more willing than I. It is nearly ten now, and I must away. I only hope that my hate and contempt for Sir Huntley will not make themselves too evident."

Laura bent over her friend, and kissed her.

"Keep up your courage," she said; "in this good cause, keep up your courage, and fear nothing."

After responding to her friend's embrace, Genevieve St. Clare glided away from the room, and made her way towards the Black Corridor, where Sir Huntley Mordaunt was already awaiting her in the recess of the great window.

She hastened to him that she, also, might be within the shadow where the play of her features would not be seen.

"You have come, then, dear Genevieve," he said, taking her hand, and raising it to his lips.

Genevieve shuddered.

But she strove to preserve her presence of mind.

"Yes, and since I have come, explain fully your meaning, for if I am seen with you, something will certainly be suspected."

He drew her further into the recess, and passing his arm around her waist, he began speaking to her in that low, serpent-like, silvery tone which he had on former occasions adopted towards her.

"Dearest Genevieve," he said, "I have come to the resolution of abandoning entirely all idea of a union with Lady Clara Mortimer. I feel that you are the only one I ever loved, and I cast myself once more on your mercy. You alone can aid me, and to you I appeal."

"But tell me, Sir Huntley," answered Genevieve, "if you are resolved to abandon Lady Clara, why do you desire to destroy Wilford Rokeby?"

"Because he is my enemy; because I hate him; because he holds in his hands papers which would be my destruction; because he has foiled me for years, and is my stumbling-block in the path of fortune. Oh, you need ask me no more reasons. He is my foe, and he shall die. And to you, Genevieve, I have come pleading for aid."

"And what aid do you desire?" asked the young girl, trembling as the arm of the assassin pressed her closely to him.

Sir Huntley took a rapid and searching glance round him, and then lowered his voice.

"You are one of the nurses of Wilford Rokeby," he said. "You administer medicine to him. I will procure a subtle and deadly drug, which you or I can place within the phial. I

know one who will give me such a poison, that no trace will be left, and no suspicion of foul play will be excited. And then, when all is over, you and I will triumph. Power, wealth, and pleasure will soon wash out all memory of this evil deed. Tell me, Viva, will you do this?"

She trembled, and dropped her eyes.

"Yes," she murmured.

"You will not fail?"

"I will not."

"You will not suffer any false fears to destroy this plan?"

"I will not," she said more boldly. "You will see when the time comes for action that I shall not be backward in performing my part of the bargain. Tell me, when is this to be done?"

"To-morrow night," returned Sir Huntley. "There is to be a grand ball here in the palace. You will be able to claim the right of nursing him through his time. While you are alone you can pour the poison into the phial, or I can do so. I will either give you the deadly mixture to-morrow, or I will bring it myself when all are busy in the ballroom."

"I understand you, Sir Huntley," said Genevieve; "and now let us part. I fancy I hear footsteps."

"Yes, someone comes, in truth," replied Mordaunt; "but tell me quickly, what have you done with my letter?"

"It is destroyed," said Genevieve; "but see, the door opens; we shall be discovered."

"I will conceal myself," returned Sir Huntley; "do you hasten away. Your presence here is natural, as this corridor leads to your own chamber.   Farewell, and remember to-morrow."

With a beating heart, Genevieve withdrew herself from him and hastened towards her chamber, where, with many a tear, wrung from her by anger and excitement, she unbosomed herself to Lady Clara Mortimer.

The latter, when she heard her story, clasped her fondly to her breast.

"Dearest Viva," she said, "yours is indeed true kindness, true love, to run this terrible risk for my sake."

"And the sake, remember, of punishing a villain," said Viva.

Meanwhile, as soon as the relief of the Night Guard had passed, under the command of Lance Courtenay, Sir Huntley Mordaunt emerged from his hiding-place, and, hurrying from the palace, made his way towards the river.

The night was very dark.

All day it had been gloomy, and nothing could be seen except where the dull light of the swinging oil lamps illuminated a small circle of space.

Well might that man of blood have hesitated to pace that pavement alone.

Well might he have started and trembled as his eyes fell upon the spot where Hubert Aveling had been murdered, and where Wilford Rokeby, too, had fallen.

But no !

His heart was steeled, his conscience seemed asleep, and he passed on eagerly, full of dark thoughts of new and treacherous crimes.

Arrived on the shore of the rushing Thames, he hired a boat, and directed the man to row him quickly to the Surrey side.

Here he disembarked, told the man to wait, and, having dived into a dark street, or rather a lane, and placed a black mask on his face, he hurried on.

The place was very dark, lit only by a swinging lamp here and there; but at length a faint light in the window of a distant house caught his eye, and he made towards it.

The tenement in which this light appeared was scarcely one which would have been imagined to be the proper destination for a courtier at the palace of King James.

It was situated in a dirty, swampy spot, surrounded by a few ragged trees, which even the blessed rains of Heaven seemed to be unable to wash clean.

Its windows were cracked, smoky, and mended with paper and rags; its door hung loose on the hinges; its battered walls seemed only to hang together in consequence of the accumulated filth upon them.

Dark stories were connected with this place.

The old man and his wife, who were the sole inhabitants, had resided there for years.

Yet, during the day, no visitor had ever been seen to enter.

Their guests came at night, and it was said that not all returned.

Those who did come and passed away in safety were always carefully disguised.

Men on foot, men on horseback, ladies in carriages came there, and, stopping for a few moments, hurried away secretly and masked.

Sir Huntley evidently had been there before, and knew the place well, for he at once knocked three times—a short, quick, peculiar knock—and in a moment after the door was opened by a thin, wizened, parchmenty old man, who stared not a little at his masked visitor.

"What want you, sir?" he asked, trying to catch a glimpse of the features of his strange visitor. "If you come for plunder, you have erred greatly."

"Fear not, Jabez Ireland," answered Sir Huntley Mordaunt. "I am one who has treated with you before, and one who can pay you well. Let me enter. I want some of the same medicine that you supplied to me once before."

"I understand," said the old man. "I understand you well. Enter, and I will bring you what you require immediately, or if you choose to mount yonder stairs, you can come with me to my laboratory."

"Lead on, then," said Mordaunt. "I follow."

The old man tottered up the creaking steps, and led the way into a dirty, murky room, where a large fire burned clearly, while upon it were various pans of copper and other metal, from which a strange and sickening odour was emitted.

The whole atmosphere of the room, in fact, was pervaded by a steam which truly seemed to be pestilential in its very self.

"I cannot bear this," said Sir Huntley. "You, who live on poisons, and in an air of poisons throughout each day and night, observe not this deathly odour, but, to me, it is unendurable. Quick, serve me and let me go."

"You desire a poison which is sudden and sure in its effect, and which is yet untraceable?" asked the old man.

"I do."

"Then here is what you seek. Six drops will be enough. Its effects are instantaneous—sure and deadly."

At this instant, a hand was thrust through an aperture, a large bat flew by, and the mask of Sir Huntley fell to the ground.

"What was that?" he shouted, angrily, as he hastily stooped and replaced his disguise. "Who dared to touch me?"

"It was that abominable bat," said the old man; "he is always in mischief. But fear not; my eyes are too old and dim to see or notice much. Here are the drops; be careful with them, for more than six drops might produce signs which would rouse suspicions of foul play."

"Here, then," cried Sir Huntley Mordaunt, thrusting a heavy purse of gold into his hand, "here is your reward. Remember, if you *did* see my features, it will be best to forget them."

The old man said nothing, but proceeded to light his visitor down the stairs, and having ushered him out into the night, he ascended the steps again as hastily as his age would allow.

Then, entering the room, he put his mouth close to the aperture.

"Did you see him, Rachel?" he asked.

"Yes," said a shrill, squeaking voice, "yes, I saw him."

"Should you know him again?"

"Yes, anywhere," replied the voice.

"Good; put his name on the list, then."

"What is his name?"

"Sir Huntley Mordaunt!" said the poison vendor.

CHAPTER XXVIII.

ON HIS KNEES TO THE KING!

THE following night was a dark and gloomy one, yet this did not deter the visitors who had been invited to the grand ball at Whitehall Palace.

The splendid reception rooms were brilliantly lighted up, and fashion and beauty crowded at an early hour into them.

Everything had been done to render this ball the most brilliant of its kind.

Musicians had been carefully selected, every nook and corner blazed with light, and the atmosphere was fragrant with the most delicious perfumes.

The noble pilasters which supported the painted roof, were wreathed in flowers, and before each bright and magnificent picture upon the wall burned a wax taper.

To anyone in the present day, it is almost impossible to conceive the brilliant appearance offered by the throng, for the dresses were of all colours and descriptions ; the bright costumes worn both by ladies and cavaliers being only parodied in our finest masked balls and court assemblies.

The king walked hither and thither with the restored favourite, Buckingham, giving a nod and a smile here and there among the throng, but generally discussing unpleasant political questions with " Steenie."

A bevy of beautiful ladies surrounded the queen, among whom none, perhaps, seemed more so than Lady Laura Clavering.

Genevieve St. Clare and Lady Clara Mortimer were conspicuous by their absence ; the former being in the sick chamber of Wilford Rokeby, the latter refusing to quit her chamber to enter a scene of gaiety while her lover was ill and in danger.

The room in which Wilford Rokeby lay had been purposely darkened early in the evening by the direction of Genevieve St. Clare, and all within was still and solemn.

On the bed asleep lay Wilford Rokeby, full dressed, except that his arm was in a sling, and his left shoulder covered only by his shirt.

By the bedside, reading, sat Genevieve St. Clare.

Opposite her, nodding in a light slumber, was the tiring-woman, who performed the menial duties of nurse.

Anyone who had watched the face of Genevieve St. Clare would have seen at once how anxious and harassed she was, and how little her thoughts were engaged with the book she was reading, or pretending, rather, to read.

Her eyes ever and anon wandered towards the door.

One hand clutched the book, the other held in a strong and eager grasp the back of the chair.

Her bosom heaved in evident emo-

WITH A LONG LEAP, HE PLUNGED INTO THE MOAT.

tion, and the roses had faded from her cheeks.

Presently a step was heard in the passage, approaching the chamber.

She cast down her book, and looked eagerly.

Then a shadow fell into the room, and a tall, dark figure entered.

This was Sir Huntley.

He made a motion as if to ask whether the old nurse was asleep.

Genevieve gave a gesture of assent.

He approached then, and, taking from the table a bottle containing a red liquid, poured into it a few drops, which did not alter its colour.

Bending over her, he whispered—

"Be courageous, and all will be well. I shall return *in one hour*."

Then he glided away like the treacherous serpent he was.

Genevieve St. Clare watched carefully his departure from the chamber.

Then she gently awoke Wilford Rokeby.

"Will you take your medicine?" she asked.

He smiled, took the red liquid from her hands, and in an instant fell back senseless.

The hour passed slowly.

But at length the clock chimed once more, and once more the heavy tread of the assassin sounded along the corridor.

This time he made no disguise, and affected no concealment, but, striding into the apartment, entered boldly.

"I come," he said, "to ask after the health of Lieutenant Rokeby."

Genevieve pointed to the bed, and Sir Huntley approaching, gently felt his hand.

The old nurse had quitted the room for a moment.

"The work is done!" he said, in a low, hoarse voice. "The work is done, and he is dead! Be careful not to raise the alarm too soon, or you may betray yourself. Let others think he sleeps, until they discover that he has gone to seek his friend, Hubert Aveling. As for yourself, be silent on your life."

"And whither go you, Sir Huntley?"

The villain smiled.

"I go, fair Genevieve," he said in a tone of bitter sarcasm, "to seek the king's consent to my marriage with Lady Clara Mortimer."

"And what if I betray you, traitor?"

"I have those who will prove that you aided me in this crime, so that if you betray me, you die also."

Genevieve St. Clare sank back in her chair as if overpowered by emotion, while he, with a smile of triumph, returned to the ballroom.

The ball was now at its height, and the beautiful women who were the gems and pride of the Court were crowding round in the mazy dance with the gaily-dressed cavaliers.

The king was still hanging on the arm of his restored favourite, talking of affairs of state, in spite of the gay revelry around them.

Sir Huntley Mordaunt, entering the room with an ill-concealed smile of triumph on his pale features, drew up in astonishment as his eyes fell upon a group near the throne.

This group consisted of Lance Courtenay, Laura Clavering, and Lady Clara Mortimer.

He hurriedly approached the latter.

"I am most agreeably surprised, Lady Clara," he said, bowing, "to see you here in this gay assemblage. I had feared we should not have beheld your beauty this night."

Lady Clara bowed coldly.

"I have a reason for being here, Sir Huntley," she answered.

"I also have a reason for being glad to see you in the ballroom," replied Mordaunt; "I intend this evening to ask the king's final consent to our marriage."

Lady Clara made no reply.

Lance Courtenay advanced towards him.

"Excuse me, Sir Huntley Mordaunt," he said, "Lady Clara Mortimer desires no speech with you. She is here by desire of her lover, and would be glad to be quit of your presence."

Sir Huntley turned angrily to him.

"What have you to do with this?" he said. "Lady Clara Mortimer is my ward—my affianced bride; how dare you interfere between us?"

"By the right of my friendship for Wilford Rokeby, I protect the one who will one day be his wife."

"Never!" said Sir Huntley; "he is even now dying or dead."

Lance smiled and pointed towards the door.

There, pale and disordered, with fierce anger in his eye, stood Wilford Rokeby.

He waited but to glance once around the ballroom, and then rushed towards Sir Huntley, who, trembling, agitated, ghastly, seemed stricken as if with some dread of an unearthly visitant.

"Villain!" cried Wilford, in a loud voice, "villain! your hour has come. Too long have you been suffered to pollute the palace by your hateful presence. You, the murderer of my dear friend, Hubert—the assassin of your uncle—you who have twice attempted *my* life—shall this night be unmasked before the king. Come what may, I will tell him all."

"My father—remember my father!" exclaimed Clara, clasping her hands.

"Aye, remember the secrets I hold," repeated Sir Huntley Mordaunt.

"I think of nothing; I remember nothing," returned Wilford Rokeby, "but that this villain's time has come! What! would you quit this room? Nay, then, wounded and weak as I am, I will drag you to the king's presence."

Seizing the unnerved and trembling villain by the throat, he dragged him upon his knees, and forced him to remain just as the king, leaning on Buckingham's arm, came upon the scene, while the ladies and the cavaliers crowded round in amazement at the strange and unwonted scene.

"What means this, Lieutenant Rokeby?" said the king, sternly, as Wilford stood before him, pale and haggard from his illness, but resolute and dauntless withal, grasping Huntley Mordaunt firmly by the throat, and holding him down on his knees. "This is not the first time you have disturbed the harmony of the palace during our quiet assemblage; explain yourself, before I order you under arrest."

"Your majesty," exclaimed Wilford Rokeby, "I accuse this man of the murder of Hubert Aveling, my friend;

I accuse him of an attempt to murder me, on the palace pavement, and I demand his arrest."

"It is false," cried Sir Huntley, springing up as Rokeby loosed his hold upon his collar. "I had no fire-arms; he knows that. He was wounded by a shot from an unseen hand. His friend may have died through the same assassin."

The king eyed both with a stern and scrutinising glance.

"How is this, Lieutenant Rokeby?" he asked.

"It is false, your majesty, false," cried Wilford. "True, he had no fire-arms; true, he fired not the shot; but he hired the assassin who fired it. And more than this, your majesty, I have proofs—proofs in his own writing—that he has been endeavouring to poison me during my illness, endeavouring to induce my nurses to destroy me. Your majesty, I swear I speak no falsehood. So Heaven help me and defend me as I speak the truth."

King James turned towards the accused.

Sir Huntley was now ghastly pale.

The letter, which he had imagined destroyed, was about to be brought against him.

"Sir Huntley Mordaunt," said the king, "how is this? What refutation have you of this statement? Can you defend yourself?"

"There is a base and cruel conspiracy against me," said Sir Huntley. "I can say no more until I see what proofs are adduced against me."

The king watched him narrowly as he spoke.

"Sir Huntley," he said, as he looked upon the ghastly and guilty face of the accused, "at another time, then, you shall defend yourself. What ho, there—guard! arrest this man, and convey him with all speed to the Tower."

Lance Courtenay at once advanced, and at his back came several soldiers, as if he had prepared them ready for the occasion.

Sir Huntley advanced, with angry and pallid features, and placed himself in the midst of the guards.

"Your revenge, Wilford Rokeby, will be satisfied but for a moment," he cried. "While Lord Ernest Mortimer lives, there is still a terrible vengeance in store for me. The scaffold which greets me will greet him also. Gentlemen, and you, fair ladies, adieu. Your majesty, I wish you, in all humility, good night. Before many hours pass, Lieutenant Rokeby will retract his own words, and your majesty will regret your hasty order."

Then, with a glance of bitter meaning at Clara, who was half fainting in Lady Laura's arms, he quitted the ball-room with his guard.

His mind was full of dark and vengeful thoughts as he strode along the passage, a prisoner between the double row of mailed troopers.

In his inmost heart, proud and defiant as he might pretend to be, he was fully aware of the terrible danger he was in.

Not only was he a prisoner, unable to concert measures for securing his safety, but he felt certain that the charges which were brought against him could be substantiated at once by more than one witness.

"Thrice accursed fool was I," he murmured, as he passed down the broad staircase and along the great hall between a throng of wondering soldiers, "thrice accursed fool, to write such a letter to Genevieve St. Clare. But no matter; I will not be daunted. The game is not lost until it is won."

But his courage somewhat failed him as he passed out into the street, and over the rugged pavement, where Hubert Aveling had died.

A tall, dark, spectral figure seemed to hover near him, stretching forth its long bony fingers, and pointing to the river, while wild voices seemed to sound in the air, and whisper, "To the Tower! to the Tower, assassin!"

He glanced round him as if expecting each moment to see the phantom of the murdered Hubert; but while he was yet thinking, they arrived at the river bank, and in another moment he was afloat on the dark river on his way to the Traitors' Gate.

CHAPTER XXIX.

THE LOVE TEST.

As soon as Sir Huntley Mordaunt had quitted the ballroom at Whitehall, on his way to the Tower of London, Wilford Rokeby—weak now and faint with exertion—approached Lady Clara Mortimer.

She sat down by him as he sank into a chair.

"Oh! Wilford," she said, "I fear that your haste has destroyed my father!"

"Clara," answered Wilford, taking her hand, "you must forgive me, and trust in Providence and the clemency of the king to save your father. Knowing what I did, I could no longer contain my anger and suffer this villain to roam at will about the palace, hiring assassins to destroy his enemies, or attacking them like a coward by poison.

Heaven will protect you and me and your father, but this man *must* be punished."

It seemed strange to both that there should be such a sudden lull after the arrest of Sir Huntley, and that the king should put no further questions to Wilford Rokeby.

The name of Lord Ernest Mortimer, however, had silenced him.

Immediately the words had been pronounced, a shadow had fallen upon his brow, and he passed away with Buckingham from among the throng.

So the ball went on, and the music swelled, and the couples whirled round in the mazy dance; and most of those present forgot that one had been taken from among them, and placed among the silent prisoners of the dark old Tower of London.

Upon few, indeed, if they had remembered it, would the arrest of Sir Huntley have produced any depressing effect, for the circle of those who admired him was but small indeed.

The great majority of the courtiers disliked, feared, and suspected him as one whose character was repeatedly assailed without ever being cleared satisfactorily, as one who never did a favour without exacting some greater service in return, and one whose manner, habits, speech and looks, were those of a traitor.

So, for a time, as I have said, the ball went on merrily, and Wilford Rokeby and Lady Clara talked eagerly of the past and the future, until the latter for a moment almost forgot her father's danger.

Presently the tramp of feet was heard once more in the corridor, and Lance Courtenay entered.

In his hand he bore a note, which he carried immediately to the king.

James I. took it, tore it open, and changed colour.

He thought a moment, then, dropping Buckingham's arm, he hastened across the room to the spot where Lady Clara Mortimer and Wilford Rokeby were sitting.

Having seen the entrance of Lance Courtenay with the note, and the agitation of the king on reading it, they were profoundly anxious to learn the meaning of his emotion.

He approached Lady Clara, and accosted her abruptly.

"Lady Clara Mortimer," he said, "you remember the terms upon which you were received at court?"

"I do, your majesty," she answered, tremblingly.

"You know that you came here under the guardianship of Sir Huntley Mordaunt, and I was given to understand that your father had retired to France, and would never more return. Is it not so?"

"Yes, sire."

"Well," continued James I., "well, you have grossly, aye, basely deceived me, madam. Your father has never left England; in fact, he is even now living within a stone's throw of Whitehall, braving my power. He is absolutely living," added the king, turning to Buckingham, who had followed him, "at Exmouth House, at Bankside, in open defiance of the edict I issued forbidding him and all like rebels to set foot in England on pain of death."

"'Tis, indeed, treasonable, sire," said Buckingham; "yet he does not seem to have used his time in fresh plotting."

Lady Clara looked up gratefully at the royal favourite.

The words, however, took no effect upon James.

"No, truly," he said; "he has not been plotting, for the very simple reason that Sir Huntley Mordaunt, for some reason best known to himself— probably from love of his daughter here —has been keeping him in strict seclusion. He has now betrayed him to me, and though I am really loath to take advantage of a communication made under such circumstances, still I am bound, as a matter of policy, to arrest him. As for you, Lady Clara, while your father is under suspicion, you must remove from court. The queen will advise you."

Lady Clara, who had now risen, and stood weeping and pale in the presence of the king, made no reply.

James turned accordingly to Lance Courtenay.

"Lieutenant Rokeby is too ill at present to undertake any duty, therefore I must depute to you, Lieutenant Courtenay, a second service. Proceed at once to Exmouth House, and arrest Lord Ernest Mortimer—take with you a guard sufficient to surround the house, and render all escape impossible. When you have secured his person, convey him to the Tower."

Lance Courtenay bowed, and, not daring to look at his friend Rokeby, or at Geraldine or Clara, walked from the room, and soon the loud tramp of his men was heard passing along the corridor.

As he went, Lady Clara raised her eyes and cast a look of appeal at Wilford Rokeby.

Wilford understood her meaning at once, and, with a deep sigh, he turned and followed his friend.

She had asked him as plainly as she could by that look to save her father.

Wishing to avoid compromising his friend, he passed quickly by without addressing a word to him, and hurrying to his own chamber, seized his hat and sword and pistols.

Then he proceeded to the refection-room, and having obtained a large glassful of strong spirit, he drank it off, to create within him some artificial strength, and then proceeded to the stables.

Here he obtained Black Meg, and having given directions to the man not to reveal to anyone the fact of his absence, he quickly galloped **away.**

CHAPTER XXX.

TOO LATE.

It was with feelings of great anguish that Wilford Rokeby made his way towards Exmouth House.

There was a war in his mind between his duty to his king, his love for Clara, and his own idea of what was best; but the love won the day, and he hurried forward with all speed in the direction of Lord Ernest Mortimer's place of concealment.

The Night Guard having to proceed on foot, Wilford Rokeby was, of course, far in advance, and on arriving at Exmouth House he found everything as still as death.

Exmouth House was a dark, gloomy, mysterious-looking building, erected on the very edge of the water, some part of it being built over the water itself upon thick piles, blackened and worn with age.

The rustling of the water against the

THE ✶ NIGHT ✶ GUARD;
Or, THE SECRET OF THE FIVE MASKS.

"THE KING'S GUARDS ARE COMING," SAID THE GIPSY GIRL; "YOU ARE SAVED."

No. 11.

wood was all the sound that disturbed the silence of the place, until Wilford Rokeby clattered up to the door, and awoke a hundred echoes as his horse stamped upon the uneven pavement.

After ringing loudly at the bell, Rokeby was answered by a man who looked upon him with evident suspicion.

"What want ye, sir?" asked he.

"To speak to the steward, the person who is here under the protection of Sir Huntley Mordaunt," replied Wilford, scarcely knowing whom to ask for.

The man shook his head and answered quickly, as if he had been schooled beforehand what to say—

"There is no such person here. You have made a mistake."

"No—no," returned Wilford, eagerly; "you know not my object, and therefore deny his existence. I know who this person is; the king has just ordered his arrest; the guards are on their road to seize him, and I am here to save him. Let me pass, lead me to him. By Heaven! I *will* enter, if I make my way with my sword."

As he spoke he leaped from his horse, and fastening his bridle to a railing, drew his sword.

The old man retreated in fear.

"Could I believe you were indeed a friend to the person who is concealed here, I would at once show you the way to his room; but you must forgive me if I have a doubt on the subject."

"This is no time to argue, old man," cried Wilford Rokeby; "I tell you his life is in danger; I tell you that the king's order has been issued for his

arrest, and by this time the guards are half way here. If you are not mad, lead me to him."

The old man shook his head, though the vehemence and earnestness of Wilford Rokeby's manner had now nearly dissipated his doubts.

"Follow me," he said, "and let us hope I am acting rightly."

Closing the door carefully after him, he conducted Wilford along a dark passage, and up a wide staircase to a room, where an old man, dressed plainly in black, was seated by the fire.

He started up in evident alarm at seeing a stranger enter.

"How is this, Jonas?" he cried, addressing the servant. "Do you not know I cannot see strangers?"

"Lord Ernest Mortimer," said Wilford Rokeby, advancing, and speaking quickly and eagerly, "let me explain, though the time to do so is short. Sir Huntley Mordaunt has this night been committed to the Tower through my instrumentality. In revenge, because I love your daughter, and I have brought the villain at last to justice, he has disclosed to the king your place of concealment."

"Great Heaven!"

"Ah, more; at this moment the guards are on their way to arrest you. Fly, therefore, while there is yet time. Ah! what is that?"

The loud clattering of horses' feet was heard below in the courtyard.

Wilford Rokeby rushed to the window, and, throwing it up, looked out.

"Great Heaven! I am too late; they have heard that I left the palace an hour back, and they suspect my errand. Alas! what now is to be done? These men are in numbers enough to surround the place. Have you no secret mode of exit?"

"None, none," said Lord Ernest Mortimer, turning ghastly pale. "It is the revenge that villain has long waited for. I am lost!"

"Not so," said Jonas, "follow me. There is a gate opening upon the river where you can enter a boat, and row off unperceived. Their horses cannot pass into the water and swim round to guard the house. Come quickly, I know the way."

"Lead on, fellow," exclaimed Wilford Rokeby; "if it had not been for your accursed delay at the door, we should have had plenty of time to escape. Quick, hark! even now they are thundering at the gate."

The man made no reply, but hastened forward, bearing a lamp to guide them down the dark staircase.

Disregarding the loud knocking at the door, which was already rousing up the other domestics who had retired long since to bed, they hurried down the staircase, and soon reached the doorway which the old servant had spoken of.

They could hear plainly the plash of the water on the piles below, and the scraping of the boat against the steps.

"Quick, open the door," said Wilford Rokeby, "I hear the tramp of troopers in the passage."

Jonas quickly undid the bolts and opened the door.

A strong gust of wind burst in at once, extinguishing the lamp and roaring up the stairs of the old house.

And after the wind came six dark forms, one of whom, in an instant more, threw forth the light of a lantern and disclosed the uniforms of the Night Guard.

They touched their steel caps respectfully, as they beheld Wilford Rokeby.

The sergeant, however, advanced.

"Lord Ernest Mortimer," he said, "we arrest you in the king's name."

"Where is your warrant?" asked Mortimer.

The sergeant pointed to Wilford Rokeby.

"There is our lieutenant," he said; "ask him if I am not fulfilling the king's commands."

"It is so," said Rokeby, sadly, "and to endeavour to save you now from arrest, would but precipitate my ruin and your own. I will return to the palace, I will see the king, and, with the aid of Heaven, I will save you."

At this moment the dark corridor was entered by six more troopers, with Lance Courtenay at their head.

"Wilford, are you mad?" said Lance. "These are our own true and faithful friends—our Night Guard—but I have others with me who have no affection for you or for me. You have imperilled yourself uselessly."

"I followed the dictates of my heart," answered Wilford; "but do your duty. I oppose no longer. I put my trust in God and the king's justice."

In a few moments more Lord Ernest Mortimer, after grasping him heartily by the hand, had descended the stairs, entered the boat, and passed away over the dark river towards the Tower;

while Wilford, standing on the steps, and watching his departure, felt as if one link in the chain of his happiness had at last been rudely wrenched away.

"I *will* save him, and *must* save him," he murmured, as he moved at length to go. "Such happiness as is now within my reach shall not be snatched from me in a moment by the hands of that itor Mordaunt."

CHAPTER XXXI.

THE LEAP FOR LIFE.

Sir Huntley Mordaunt, on arriving at the Tower of London, was placed in the cell which had on a former occasion been assigned to Wilford Rokeby.

Bitter and vengeful were his thoughts during that first night.

Oh! how he regretted the few words which— spoken —would have passed away with the wind, but which —written—were his ruin and destruction.

Yet he did not give way absolutely to despair.

There was one ray of hope yet.

He might declare the letter to be a forgery, and might defy Genevieve St. Clare to bring forward any other proof of his villany.

But as that night passed, and the next day came and went, and the next evening arrived, without his hearing anything about his ultimate fate or seeing a face he knew, he began to be alarmed; began, in fact, to fear that he would be left to pine away, neglected, and unknown, and untried, as many a prisoner has been left in the *oubliettes* of the French Bastille.

It was about nine o'clock that the door opened, and Ben Lockster entered.

This was the first time that the two confederates had met, for a stranger had hitherto brought Sir Huntley's meals.

"So they've caged you at last, Sir Huntley," said he, with his hideous grin.

"Peace! be not insolent!" cried Mordaunt, angrily. "Although I am a prisoner here, I shall not suffer that. Where is Leonard Fairfax?"

"He is at hand," returned Red Ben, surlily.

"Let him know I wish to see him," continued Mordaunt. "I must escape from this place. I have a plan by which it can be done, and by which you can place a hundred and fifty golden pieces in your pocket."

Red Ben's eyes glistened.

"That would be a good night's work," said he.

"It would; but remember, I offer nothing that I cannot perform. If you follow my instructions, the money is yours. Go now, and tell Sir Leonard Fairfax I would speak with him."

Red Ben hastened away, and in a few minutes Sir Leonard Fairfax made his appearance.

"Well, my friend," said Fairfax; "we meet under strange circumstances."

"We do," returned Mordaunt; "but it is stranger still that you have not visited me before this."

"Not so. I have been absent, and did but return to-day."

"Well, we will waste no time in that discussion," said Sir Huntley Mordaunt. "I have to speak to you of something of great importance. I must escape from this place."

Sir Leonard Fairfax smiled.

"You must!" he said. "That leaves, then, no room for question. Know you not that such an escape from this well-defended fortress would bring disgrace and ruin on me?"

"I know all," returned Sir Huntley Mordaunt. "But know what I may, I still adhere to what I have said. I must escape from this place, and that this very night."

"It cannot be done."

"It must and shall."

"You command me?"

"I do; and for this reason. If you refuse to aid me in leaving this place, I will disclose to the king the history of all your transactions since you were appointed deputy-governor. I may be executed like a gentleman, on Tower Hill, but you would be strung up like a dog. Come, let us not argue. I *must* escape to-night, and I will tell you how it is to be done."

Sir Leonard Fairfax muttered something very much like a curse, but, nevertheless, he sat down acquiescently.

"Well," he said, "say on. I doubt me, though, whether any plan *you* could suggest would be better than what I, who know the Tower, could arrange in such a matter."

"We shall see," returned Sir Huntley, with a smile. "You are not aware, perhaps, that I have studied my plan, and understand thoroughly its strong and weak points. It is very simple, and therefore more likely to be successful. Listen."

Briefly Sir Huntley Mordaunt told his plan.

Sir Leonard Fairfax listened intently.

"You are right," he said, when Sir Huntley had finished, "the plan is good and simple. It shall be done. At twelve o'clock the guard is changed. From your window you can hear the sound of the loud gong, which proclaims the hour. I will leave your door open. When you hear the quarter after twelve strike, quit this cell, and hurry up the stone corridor to the left. Then turn quickly to the right, and you will soon find yourself upon the battlements. Once there, you follow your own ideas."

"I understand you well," said Sir Huntley Mordaunt, as he drew out a purse, "and now for the reward promised to Ben Lockster."

"You pay well."

"Life is worth it—life is worth anything," replied the fallen courtier.

"Then, you really imagine your life to be in danger?"

"I do. I know it. Were I to remain here, I should mount the scaffold," said Sir Huntley.

"And if you fly, will not the king's resentment follow you?"

A dark smile crossed the features of Sir Huntley Mordaunt.

"It *may* follow me," he said, "but I know of certain means by which I can laugh at his anger. I can force my enemies to aid me, when once I am away from this accursed prison. Neither you nor any of them know what power I hold in my hand. I am gifted with a strong arm and a clear brain, and once upon the outside of these walls, you will see how I shall use them."

Sir Leonard Fairfax smiled.

"You appreciate yourself?" he said.

"I do; a man is a fool who cannot appreciate the gifts which have been bestowed upon him. But tell me this —the night I was brought here, I remained awake, and some hours after my arrival, I heard the grating of rusty hinges?"

"Yes, another prisoner was brought here by Lieutenant Courtenay."

"And who was it?" exclaimed Sir Huntley, in eager tones.

"The name was given Lord Ernest Mortimer," replied Fairfax.

A smile of pleasure showed itself upon Mordaunt's face.

"Good—good," he said, "then I am content. With such a game as that I now have in my hands, I need fear nothing. You can go now, my friend. What you have just told me, makes me all the more eager to escape."

"You understand my directions?"

"Yes, perfectly."

"Follow them then, and you will find that, as regards my part of the play, *I* shall not fail."

He rose as he spoke, and quitted the cell, leaving the door open as he had said.

On reaching his own room, he sent for Red Ben, and quickly gave him the details of the plan.

"Ben," he said, "Sir Huntley Mordaunt must quit the Tower this night."

Lockster stared.

"It's ruin," he cried; "both I and you will lose our lives for it."

"No, no," returned Sir Leonard Fairfax, sternly; "and if there were that risk it must be done. Sir Huntley knows too many of our secrets to render it safe to disobey him."

"And how is this to be done without casting suspicion upon us?"

"Easily. The plan which he has invented himself runs thus: at twelve o'clock the three men who are now sleeping in the guard-room will take the place of those who are now guarding the western drawbridge. At a quarter before twelve you must rouse them and send them into my room here. I shall detain them, explaining that we have some suspicion that an escape will be attempted to-night from the Tower, and directing them to fire upon any one who may be seen upon the battlements."

"Yes; and then?"

"While I am conversing with them you must proceed to the guard-room and draw the bullets. Then, when the alarm is given, you must also rush out upon the battlements and fire at Sir Huntley as he leaps over into the moat."

"And what am I to receive as my

reward for doing this, which may cost me my life?"

"Fifty pounds for every bullet you extract."

Ben's eyes glistened.

"And who will pay me?"

"I will, as soon as Sir Huntley Mordaunt is safe beyond the reach of his enemies."

"Very good," replied the gaoler, "I will see that this is done. It is now past eleven; at a quarter before midnight expect the men here."

He proceeded at once to the guard-room, on leaving the presence of Sir Leonard Fairfax, and found the men fast asleep on the benches.

One old fellow, who was there as watcher, was nodding over the fire.

"Sir Leonard has reckoned without old Robert here," muttered Red Ben. "Never mind, a good tankard of ale will make him sleep as heavily as they. I'll go and fetch some."

So saying, he passed out once more, and returned, after a few moments, with a large tankard of white foaming ale, as strong as a spirit.

"Here, old Robert," he said, clapping him on the shoulder, "here's some ale. Will ye drink with us?"

The old man grinningly looked up at Ben.

"Aye, that I will, good Master Ben," said he, "though if the deputy-governor were to know——"

"Hush, man! Drink, and don't be noisy over it. The deputy-governor won't know it. I get as much as I like, as you're aware, by which token you needn't spare it. Drink as much as ever you like, only be quick."

The old man required no further admonishing.

Raising the tankard to his lips, he took a draught which nearly emptied it.

"Ah, ha! this is some of the right sort, Ben," said he, smacking his lips.

"Yes," said the gaoler, seating himself, and finishing the ale, "yes, the governor does not supply us with bad provisions."

"No," yawned Robert, once more settling himself.

In a few minutes more he was asleep, snoring loudly.

The clock presently struck the quarter to twelve o'clock.

Red Ben at once rose, and roused the slumbering sentinels.

The men, accustomed to be awakened on the moment, at once sprang to their feet, and made towards their muskets.

Lockster, however, waved them back.

"Stay," he cried. "Before you go on duty, the deputy-governor desires a word with you. He is in his room, and has some important communication to make to you."

The three men, unsuspicious, of course, of anything, at once quitted the room.

Red Ben watched them out, and then hurried to the corner where their muskets were piled.

He had no time to spare.

Eagerly he glanced at the old man, who was seated by the fire.

"Good ale that, Ben," he muttered, in his drunken slumber.

"Aye, right good ale, Robert," said Ben, to himself, as he drew the first bullet, and adroitly placed it in his pocket, "and good work this that brings in fifty pounds a minute. Now to make it a hundred."

Another bullet was extracted.

"Ha, ha!" muttered Ben, as he took the third musket, "I should like this game every night. Ha!"

In his exultation he had been somewhat careless, and the bullet fell on the ground.

"Ha!" cried the old watcher, "what are you doing there with the men's guns, eh?"

"Silence! madness!" exclaimed Red Ben, savagely, "I am but loading my own."

"All right," said Robert, relapsing once more into sleep and insensibility.

Ben had just succeeded in drawing the bullet from his own musket, when the guard returned.

"Now," said Ben, "we will relieve guard. Midnight is striking."

Ben Lockster, who at the western drawbridge had charge of sentinels as well as the prisoners, at once proceeded along the echoing corridors out into the cool night air; and in a few moments the tired sentinels had quitted their posts, and been replaced by fresh men.

The moon was shining brightly, and illumining the rushing river, and the housetops, and the far-off country, and a pleasant breeze was blowing from the south as Ben Lockster stood by the drawbridge and eagerly listened for footsteps.

"It is a lovely night," he said to one of the men. "I think I shall remain here for awhile; it is fresher, cooler, and more enlivening here than sitting in that hot guard-room, and listening to the snoring of old Robert."

He had hardly spoken when there was a rush of feet behind him, and then a dead stop.

"What was that?" asked the sentinel, starting round to listen.

"Nothing, nothing; only the plash of the water, and the roaring of the wind round the old towers."

"See yonder light! What is that, I wonder? It looks to me like the lantern on the prow of some barque; perhaps, one that has come hither to carry away the prisoner who hopes to escape this night."

"And who is he?"

"Sir Huntley Mordaunt. Ah! what is that? See—see! a man is running along the upper terrace! How he runs! Ah! he nears the drawbridge! Quick! quick! follow me, and fire if he dares to leap!"

Sir Huntley Mordaunt paid no heed to these cries, but dashed along at full speed.

Ere the sentinels could reach him, he had reached the parapet, and with a long leap, he plunged over into the moat.

"Fire!" cried Red Ben, presenting his piece.

Four reports rang out simultaneously on the night air.

But Sir Huntley Mordaunt swam across untouched—unchecked!

"Ha! ha!" he cried, as he rose upon the opposite bank. "Ha! ha! you are foiled!—foiled again! I am free once more—free for love and revenge!"

The night was, as I have before said, a clear, bright, moonlit one, and most unfavourable, therefore, for anyone attempting an escape.

But there was no time to think.

Little caring which way he went, provided that he could find a momentary hiding-place, Sir Huntley Mordaunt, who was but badly acquainted with the neighbourhood, dashed across the open space before the grand old Tower, and made for a narrow street.

Seeing one turning where the lamps were conspicuous from the fact of their having been blown out by the somewhat high wind, he rushed into it, hoping here to be able to rest and think awhile.

He had scarcely entered it when the clattering of horses' feet was heard, and in another moment the glittering body armour of some mounted soldiers flashed in the light of the solitary lamp at the extreme end of the street.

CHAPTER XXXII.

THE GIPSIES.

THE place in which Sir Huntley Mordaunt had secreted himself was so excessively dark that he could not tell whether it was a blind alley or not.

He knew well, however, that it would not do to rush into the arms of the mail-clad soldiers at the end where he had entered, and he, therefore, without calculating whither he was going, rushed in an opposite direction.

The light as he advanced became brighter, and at length he found himself on the margin of the Thames, where the water plashed up darkly against a rough breakwater, and where a broad and roughly-built boat rolled against the stone-work.

" In luck, by Heaven!" cried Sir Huntley, as he swung himself from the dark pavement into the boat. " Oars, too, all ready to my hand! Now, then, for freedom and revenge."

It was wonderful with what celerity, and yet with what quietude, the villain settled himself to his work; with what ease he pulled over the bosom of the silent highway.

It was all his own that night.

Not a soul was out on the river, and the tide was just on the turn.

So away he sped towards London Bridge, and arriving at the point he wished to reach, he sprang ashore, and, without troubling himself even to fasten up the boat, he sprang up the high embankment, and made for Blackheath.

His plans for the next few hours were certainly undefined.

He could only think that he had escaped from the Tower.

He could only remember the cold edge of the axe which he had dreamed of each night, and which now had vanished.

There was an elasticity, a joyfulness in his mind which overcame everything else, and he ran up the rising ground and along the highway like a boy.

Suddenly a thought struck him.

"Whither am I going? Ah! the old poison vendor, he will find me an asylum. It is a long way," he murmured; "but he will do anything for money, and I can therefore trust him."

False reasoning.

He would do anything for money, and therefore might betray him.

Those whom money governs are those in life who are the most inevitably to be avoided.

However, Sir Huntley Mordaunt was of a far different opinion.

With a light heart, therefore, as if he had just discovered some great friend, he hurried away across the dark cross roads.

For a time all went well.

The night, truly, had now become overcast; the bright moon which had rendered the escape from the Tower so dangerous, had hidden her face behind dense clouds, and the great, spectral trees by the side of the road cast no shadow over the highway.

But the villain, whose heart should have sunk in the darkness, quailed not.

His thoughts were so full, indeed, of anticipations of revenge, that he never noticed those who followed in his footsteps, and dogged him everywhere.

He was rudely, however, roused from his reveries.

He had arrived at a point in the road where a dense woodland began.

Great trees spread their giant branches across the highway.

Beneath these trees, on either side, was dense undergrowth, forming, as it were, a wall of darkness on either side, with here and there openings, where murderers might have leaped aside from justice, and hidden themselves away like loathsome things amid the ooze and slime of the forest.

Rugged paths led from these openings, paths that crept along the margin of greasy pools and treacherous swamps, and rose suddenly towards hillocks to descend as quickly into quiet dells, where men might have lain dead for years, unknown, clutching with their skeleton hands the reeds that nodded over them and whispered their requiems, while the frogs, and the toads, and the lizards, danced a funeral dance upon their breasts.

A dreary, horrid place this; but yet, as Sir Huntley Mordaunt came to it, the sounds of rough music were heard, and the murmur of many voices.

"What can this mean?" said Sir Huntley aloud, as he stopped to listen.

As he spoke, a heavy hand was laid upon his shoulder, and a rough voice said—

"It means, my friend, that you have come into Gipsyland, and must pay toll to pass through it."

Starting back, he beheld two strange beings.

Both were of the true Bohemian type, swarthy and dark-haired, with large, bright, meaning eyes, and heavy mouths and broad shoulders, and dressed in what seemed the left-off habiliments of some cavaliers.

"I will pay no toll," exclaimed Sir

Huntley, drawing his dagger. "Come on, and meet your death!"

The gipsy drew back, at the same time muttering a few words to his comrade.

Then he advanced with a long knife; but, ere Sir Huntley was aware, a blow from a heavy stick, dealt from behind, stretched him senseless upon the earth.

"That was well done, Josef," cried the first gipsy. "Bring the fool into the camp. I hope you have not killed him, for I expect a rich ransom here."

"Oh, no, Ishmael," returned Josef. "I've only given him the usual tap; he'll recover right easily as soon as Corah attends to him."

"Bring him along gently, then," said Ishmael.

And, as he spoke, some other figures seemed suddenly to spring from the dark undergrowth.

They had been lying there awaiting the signal from their chief, and, now that it had been given, they assisted in raising the insensible Sir Huntley, and bearing him away along one of the dreary paths that I have before described.

The spot towards which they were making their way was hollowed out, partly by Nature and partly by artificial means, and was, in consequence of the surrounding trees, adapted admirably for the homes of these nomad tribes.

At this moment women and men had retired to their tents, with the exception of those who watched; but even now a bright fire blazed in the centre of the circle.

A bright big fire it was, that sent its glowing warmth into the ends of the low tents which were placed in a semi-circle round it.

Yet, bright as it was, and high as the flames reared their heads, not a sign of light was observable by anyone who passed along the highway.

"What have we here?" cried one of the watchers, as they approached.

"A grand discovery—a cavalier," said Ishmael. "Where is Corah?"

"Asleep. What want you with her?"

"To arouse the stranger."

"Rob him first."

"No, no," said Ishmael. "I know something better than that. We will not rob him now; we will rouse him, threaten him, promise him death, and then he will be ransomed."

"Good; then Corah need not come. I will arouse him myself."

The speaker, who was an old gipsy, with long white beard, then approached Sir Huntley, who was still lying insensible, and, drawing from his pocket a small phial, held it to his nose.

Sir Huntley Mordaunt shivered, and then opened his eyes.

"Where am I?" said he. "Ah! I know I am among thieves and murderers."

"Well," said Ishmael, coming to his side, "I don't know whether you call us thieves or not, but, if you look at your pockets, you will find we have taken nothing."

Sir Huntley roused himself, and examined his pockets.

Not a coin was taken, nor a piece of jewellery displaced upon his person.

"Then, what want you?" he cried. "What is it you require of me?"

"A ransom."

Sir Huntley smiled, as he rose to his feet.

"You have made an error," he said. "You have caught me, truly, when I desired to make my escape, but you are quite wrong in imagining that I could pay a ransom; I could not."

"Then, my friend," said Ishmael, "you will have to remain here until your friends ransom you. We are used to poor gentlemen; they always have rich friends."

While the man was talking, a thought seemed to strike Sir Huntley.

"Look here, fellow," he said, "what is your name?"

"Ishmael."

"You are a gipsy—a rover—an outlaw?"

"I am, ready to earn money in any way which comes first to hand."

"You have used me ill," continued Sir Huntley. "I feel even now the effects of your ill-usage; but, as I have a desperate enterprise in view, and can pay you well, I will place it in your hands, if you are willing to undertake it."

"What will you pay?"

"You ask the price before you know what the enterprise is."

"Yes; what then? I know we will do anything; it depends upon the price."

Sir Huntley smiled.

"You are a bold villain," he said. "How many do you number in your tribe?"

"Twenty."

"Then, I will give ten gold pieces to every one among you."

"Or, rather," said Ishmael, "you will give me two hundred, and permit me to distribute them as I please."

"Be that as you please," returned Sir Huntley. "And now I will explain to you my plan. It relates simply to the carrying off a lady; but the accomplishment is surrounded by great difficulties. Listen."

Briefly, but clearly, Sir Huntley Mordaunt gave the details of his proposed scheme of villany, the working out of which we shall presently see, and the gipsy listened with many a nod and smile.

"You smile," said Sir Huntley Mordaunt, with some sternness.

"I do," returned Ishmael. "We have in our time had so many jobs of this kind to assist in; but come, when is this to be done?"

"To-morrow night."

"And the money, when is that forthcoming?"

"Half now, at this moment, if you wish it," said he, drawing out his purse.

The gipsy's eyes glistened as he glanced at the glittering pieces.

"Good," he said; "it shall be done. To-morrow, as soon as darkness comes on, you shall accompany us to London, and if we do not carry off this lady, why, we will die in the attempt."

"And where am I to sleep to-night?" asked the courtier.

"I will lend you my blankets," returned Ishmael, "and beneath the shelter of yonder overhanging tree you will be able to sleep in peace."

He brought out his blankets, laid them on a sandy piece of ground beneath the boughs of a young oak, and left the cavalier to his thoughts.

And here, amid these lawless spirits, Sir Huntley passed the night, dreaming of the villanous scheme which would, on the following night, deliver into his hands one of his enemies, on whom he would wreak his vengeance.

CHAPTER XXXIII.

THE WILL.

It was on the day following the escape of Sir Huntley Mordaunt from the Tower of London that a gentleman presented himself at the Palace of Whitehall, and requested to be permitted to see Lady Laura Clavering.

Admitted to her presence, he glanced round nervously at the ladies who were with her, and then, drawing a piece of paper from his pocket, said, with a smile, which was intended to be very bland—

" I presume I am in the presence of Lady Laura Clavering?"

" Yes, sir."

" The daughter of Lord Herbert Clavering, of West Trowis, Yorkshire?"

" The same, sir."

" Well, then, my lady," said the new comer, bowing, and drawing up his mouth in strange contortions, " I am Master Anthony Joiner, attorney-at-law, of 5, Little Capel Lane, at your service. I have the honour and pleasure of informing you that there has been just placed in my hands a will, the will of Sir Edgar Farnleigh, of Farnleigh House, who died some little time since by the hands of a cruel and cold-blooded assassin."

With an eye to future business, Mr. Anthony Joiner banished the smile, and substituted in its stead a snuffle and a grimace, meant to be expressive of sorrow and disgust.

" I am aware, sir, of Sir Edgar's untimely end, though it seemed as if his system was fast breaking, and he would in the course of nature have died before many hours. But how does his death affect me now?"

" I will explain it clearly. His favourite heir was Hubert Aveling, who also died by an assassin's knife. Hubert Aveling's father was a very rich man, who, however, dissipated his wealth, and left his son penniless. Sir Edgar Farnleigh, his uncle, took him in hand, and made a will, leaving to Hubert the entire of his immense property. Now, at Hubert's death, the next heir was Sir Huntley Mordaunt, and it seems clear enough to me that Sir Huntley destroyed the old man under the supposition that no will was made, and that the property would therefore naturally and quietly pass to him. He was wrong; a will had been duly drawn out, and attested on the preceding evening."

"And that will?"

"Leaves everything to you."

"To me!" exclaimed Lady Laura Clavering, in astonishment. "Why, what claim have I upon him?"

"A claim which he recognized, though some truly would not have done so—a claim founded upon the known love borne you by the murdered heir, Hubert Aveling. Yes, my lady, to you the whole of the magnificent rent-roll of Farnleigh is left, and I trust you may long live to enjoy it."

A deep pallor overspread the face of Lady Laura, and a sigh escaped her bosom.

"Alas! sir," she said, "there is no enjoyment left for me. Wealth has no charms for me since he whom I loved is dead."

Mr. Anthony Joiner bowed consolingly.

"These afflictions are very hard to bear," he said, "but I trust you will be able to find some means of using your money which will give you pleasure and comfort. Allow me now, for instance, to be the manager of your affairs, and to direct your expenses, and you will, I am sure, have no cause to regret employing Mr. Anthony Joiner."

The artful, wheedling way adopted by the attorney did not in any way deceive Lady Laura Clavering, and in spite of the grief which naturally filled her heart, she at once resolved to take the advice of others before placing the entire management of her fortune in the hands of a stranger.

"I will communicate with you in a day or two, Master Joiner," she said; "in the meantime I will consult my friends, and be assured that I shall not be forgetful of your zeal."

The lawyer shuffled about in his pocket, and produced a card.

"There is my card, my lady," he said, bowing; "Anthony Joiner, Little Capel Lane, at your service."

And with a sweeping bow, intended to include all, he quitted the room.

Lady Clara Mortimer and her sister, who were present, came at once to the side of Laura.

"We quit the palace this evening with our brother," said Clara; "but we have the pleasant thought that you, at least, have found good fortune to solace you even if you lose the companionship of those whom you have always kindly called your best friends."

Lady Laura burst into tears, and hid her face in Clara's bosom.

"Alas," she said, "this wealth is of no avail to me; Hubert Aveling being dead, the world is a blank and a desert, and what care *I* for gold? Farewell now; we shall meet, I hope, soon again."

After kissing their companion tenderly, Clara and Geraldine Mortimer quitted the room, to take leave of Wilford Rokeby and Lance Courtenay.

Both were in the Black Corridor, waiting with Lord Claude Mortimer.

"Clara," said Wilford Rokeby, as he advanced to meet her, "this parting is made truly as if we were separating for years, whereas it is but for a few hours.

The king's anger will soon pass over, and when that accursed traitor, Mordaunt, is disposed of, we can hope for many happy days in the future."

"You are always so sanguine, so full of hope, dear Wilford," she said, smiling, "but while that villain Mordaunt lives, I shall always fear for your life. Either by poison or by steel, he will attempt your destruction."

"He must do so through others, then," said Wilford, "for at the present moment he is in safe custody. The Tower is a strong place."

"Yes, but you contrived to escape."

As she spoke, the door was flung open, and a page entered, bearing a letter.

He looked hot and excited, as if disturbed by some strange news.

"What ails you, Henry?" cried Rokeby, advancing to meet him.

"Stop me not," said the boy. "I have been seeking everywhere for the king. I bring him strange and terrible news."

"What news?"

"The news that Sir Huntley Mordaunt has escaped from the Tower."

Then he passed away at a run, before they could ask another question.

For a moment the three friends glanced at one another in complete astonishment, while Clara and Geraldine turned pale and sick at heart.

"This is bad news, indeed," said Wilford Rokeby. "This villain seems to possess a charmed life. We must guard against him as we would against an invisible foe, for the next time he strikes it will be in the dark."

"As he always strikes," said Lord Claude. "To you and your friends, Rokeby, I leave his discovery and punishment. Trust me to protect my sisters."

"There is another thing which you forget, Claude," said Clara.

"What is that?"

"The safety of our dear father."

"That I will secure at the peril of my own life," returned Wilford; "and now, dearest, farewell! Be of good cheer, and trust in me."

He stooped, gently kissed her on her blushing cheek, and Lance having taken leave of Geraldine, they parted.

It was about eight in the evening when Lucy Manvers, one of the tiring women, entered Clara's chamber with a note.

It was signed "Wilford," and ran as follows:—

"MY DEAREST CLARA,—I have news of great importance to communicate to you. You leave the palace at nine. I shall then be relieving guard, and shall be unable to speak with you; but if you can quit the palace a few moments sooner, I will await you near the western gate, and tell you all ere you enter your carriage. Do not fail, as I shall be in a state of great trouble and excitement till I see you.

"Your own, ever,
"WILFORD."

"This is strange, most strange," she murmured, as she placed the note in her bosom. "He must, indeed, have important news if he desires so anxiously to see me, and in such a secret manner, too. Did Lieutenant Rokeby give you this?"

"He did, my lady," replied the girl.

THE ⋆ NIGHT ⋆ GUARD;

Or, THE SECRET OF THE FIVE MASKS.

"SEE!" CRIED WILFORD, "HE IS ESCAPING.   THIS MUST NOT BE."

No. 12.

"Then you may go now. What a strange letter," she added, to her sister, as Lucy left the bedchamber. "See, Geraldine; read it."

Geraldine read it through, and shook her head doubtingly.

"I do not like this," she said; "there is something unreal about it. Does it not seem so to you?"

"I know not what to think. Lucy says she received it from Lieutenant Rokeby's own hands; I must go, therefore. Love bids me go, and Providence will save me from harm."

CHAPTER XXXIV.

THE TRAP.

NIGHT had fallen once more over the old palace of Whitehall.

Again the shadows had crept along the pavement, and hidden away behind the buttresses; again the windows glittered with lights; again the river plashed and gurgled unseen.

At a quarter before nine, a coach, with two horses, drew up near the western gate of the palace.

"Why do you not draw up nearer the gate?" asked Wilford Rokeby, advancing from the guard-room.

"Lord Mortimer's orders were to remain here," growled the coachman.

"Very well. I suppose he has his reasons," said the lieutenant of the Night Guard, as he re-entered and passed into the room where his men were getting ready to relieve guard.

Hardly had he done so when a veiled figure hurried by, and passed forth into the open air.

This was Lady Clara Mortimer.

She glanced round her in doubt and alarm as she found herself alone.

"I am betrayed," she murmured, "and must return at once."

The words had scarcely left her lips —she had hardly, in fact, turned to leave the spot—when a large shawl was thrown over her head, her cries were stifled, her arms pinioned, and she found herself surrounded by a number of ruffianly-looking men.

She could ask no questions—utter no sound—make but slight resistance.

Her captors, led by a masked man, who was no other than Sir Huntley Mordaunt, had her entirely at their mercy, and, in spite of the feeble attempts which she made to escape, she was borne off to the coach which stood waiting for her at the western gate.

Into this coach she was placed.

Sir Huntley entered with her, and the coach drove off.

Not a word was spoken until the soft running of the wheels proclaimed that they had left London, and were passing along a country road.

Then Sir Huntley reached forward

and removed the gag from Clara's mouth, and released her arms.

"So, so, my pretty one," he said, "you began to hope that you had for ever escaped me, did you not?"

"I hoped so, indeed," said Clara, with a shudder.

Sir Huntley laughed coarsely.

His troubles and his desperate position seemed indeed to have taken from him his courtier-like gallantry and politeness.

"You fear me. I know it; I glory in it," he said. "It is for that reason I have made you captive; it is to save myself that I have endangered you, and through you I shall have my freedom and my life."

"Never!" said Lady Clara; "never, while I have life, will I do aught to save you."

"You are deceived; you will," returned Sir Huntley. "Listen to me. There is at this moment in existence a conspiracy against the king's power. Five men leagued themselves together to destroy King James, and one of their first rules was that they should remain unknown to one another. Do you follow me?"

"I do."

"Well, this first rule was not kept; it was impossible to keep it. I was one of the five."

"You!"

"Yes; and two others were Lance Courtenay and Wilford Rokeby."

"I believe you not!" cried Lady Clara. "Wilford Rokeby never plotted against King James."

"I can prove he did, and his friend Lance, also. Yes, he plotted against the king, and, before many hours have passed, the king will know all."

"He will not believe it," returned Lady Clara Mortimer, boldly.

"You trust too much in the king's clemency," returned Sir Huntley; "the proofs which will be adduced are of such a nature that he cannot help believing all, and if *I* perish, I shall have the pleasure of knowing that Wilford will perish also."

"You seem to take a pleasure—a fiendish pleasure in evil," said Clara; "and yet you gain nothing by it. I know of something that has happened only to-day which proves how useless are your machinations."

"And pray, my lady, may I ask what this is?" asked Sir Huntley Mordaunt, sneeringly.

"Simply this. Sir Edgar Farnleigh died some time since by the hand of an assassin. That assassin imagined that, having removed from his path Hubert Aveling, who was the heir to the property, he himself, being the next heir, would inherit the wealth."

"Well!"

"He was mistaken."

"Mistaken! How so?"

"You seem interested, Sir Huntley. I will tell you how he was mistaken. He fancied that he arrived in time to kill the poor old man before any will was made. He was wrong. The will had been already made and attested."

"Yes, yes; and in whose favour?"

"In favour of Lady Laura Clavering, the betrothed wife of the murdered Hubert."

Sir Huntley grasped her so tightly by the wrist that she cried aloud.

"Coward!" she cried. "Would you add brutality to your many wrong doings?"

"Listen to me," said Sir Huntley, releasing her, and speaking in a hissing tone, which betrayed the intensity of his feelings, "listen to me. You are in my power. I am, as it were, an outlaw, and, therefore, desperate. I am about to take you to a place from which there is no escape. You must write to Wilford Rokeby, begging him to withdraw all his accusations against me, and saying, that upon my being reinstated in the favour of the king, depends your honour and your happiness. Fail to do this, and you will be my wife in a few hours. Among the lawless band with whom I am now connected, there are those who will think nothing of dragging a priest to the forest glades, and compelling him to perform the marriage ceremony. Your nineteenth birthday approaches, and ere then, if you refuse, you shall be mine."

Before she could answer, the coach, which for some time had been passing rapidly along a dark country road, overshadowed by trees, came to a standstill, and a rough head showed itself at the window.

"We are arrived," said Ishmael, as he opened the door.

Sir Huntley leaped out, and proffered his hand to Clara, who, declining it, descended unaided.

"This way, lady," cried the gipsy, and surrounded by her savage captors, she was led through the heavy trees, into the midst of the gipsy tents.

The shades of night were now settled thick and heavy upon the country, and not a ray of moonlight broke through the branches.

The only light was from the large fire, whose flames cast a red glow upon the groups around—tall, wiry-looking men in rough, picturesque costumes, and women, young and old, in gaily-coloured dresses, and red handkerchiefs crossed over their swarthy bosoms, and long, black hair streaming down their backs.

It was a scene worthy the pencil of a painter, and in spite of the imminent peril in which she stood, Lady Clara Mortimer glanced for one moment round her in wonder and admiration.

Her study was cut short by the approach of an old woman.

"This way, lady," said the gipsy; "we have but humble accommodation here, different far from the home of which you could boast in the palace, but still the best we have we will give you."

"Thanks, good woman," said Clara; "it matters not to me what home you give me here, what I desire is freedom."

The old gipsy took no heed of her words, but led her forward towards a tent which was pitched beneath the shelter of a stalwart oak.

Here she showed a rough straw bed, which was to be her lodging for the night; and here Lady Clara Mortimer, after a long fit of weeping, contrived to snatch a few hours' repose.

Her trials began afresh with the arrival of the dawn.

Corah, a young gipsy girl, the daughter of the chief, had spoken kindly to her, and whispered words of comfort; but no sooner had the frugal morning meal been partaken of than Sir Huntley Mordaunt was by her side.

"How like you our forest life?" he asked, tauntingly.

Clara replied not.

"Are you ready to write as I desired to Lieutenant Rokeby?" he continued.

"I have before refused," she answered. "Nothing shall induce me to do it."

"Not the knowledge that your father will die, when I could save him? Not the knowledge that, if you refuse, Wilford Rokeby will be placed in the Tower, and that before two days are gone you will be mine?"

"I believe you not," said Lady Clara. "If you could save my father you would not. And again, I do not believe that you have the power either to save him or harm Wilford. Providence will protect me. I fear you not."

Sir Huntley Mordaunt turned pale with anger at these brave words.

"Very good," he said, "very good; you brave my power, and you will soon see how foolish, how mad, you are to do so. It is Wilford Rokeby who has taught you to believe that my influence with the king is gone. He has told you wrongly; I have friends, powerful friends, whom he fears, and who, if *I* perish, will light such a conflagration as he will find it difficult to extinguish. Mark me, while you have the chance it will be better to accept it."

"Again I refuse," said Lady Clara.

"Very well, then," returned Sir Huntley Mordaunt; "I will send at once to the king."

He had hardly uttered these words when he started and turned his head to listen, for the steady tramp of soldiers was heard advancing along the high road.

Corah at the same moment came suddenly behind Lady Clara, and whispered in her ear.

"The king's guards are coming," she said. "You are saved."

She had scarcely spoken when a young gipsy boy came rushing in among the tents.

"To arms!" he cried, "to arms! all of ye. The king's troops are upon us!"

CHAPTER XXXV.

THE BATTLE IN THE FOREST.

THE gipsies at once started to their feet, and rushed to seek their arms.

Rushing to their tents, they each seized whatever weapon came nearest to their hands—daggers, clubs, muskets —and prepared to resist their enemies.

Sir Huntley Mordaunt, at the first intimation of danger, sprang from his post of observation to the spot where Lady Clara Mortimer sat upon the fallen tree.

"Come," he said, "let us away; in such a scene you will be out of place and in peril."

Clara moved not.

"I am in less peril here," she answered, "than in your company, no matter who it may be who is coming hither. If they are the king's guards, they are my friends, and are here to save me."

There was no time for further colloquy.

The crashing of small branches, and the crackling of leaves, showed that the soldiers had already made their way into the forest, and were advancing rapidly along the dark and rugged paths.

"Keep in line, my men," cried Ishmael; "protect yourselves in the shadows as far as possible, and, as they advance, give them a hearty shower of stones. They won't like that, I warrant."

It required but a few moments to collect from the rough ground some large, sharp flints, and, when the soldiers neared the encampment, each man was ready for action.

Wilford Rokeby, who was in command of the guards, having ordered his troops to halt, advanced and raised his hand, as if to stay an offensive movement on the part of the gipsies.

"My friends," he said, "yonder stands a proscribed traitor—an outlaw—a man upon whom the anger of the king has fallen heavily. By his side stands a lady whom he has stolen forcibly from her friends. Deliver them to us and we shall no further molest you; refuse, and your blood will be on your own heads."

"We refuse," said Ishmael. "Now, boys."

In an instant the heavy stones which they had picked up from the ground were flung into the troopers' faces.

Coming from all quarters, they quite bewildered the soldiers, who fired at random and wounded no one.

"Now, boys!" cried Ishmael, "rush in at them before they recover."

"Steady, my men, steady!" shouted Wilford, as a shot from the pistol of the gipsy chief whistled through his plumed hat, "steady, and cut them down."

The gipsies were greatly superior in number to the troopers whom Wilford and Lance had brought with them to the forest, and rushing in with their knives before the troops could reload, they entirely prevented the approach of either Wilford or Lance to Sir Huntley Mordaunt.

While the soldiers, assailed by enemies who outnumbered them almost two to one, were thus kept at bay, Josef suddenly appeared upon the scene, bringing with him a wild-looking horse, ready saddled and bridled.

"Here, sir," he cried, "leap up here, and make your escape."

"The lady! the lady!" said Sir Huntley Mordaunt, seizing Clara's hand; "she must go with me."

"No, no, leave her to us; you go. Delay not, or you may be too late. See—see, even now, the fate of our chief!"

Sir Huntley, ere he placed his foot in the stirrup, glanced in the direction of the gipsy chief, and saw Lance Courtenay in the act of running Ishmael through the body, while Wilford, who stood near him, was engaged hotly with two members of the wild forest tribe.

"See, Lance, see," cried Rokeby, "he is escaping! This must not be."

But there was no possibility of reaching him.

The gipsies at this moment, in spite of the fall of their chief, had everywhere the best of it.

The troops were brave enough, and fought sturdily and valiantly, but they were no match against treacherous blows dealt from behind by men who crept upon them stealthily with heavy bludgeons.

Several of them were on their knees, with the rough grasp of the gipsies at their throats, and altogether affairs seemed distinctly to forewarn the defeat of the king's guard.

"Gipsies!" cried Sir Huntley, as he prepared to fly, "save her for me, and a rich reward shall be yours. Wilford Rokeby, we shall meet again!"

With these words, he dashed off, followed by several bullets, which, however, seemed to take no effect, for the next moment the clatter of his horse's feet was heard plainly from the high road.

Clara, meanwhile, stood by Corah's side in great terror, while behind was a group of swarthy gipsy women, watching with intense eagerness the different phases of the fight.

The sight of her beloved face roused the friends to still greater exertions, and the tide soon turned.

Lance Courtenay, having disposed of the gipsy chief, who was by far the most formidable opponent, flew to the rescue of Wilford, who, relieved thus of one of his adversaries, ran the other through and dashed towards Josef.

The king's guard now recovered itself, as it were; and, incited by the success of Wilford Rokeby and Lance, they gathered once more into a compact body, and rushed upon the gipsies with their long, heavy swords.

Resistance was now useless, and a horrible carnage would have taken place, had not Wilford Rokeby cried suddenly, in a loud voice—

"Hold! guards—forbear!"

The troopers at once desisted from their dreadful work.

"Gipsies," cried Wilford Rokeby, "I give you your lives. You have protected, at the peril of your lives, an outlaw and an assassin, but the king no doubt will take no further notice of this night's work, if you now make your peace. You must deliver this lady to us quietly, and lay down your arms. Beware of treachery; for if one stray shot follows my men as they depart, not a man of you shall be left alive to tell the tale."

"We yield," said Josef, sullenly, as he gazed round at the dead bodies of his friends, and those, too, who lay groaning with the agonies of fearful wounds; "take the lady and begone."

Wilford now approached Clara, who, in spite of the rough soldiers around them, threw herself upon his breast and wept with joy.

"Come, dear one," he whispered, "let us leave this place at once. Lance, keep a watch upon these fellows, for those who would hire themselves out in such a cause cannot be trusted in anything."

"Farewell, Corah, farewell," said Clara, turning to the gipsy girl, and placing a gold locket in her hands, " for your kind wishes, take this in remembrance of me."

The gipsy maiden seized her hand and pressed it to her lips, and in a few moments after Wilford Rokeby was leading his betrothed bride through the tangled forest towards the highway.

The forest tribe did not make any attempt at treachery.

The stern, resolute words of Wilford had made an impression upon their minds, and they watched, therefore, in gloomy silence, the departure of their conquerors, and then, amid the wailing of the women, prepared to bury the dead and succour the wounded.

At an inn, not very far from the scene of the conflict, a coach was waiting in readiness to convey Lady Clara Mortimer to her brother's house.

"You are always sanguine, always sure of success, dear Wilford," said the young girl, smiling as she caught sight of the carriage. "You were certain that you would save me."

"Without confidence, of what use is courage?" said Wilford. "I knew also, dear Clara, that if I perished, Lance would save you." •

Leaving Rokeby and his guards to escort Lady Clara towards Westminster, we must return to the Tower of London, and see how it fared with those who had aided—some consciously and some unconsciously—in Sir Huntley Mordaunt's escape.

It was on the evening of the rescue of Lady Clara from the hands of her persecutor, that Sir Leonard Fairfax sent for Ben Lockster.

Sir Leonard was seated in his room by the fire, reading a paper.

"Close the door, Ben," said he. "I have important news for you."

Ben closed the heavy portal, and joined Sir Leonard near the fire.

"What is it, Sir Leonard? You seem agitated. Is the news, then, so bad?"

"It is, indeed. You know that I have a spy in the palace?"

"I do. A lady."

"The same. Well, I learn this evening that suspicion has fallen both upon you and me, in consequence of the escape of Sir Huntley. I shall receive an order this very night for your arrest, and——"

"My arrest!" exclaimed Ben.

"Yes, 'tis the truth. If you believe me not, read this letter yourself."

"Yes, yes, I believe you," returned the gaoler. "But what is your advice? What am I to do?"

"You had better leave at once. Let it be supposed that you asked me for permission to be absent, and keep out of the way. It is quite certain you are not safe here."

"I will take your advice, and go at once," said Red Ben. "And yourself?"

"I must remain here. At present, there is no order for my arrest."

"I am extremely thankful, Sir Leonard," said Red Ben, as he prepared to quit the room. "I will send to-morrow, and see how matters have turned out."

In ten minutes he was clear of the gates of the Tower.

Hardly had he fled away into the darkness when the order for his arrest arrived from Whitehall.

Sir Leonard read it gravely through,

when the porter, who brought it, delivered it to him.

"Seek for Ben Lockster," he cried, as he turned to one of the Tower guards. "He's wanted at once."

"He is not in the Tower, Sir Leonard. I just now passed him through the western gate, and he hurried away with all speed towards the river-side."

"Ah! he has fled," exclaimed Sir Leonard, in assumed surprise. "He has had tidings of his danger, and, knowing well his guilt, has made his escape. Inform his majesty that instant search shall be made," he added, turning to the trooper, "and I hope that we shall not be too late to secure him. Quick, there, guards, follow me."

In a few moments Sir Leonard Fairfax, with ten men, passed over the western drawbridge, and hurried towards the river—in other words, in the very direction which he *knew* Ben Lockster had not taken.

CHAPTER XXXVI.

THE GOLDEN TEMPTER.

RED BEN, haunted by the vision of the scaffold—for such he knew well would be his fate if he were caught, and placed in one of the Tower dungeons—hurried away towards his own home.

The pale ghastliness of fear was for the first time visible upon his ugly features, and in his dark and treacherous mind he endeavoured to conceive some plan by which the destruction of some one else should be made the means of securing his own safety.

He cared not to trust Sir Leonard.

Long association with criminals had taught him *this* lesson—that there is *no* honour among thieves, and that the man who would be guilty of treachery to one would be guilty of treachery to another.

If he were once arrested and placed in one of the stone cells, he felt certain that Sir Leonard Fairfax would place all the blame upon him, and trust to his own title and position to save himself.

"No, no," he muttered, "no, no: I cannot trust Sir Leonard. I have no powerful friends as he has. I have no power or influence, and I cannot betray him without implicating myself. I must—yes, I have it—I must seek Sir Huntley Mordaunt, and—yes—betray him to the king. He will pardon me, and reward me well. Aye," he added, rubbing his hands as his heart beat more quickly, and his ferret eyes glistened, "aye, the reward, the gold is the thing. Ever since I handled those bright coins that Sir Huntley paid me for extracting the bullets, I have hankered after more. I must secure them in my belt, and quit this place in search of my victim."

As he spoke thus, he reached the door of his house, and letting himself in with a key, he bolted and barred the door behind him.

Then he hurried into a room on the ground floor.

As he did so, he started back with an exclamation of surprise, not quite unmixed with fear.

The lamp stood alight upon the table, and by the fire, which blazed cheerily up the wide chimney, sat a man in ragged, dirty clothes, a torn slouched hat surmounting his long, shaggy locks, and a huge beard, nearly concealing his face.

"Pray, who are you, sir?" cried Ben Lockster, as he advanced.

"Don't you know me?" asked the other, in a gruff voice, which seemed quite unknown to him.

"I do not. Be good enough to tell me your business."

The unknown burst into a loud laugh.

"Ha! ha!" cried a familiar voice, "my disguise is complete, then, indeed."

"Sir Huntley Mordaunt!" exclaimed Ben Lockster, in undisguised pleasure.

"Yes, I am he. I knew of no one else but you whom I could trust, and so I came hither."

"You have come into the very heart of danger, then," said Ben, who had no desire to be taken with his victim, and thus lose his chance of reward. "I am discovered as having aided you in your escape; and I am even now flying from the king's troops."

"Then where can I take refuge? Whither can I fly?"

"To Claverstone; you can remain in safety there. No one will dream of your taking refuge in your own house."

Sir Huntley Mordaunt thought for a moment.

"Yes," he said, "you are right. In this disguise I can safely make my way thither. So let us go at once. When we reach the 'King's Arms' we can procure horses, and post thither at once."

"We will," returned Ben Lockster, "we will. I have only one thing to do."

With that he hurried upstairs, and going to his drawer, took out his hoarded gold, and having gloated over it a moment, placed it in his belt.

"Now, then," he said, as he re-entered the chamber where Sir Huntley eagerly awaited him, "now, then, I am ready."

Opening the door they glanced rapidly up and down the street, to see if anyone was on the watch, and no one being moving anywhere, they closed the portal behind them, and walked rapidly away.

On reaching the "King's Arms" they stopped.

"It won't do for me to be seen," said Sir Huntley. "I don't much look like a man who can afford to pay for horses. Here, take my purse; go and procure them yourself."

"I don't know that I look much like a nobleman myself," thought Red Ben, as he made his way towards the inn; "however, money will overcome everything."

The landlord of the inn certainly did look askance at him when he demanded the two horses, for neither his appearance, nor his dress, nor his features were such as to commend him to any one.

The sight of the gold, however, had, as he had said, a magical effect upon the man, and having received beforehand a goodly reward for his trouble, he led out from the stables two tall and finely-made horses.

"I expect, master," he said, with a grin, "that you require speed in these animals more than anything else; and for running along a hard country road, there's none can beat these."

Red Ben scowled angrily at the landlord, but forbore to make any reply.

It was not policy now to quarrel with anyone.

"We will return them," he said, as he leaped on the back of one, and prepared to quit the court-yard. "Good-night."

He soon rejoined Sir Huntley, and they set out together towards Claver-stone.

Eager for gold; eager to save himself from the anger of the king, he was as anxious as Sir Huntley to arrive at his destination, and he urged the horses, therefore, to their utmost speed.

It was early morning when they reached the place, and clattered over the drawbridge, which the astonished servants let down for them to pass.

"Ha!" cried Sir Huntley, as he dropped wearily into an armchair in his comfortable study, "ah! I am glad indeed we have arrived in safety. After the Court and its glitter, and the power I enjoyed when I was there, the hunted life of an outlaw would never suit me. With my retainers, and you, my faithful friend, I will defend this place, even against the king's troops."

Faithful friend!

Thus he sincerely termed the one who was even then plotting to betray him.

"Yes, truly," said Red Ben, "this place is strong enough to bear a siege. Fill the moat with water, draw up the drawbridges, place armed men upon the battlements, and you need fear nothing."

"Aye, and give me but the chance of destroying Wilford Rokeby, of shooting him with my own hand, and then I should die happy."

"There is another wish," said Red Ben, "which you have, that is even stronger than that."

"And that——"

"Is the wish to marry Lady Clara Mortimer."

"You guess aright, Ben," said Sir Huntley, "you guess aright. But that, I fear, is now beyond my power. To ruin Wilford Rokeby—to destroy him with my own hand—that is now my first desire in life."

"And in that," said Red Ben, "I will do my best to aid you."

CHAPTER XXXVII.

IN THE FOREST.

It was night—still, solemn night—at Claverstone, two nights after the return of Sir Huntley Mordaunt.

Sir Huntley was busy in his study.

In a room near sat Red Ben, writing.

His eyes glistened as he scrawled out the treacherous lines.

His heart beat high as he dreamed of the blood-money which would be his.

Presently he rose, and paced the room rapidly.

To and fro, to and fro, he went, until he presently stopped, and unlocked a drawer.

This room was one which had been assigned to him as his own by Sir Huntley.

In one corner was a bedstead, and in the centre a large table, on which lay the open letter, and in this drawer that he had now opened was a heap of gold, the reward which had been paid to him for drawing the bullets from the sentinel's guns at the Tower of London.

"Gold, gold!" he murmured, as he plunged his hand into the glittering heap and let the coins slip through his fingers. "Gold, gold! How beautiful it looks! What power it gives! what happiness! what pleasure! I must have more—more, and how? If I betray him not, I shall be destroyed, and I shall lose the enjoyment of all I have. If I betray him, I shall earn the king's favour and his money. It must—it must be done!"

"How now, Ben Lockster!" cried a voice, that of Sir Huntley Mordaunt.

"What's that?" cried the ex-gaoler, in affright, clutching the gold and looking up, in horrified accents, his eyeballs starting, his mouth half open, his cheeks blanched with the terrors of a guilty conscience.

"Ben Lockster," again cried the voice of Sir Huntley.

He was calling from his study.

"Fool!" cried Red Ben, as he closed the drawer and drew himself up, "fool, to be alarmed at a voice. Ben, if you are to be terrified at a sound, how can you carry out your grand projects? I am coming, Sir Huntley," he added, in a loud voice, and, leaving the letter open on the table, he made his way towards the study where his master was sitting.

Sir Huntley was standing with his back to the fire.

"Ben," he said, "a messenger has just come from London with intelligence which has much disquieted me. Go, Ben, to the sentinel at the postern, and tell him to keep a sharp look-out; go also to the sentinel on the outward wall, and bid him fire upon anyone who approaches."

"I will go," observed Red Ben, and hurried away.

Sir Huntley watched him until he was fairly gone.

"I like not that man's manners," he

said; "I like them not. He is too cringingly servile, too respectful, too anxious to please. I believe it is all put on. I believe he would willingly betray me. What could he have been writing when I approached his room just now? I will go and see if I can even now discover what he was doing."

As noiselessly as he could, Sir Huntley made his way towards Red Ben's room.

No one was near to observe him, and he entered the chamber unobserved.

The letter lay open on the table.

Taking it up eagerly, he read as follows:—

"To Master Wilford Rokeby, Lieutenant of the King's Guard.

"On the night of next Monday, at ten o'clock, I will induce Sir Huntley Mordaunt (who is now at Claverstone) to quit the abbey and make his way along the Torrent High Road towards Lansdowne. If you can bring down a guard you can easily seize him if you lie in ambush near the 'Farmers' Arms,' which stands on the edge of the highway. For this capture I expect the king's pardon and five hundred pounds.

"(Signed)   Ben Lockster,
"Late gaoler in the Tower of London."

"So, so," said Sir Huntley Mordaunt, with a ghastly smile; "so, so, my friend, this is the end of all my confidence in you! But it matters not. You have laid a trap for *me*—*you* shall fall into it yourself."

Carefully he perused again the treacherous paper, and then replaced it in exactly the same spot where he had found it.

He had scarcely done so when he heard the steps of Ben Lockster returning hurriedly.

"What is to be done?" thought Sir Huntley Mordaunt, glancing eagerly round; "he must have no suspicion that I have cognizance of his villany. Ha! yonder curtained recess. There I can conceal myself."

Hurrying behind the curtain, he concealed himself, and stood motionless while Ben Lockster rushed breathless into the room.

"The letter," he cried, as he approached the table; "ha! it is still there; and he knows nothing. This must be sent at once. Ha! ha! Sir Huntley, I have had the last of *your* gold, now I will have the king's."

"Ruffian," thought Sir Huntley, "neither my gold, nor the king's, shall be yours."

Carefully Ben Lockster enclosed the letter in a cover, and placed it in the breast of his doublet.

Then he passed out, and made towards the postern.

He had not yet delivered his message, in fact, for immediately upon remembering that he had left the letter open upon the table, he had rushed back in terror.

Sir Huntley now issued from his hiding place, and made towards his own room; and not long after Red Ben entered.

All signs of agitation had now left his face, and he walked with a firm and confident step into the room.

"Have you executed my orders, Ben?" said Sir Huntley, in a friendly tone.

"Yes, Sir Huntley," said Ben; "all is prepared against any attack."

"Very good," replied Mordaunt, "but yet I do not care to remain here.

It would be better if I were concealed somewhere in the neighbourhood, somewhere near where you could bring me tidings of the actions of my enemies."

Ben Lockster's heart leaped within his dastard breast.

Little knowing that his infamous plan was discovered, he imagined that Sir Huntley was about to play into his hands, and fall a willing victim to his villany.

"Well, Sir Huntley," he said, "I fancy I could contrive that for you."

"How soon?"

"Before Monday. I know an old man who would willingly conceal you if you paid him well. His house is a humble one indeed—the hut of a wood-cutter, but he is honest and faithful."

"I will gladly then avail myself of the chance," said Sir Huntley Mordaunt. "See him, and prepare him for my coming, and in the meantime we will keep good watch at Claverstone."

At length the Monday came, when the villanous traitor expected to be able to cast Sir Huntley Mordaunt into the power of the king.

Sir Huntley acted his part well, and not a single suspicion crossed the mind of the treacherous gaoler.

They set out as soon as night had closed over the earth, Sir Huntley armed to the teeth, but Ben Lockster having with him only a heavy horse pistol.

Little dreaming of the awful doom that was impending over him, he imagined it unnecessary for him to arm himself, as those who came as the enemies of Sir Huntley were his invited friends.

Their way lay through a dark and dismal wood, replete with heavier shadows and more rugged pathways even than that in which the battle with the gipsies had taken place a few nights before.

Huge trees spread their interwoven branches above their heads, tangled brushwood impeded their passage, and from among the dense bushes sprang forth hideous bats and noisome birds of night.

It was just the place for a black and horrible crime, and though suspecting nothing, a shudder passed through Red Ben's frame as they passed onwards.

Along these dark paths they passed for some time in silence, until presently they emerged upon an open glade, where the bright moon shone in undisturbed brilliance over a plain of velvety turf.

As they did so, a huge raven came sailing—swooping over them.

"Your pistol a moment, Lockster," cried Sir Huntley, "I will shoot that ill-omened bird of night."

Unsuspectingly, the treacherous gaoler delivered into his hands the fatal weapon, and as he did so, Sir Huntley burst into a loud laugh.

"Now, then, Ben Lockster," he cried, "this farce is over. Your hour has come. I know you for a false villain. I have read your letter to Wilford Rokeby. I have led you into your own trap."

"Indeed, indeed," began the man, speaking in a gasping tone, and falling on his knees as the cold steel touched his forehead, and the horror of his position suddenly burst upon him.

"Nay, speak not, entreat not; it is useless," pursued Sir Huntley Mordaunt. "In this deep, vast forest glade you die. In this spot, near which you intended to betray me into the hands of my enemies, you will lie dead, and at the mercy of the crawling things that make this forest hideous. You, too, shall bear for me my triumphant message of scorn and hate to my enemies; for, when I have killed you, I will place in your belt a letter, which shall tell Wilford Rokeby and the king what little dependence they should place upon the cleverness of traitors such as you."

"Oh, mercy! mercy!" murmured the wretched man, clasping his hands together in wild entreaty.

"Mercy!" laughed Sir Huntley, "take the same mercy you intended for me. Ah! in this short moment how bitter must be your thoughts and regrets. I, who throughout your life have been your best friend, should have been the last whom you should have desired to betray. I, too, whom you know to be ever on the alert, should have been guarded from treachery by your own cowardice—your own fears of discovery. But it is done; you have acted the traitor; you have sealed your own doom—signed your own death warrant. Ha! I hear the sound of horses' feet; it must be done."

Then, without another word of explanation, he fired, and the wretched man fell back ghastly and blood-stained upon the velvet turf.

Throwing away the pistol, Sir Huntley Mordaunt knelt and thrust a letter into Red Ben's belt.

As he did so, the moon broke out fully, and he saw on the back of his hand a patch of blood which had gushed upon him when the fatal ball had pierced Ben Lockster's brain.

"The blood on my hand!" he cried, aloud, as he sprang up in terror. "Oh horror! is this to follow me for ever? Oh! Heaven pity me, and save me from these haunting visions!"

Then, without daring to glance again at his hand, and at his cold and senseless victim, he fled away among the dark trees, just as Wilford Rokeby and ten mounted men galloped into the forest glade.

CHAPTER XXXVIII.

THE STORMING OF CLAVERSTONE ABBEY.

"WHAT have we here?" cried Wilford Rokeby, as his eyes fell upon the ghastly face and inanimate body of Ben Lockster. "A murder in very truth!"

He leaped to the ground, and approached the slain man.

"Dead, quite dead!" he murmured, as he placed his hand over his heart, and assured himself that all pulsation had ceased. "Ah! I recognise, now, the features—those of Ben Lockster, the treacherous gaoler, who sought my

life in the Tower. It is well; he has earned his reward at last. Ha! What is this?"

He caught sight of the letter, as he spoke, and withdrew it from Red Ben's belt.

The bright moonlight, which was now falling gently over grove and dale, enabled him to read the lines.

"Once again, Wilford Rokeby"—so the letter ran—"I have escaped from your treacherous ambuscades. Once again, I am enabled to defy you and laugh at your threats. The miserable wretch who was the means of bringing to this part of the country you and your retainers lies dead here—dead by my hand, and is the instrument of bearing to you my scorn and defiance. Tremble, Wilford Rokeby, for when you fancy yourself most safe you will be nearest to your destruction.
"HUNTLEY MORDAUNT."

There was no doubting the authenticity of this document.

There was no denying the fact, moreover, that the arch traitor had once more proved more than a match for his enemies.

He had not given his foes the slightest chance of discovering him.

As I said in my last chapter, he fled rapidly and eagerly away when he heard the approach of the mounted guards.

But he soon stopped.

The dried branches beneath his feet and the leaves crackled loudly as he sped along, and there was every chance, therefore, of his path being discovered.

He waited, accordingly, for some time, cowering down among the thick undergrowth, while some of the soldiers made a hurried search among the trees for the murderer of the still warm victim.

Their search, however, was in vain.

Not a sign of the fugitive could anywhere be seen.

Wilford, therefore, slowly turned from the sickening spectacle of death, and remounted his horse.

"Take up the body, and bear it onward with us," said he to his men. "We must hasten on towards the abbey. No doubt we shall find him concealed somewhere in Claverstone."

The men, who knew nothing of Ben Lockster and his villanous deeds, reverently raised the dead man and placed him on a horse, and then the whole of them, with Wilford Rokeby at their head, proceeded towards the abbey; while Sir Huntley Mordaunt, as soon as they had gone, went leaping away across the wooded country in the direction of the abbey.

It was, of course, dark night when they neared it, and they resolved accordingly to keep watch till daybreak, and see that no one quitted the precincts of the castellated mansion.

No one seemed stirring or desirous of stirring during this night.

There was solemn darkness, solemn stillness everywhere.

The moon's radiance only served to show how quiet, how gloomy, how old and mysterious was the ancient abbey.

Not a light burned in any window.

The place seemed truly as if it had been deserted by its inmates.

Dawn at length broke in golden tints over the country, and inundated the valley below with his brilliant radiance, while it lighted also the turrets of the abbey and the high forest trees.

As soon as it was sufficiently light

to permit of precise action, Wilford Rokeby approached the drawbridge and blew a horn loudly.

The gate was at once opened and an armed retainer appeared.

He turned visibly pale at the sight of the armed men, anticipating, no doubt, a repetition of the attack which had caused the blood to flow so gushingly in the dark corridor of the abbey, and which had resulted in the discovery and release of Lady Mordaunt.

"What is your wish, gentlemen?" he asked civilly.

"To see Sir Huntley Mordaunt," answered Wilford Rokeby.

"He is not here, sir. He quitted the abbey last night at a late hour and has not since returned."

"Then I demand entrance in the name of the king!" returned the young lieutenant of the Night Guard. "I have here the king's order to enter the abbey and retain it for King James. Therefore, let down the drawbridge, and let me and my men enter at once."

The man shook his head, as he drew back behind the door.

"Not so," he said. "I am left here by my master to protect his property. I am responsible to him for the safety of this house and all it contains. I owe no allegiance to King James, and I shall refuse to open."

"You are acting the part of a madman," said Wilford Rokeby. "Do you not know that for such an act as this your head could be struck off, and placed on London Bridge, or on the gates of yonder town?"

The man made a gesture of indifference.

"What does it matter to me?" he said. "If I remain here, and place at defiance the king's power, I can but lose my liberty and life. I should lose both if I were to yield up this place to you. Sir Huntley Mordaunt is a man who never forgives."

"You refuse, then?"

"I do; it shall never be said that I betrayed my trust when but a few enemies are near me. Claverstone Abbey, even against the king's troops, shall be defended to the last."

So saying, he slammed to the door, and Wilford Rokeby and his men were left to their own resources.

"Well," cried he, to his sergeant, "well, we must wait awhile. Lieutenant Courtenay will be here with the troops, and we can then take this place by storm. Until then you must keep a strict look-out."

Patiently the little troop kept their watch over the castle.

The day passed away slowly—very slowly for those who watched and waited.

Another midnight came, and then the low roll of military music swelled out upon the clear night air.

"They are coming," cried Wilford Rokeby. "This place, ere morning, shall be ours, no matter how it is defended."

As he spoke, he passed out on the high road, and listened.

The tramp of the men and the roll of the music came nearer, and at length the soldiers, with Lance Courtenay at their head, marched to the spot where their friends awaited them.

"Well," said Lance, as he greeted

his friend, "what cheer? Have you caught the villain?"

"No. He has again escaped us," said Wilford; "but it matters not. We will attack and seize Claverstone, and I have no doubt we shall find him within the walls."

"We must wait until the morning," said Lance; "but when the dawn breaks we shall not be delayed long. With the cannon I have brought with me, and the brave hearts, too, that fill my host, Claverstone Abbey will be ours in an hour."

At length the second dawn broke over the abbey, and the troops of King James gathered around it.

Again a loud summons was blown on the horn.

Again the armed retainer appeared at the door.

"What want you, gentlemen?" he asked once more, as he glanced in evident alarm at the assembled troopers.

"As I said before, I demand an entrance in the name of the king," replied Wilford Rokeby, resolutely.

"And I," said the man, "in the name of my master, refuse to admit you."

With these words, he rushed back, closed the massive door, shot the bolts, and prepared for a siege.

In another moment a loud bell rang the alarm, and armed men rushed out upon the battlements.

"We shall have to take this place by assault," said Wilford, turning to Lance, who stood by his side. "Bring up the heavy guns and break down yonder gateway. Let the men with ladders swarm into the moat. Such a

siege as this must not be permitted to last long."

Scarcely ten minutes elapsed before the calm serenity of the landscape was disturbed by the din and bustle of active war.

Men hurrying forward, cannons labouring up to the front, horsemen dashing hither and thither with commands, guns belching forth flame from unexpected places, and then the roar and crash of battle; such made up the scene before Claverstone Abbey on that memorable morning.

The defenders of the abbey fought well and bravely.

Urged on by the eager orders of Wilford Rokeby, the besiegers again and again assaulted the place, but were hurled back by those who had the advantage of position.

Over the country-side strong men and gentle maidens swarmed out from their homes, terrified by the sudden roar of battle.

Throngs were on the hill-side; eager faces peered from windows, wives and sweethearts clung to the arms of husbands and lovers, as the cannons boomed and the red flame came forth in volumes from their iron mouths, and the smoke curled aloft and swept among the trees, and the crash of the heavy shot echoed away through the woodlands.

Such a scene as this the neighbourhood of Claverstone had never, for long years before, beheld; and well might the quiet rustics stare in fear and wonder as the men yelled and struggled, and clashed their weapons, and fought hand to hand on the battlements, or clutched each other's throats on the summit of the high ladders, and fell back with curses down into the green water of the moat.

Not long, however, did this last.

The numbers of the assailants soon began to tell, and the heavy shot from the cannon told fearfully upon the gateway.

At length the critical moment came.

The iron-bound portal gave way with a crash, and the king's guards, headed by Wilford Rokeby and Lance Courtenay, began to swarm into the abbey.

A desperate effort at defence was made within, and the swords of the troopers and the retainers crossed with a ring and a clash.

But it was all in vain.

Amid shouts of victory and groans of despair, amid the roar of musketry and the curling of the blue smoke, and the ring of steel and the shouts of eager commanders, the little band forced their way into the inner courtyard, and the Abbey of Claverstone was theirs.

The great object, of course, in seizing upon this stronghold was the discovery of Sir Huntley Mordaunt, who, they felt convinced, was even at this moment concealed within it.

By the manner in which the defence had been conducted, and the desperate courage which the defenders had evinced Wilford felt convinced that Sir Huntley had been the director of every movement, and a diligent search was at once instituted. It was in vain.

Not the remotest and most secret nook was left unexamined, but still there was no discovery of anything which gave the slightest cue to the whereabouts of the assassin of Hubert Aveling and Sir Edgar Farnley.

Meanwhile, while they were seeking everywhere, a tall, stern-looking retainer had stood sullenly leaning on his gun, watching the movements.

He had stationed himself at the door of the guard-room, and had said nothing to anyone, only regarding those who passed him with a kind of stubborn, dogged anger.

This man was no other than Sir Huntley Mordaunt.

He had disguised himself well; his figure seemed changed.

High boots had added to his stature.

His hands and face were stained.

With a feeling of triumph he saw the discomfiture of Wilford Rokeby, and with avidity he listened when he heard the young lieutenant of the Night Guard state his intention of returning to London, and leave the place occupied by the royal troops.

"I will give the king a lesson he will never forget," he muttered. "There shall be a conflagration here which shall light up the country for miles, and the red light that shall shame to-morrow's dawning shall be a warning to tyrants who brave the anger of their powerful nobles. If Wilford Rokeby cannot yet fall my victim, at least his friend shall die."

He was wrong.

"As you are returning to London," said Lance Courtenay, as they stood within the guard-room, "I will accompany you. I have urgent business to-morrow night—business I cannot well delay."

A look of strange inquiry passed

between the friends, but neither seemed inclined to speak his thoughts.

"I must leave the place, then, in the charge of Giles Lambert," said Rokeby, "for I must return at once."

So saying, he passed out, and having found Lambert, who was telling off the sentinels for the night, he gave him his instructions, and soon after the two friends had mounted their horses, and were hurrying off towards the old city on the Thames.

As soon as they were gone, and the abbey of Claverstone had relapsed into its usual quiet, Sir Huntley Mordaunt took up a large flambeau, and proceeded with it to one of the lower rooms.

"My servants must die with them," he muttered, as he descended. "No matter; my revenge must be accomplished."

The light of anticipated revenge gleamed upon his features, ghastly and horrid as they were from the raging of his inward thoughts.

A smile was upon his pale lips—a grim and deadly smile, such as that which must have hovered on the lips of them who, in the treacherous darkness of the Tower of London, glided to the murder of the young princes.

The horrid purpose he had in view could be read upon his face as he passed slowly and with measured tread towards the western wing of the abbey.

In this wing he knew well that his horrid design could be best carried out.

This part of the building, in fact, was far more ancient than the rest, and was composed almost entirely of wood, which he expected would burn fiercely and resistlessly.

Besides, in this part were also kept the stores of the castle, and large kegs of spirits could be broken open, and allowed to flow over the floors.

"Ha! ha!" he murmured, as he passed, flambeau in hand, into the store-room, "now for a flame which shall wake up the whole country side, and cast defiance in the teeth of King James and my enemies."

CHAPTER XXXIX.

THE LAST MEETING OF THE MASKS.

On reaching London, Wilford Rokeby lost no time in seeking the king, and laying before him the history of his proceedings at Claverstone Abbey.

The king listened gravely to the details, and when he had heard all, turned to the Duke of Buckingham.

"What think you of this, my lord?" he said. "Is not this open rebellion?"

"It is, your majesty," returned Buckingham; "but it is, at the same time, only what I prophesied to you long since. Had my wishes been carried out, this wretched and rebellious assassin would long since have graced with his head the archway of London Bridge. It seems now as if you would have some difficulty in tracking him. Were I to meet with him, however, I would give him short shrift. The first tree would be good enough to hang such a cur as he is."

"You are right, Steenie," replied James. "Lieutenant Rokeby, you have done us good service, and we will not forget you. To-morrow, in all probability, I shall be able to settle upon a plan of action. Meanwhile, remain near me, that if anything occurs, I may have a brave sword at my service."

"As it will be ever, your majesty," said Wilford Rokeby, bowing, and taking his leave.

As he passed along the corridor, a page met him, and placed in his hand a letter.

He opened it eagerly, and to his astonishment saw that it was from Lady Clara Mortimer, enclosing one from Lady Huntley Mordaunt.

The first note ran thus :—

"DEAREST WILFORD,—You see by the enclosed letter from Lady Huntley Mordaunt that she has quite recovered her reason. The patient attention of Mistress Fortescue, and the absence of her husband's tyranny, have succeeded at length in restoring to her her reason ; she has received a visit, moreover, from her father, Captain Malcolm, and he has recognised her as his daughter, whom Sir Huntley had stated to be dead. If you will come to my brother's house, we will visit her together.

"CLARA."

The enclosed note was a repetition of what Clara had stated, and bore evidence of deep gratitude for her providential recovery.

"Thank Heaven, Clara is now safe," cried Wilford Rokeby ; "no matter now if the king, in his caprice, should pardon this assassin, he cannot marry my betrothed wife. No matter what threats he may hold out, she is for ever beyond his reach."

He at once proceeded to the house of Lord Claude Mortimer, where Clara received him joyfully.

She looked as beautiful as ever, be it said, though grief for her father's continued imprisonment had stolen away some of the roses from her cheek, and saddened her bright eyes.

Very little time were the lovers allowed to themselves on this day ; the visit had to be made to Lady Mordaunt, and in the evening Wilford Rokeby had to pass across the river, and attend a meeting of the Five Masks at the old house in Surrey.

The first glance at Lady Mordaunt was enough to show that the reason which had been long banished by cruelty and sorrow had taken possession of its seat.

She raised Rokeby's hands to her lips, and, with tears in her eyes, thanked him for his brave rescue of her from her wretched prison.

"I have you to thank," she said, "for life—for honour—for reason."

"And I have you to thank, madam," answered Wilford Rokeby, "for placing it for ever beyond the power of Sir Huntley to offer his bloodstained hand to Lady Clara Mortimer, my betrothed wife. But, tell me, madam, for what reason did Sir Huntley place you in that horrid dungeon?"

"My father," replied Lady Mordaunt, "settled upon me a fortune, which fell to my husband at my death ; on the other hand, an uncle left to me a sum of money which Sir Huntley could only have the benefit of while I lived. He at once concocted a hideous scheme of villany. He never loved me; he took me from the one I really loved merely because he desired the use of my fortune, and he spread, therefore, a report that I was dead. This report was only circulated where my uncle's executors would never hear of it; so that, while obtaining from my father the money which fell to him on my death, he still continued in the enjoyment of the other fortune which was dependent on my life. His horrid plan, he knew well, could be the better carried out if I were to lose possession of my senses, and he therefore immured me in that foul and loathsome dungeon where you found me, and from which you saved me."

"How you lived at all," cried Wilford Rokeby, "is a mystery. Providence seems, indeed, to have preserved you, in order that you might be an instrument in his destruction."

The lady shuddered.

"The remembrance of the place horrifies and terrifies me still," she said; "each night brought its own fear—each corner in my dungeon had its own shadow—each shadow formed its own spectre to affright me. Oh! those long —long—hideous nights of watching and waiting, of hoping against hope, of battling with myself; and oh! the terrible day, when the light of reason fled, and all seemed a blank and a waste, until I became part of an invisible crew, whose gibberings and tauntings were my only companions. It would make me mad once more, were I to re-member and dwell upon these scenes for long."

She pressed her hand to her brow as she spoke.

"Drive them from your memory," said Wilford Rokeby; "think only of the future."

"Yes, yes," said Lady Mordaunt, "may Heaven reward you and punish him."

"The king's vengeance will fall heavily upon him," replied Lady Clara Mortimer, as she drew the trembling woman to her breast.

Wilford smiled.

"I trust," he said, "that the king will have nought to do with his punishment. My prayer to Providence is as it has been always, that my good sword here may avenge my murdered friend, Hubert Aveling, whom he slew in the pride of youth and love."

The two lovers now took leave of Lady Huntley Mordaunt, and returned towards the house of Lord Claude Mortimer.

Darkness had already fallen over the city when he parted from Lady Clara, and proceeded to Whitehall.

Having placed the guard, and wrapped himself in his cloak, he quitted the palace once more, and was making his way towards the river, when he saw a second form quit the palace, and follow in his footsteps.

This one was presently followed by another, who also took his way towards the river, where they entered separate boats.

"This is very mysterious," said Wilford Rokeby, to himself. "I must keep good watch here. I know not where

Sir Huntley may have his spies watching me and ready to compass may death."

He found, however, that his watchfulness was not required.

No one offered to molest him, or even follow him.

Hastening down to the river's side, he entered a boat, and was pulled rapidly towards London Bridge.

Here, at the usual place, he procured his horse, and was soon riding along the dark high road, towards the old house where the secret meetings of the Five Masks were held.

He could not make any very great haste, however, for in advance of him, during the whole ride, was a horseman, who showed no desire to hurry himself.

In due time, however, he arrived at the old house.

" Am I the first ?" he inquired of the trooper who held the door.

" No, sir. The others are here before you," replied the man.

There seemed an unusual solemnity about the old place.

The air seemed cooler—the silence more profound than ever.

However, Wilford was not one to give way for a moment to superstitious fears.

Advancing boldly, he entered the room, and found himself in the presence of three Masks, of whom the White Mask was one.

" I am glad you have arrived," said one of the masks, rising, " because there is very important business to discuss this night. We all know that he who wore the White Mask is dead, and

yet there is another White Mask, who knows of our meetings, and is here among us in our councils. I challenge him to declare how he became acquainted with our secrets."

The White Mask rose, as a murmur of approbation followed the mask's speech.

" Gentlemen," he said, " you are certain that I have not betrayed you."

" We feel certain of that," was the reply.

" On one occasion I saved you from arrest, and perhaps death."

" You did."

" Then question me not.   Let us proceed at once to business.   Sir Huntley Mordaunt, our treacherous ally, is now for ever cast from the king's favour, and it behoves us now to be more guarded—more vigilant—more energetic than ever.   Buckingham is now higher than ever in the good graces of King James.   While the country is groaning beneath overwhelming and unnecessary taxation;   while Spain threatens war, and Buckingham foments the flames of discord, the king promotes him to higher offices. If we want peace and less taxation, we must use our voices against Buckingham, who, when he has power, always uses it———"

" For the best !" cried the Black Mask, as he sprang to his feet and ascended to a part of the room where a table was raised somewhat above the rest of the apartment.

For an instant a dead silence prevailed throughout the room.

A dead, deep, ominous silence it was.

Then the three other masks drew their swords.

"What means this? We have treason here," cried Wilford Rokeby, fiercely.

The Black Mask waved them sternly back.

"You have no treason here," he said. "You have some one present who will protect and aid you. At this very moment this house is surrounded on all sides. The secret of these meetings has been revealed to the king, and every shrub and tree near this building contains an armed trooper. Definite orders have been given, and they only await a signal."

"You, then, have betrayed us," said Wilford, while a loud murmur from the others proclaimed the unanimity of their thoughts.

"Not so," returned the Black Mask. "Had I desired to betray you, I should have given to the king your names and stations."

"Which you know not."

"You are wrong; I know you all. Yonder is the White Mask—the representative of Hubert Aveling. Think you I know him not for Malcolm, the Captain of the Night Guard at Whitehall; and you, Wilford Rokeby, and you, Lance Courtenay, his lieutenants, who have been plotting against Buckingham for months unsuccessfully, aided in your counsels by that assassin and arch-traitor, Sir Huntley Mordaunt! I know you all. Yet would I not betray you."

"Who, then, are you, mysterious man, who thus hold us in your power?"

"I will tell you," said the Black Mask, and, as he spoke, he removed the covering from his face.

"Buckingham!" exclaimed the three friends, in astonishment.

It was, indeed, the duke himself who stood before them.

"What say you now, Wilford Rokeby?" cried he. "Do you wonder why your plans have failed? Do you wonder now how it was that secret—masked and mysterious as you supposed your meetings to be—you were yet known so well, that a letter, summoning you hither, was given you at Whitehall Palace?"

"I say nothing, my lord duke," said Wilford, "except that I and my friends must fight our way out of this place, and that right quickly."

"Stay, rash man," exclaimed Buckingham, drawing a pistol from his belt, and raising it aloft. "There is a signal agreed upon; one shot from this pistol, and the king's troops will attack this place, and not one among you will escape. There is no possibility of departing until I please. I declare this society dissolved; I forbid its reassembling; I warn you against joining in such intrigues as these. On the other hand, I offer you my friendship, and am willing to grant you my forgiveness for all that is past. Let us leave this place secretly, and masked, for the last time. The next time we meet let it be as friends, undisguised, and in the open day."

As the wily statesman concluded his speech, the door was flung open, and the sentinel appeared.

"Gentlemen," cried he, "you are

betrayed! The house is surrounded by the king's troops; all escape is cut off?"

"Was I right or wrong, gentlemen?" said Buckingham. "Come, let us depart. To-morrow we will consult upon the best means of freeing Lord Ernest Mortimer, and discovering and bringing to the scaffold our mutual enemy, Sir Huntley Mordaunt. To horse, gentlemen, to horse. I will be answerable for your safety."

In a few minutes they had mounted their steeds, and, with Buckingham at their head, passed through the ranks of the king's guards, and dashed at a merry pace over the high road towards London Bridge.

CHAPTER XL.

THE REWARD OF THE BRAVE.

IT was not until the morning after the meeting which had so abruptly dissolved the Five Masks that the Duke of Buckingham mentioned anything to Wilford Rokeby in regard to the capture of Sir Huntley Mordaunt or the release of Lord Ernest Mortimer.

On this morning he sent for Rokeby to his chamber.

He gave one rapid, searching glance at the features of the young lieutenant, and then held out his hand, which Wilford took and shook heartily.

"I trust," said Buckingham, "that no ill feeling exists between us in regard to the proceedings of last night?"

"None, my lord," answered Wilford; "though you will allow that it is unpleasant to be compelled to admit oneself so thoroughly outwitted and deceived."

Buckingham smiled.

"It is for your good," he said, "solely for your good, that I have acted as I have. With others I might have acted differently, but knowing you and Lance Courtenay and Captain Malcolm to be true and loyal men, I could not betray you to the king, even though you were plotting against me. Besides, by remaining inactive, I learned the schemes of that arch traitor, Sir Huntley Mordaunt, and was enabled easily to defeat them. What you and your friends have done I regard purely as the result of a mistaken loyalty. The king, in his present weak and undecided state of mind, could have no better adviser than myself. I shall do all, therefore, which lies in my power to aid you and assist your friends; but I must also obtain from you a promise that you will no longer seek to thwart me."

"Enable me to destroy the assassin of my friend," cried Wilford; "aid me in releasing Lord Ernest Mortimer, and I will willingly promise to quit political intrigues for ever. I look forward to my marriage with Lady Clara, and a quiet, happy future with her, as far

"IF I FALL, LANCE, TAKE MY DYING LOVE TO CLARA."

better than all the ferment and constant torturing passions of political life. But tell me, what of Lord Ernest Mortimer?"

"I will tell you," replied the duke. "Proceed to the king, ask him for an audience, and plead to his majesty. If he remains resolved, and you see no show of yielding, tell him that the Duke of Buckingham has a favour to ask, and he will then send for me. There is a chance then that you will see the father of your betrothed free before nightfall."

"Why, then, my lord, do you not proceed at once to King James, and procure this pardon for my friend?" asked Wilford.

"Because," returned Buckingham, "because the king has said to me,

'When you require a favour, ask and you shall have.' I had wished to secure for myself a favour of another kind altogether, and until all else fails I do not desire to avail myself of this offer. Go then first; but if you find your entreaties in vain, send without hesitation for me."

After thanking the duke, Wilford Rokeby retired to the guard-room, and dispatched one of the troopers to crave an audience for him with the king.

It was not long before he stood in the presence of King James.

"Well, my brave lieutenant," he said, "have you come to crave promotion?"

"Not so, your majesty," said Wilford Rokeby, bowing respectfully, "I came to ask nothing for myself; I came to crave a boon, a boon which to me, I can assure you, will be of inestimable value."

"Modesty should always be rewarded," said James. "This morning Howard Malcolm, the captain of my Night Guard, has placed in my hands his resignation, and in his letter has mentioned your name. I have, therefore, the pleasure of placing you in his post. Be as brave and vigilant as ever, Captain Rokeby, and other honours will arise for you."

"I cannot too greatly thank your majesty," he said, as his face flushed with gratification, "for the kindness you show me, and yet I could have wished that this honour had fallen on me at any other time."

The king frowned.

"How now?" he said; "do you then refuse the promotion I offer you?"

"Not so, sire," replied Wilford; "my regret was that in the face of the kindness you have just shown me, I should be compelled to ask you a second favour."

"Speak on," said James, kindly; "to such a brave soldier as you I should be sorry indeed to have to refuse any reasonable boon. Speak on freely."

"I will, sire," said Rokeby. "Your majesty is aware that I love, and am betrothed to Lady Clara Mortimer, the daughter of Lord Ernest Mortimer, who is now a prisoner at the Tower. She will soon become my wife, for even if Sir Huntley Mordaunt were not a proscribed felon, all fear of his interrupting the union would now be removed by the fact that I have discovered, and can produce the lady who is his legal wife, and has been for some years."

"What want you, then?" asked James, whose brow had again contracted into a frown, and whose voice had assumed a sterner intonation; "my consent to your marriage with the daughter of this rebellious nobleman?"

Wilford Rokeby bowed low as he spoke again pleadingly.

"No, sire, that is not what I desire to ask now, though your majesty may be well assured that I would not marry her without it. The boon I crave is of greater import, far greater. I seek the pardon and release of Lord Ernest Mortimer himself."

"That, Captain Rokeby, is a boon I cannot grant," returned the king. "Such an act of rebellion as that of which Lord Ernest Mortimer was guilty, deserved death, and would be ill rewarded by a long and solitary imprisonment. Ask me anything but that, for it is more than I can do."

Wilford Rokeby was about to make reply, when a knock came to the door, and when the king said, "Enter," Lance Courtenay walked in, and bowed respectfully before King James.

"I have ventured," he said, "to intrude upon your majesty, for most important news has arrived from the north."

"In regard to what?" asked James, who was now in no good humour.

"In regard to Sir Huntley Mordaunt. See, here is the letter, which has just been placed in my hands. It was addressed to me and to Lieutenant Rokeby."

The king took the letter, and read it aloud.

It ran thus :—

"DEAR WILFORD,—I have every reason to believe that Sir Huntley Mordaunt is, at this very moment, concealed in Claverstone Abbey. He has, I fancy, attempted to destroy the place, but has been prevented by one of his own retainers. I will keep watch until you return, and the one whom I suspect to be him, I will, on no account, allow to quit the Abbey. I would wish you to inform the king and return as soon as possible.

"Your friend,
"GILES LAMBERT."

A gleam of pleasure overspread Wilford Rokeby's features.

"If I return and succeed in destroying this arch traitor," he cried, "I shall be doing your majesty a service, for which, I trust, you will give me a reward. May I hope that you will grant me the favour I have asked, when I return from Claverstone?"

Before the king could reply, the door was opened, and the Duke of Buckingham entered.

"Your majesty," he said, "I have come to ask of you a favour."

The king smiled.

"You are about to follow the example of Captain Rokeby; but proceed. I am aware that I have promised to grant you one, but I hope it is not of the same nature."

"Your majesty remembers and repeats your promise?" said the duke.

"Yes."

"Then I ask for the release of Lord Ernest Mortimer."

The king's brow grew dark as night.

"Steenie," he said, in peevish anger, "you are taking an advantage of me to induce me to do an injustice."

"No, sire; I can assure you that it will not be an injustice. Lord Ernest is really repentant. He sincerely regrets the past. He desires to lay his loyal sword at your feet, to pass the remainder of his years, the winter of his life, near your person. He has children whom he loves, and whose future is dear to him. He has spent, within a prison, years which might have been given to pleasure or his country's service. Think of these things, your majesty, and forgive him for my sake."

"Steenie," said the king, "I cannot refuse you, for my royal word is pledged, though I would that you had asked for any other reward for your many services. Let Lord Ernest Mortimer be released, and let Lady Clara and her brother and sister be restored to Court. But, from you, Wilford Rokeby, I must demand, in return, the death, or the living body of Sir Huntley Mordaunt."

Wilford Rokeby's heart beat wildly, and his eyes beamed with pleasure, for now, in one moment, two dear wishes were about to be accomplished.

Lady Clara's father, who, in the king's mind, had evidently been already condemned, was about to be released, and Sir Huntley Mordaunt was to be left for Wilford to dispose of.

"Your majesty," he said, kneeling before the king, "in the name of Lord Ernest and his children, I thank you for his pardon. All I hope for is, that I may be the one to lead him forth from his prison, and conduct him to the presence of his daughter. In my own name I thank you for your last words. Sir Huntley Mordaunt's death shall repay your majesty for your kindness and forgiveness."

"You can proceed at once to the Tower," said the king, "and thence to

Claverstone. I will give you now my royal warrants for his release, and for Sir Huntley Mordaunt's seizure."

In a few minutes more Wilford Rokeby, armed with the royal warrants, was proceeding with beating heart towards the Tower of London.

Sir Leonard Fairfax gazed with no eye of pleasure upon the young lieutenant when he presented to him the warrant for the release of Lord Ernest Mortimer.

Nor was he more satisfied when he heard of the discovery, which it was firmly believed had been made at Claverstone, by Giles Lambert.

He knew Sir Huntley Mordaunt well, and was quite convinced in his own mind that to save himself from an ignominious fate upon the scaffold, the arch traitor would reveal any secrets, no matter if he compromised and ruined his best and most faithful friend.

Wilford Rokeby, who knew the character of the man before him, spoke to him with hauteur, and with an imperativeness which was infinitely galling to the deputy-governor of the English Bastille.

"I must see your prisoner at once," he said; "let no formalities be gone through. When I release Lord Ernest Mortimer, I have an important mission to fulfil for the king, which admits of no delay. If, by the death of Ben Lockster, the treacherous gaoler, you have lost your turnkey, conduct me to Lord Ernest Mortimer yourself."

Sir Leonard Fairfax flushed crimson with anger.

"This insolence to me, sir!" he cried. "Do you know that I am a nobleman, the son of a nobleman, and deputy-governor of this Tower of London?"

Wilford Rokeby gazed contemptuously at the speaker.

"Nobleman or not, I know well your character," he said. "You are a traitor to the king, and the friend of assassins. You nearly, upon one occasion, compassed my death, in connivance with Ben Lockster, and having failed in this attempt to gratify that villain and murderer, Sir Huntley Mordaunt, you released him from the Tower, and thereby placed yourself among the ranks of King James's enemies."

"Knowing all this, why did you not inform the king?" asked Sir Leonard Fairfax, with a sneer. "I will answer my own question for you—because you feared to do so, knowing that you had no proof."

"You are wrong," replied Wilford Rokeby; "I had other reasons for my silence; but lead on at once. I can give no further time for speech. The king's justice will soon overtake you."

Sir Leonard Fairfax, after a moment's hesitation, himself led the way towards the cell where the unfortunate father of Rokeby's mistress had passed so many weary hours.

It was a small, dark, dismal cell, where the light of day never penetrated; and, as they approached, they could see through a grating in the door the whole miserable scene.

The place was no larger than that in which the father of the French Bastille was found—a living tomb, in fact, which seemed truly calculated to crush out the present life of man, and dim for ever his perception of the future.

Dank, dark, murky walls, where the ooze of the river traced green fantastic forms—black corners, where no light appeared to have gleamed for hundreds and hundreds of years—a stone floor—a stone ceiling—no window—no sunlight—such made up the place where the misled patriot had been placed to appease a king's wrath, and show an example to the people.

It was truly a burial here.

No sounds of busy life penetrated this dismal abode of silence; no sounds of human feet or human voices, not even the tramp of warders, for the walls were so thick, and the cell so buried beneath the earth that nothing but utter stillness reigned around it.

At a table in the centre of the wretched cell sat Lord Ernest, the light of a dull lamp above him falling on his poor old head as he pored over the pages of a dark-lettered volume.

It was a picture of silent misery, in which the soul and mind of the good old man were the only lights to redeem the darkness.

He started up with a glad and wondering look as he saw Wilford Rokeby enter.

The welcome news was soon imparted to him, and he walked with a firm and elastic step from the place which had been both the culmination and the end of his misfortune.

" Joy never kills," the proverb says, and in this instance it seemed to impart fresh vigour and energy to the released prisoner.

Within an hour from the time of his interview with the king, Wilford Rokeby had conducted the surprised and delighted nobleman to the presence of his son and daughters.

The joy of Lady Clara Mortimer and her sister and brother may be imagined when they so unexpectedly beheld the face of the father who had so long been separated from them, and who had suffered so severely, and through so many years, for his participation in a mistaken revolution.

The son, more strong-minded, of course, than his sisters, grasped his father's hand, and, with a voice which trembled somewhat with emotion, congratulated him upon his rescue from what had appeared truly an inevitable doom.

The daughters acted differently.

They clasped him in their arms, and kissed him, and, leading him to a seat, stroked his white hair, and whispered words of glad consolation and welcome, until the tears, which had been almost dried up with constant misfortune and the unceasing assaults of the world, flowed again, and the old man burst into tears of joy, and clasped his children to his heart, as if he had even now a fear of losing them again.

But we must not pause to dwell now upon this scene.

There are other and more stirring scenes to describe—other characters whose fates we are bound to follow.

It will suffice to say, that after an affecting welcome came an affecting parting, for both Claude and his father insisted upon accompanying Wilford on his journey towards Claverstone Abbey.

" I will be there," said Lord Ernest Mortimer, " to see the discomfiture of my worst and most hated foe."

CHAPTER XLI.

IN WHICH THE ASSASSIN OF HUBERT AVELING IS AT LENGTH BROUGHT TO BAY.

FIERCE and eager riders were those three who pressed on towards Claverstone, and strong was the hope within their hearts that they would reach the Abbey in time to prevent the escape of the miserable traitor whose doom had been pronounced by the king.

Yet they little thought how greatly Sir Huntley Mordaunt was playing into their hands.

Our readers will remember that we left the traitor when he had glided serpent-like into the store-room, with the intention of setting fire to the Abbey, and destroying his own friends and retainers, rather than fail in compassing the death of Giles Lambert and securing his own escape.

But he was not alone.

All through his glidings along the dark corridor, and his stealthy descent of the winding stairs, he had been watched by eager eyes.

One of his retainers, Robert Urleswood, had heard his mutterings, had watched the eager triumph in his eye, and had followed him.

"How now, Sir Huntley Mordaunt," he cried, as he saw his master stooping down, "would you destroy your best friends? How have I and my fellows offended you, that you should wish to despatch us thus, unwarned, to our last homes?"

A flush of anger and shame, too, overspread the features of Sir Huntley Mordaunt.

"Why have you followed me?" he cried. "Am I not master here?"

"Yes, Sir Huntley, but not the master of our lives. Why not trust in us, who have fought well and often for you? If you desire to destroy these men there is no one who would assist you more readily than Robert Urleswood."

"Destroy them—we cannot, except in some such way as this."

"Let it be so, then," said Urleswood. "Look you here. In this room, and in several of the vaults of Claverstone, there are, as you know, large stores of gunpowder. One night's work would connect all these stores, and a large and unerring train could be laid from this room. Wilford Rokeby and his friend will soon return to assume possession of the Abbey in the king's name, and we retainers can claim permission to retire to our homes. Before going, I will place in this store-room a slow match, which shall burn an hour, and give us all time to escape out of harm's way. Then, in the midst of their triumph, while we and you are out of harm's way, they will be blown to atoms, and their mangled bodies will be crushed in the ruins of the Abbey."

Sir Huntley Mordaunt listened with

fiendish satisfaction to the words of his retainer.

"Good," he said, "I will take your advice. Only despair, and a resolve to destroy my enemies at any cost, would have led me to dream of risking the lives of my best friends."

All through that night the two men worked silently and slowly, until the vaulted receptacles of the deadly material, from one end of Claverstone Abbey to the other, were so connected that one slow match, ignited near the store-room door, would be the beginning of a dozen terrible explosions, which would rend the building into a hundred pieces.

"Well done, my faithful retainer," said Sir Huntley, as he desisted from his work, and saw already in anticipation the hideous ruin he was preparing; "now let them come, for they will rush into the very arms of death."

It was in the grey of a bright morning that Wilford Rokeby and his two friends arrived at the Abbey, and were eagerly greeted by Giles Lambert.

"I believe Sir Huntley to be at this moment in the Abbey," he said; "in fact, I feel sure of it."

"Then why have you not seized him?"

"He is now virtually a prisoner," said Giles; "no one has been permitted to leave the place, and the only secret entrance has been discovered and blocked up by my men. We can send the retainers away now, and during their departure we shall inevitably discover our man."

"Be it so, then," said Wilford, "be it so. Let them at once be mustered; withdraw our men from the building; let the retainers be assembled in the corridor, and let them pass one by one through the ranks. Out there in the light of the morning we may recognise his features, whereas in this dark old house we might easily be deceived."

Within half an hour the retainers, including Sir Huntley, and numbering some twenty men, were assembled in the hall.

Urleswood came last.

He had just applied the slow match to the train which was to be the destruction of the king's friends.

Outside, beyond the moat, the king's guards were assembled.

Wilford Rokeby, Lance Courtenay, Giles Lambert, and Lord Ernest Mortimer, with his son, stood on the drawbridge along which the domestics had to pass.

"When I say 'he is here,'" whispered Giles Lambert to Rokeby, "your enemy is near."

One by one the retainers passed out of the old building.

They came quickly, and quickly too beat Wilford's heart.

At length came one who wore a cloak and walked erect and boldly.

"He is here," whispered Giles Lambert. "Now then for vengeance."

Not a moment was lost.

Wilford Rokeby sprang forward, and tore off the cloak of him who advanced.

He knew him at once; despite all disguise he recognised the features of his foe; the bright, savage eye, the angry, curling lip, the broad brow.

"Sir Huntley Mordaunt, you are mine at last," he said; "Heaven has delivered you into my hands. Tremble, coward and traitor, the hour of vengeance has come."

Sir Huntley Mordaunt was no coward, but he could not help seeing that the decisive moment in his existence had come.

Folding his arms proudly, he glanced round upon the men-at-arms.

"A brave thing, truly," he said, "to threaten me when you are surrounded by the King's Guard. Is this your vaunted courage, Wilford Rokeby?"

"Vaunting," said Wilford Rokeby, contemptuously, "is not my custom. What I am about to do is consistent with justice, and is, moreover, far too good a chance to offer to one who is a traitor and an assassin. The king, in pardoning and releasing Lord Ernest Mortimer, who stands yonder, demanded of me either your death or your living body. He gave me the choice, and I will take him the news of your death."

Sir Huntley Mordaunt remained standing with his arms folded.

"In other words," he said, "you are about to murder me."

"Not so; it shall be a fair and open fight—a fight to the death!" said Wilford.

Then turning to his friends and soldiers, he added—

"Gentlemen, let no man interfere. No matter who obtains the best of this battle, I command that no one shall interrupt its fair and just proceedings. I trust in Providence to defend the right, and to guide my good sword to the heart of this unworthy traitor!"

Then he took the hand of Lance Courtenay and pressed it.

"If I fall, Lance, you will take my dying love to Clara, and my loyal wishes to the king. But as you value my friendship, let no man step in to save me. My own right arm shall avenge me on this traitor, or I will die by his hand. And remember, if I die, this man must be permitted to go scot-free. Let no one molest him—let him go in peace."

After this, he turned towards Sir Huntley Mordaunt, who was standing with his sword drawn, and his cloak at his feet, ready for action, and wondering at the chivalrous words which had just fallen from the lips of his antagonist.

At this moment Robert Urleswood rushed forward, and whispered in his master's ear—

"Hasten this fight," he said, in tones of agitation, "and back away from the Abbey. In less than twenty minutes the match will fire the train, and Claverstone will be blown into a thousand atoms."

"Away!" cried Wilford Rokeby, angrily motioning the man away, and advancing towards his foe. "And now, Sir Huntley, for justice and Hubert Aveling!"

Then, as the morning's sun glistened down upon the scene, the swords of the deadly foes were crossed, and Wilford Rokeby and Sir Huntley Mordaunt stood face to face for the last time.

The day dawned with unusual splendour.

Over the country side, and the forest and the valley, and the grey turrets of the Abbey, and the far-off church, and the white cottages dotted here and there over the landscapes, and golden rays descended, and united to form a scene of unutterable beauty.

But no one cared to gaze upon it.

Their hearts were bound up in one subject, and their eyes were riveted upon nothing but the two fierce, angry men, who, with pale faces, stood opposite one another, and began, with a quivering clash of swords, their last fight to the death.

CHAPTER XLII.

IN WHICH WILFORD ROKEBY AND SIR HUNTLEY MORDAUNT MEET FOR THE LAST TIME.

To say that the hearts of the brave men who stood without Claverstone Abbey trembled at the sight of the two combatants, would be false.

But there was not a face among those who looked at them which did not pale as their eyes wandered from one to the other of those desperate antagonists.

There was no haste or eagerness displayed on either side.

They were both intent upon death; you could see it by their eyes, by their stern grip upon their swords—their firm attitudes—their pallid faces—their set teeth.

Strong men clutched each other's arms, and, although foes and friends, alike gazed eagerly.

As had happened when the fine old building had been attacked so vigorously by the king's guards, there were others near at hand, besides the combatants and the mail-clad troops and retainers.

Men and women going to their early work in the fields, stopped, arm-in-arm, to look upon the gay assemblage, wondering at the meaning of the strange duel.

Through the throng, indeed, they could see but little, but the murmurs of the spectators showed that something of great import was in progress.

The two men who were the principals in the deadly fight were the coolest of all—although their lives, their liberty, their honour, depended on the issue of the combat.

Their clashing swords scarcely parted for a moment, as if truly, while the blades were evenly crossed, each held his adversary's life in the balance.

But this did not last long.

There was far too much at stake to permit of child's play.

On the one side, Sir Huntley Mordaunt, seeing freedom before him if he only succeeded in slaying his adversary, thought not of the murder he had done—thought not of the sorrows he had caused—thought not of the friends he had betrayed.

All he dreamed of in that supreme moment was, that by being bold and preserving his presence of mind, he could secure to himself a free pass, as it were, through the body of Wilford Rokeby.

Never before, by Claverstone Abbey, had such a fierce combat been seen, and never even had the young Captain of the Night Guard been face to face with an enemy so bold.

True it was that beneath the walls of the Tower they fought a duel to the death, but the interruption had been sufficient to take from it all its serious character.

Now, however, it was far different.

There was no chance of escape for him, nor could he, if he would, have accepted it.

On the one side, as I have said, the chance of escape for ever; on the other, the memory of the death of Hubert Aveling—the long sufferings of Lord Ernest Mortimer—the hideous mental captivity suffered by Lady Clara Mortimer—the murder of Sir Edgar Farnley—the silent sorrow of the poor maniac wife—the gloom and horror, and the dim, dull atmosphere of treachery which had hovered over the Palace of Whitehall, and banished from his heart for ever the hope of happiness.

There was real happiness now to be achieved by the young Captain of the Night Guard through this desperate fight. A lunge to Sir Huntley's heart, and the world was free before him for ever.

Clash, clash! parry, parry! Bright sunlight gleaming on the sword-blades, and the jewelled collars, and the golden handles of the weapons! Clash! clash! Hearts beating with every stroke, and heads burning at each failure. Clash, clash! parry, parry!—friends clutching wildly each other's arms, and the madness of battle infecting the lookers-on as well as the fighters—such was the scene.

They both fought well; and Sir Hunt-ley, fighting for dear life, for a long time had the advantage.

He had another motive, moreover, in pressing forward.

He knew well that in a very few minutes the train which he had laid for the destruction of Claverstone Abbey and those whom he had hoped would be its inmates, would explode, and he had no wish to be one of the victims of such an ignoble death.

His desperate efforts enabled him for some time to gain the advantage.

Wilford Rokeby, in face of this resolute man fighting for his worthless life, was compelled to give way.

The king's guard silently—quietly yielded ground as he did, sorrow and despair at their hearts, as they beheld their beloved leader worsted in the fight.

But suddenly Wilford Rokeby recovered himself.

A spirit from another world seemed to whisper to him of the vow he made long, long ago—that vow registered before Heaven over the dead body of Hubert Aveling, when it lay in the stillness and majesty of death in the guard-room at Whitehall.

His sword seemed to gleam more brightly—his wrist seemed to form itself into steel—his eyes darted strange fires—the point of his sword appeared to flash everywhere, and, inch by inch, Sir Huntley Mordaunt was compelled to retreat.

But, in retreating, he executed a feint.

Instead of breaking ground towards Claverstone Abbey, he worked round so that they fought on a level with the battlements.

Again, again; clash, clash, and the sword of Wilford Rokeby was raised to strike a deadly blow.

Even now his evil genius was near him.

Robert Urleswood was, as we have seen, a faithful servant to Sir Huntley Mordaunt.

Villain as his master was, traitor as he had openly confessed himself to be, selfish as he had proved himself, this man clung to him with a kind of dog-like devotion, and was willing to sacrifice himself for one who was unworthy of his simplest thought.

He had known Sir Huntley Mordaunt from a boy.

He could remember him in the flush and pride of his youth, when he was the admiration of the country side, and the pride of his doting parents.

He could remember him when his heart was not blackened by a false ambition, when his eyes were not for ever gleaming with sinister fires, when he had a cheery word for all, and was not the unapproachable, gloomy traitor, living only for himself.

He could picture to himself the day when Claverstone Abbey was decked with bright flags; when banners streamed from the windows; when loud, ringing shouts rose from the courtyard and echoed away along the country side—that day when Sir Huntley came of age.

Urleswood thought of all this; and the sight before him, and the knowledge of what was coming, maddened him.

Claverstone Abbey, his birth-place, and the home he had for years called his own, was presently, by his own act, to be blown into the air.

And, then, the man before him, who, villain as he was, had always been a kind and lenient master to him, was there at bay, with not a friend near him—the hated of all—fighting to the death with one who justly sought his life.

These memories took from him all fear of that fate which he must have known would be his.

He only thought that the one who had been for long years master and kind friend was in danger, and that it was his duty to save him.

So, in the midst of the fair fight there was a flash, a report, and Wilford Rokeby's left arm fell powerless to his side, as he tottered into the arms of Lance Courtenay, who rushed forward to receive him.

"Treason! treason!" shouted a hundred voices, while twice a hundred swords flashed in the brightening sun of morning, and the king's guard advanced threateningly towards Sir Huntley.

This time, however, as we have seen, they were in error.

The arch traitor had not been the planner of this piece of foul treachery.

Hardly had Wilford fallen back, hardly had the threatening swords been raised, when there was another flash, and another report, and Robert Urleswood fell dead upon the green sward.

One of the Night Guard, Wilford's faithful friends, had seen the flash, and noted whence the shot proceeded, and, from that instant, the retainer was marked for dead.

High up among the thick branches of an overhanging tree, the devoted retainer had perched himself, carefully biding his time until he could fire at Wilford Rokeby without running the risk of injuring his master.

"This treason," cried Lance, "does away with all previous arrangement. Seize this traitor! convey him back to the abbey, and let this duel wait until Wilford Rokeby is well enough to carry it on."

"Hold!" cried a loud, hoarse voice, as Lance Courtenay spoke, and the men were about to rush upon Sir Huntley Mordaunt.

It was the voice of Wilford.

Pale, blood-stained, with his arm bound up hurriedly by a friendly trooper, he stood ready for the fight once more.

"I will allow nothing of the kind," he said; "I challenged Sir Huntley to a fight of which I must take the consequences as well as he. I am well and able to continue the fight. Sir Huntley, come on."

In vain his friends interfered.

In vain they endeavoured to persuade him to delay the conflict till the morning.

He was resolute.

For the first time in his life he had got his enemy, the assassin of Hubert Aveling, to himself; for the first time there was a chance of a desperate, unfailing fight, and he was resolved that it should not be interrupted.

The swords were crossed again, and they had hardly done so, when, in a desperate lunge, Wilford's weapon slid off Sir Huntley's guard, and inflicted a wound upon his hand.

The sight of the blood seemed to madden Wilford.

"Ha, ha!" he cried; "traitor and assassin! You have lived through life with the blood of the innocent upon your hands; you will die also with it last in our thoughts, and last in your own!"

Again the weapons crossed with a ring and a clash, and the spectators once more held their breath.

Now, however, the issue of the battle was no longer doubtful.

Desperation, determination, hate was in his face, and deadly and rapid were his thrusts.

At length the final moment came.

A wound in Sir Huntley Mordaunt's arm began to tell its tale of destruction.

The blood streamed from his opened flesh, and poured down his doublet.

His strength began to fail; his eyes to glare; his cheeks paled, and ever and anon mutterings of terrible curses broke from his quivering lips.

"The curse of Heaven and Hell be upon you," he cried, as his senses wandered, and he began to see before him those Eternal plains along which he would have to wander for ever in humility, and shame, and horror; "kill me if you will, but you cannot restore to Lord Ernest Mortimer the years of suffering he has undergone, nor to Hubert Aveling the life I wrung from him on the dark pavement of Whitehall! Die by your hand I may, but for you it will be a poor triumph. You may cut short the thread of my life, but you cannot renew it for others."

His face became more deadly pale now, and his breath came short, and still the one-handed avenger pressed upon him.

Then at length the bright blade was drawn back, and with the words, "Hu-

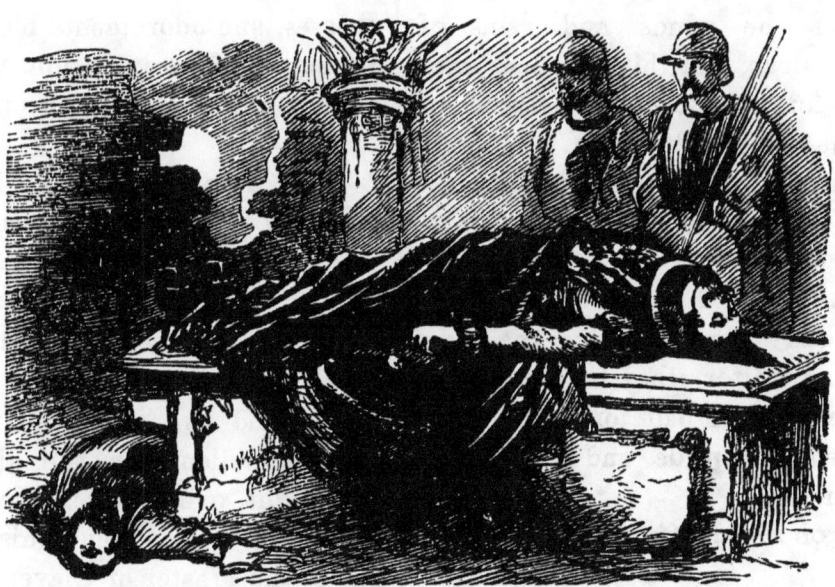

THE LAST OF SIR HUNTLEY MORDAUNT.

bert, you are avenged!" Wilford Rokeby drove his glittering sword up to its hilt in the breast of the arch traitor.

One upward glance of deadly hate; one wandering look towards Claverstone; one gurgling curse, whose purport none could hear, and Sir Huntley Mordaunt rolled over in the mire—DEAD!

Scarcely had he done so, when the earth was rent as with a terrible convulsion; a flash of crimson flame rushed upwards to the heavens; a roar as of a huge park of artillery shook the forest glades, and tossed to and fro the branches of the trees, and cast in a hundred pieces the huge walls of the old Abbey.

Great blocks of masonry tumbling, crumbling to dust; towers torn from their climbing ivy, and falling in vast pieces into the moat; huge beams swaying to and fro in fiery tangles amid long lapping tongues of fire; old nooks and corners, rendered venerable and honourable by age, disappearing amid dense white steam and blackening smoke; rooms where lovers had whis-pered and children had prattled, extin-guished by a touch, and made into horrid heaps of ruin; such was the scene where devastation ran riot on that bright May morning, and which seemed a fit consummation to the desperate life just ended.

Wilford Rokeby, weakened by excessive loss of blood, fainted in Lance's arms, as the explosion rent the air, and the grey old towers were torn asunder, and Claverstone Abbey sank into ruins for ever.

Tenderly, triumphantly, lovingly, he was borne away by his men towards the village, while Giles Lambert and some of the Night Guard remained behind to guard the smoking ruins.

"What are we to do with this?" said one of the troopers, as he kicked, contemptuously, the body of Sir Huntley Mordaunt.

"See yonder chapel," replied Giles Lambert. "It is ruined by the explosion he created, but there is still enough of it remaining to preserve his body from the winds and rains of Heaven. Bear him thither—bear him tenderly, for, murderer and assassin as he was, he was of noble birth. He was, indeed, our worst and most treacherous foe, but he has paid the penalty with his life."

The men bowed in obedience, and silently and reverently raising the body of the dead traitor, they bore it to the old chapel, which had for a hundred years been the pride and honour of Claverstone.

There, on a slab of marble, they laid him.

Over him were fragments of a frescoed roof, with figures of angels smiling coldly on him, and marbled flowers and crosses, and adornments blackened with the smoke of the explosion, and glintings of moonlight falling through strange crevices.

And here through the long day he lay, and through the succeeding night, when the pale moon fell through the broken arches upon his pale, ghastly face, and the body of his retainer, Urleswood, flung carelessly near his marble couch, and two of the King's Guard watching silently in the gloom of the still night, over his dead body.

It was a solemn scene, this last closing one of the Master of Claverstone.

More solemn still when we think of the avenged spirit of Hubert Aveling smiling over the place of atonement!

CHAPTER XLIII.

CAUGHT IN THE TRAP.

Sir Huntley Mordaunt had died in battle, and through the generosity of his enemy had been saved from the disgrace and shame which rightly should have been his.

So the third day after the terrible duel, and the still more terrible scene which had succeeded it, the body of the Master of Claverstone was borne to its last resting-place.

There was a goodly number to follow it to the grave, solid-looking retainers and tenants, and many coming from curiosity to see how the funeral pomp was carried out, and what portent might appear at the burial of one who was accused of so many strange misdoings.

But nothing out of the way occurred, at least until they reached the churchyard, and the body was about to be lowered into the grave.

A crowd was standing here—some friends, some strangers—and one whose face could not be seen, so low was his plumed hat drawn over his face, and so high was his cloak raised.

The service was read slowly and solemnly—the coffin was slung—the man of many sins was about to be lowered, when one of the men missed his footing and fell, striking his head against a stone.

In an instant the warm blood gushed forth, and fell dripping upon the coffin.

A thrill of horror ran through the assemblage, and the cloaked figure who had stood so mysteriously by, advanced, and glanced down into the grave.

" Fit emblem of his career," said he, as he bent over the yawning pit where the body of the traitor lay. " The blood of the innocent clung to him through life, and blood has rained upon him in his grave. As it lay upon his hand in his last battle—as it lay upon his heart always, so it will now lie upon his heart within his Eternal Home."

Then, after this one look, he passed away slowly, leaning, as in pain, upon the arm of a trooper.

As he moved from the place, his cloak was slightly taken from his face, and the retainers of Claverstone Abbey, who well knew the noble features, saw at once who it was.

It was Wilford Rokeby.

His face was pale, and his pace was slow and nervous, for the wound he had received from the treacherous shot of Robert Urleswood had taken a terrible effect upon him.

An avenging and justly angered Providence seemed truly to have saved him long enough to consummate the punishment of Sir Huntley Mordaunt, to carry out the vow he had taken over the dead body of Hubert Aveling, and then, as we have seen, exhausted nature gave way, and he fainted on the very field of battle, as the last roar of the explosion which sang the requiem of the traitor burst through the riven walls of Claverstone.

In pain, and weak as he might be now, he had crawled towards the old churchyard to take a last view of his enemy, not in any spirit of triumph or exultation, but merely to see how the man of many crimes was placed in his quiet home with the dark boughs of the cypress nodding over him, and the grey old tower of Claverstone church frowning sternly upon his tomb.

On reaching the inn where he had rested, and where he had received the attentions of a skilful leech, the wounded Captain of the Night Guard was met by Giles Lambert.

His horse was ready saddled and bridled before the gateway, and he was evidently prepared for a lengthened journey.

" Whither go you ?" cried Wilford, as he reached the doorway, and sat down somewhat wearily beneath the porch.

" To London, Wilford," returned Giles. " Now that you have performed the great wish and duty of your life, now that Claverstone is destroyed, and its master dead, I go to apprise the king of your glorious duel, that when you reach the metropolis you may be received with the honour that is due to you."

Wilford smiled.

" My friend," he said, " I appreciate your motive ; but there is one great objection to your plan, so great that I must beg of you to postpone your visit to London for some time."

Giles looked somewhat chagrined.

" What objection can there possibly be ?" he asked.

" A great one," replied Rokeby. " If you were to go to London, the king would know of the defeat and death of Sir Huntley Mordaunt, would he not ?"

"He would; that would be my purpose in going."

"Well, the news of such an event would soon spread over London."

"It would."

"And it would reach the ears of Sir Leonard Fairfax."

"The deputy-governor of the Tower?"

"The same."

"And what of him?"

"He is another who must be crushed like a viper—one who must die on the scaffold, for to slay him in fair fight would be an insult to humanity. He is not even like Sir Huntley Mordaunt; he has no boldness—no shadow, even, of courage. He is a villain—a stabber in the dark—a digger of pitfalls! I have marked him for vengeance, and I will be the one to accomplish it. If he were to hear of the death of Sir Huntley Mordaunt, he would fly at once, and justice would be defeated. So, Giles, though I appreciate your friendship, I must beg of you to defer this visit to London."

"Be it so, Wilford," said Lambert, "be it so. I have no desire to spoil you in punishing any of these villains, but I hope you will soon be able to proceed on the journey yourself."

A full week more was required ere Wilford Rokeby was considered fit for the journey to the metropolis, and even when he did set out, his face was ghastly pale and thin, and he was still evidently suffering from the effects of the deadly shot.

And thus, like a knight of old, wounded in far-off battle, he entered the metropolis, on the horse which he had named after the dead Black Meg, surrounded by his friends and companions in arms.

It was with a pleasure unmistakable that King James listened to the story.

His mind was full of ideas of chivalry and stern justice, and when Lance Courtenay (for he it was who told the tale) had completed his narrative, he held out his hand to the young captain.

"Captain Rokeby," he said, "you have done well and valiantly. All I blame you for is treating that villain too honourably. He was not worthy that he should cross swords with a noble soldier such as you."

Wilford bowed respectfully, and raised the king's hand to his lips.

"Your majesty," he said, "this man was of noble birth; I could do no less. But now that he is dead, and I have performed your majesty's bidding upon him, there is another traitor, whose name I will disclose to you, and for whose arrest I shall ask your majesty's warrant."

The king's countenance changed in a moment.

"It seems truly," he said, "as if I were beset by traitors. What is the villain's name?"

"Sir Leonard Fairfax, deputy-governor of the Tower," replied Rokeby.

The king thought for a moment, earnestly as it were.

Then he turned to Buckingham, who was standing near.

"Steenie," he said, "I am not surprised. You, yourself, have before now warned me against this man; and, pray, Captain Rokeby, of what special crimes do you now accuse him?"

"Of attempting my assassination; of

compassing the escape of Sir Huntley Mordaunt from the Tower; of numberless murders, committed within and without the fortress. I do not state this unadvisedly. Of whatever I may accuse him, be assured I can give your majesty the proofs. If he be innocent, then let all the blame and responsibility fall upon me. But as I am certain he is guilty, I pray your majesty to lose no time, since if he hears I am here in this palace, he will fly at once, and thus escape the traitor's death he merits."

"I would grant the warrant at once, your majesty," said Buckingham.

The king required no further inducement.

He sat down at once, and wrote out the requisite paper.

"Here," said he, as he handed it to Wilford Rokeby, "here is the warrant. You, however, are far too ill for any duty now. Let Master Lance Courtenay take it for you."

Wilford smiled.

"Your majesty," he said, "I prefer being the bearer of it myself. I once promised this man, when he endeavoured to compass my life, that I would be the messenger to bring him news of his coming punishment, and if your majesty will permit me, I will accomplish my vow, and take my rest afterwards."

"Be it so, then," said King James; "take a file of soldiers, and proceed to the Tower at once. Such a villain as you describe him to be I should be loth to see escape."

On quitting the king's presence, Wilford was met by Lady Clara.

"How pale and ill you look, Wilford," she said; "you need rest, anyone can see that you do. You look as wan and ghastly as after that treacherous shot wound, when I, and Genevieve, and Clara had to nurse you night and day."

He kissed her fondly, but put her away from him.

"I have one more stern duty to perform," he said, "and then, Clara, I will return and rest awhile. While Sir Leonard Fairfax, deputy-governor of the Tower, and Sir Huntley's abettor in all his villanies, is still alive, there is no peace of mind for me."

Sir Leonard Fairfax sat in his room in the Tower.

A fire burned in the grate—a large wood fire—and the flames lapped merrily over the charred wood.

Opposite this Sir Leonard sat and nodded in a deep sleep.

A deep sleep, truly, but not the sleep of the innocent.

It was a heavy slumber, in which dreams succeeded one another with frightful rapidity—dreams of horror; dreams of victims slain in dark cells; of dead men's hands clutching at his garment; of drowning wretches gasping for the help he would not give them; long rows of phantoms trooping by, pointing at him, and gibbering horrid things.

He was startled from his sleep by a heavy hand on his shoulder.

Springing up, he gasped forth in frantic accents—

"No, no, it was not I, not I! Ah! Woodford, what ails you? Why do you look so pale and haggard? Why do you come to me in my sleep to rouse me thus suddenly?"

The man's aspect, truly, was calculated to affright anyone.

His lips were pale, his cheeks death-like.

"What ails you, fool and coward?" shouted Fairfax, as the man still did not speak. "If there is danger, speak; if death is at the door, speak; but do not curdle my blood by standing thus, grim and ghost-like, before me!"

The man took one furtive glance round the room.

Then he said, in a hoarse, hurried whisper—

"There is peril; there is death at the door. You must fly!"

"And wherefore this?" asked the deputy-governor, trembling.

"My son, who, as you know, is in the king's guard, has just posted hither in all speed, to tell me that the king has granted a warrant for your arrest."

"Well?"

"This warrant is in the hands of Wilford Rokeby, and he and the Night Guard are on their road hither to arrest you."

Sir Leonard clutched the back of his chair convulsively.

"Are you jesting," he said, "or is it really come to this?"

"I swear it," said Woodford. "I, as you know, am much compromised in your affairs. All I trust is that you will not betray me to anyone. I have endeavoured always to serve you well."

"To me the past is a sealed book," said Sir Leonard Fairfax. "But hark! what noise is that?"

Woodford, the turnkey, ran at once out into the passage, and hurried up to the other end.

In a few moments he returned.

"You must fly!" he said. "There is not a moment to lose. The Night Guard are thundering at the gate."

A look of despair overspread the features of the guilty man, and, as he seized his plumed hat, he gazed round him as if his senses had wandered.

"Which way can I go?" cried he. "The front entrance is barred to me, and I must pass that to reach even the eastern gate."

"The stairs!—the secret stairs!" cried the man. "You forget them. A boat is always ready there. Fly, fly, at once!"

Without another word, Sir Leonard Fairfax quitted the room, and made his way at a run along the corridor.

It was a memorable corridor that.

Once, not so very, very long ago, Red Ben, the treacherous gaoler, had held aloft his torch for Wilford Rokeby to traverse its gloomy depths, and muttered to himself, in triumph—

"He is walking to his death!"

Sir Leonard Fairfax thought not of this.

He remembered not the pitfall.

All his mind was engrossed by the recollection of his horrible dreams—the thought of those who pursued him, and the fear of what would most certainly be his fate if the king's guards caught him.

Along the dark corridors he sped towards the fatal spot.

The clanging of the mailed feet could be heard distinctly hurrying up the stone corridors, and each echo struck home to the heart of the trembling dastard, as he crept along, afraid of his own shadow.

Presently he neared the place.

The glimmer of the river was before him—down the steps, and towards this he plunged.

Suddenly there was a despairing cry which re-echoed throughout the vaulted corridor, and struck dismay into the hearts of those who heard it.

Down into the hideous depth he plunged—down into the black yawning gulf which had received so many victims—down among the oozy slime, where the creeping things crawled and leaped over his face—where he sank inch by inch into the horrid black mud, until his gurgling cries were lost for ever!

Just as he disappeared gasping for life, Wilford Rokeby and his guards rushed up, torch in hand, and threw the glare of their red flambeaux upon the hideous death-trap.

"Another traitor caught in his own snare," murmured Wilford Rokeby, as he gazed at the black abyss. "Never mind, he has saved the headsman his office, and now there is nothing for us to do but to make our friends happy, and to receive the reward of life-long service ourselves."

With these words, whispered only to his own heart, as it were, he quitted the place, leaving the warder of the Tower to drag out the body of the deputy-governor from among the decay and ooze which had surrounded a hundred victims.

CHAPTER THE LAST.

IN WHICH THE REMAINING CHARACTERS ARE HAPPILY DISPOSED OF.

WE have seen the end of the traitors.

We have seen Sir Huntley Mordaunt at bay without his old fortress of Claverstone.

We have seen the avenger of Hubert Aveling performing his vow, and we have seen also the hideous fate which befell Sir Leonard Fairfax, the deputy-governor of the Tower, and the aider and abettor of Sir Huntley.

With one exception, we have now to speak only of those who throughout our history have passed along the path of honour and rectitude.

The one exception is the dark-visaged old man, of whom Sir Huntley Mordaunt had bought the poison that was intended to destroy Wilford Rokeby,

Plying a vocation which he knew to be terribly dangerous, he had always emissaries who informed him of all the doings of the great—so many of whose names appeared upon the fatal list upon which he had inscribed the name of Sir Huntley Mordaunt.

No sooner, therefore, had the king's order been given for the arrest of the traitor, on the charge of attempted poisoning, than word was brought to the old man, and he at once resolved to fly.

He had made a sufficient fortune to live on by his nefarious trade, and he determined to pass over to Paris, where he might remain quiet and unknown.

Before doing so, however, he made up his mind to avenge himself upon those who, while being purchasers of his noxious drugs, had nevertheless spurned and reviled him; and, accordingly, on the very day on which he quitted England, there was given to the door-keeper of the king's palace at Whitehall a large packet, which fell into the hands of Buckingham.

It was intended for the king's eyes only; but, as usual, it passed, almost as a matter of course, into the hands of the favourite.

It was well for the king, and well for the Duke of Buckingham, that it so happened.

Names, the most illustrious, were included in that terrible black list of misdoers.

King James, therefore, was spared the necessity of parting with some of his most useful friends, and Buckingham was enabled to place a black mark and a watch against many of his enemies.

Lady Huntley Mordaunt, still young, having nothing to remember of her husband, except ill-usage—not even having a first dream of love to set against the dreary blank of misfortune and cruel indignity—may be excused if she did not permit the memory of Sir Huntley Mordaunt to render wretched and useless the remainder of her life.

Retiring for a time to her father's house, until the recollection of his violent death had passed away, she once more entered society, and at the end of some twelve months became the wife of Lord Claude Mortimer, who, though only the son of a nobleman, had been given his title of baron for his eminent services to the king.

Lady Laura Clavering, the beloved betrothed of the dead Hubert Aveling, never married.

Faithful to the vow she had registered in her own inmost heart, when her hot tears had dropped upon the cold face of her murdered lover, she lived through her short life merely as the minister of good to others.

Giles Lambert had loved her long, honestly, and strongly enough.

But, although she esteemed him highly as a friend, he pleaded in vain.

The passion which had concentrated itself upon Hubert Aveling could never be aroused for another, and kindly, gently, firmly, she told him that with the last sigh of her murdered lover had died away from her heart all power of love for ever.

Time was, however, more kind to him than to her.

There was one in the palace who had suffered through Sir Huntley Mordaunt, and who, after a time, consented to become Giles Lambert's wife.

Need we say that it was Genevieve St. Clare, who thus crowned with happiness the brave companion in arms of Lance Courtenay and Wilford Rokeby? There was little delay to the marriage of our heroes to the ladies of their love.

Their enemies were disposed of—their troubles were over.

Sir Huntley Mordaunt being dead, and Lord Ernest Mortimer being restored to the king's favour, nothing remained but to celebrate the marriage, towards which they had looked so long and so ardently.

It was some weeks after the destruction of Sir Leonard Fairfax that Wilford Rokeby met Lady Clara Mortimer, in the same corridor where they had met upon so many previous occasions, where Sir Huntley Mordaunt had received upon divers occasions so many rebuffs, and where the voice of Lady Laura Clavering, hidden in the wall behind the revolving coat of mail, had, upon one occasion, so startled the traitor.

Eagerly he advanced towards her, and took her hand in his.

"We are well met, Clara," he said; "I have a question of great importance to put to you."

She blushed deeply.

Well she knew what the important question would prove to be.

"And what is that, Wilford?" she murmured, in gentle accents.

"Need you ask it?" he said, tenderly, as he passed his arm around her waist, and pressed her yielding form to his. "Need you ask what, after all my trials and perils, I desire as my reward? What can I desire—what can be my reward, but your consent to be my wife?"

"You have it, Wilford," she said. "You know you have it."

"Then, dearest, shall our marriage take place this week? There is now, I think, no reason for delay. Your consent is given—the king's consent is given. Your father, too, I have already asked. Tell me, then, dear one, shall it be as I wish?"

A smile, a tear, a blushing face pillowed upon a manly breast—a fervent embrace—a meeting of mutual lips—such was the answer.

Of Lance Courtenay's courtship we need say nothing here.

It would be a mere repetition of the interview which had already set the seal to Wilford Rokeby's happiness through life.

It will suffice to say that Lance found Geraldine Mortimer quite as yielding as her sister, and the marriage day was fixed for a week from the time of the meeting.

What a joyous day was that when the two couples, happy in each other's love, were united for ever in the king's chapel in Whitehall Palace.

Bevies of lovely demoiselles, throngs of gaily-clad courtiers, lined the corridors and chapel that day to do honour to the union of the Captain of the Night Guard, and his friend, with the ladies they had loved so long and defended so bravely.

The king himself was there, and Buckingham, with Lady Laura and Lord Ernest Mortimer, and his sons, while among the crowd of servitors might have been distinguished the pleased faces of Master and Mistress Markham, the faithful domestics of Wilford Rokeby's father.

A sunny sky smiled down upon the

palace that day, and a sunny path of happiness was from that moment begun.

Happy in his wife—happy in the favour of the king, and the respect of his friends—happy in a past, which was full of recollections of honour and glorious peril for him, Wilford Rokeby lived on ; and so, may we trust, that though Whitehall and its inmates are things gone by for ever, and their very memories have nearly died out from among us, that you, dear readers, may never forget the death of Hubert Aveling, and the vow of vengeance so grandly fulfilled by him whom you have known as the gallant CAPTAIN OF THE NIGHT GUARD.

THE END.